THE SHELTER of the DOVE'S WINGS

MELODY S. DEAL

Scripture taken from the King James Version of the Bible.

Balboa Press books may be ordered through booksellers or by contacting:

Balboa Press
A Division of Hay House
1663 Liberty Drive
Bloomington, IN 47403
www.balboapress.com
1 (877) 407-4847

Print information available on the last page.

ISBN: 978-1-9822-2476-9 (sc)
ISBN: 978-1-9822-2477-6 (e)

Balboa Press rev. date: 04/11/2019

Contents

For my grandchildren,
Alexandra, Bonnie, Madison, and Justin

Acknowledgements

Continued appreciation to Maxine, who provided the inspiration to write Sarah's story, to my husband Robert for his patience and support, to Alice, Pat, and Shel for being my sounding board, to friends and family who encouraged me, and to God who brings clarity and lights my pathway.

Chapter 1

"Joy, you good for nothing piece of cow dung, where the devil are you?" Edward J. Humes, lost his balance and landed on his backside, jug in hand. He got to his knees, put the jug to his mouth, and drained the contents.

Humes wobbled in that position while surveying the tree line and thicket before him. He put the clay vessel to his mouth, remembered it was empty and tossed it to the side. The inebriated man fumbled with the garish silver buckle on his belt. "Girl, you best show yourself." The buckle released and in one fell swoop he pulled the belt free from the waistband on his trousers and whipped it in a circular motion above his head. "Run from me, will you? After I work you over with this, you'll never be able to run from me again."

Tiring quickly, Ed dropped his arms, his head slumped forward, and his chin fell to his chest. His large frame slowly listed to the left and melted to the porch floor. He pulled himself into a fetal curl, belt still in hand.

He maintained that position for a short time, then his body jerked, his eyelids fluttered, and he raised his head slightly. "Man has a right to expect a hot supper on the table when he comes home. That High and Mighty mother of yours didn't teach you jack shit."

His head flopped back down on its side. Saliva drooled from his mouth making a pool of wetness. In a barely intelligible whisper he said, "Joy, name is wasted on you. You've never been anything other than a burden." Then the potent elixir took its toll.

***

Crouching behind a mulberry bush nearly barren of fruit, Joy used the hem of her dress to dab blood from her swollen cheek. *I'm going to have another black eye.*

Her tall skeletal frame shivered in the cool night's air. *I wish I'd grabbed Ma's shawl.* A tear spilled from her eye and trickled down her cheek. Using her tongue, she captured the moist drop, savoring the salty taste. *Can't cook without food. Pa doesn't look like he's gone hungry, must be getting something to eat somewhere.* With quivering fingers, she plucked a shriveled mulberry and reluctantly popped it into her mouth. *Stomach hurts, likely from eating nothing but these dried out berries for days on end.*

Joy folded her arms over her shoulders. *I'm so cold. Pa's going to be mad when he finds out there's no more firewood. If he didn't keep the axe and saw locked up, I could have cut some. He's likely afraid I'll use one of them on him.*

She rubbed at her sore shoulder, as she recalled the beating the week prior. *I thought I was going on to Glory. Can't keep counting on him passing out before he goes too far with his fists. I should have left before he came home this time. I was so stupid to hold on to hope that he'd change.*

I must leave. Got to find food. Mama, Mama, why did you have to die? Joy buried her face in the skirt of her tattered dress and softly cried.

An owl, perched on a large limb that stretched out over the mulberry bush, called out, "Whoo, whoo."

Joy's long golden hair was aglow in a bright moonbeam when she looked up and waved. *Goodbye, old friend.* Two squirrels popped out of nearby brush and stood on their hind legs. They wiggled their noses at her while they held their front paws together, as if begging. Joy took two acorns from her pocket and tossed them within reaching distance of the pair. *Thanks for your daily chatter. Without you I wouldn't have had anyone to talk to.*

Several crickets accompanied by a few katydids, sounded their presence. Joy turned her neck to the right and then the left watching the subtle movement of the foliage which indicated that the insects were working their magic to make their unique music. *Yes, I hear you singing, it's been appreciated.*

A snort came from dense thicket just a few feet from where the girl cowered. Joy had more frequently heard, than seen the buck. On this night he moved so that his head and magnificent rack were visible. Joy reached out. *Oh, beautiful big boy. I was close to getting you to let me touch you. Curious how your huge size has made me feel protected, rather than threatened. Stay safe.*

She reached to the back of her neck and tightened the knot in the cord that held a small, thin journal that she kept hidden beneath her dress. She clutched the treasure and stiffened her spine. *I'm not leaving without Mama's shawl. It and this are the only things of hers that didn't get destroyed by Pa.*

In her bare feet she padded through the shadows toward the house. Once close enough to assure herself that the monster still slept, she stepped up on the porch, over her father's snoring body and into the house. Joy pulled the shawl out from under her straw mattress.

I'm glad Ma never knew that Pa gambled away her family's farm and that we had to move to this place. Joy surveyed the unadorned space that had been her prison. *Without Ma this shack was never my home…never held a shred of hope or happiness for me.*

The frail child's eyes fell on the banjo that was propped against the wall. It was the monster's prized possession. She turned and stared at the breathing hulk that lay splayed near the door's threshold. *I needed a father…why couldn't you love me?*

She picked the banjo up and swung it back over her shoulder, aiming it at the wall. The gravity of what she was about to do so burdened her that her body quivered.

She slowly lowered her arm, carried the banjo to the table and picked up a fork. Using the utensil's handle as leverage, one by one she popped the instrument's strings until all four fell slack. As her parting message she placed the tines of the fork against its fine-grained polished veneer and scratched her name. Tracing a finger over the three carved letters she spoke to her father's constant companion. "Just once, I wish I could have felt the tender loving embrace you got every time he picked you up to play."

The girl drew in a deep breath. *Pa and I moved here in the spring of 1903, I was thirteen years old. If I've marked the passing of the seasons correctly it's 1905. Leaves have changed color, getting cold…must be September or October. My birthday is October the 15th… I'm sixteen or about to be. I can survive on my own if I make it out of these woods and find a town where I can work.*

Joy slipped out of the house and kept to the shadows as she made her way back to her hiding place behind the mulberry bush. She looked toward the porch and the hateful man who lay sleeping. His leg gave a jerk, then another followed by a third…*reminds me of a hound dog dreaming of a hunt. Difference is…touch this one and he'll bite you, touch one with long ears and a tail and he'll lick your hand with affection.*

She wrapped the shawl around her shoulders and tied it securely. Joy took a last look at the ramshackle cabin before starting her journey to freedom.

***

Bone weary and bruised with bloody bare feet Joy pushed aside a low hanging branch and stumbled onto the side of a dirt road. It had taken her hours to claw her way through the dense woods. She had no inkling of how far she'd traveled.

A light rain was falling, and water was collecting in wagon wheel ruts that could be seen going in both directions. *A well-traveled road…might lead to a town, but which way?*

A dark cloud eclipsed the moon. Thunder boomed down from the heavens. The light rain became a torrent and lightening tore at the sky. *I must find a place to get out of the rain.*

A lightning strike spat forth a measure of brightness enough to momentarily illuminate a farmstead that was situated across and down the road. A long lane led to a house and out buildings. *There's a barn. I can hide in it until the storm blows over. Don't know how much longer until daylight. Maybe I can sleep a bit. Need to leave before someone comes to do morning chores.*

The girl ran up the lane splashing mud on her legs. Brown muck caked the hem of her dress making it heavy-laden. As she approached a large structure on her way to the barn, she heard the flapping of wings followed by repeated cackling coming from within.

Joy's heart caught in her throat. *Chickens. S*he took refuge behind the trunk of a nearby tree where she stayed frozen in place until she was satisfied that no one from the house was coming to investigate the ruckus. The chickens got quiet and she moved to the barn.

The large beam of wood that served as the barn door's latch was heavy and hard for her to move. Once she got the door open, she stumbled in and pulled it closed.

Joy stood still letting her eyes adjust to the changed level of darkness. A welcoming pile of straw was the first thing that caught her attention. The second was the mooing of cows. "Hush now. I'm just going to use your straw for a bit."

She collapsed on the sweet-smelling mound and started to pull the golden comfort over her body, then stopped. Joy got up and walked to the closest stall where she patted the cow's side and softly cooed, "Cooperate with me old gal, all I'm after is a couple of squirts."

She knelt and grasped the bovine's teats. With a few skillfully executed pulls she was able to produce streams of milk. Angling her mouth under the animal's udder she drank her fill. The richness of the sustenance was a delight to her deprived taste buds.

Joy laid her cheek against the cow's protruding stomach and savored the long-missed comfort of touching another living being. "Thank you kindly."

Clasping one of the stall's rails she pulled herself up and moved the short distance to the straw pile where she immersed her body in its warmth. Sleep came instantly.

Chapter 2

Abe scrambled down the stairs, two at a time. Before entering the kitchen, he jumped and tapped the transom above the door. "Good morning, Ma, uh...Ben."

Ben quickly released Sarah from his embrace, took a seat at the table and picked up his issue of *Forest and Stream*. He cleared his throat before greeting his step-son. "Good morning, Abe. You look chipper today."

Sarah spread her arms wide for her morning hug. "Come here, you."

The fourteen-year-old let himself be folded into his mother's love. "Sorry to interrupt, Ma."

"What's got you raring to go so bright and early?" Sarah said tilting her head slightly to rub noses with her oldest child before releasing him from her arms.

"When I woke and looked out the window and saw frost on the chicken house roof, I just felt like jumpin' out of bed. I reckon there's somethin' about the first real nip of fall that fills me with the get-goes. Don't know why, maybe because harvestin's done."

"I know what you mean, Son." Sarah said. "I've always been partial to the autumn season too. The Lord blessed us with a bountiful crop this year, fields and garden."

"I'll grant you that, Ma," the boy said. "The green beans and tomatoes you put up will taste good this winter. Hey Doc, I mean Ben, what you studyin' there?"

"Fishing," the boy's stepfather replied. "You boys best me every time we go to the river. I'm determined to remedy that."

Abe couched, "Now don't go bein' too hard on yourself, Ben. We've been a fishin' all our lives, you're just learnin'."

"Being raised a city slicker did have its disadvantages," Ben said. "I found an interesting advertisement for a fine-looking rod. Listen to this... weighs 5.2 ounces. Half Wells cork grip with ¼-inch rings. Down-sliding blued nickel silver hardware over wood insert reel seat. Red thread wraps with black tipping. Comes with a cloth bag."

"Boy howdy," Abe replied. "What's a rod like that cost?"

"Five dollars," Ben said.

"Whew." Abe cut a look at his mother. "Luck to ya, Ben."

The newly-married Ben, gave his wife a puppy dog plea. "Did I say it came with a cloth bag?"

Sarah had a smile on her face while she gave a pancake a masterful flip.

Abe grabbed his jacket. "I'd best get to the milkin'. It'd be nice to have a good start by the time Gerald gets here."

"Oh, that reminds me," Ben said. "Gerald told me yesterday that he's going to wait for Parker's General Store to open before he comes out today. Said he needed to pick up supplies for fence mending."

"Okay." Abe started to leave then paused, "I didn't know how I was gonna make it when Sam left. Then Gerald came along. At first his ways had me a thinkin' that I just couldn't work with him."

"You've never told me this before Abe," Sarah said. "I had no idea you were uncomfortable working with Gerald. What do you mean by his ways?"

"Oh, Ma, Gerald's a good worker, I'm sorry I mentioned it," the boy said.

"Don't be," Ben said. "You handle a man-sized load here on the farm and your mother and I want you to be happy in your work. If there's something about Gerald that troubles you, we want to hear it."

"Well, I knowed right off that Gerald wasn't as smart as Sam. Sam could figure out anythin' and everythin'. I learned a lot from working with him. But that ain't what troubled me. It was that Gerald, well, Gerald..., now I don't mean to be disrespectful, but Gerald seemed sissified to me when I first met him."

Sarah couldn't stifle a chuckle. "Sissified?"

"It wouldn't be fair to compare anyone to Sam," Ben said. "By the time he left he knew this place inside and out. Even a greenhorn like myself could see that he was knowledgeable about many aspects of farming."

"Gerald knows enough," Abe responded. "I'm used to his ways now, but at first, it got on my nerves how he talked to the cows. I ain't never heard a man talk baby talk to critters before. Aside from that he flops his hands around when he talks.

"Like I done said, all them concerns was when he first come to the farm. I don't pay them no never mind these days. Gerald's reliable and I'm happy to have his help with the work around here. Ma, I don't think I ever said thank you for hiring him or to you, Ben, for recommendin' him."

Gerald Keller stood five-foot eight inches. His build was stocky, and he sported a bushy black, beard. His eyebrows grew in one continuous dark line across the bridge of his nose. He wasn't a handsome man but his massive facial hair, juxtaposed against his shiny bald head, made his appearance memorable.

"I'm glad that hiring Gerald has become agreeable to you, Abe," Ben said. "When I married your mother and moved out here to the farm, offering my house in town as a place for Gerald to live worked out for all of us. He's been a good tenant."

When Sarah responded, "You're welcome, Son," Sam Hartman's face appeared to her and her mind wandered. *Abe didn't know how he'd make it without Sam's help and there was a time when I couldn't see myself making it without Sam either. Him coming to live and work here at the farm after Henry died was a Godsend.* Sarah felt Ben's intense gaze. She turned to see concern in her husband's eyes, and she knew she'd been staring off in the distance. Likely he thought she was remembering his once arch rival.

No worries, Doctor Ben Adams. Sam was a handsome man and I knew we had feelings for one another. But me going into labor, while trapped in the root cellar after the tornado blew through, changed things. If you hadn't come to my rescue, Naomi would have died. When you looked deep into my eyes and asked me if I trusted you to reach inside me and turn her, so she could be born, I said yes. I knew then that you truly loved me and that I loved you back.

When Henry died, I thought I'd lost the only man I'd ever be able to love without reservation. That day I saw in your eyes the man behind the polite, always correct facade and I knew I'd been wrong. I realized that my love for you could grow into that all enduring, life sustaining kind of love. And, it has. I know you often need reassuring; I'll see to that.

***

Abe picked up a handful of acorns and playfully pitched them hither and yon as he made his morning trek toward the barn. As he neared, he noticed the beam closure to the barn's door was slid to the open position. *Did I forget to latch the door last evening? I'm the first one out of the house this mornin', Ben said Gerald's comin' late, wonder what's goin' on?*

Abe tentatively swung the barn door open, entered and stood motionless. Dust particles swirled in the beams of light that streamed through the barn's siding. The boy commenced a thorough, visual sweep of the space. He looked left, nothing, except for Moon Blossom and the other cows who mooed their morning greeting. He tilted his head back to inspect the hayloft. What little of it he could see without climbing the ladder looked undisturbed. Nothing appeared amiss directly in front of him. As he tracked to the right, his breath caught, his body jolted, he slipped and fell.

Not wanting to waste time to stand, the boy made a mad crawl out the door, stood and fell again before gaining traction for a full-out run to the house.

Naomi and Henry were banging their spoons against their highchair trays. Three-year-old Hathaway stood in front of them, cajoling and cooing. "Ma's a gettin' you breakfast." Her voice had a sing-song lilt when she said, "Omi, lay down you spoon. Me play wind the fred wif ya."

The fifteen-month-old complied and her twin Henry played copycat. Hathaway alternated between one baby and then the other, taking turns in holding her siblings' miniature hands in her still chubby dimpled ones to teach the age-old game. "The pull, pull, pull part is hard ta learn, ain't it, Pa?"

Ben leaned over and kissed the toddler on the cheek. "It certainly is, but you're a really good teacher, Hathaway."

Hathaway beamed, basking in the warmth of her stepfather's attention. The small girl turned and called to her brother who had just entered the room. "Zeke, come help wif wind fred."

The six-year-old boy rubbed at his eyes, still filled with sleep. "Wind-the-thread. I ain't had my mornin' bacon yet. I can't play no dern wind-the-thread until I've had me some bacon."

"Language, please," Sarah called out.

"Good morning, Zeke," Ben greeted to his stepson.

"Mornin' Pa." The boy responded.

"Bacon's almost ready, Zeke. Come here and give me a hug." Sarah said, beckoning with her widespread arms.

The boy responded to his mother's invitation then cut a look at his youngest brother who was squealing and reaching out to him. As always occurred, Zeke's heart melted. "Ok, I'll play wind-the-thread with ya, but just 'til my bacon's ready."

Eleven-year-old Luke and nine-year-old Josh shuffled into the kitchen, in unison pulling suspenders up over their shoulders in readiness to tackle morning chores. "'Mornin', Ma, 'mornin', Ben." One, then the other said.

"Good morning, boys." Ben replied to his stepsons.

"Good morning, you two." Sarah called out to her sons. "Come here and give me a hug, then go gather the eggs. I'm anxious for you to find out if our newest pullets have started laying yet."

The kitchen door flew open and Abe stumbled in. He bent at the waist and rested his hands on his knees while he gulped air.

Ben abruptly laid down his magazine and Sarah's long handled cooking fork froze midair. "What's wrong?" The pair simultaneously asked.

The adolescent's voice cracked and went up an octave. "There's a dead body in our barn."

Chapter 3

"What?" Ben said jumping to his feet.

Abe, still trying to catch his breath responded, "I said I think they's a dead body in the barn. I saw a bloody foot a stickin' out of the hay pile."

Ben was putting on his jacket as Sarah took the skillet of bacon off the stove and closed the distance between herself and Abe. "Abe, take a deep breath, Ben and I will go back with you."

Ben put a hold on Sarah's arm. "Stay here with the children until I see what's happened."

"Ben," Sarah said, giving her still learning new husband a stern look, "I'm coming."

Abe led the way with Ben and his mother close behind. As Sarah was closing the door she called out, "Josh, you're in charge."

Josh, Luke, and Zeke stood as if stunned. Hathaway was oblivious and Henry and Naomi continued eating their breakfast, fist to mouth, while grunting like contented little piglets.

Zeke was the first to find his voice. "I'm goin' too. It ain't every day we get ta see us a dead body."

Luke jerked his coat off its hook. "Me too."

Zeke was jumping, trying to reach his jacket that hung fingertips too high. "Luke, give me a hand."

"Sure thing. Here."

"Hold on," Josh called out. "Ma put me in charge, and I say you two need to stay here in the house and help me tend to the babies."

Zeke yelled as he opened the door and ran outside, "You may be in charge of them babies but you ain't in charge of me."

"Sorry, brother," Luke said giving Josh a taunting wave as he ran out behind Zeke leaving the door open.

Josh yelled, "Dag burn it," as he slammed the door shut so hard that the glass in the kitchen's windows rattled. Hathaway's eyes grew big. Henry and Naomi began to wail in unison.

***

Ben stepped in front of Abe as the boy reached for the barn door. "Let me go in first." Ben swung the door fully open allowing a flood of morning light to illuminate the scene before them.

Abe pointed to the hay pile. "There, see that foot?"

Ben knelt and began to brush away the golden stubble. Joy's long legs were exposed first, followed by her torso and then neck and head. "It's a girl."

Abe spoke in a whisper, "She's dead, ain't she?"

Sarah put her arm around Abe and pulled him close.

Ben placed his fore and middle finger at the base of Joy's wrist. "Heartbeat's strong."

Sarah knelt on the opposite side of the girl. "Dear Lord in heaven. What's happened to this child? Ben, look at her face. She's been struck hard…one eye's swollen shut and turning black.

"That'll heal. It's her pallor that concerns me; she's emaciated. Let's get her up to the house."

Ben took off his coat and spread it over the girl. As he slid his arms under her and started to lift, Joy's lids popped open and she bolted to a sitting position. Her eyes darted from Sarah to Ben to Abe and back to Sarah. *Can't let them know who I am. They might try to find Pa.* Joy hung her head low as she tried to gather her wits.

Sarah ran her hand back and forth across the girl's frail shoulders. "Don't be afraid. You're safe now. My name is Sarah. Can you tell us yours?"

Joy didn't respond.

Abe leaned down low so he could look at the girl's face. "Maybe she's a mute, can't talk. Might be deaf too." He yelled, "Can you tell us your naaaame?"

Ben pulled Abe back. "Give her a minute to calm herself. We've startled her awake and she's likely disoriented, trying to remember where she is."

"You're safe," Sarah assured again. "You can trust us." She gestured toward Ben. "This is my husband Ben, he's a doctor." Pointing to Abe she said, "This is Abe, my oldest boy. He found you here in the barn."

I've got to give tell them something. Jane, my mother's name. With her voice barely above a whisper she said, "My name is Jane. My apologies for sleeping in your barn without permission. I needed a place to get in out of the rain last night."

"Ain't no apologies needed." Abe said looking at Ben and his mother for confirmation. "Ya did scare the daylights out of me though. I found you when I came to do the milkin'."

The cow tethered nearby took the opportunity to sound her displeasure. "That's our cow named Moon Blossom. She ain't been milked yet and her teats are likely a throbbin'." Abe's face turned bright red as he heard himself making the ill-considered explanation.

Sarah patted the girl's hand. "Jane, you're more than welcome here. I think we can show you better hospitality than letting you sleep in our barn."

"Of course, we can," Ben said. "Jane, do you think you can stand? We'll take you up to the house and get you something to eat and cleaned up. I'd like to look at your injuries if you'll let me. Can you tell us what's happened to you?"

Abe interrupted, "Where's your ma and pa? Do they know you're hurt?"

Sarah saw a tear run down the girl's cheek and took charge. "Enough talking for now." She took Joy by her left arm and Ben took the girl's right arm. The pair helped the child stand.

Joy's legs buckled. Ben caught her on her way down and swept her up in his arms. As he did, the journal she was carrying under her dress slipped out. It stayed attached to the cord around her neck and dangled at her side.

"She's fainted," Ben said. "She's likely dehydrated and weak from exposure. Sarah, tuck my coat around her, we need to get her warmed up."

When the trio plus the stowaway exited the barn, they were met by the posse of two. Zeke saw the girl limp in Ben's arms and yelled. "It's a girl and she's dead. I ain't never seen me a dead girl before. Ma, are we gonna lay her out at granny Riley's house like we did my first Pa?"

"Zeke, shush!" Sarah scolded as she rushed past him. "She's not dead, what if she heard you." Sarah called over her shoulder as she tried to catch up to Ben. "Abe, keep Zeke here and give him some chores. Luke, you've got to make today's egg deliveries."

"I'm comin'," Luke yelled. "Tell Josh to gather today's eggs."

"Knucklehead," Abe said to Zeke as he good naturedly grabbed him by the collar at the nape of his neck. "I'll put you to muckin' the stalls while I do the milkin'." Zeke squirmed to get free of Abe's hold.

Abe kept a firm grip on his brother's collar as he ushered him into the barn.

***

Josh was watching out the kitchen window. He saw his mother rushing to catch up with Ben who was carrying a body. Josh opened the door and held it so Ben could pass through.

"Thanks, Josh. Open the door to my and your mother's bedroom. I'll put her on our bed for now."

"Is she dead?"

"No, she's fainted. I suspect she's just weak from hunger and thirst. Ask your mother to come help me when she reaches the house."

When Sarah rushed into the kitchen, she saw that her three youngest were corralled in the corner of the kitchen in a pen made from turned over chairs. Hathaway called out, "Mama, me teach 'Omi and Henry blocks."

"Thanks, my sweet girl," Sarah responded.

Josh came back into the kitchen. "Ma, Ben put the girl on your bed. He said to have you come in to help him with her."

Sarah took off her coat and hung it on her peg by the door. "Josh, thanks for looking after the little ones. Did you change the twins' diapers?"

"I gave their butts a sniff when I pinned them up. They weren't at full load yet."

"Oh, my goodness," Sarah said looking at her babies. "Stay with them until either Ben or me can come out and take over. You've still got today's eggs to gather."

"Sure, wish somebody would tell me what's happened. I feel left out."

Sarah talked as she hurried to join Ben, "We found the girl sleeping in the barn. It appears she's been hurt and needs food and water. That's all any of us know except that she told us her name is Jane." Sarah's voice cut off as she entered the bedroom and closed the door.

"Sarah, we need to get Jane out of these dirty clothes and washed up so we can assess her injuries," Ben said. "She looks to be about fourteen or fifteen. I'm sure modesty is important to her. It'd be best if I stay out of the room and let you clean her up. I'll go fetch a pan of warm water, some soap and cloths."

Sarah gave Ben a tender kiss on the cheek. "I expect you're right. If she comes to, she'll be more comfortable with just me tending to her personal needs."

Sarah's eyes teared up after Ben left the room and closed the door. She knelt beside the bed and took the girl's hand in hers. "Dear Father in heaven. What kind of monster has hurt and neglected this child? Ben can patch up her body, but I suspect that's not the only healing she needs. Father give us the wisdom to help her heal from her wounds that the eye can't see."

As Sarah held the frail child's hand in her capable grasp, she felt a slight return caress.

Chapter 4

"Zeke, would you run down to the barn and let the boys know I'll have supper on the table by the time they get here and wash up?" Sarah asked.

"Why don't I just ring the dinner bell?" Zeke asked.

"Because Jane is still sleeping, it might wake her," Sarah answered.

"Okay, I'll go Ma," Zeke replied. "Henry and me's been playin' with my toy animals. Someone's gotta guard them while I do it."

"Guard them?" Sarah questioned.

"Yeah, guard them from Henry. If I had me a penny for every time, I've pulled one of 'em out of his mouth, I'd be rich. He's done gnawed on one of my cow's legs so much I'm scared it might break off."

Ben came from checking in on Joy just as Zeke was telling about the perils of toy sharing with a teething baby. "Go on Zeke, I'll look after Henry," Doc said. "It's really kind of you to share your wooden animals with him but he's just too young to understand about not putting them in his mouth. If the cow's leg would happen to break off when he's chewing on it, it might cause him to choke."

Zeke kissed Henry on his bald head. "Well, I wouldn't want that to happen. After all, I am his big brother."

Ben knelt next to the baby. "Hey, little buddy. How about you put down that cow so I can get you ready to eat your supper." Henry wouldn't surrender the toy and Doc had to pry it out of his tiny hand. The little guy screamed in protest, flailed his arms and kicked his feet. Doc got him in his high chair and gave him a dried biscuit left from breakfast. Henry made baby griping sounds as he pounded it on his tray. Eventually he surrendered to his oral obsession and stuck the biscuit in his mouth.

Hathaway was in her chair with it positioned so that it butted up against Naomi's high chair. She intentionally leaned her head toward the baby, close enough for Naomi to grasp on to one of her pigtail braids. Naomi pulled on it and Hathaway said ouch. Her mock cry of pain was funny to the baby and she giggled. The jerk, ouch, giggle repeated over and over until Sarah called a halt to the play. "Hathaway, tell Naomi a story while I finish up supper."

Ben came up behind his wife and rubbed his hand across her shoulders. "Is all this ruckus getting to you?"

"Just a bit," she replied. "I'm concerned about the girl. I thought that without the chatter I might be able to get my head around the situation."

Doc chuckled.

"What's so funny?" Sarah asked.

"Oh, nothing really," Ben said. "It's just that your comment about all the chatter caused me to remember one of my greatest fears about marrying you. I was concerned that after living alone the noise made by seven children would keep me from having even a moment's peace."

Sarah wiped her hands on her apron and turned to face her husband. "So, you were afraid to marry me. Noisy children were one reason. How about you spill-the-beans and tell me about the rest of your great fears over tying the knot with me."

Doc blushed, then chuckled again. "Oh, I think not."

Sarah moved in close and fidgeted with the button on Ben's shirt while she looked up at him. "Are you sure you wouldn't like to tell me about these concerns of yours?"

Doc's eyes darted around the kitchen and he swallowed hard. "Not now, but I would like to *talk* about it later."

It was Sarah's turn to giggle. "Okay, I'll let you off the hook, for now." Nodding toward their bedroom door she said, "I saw that you just came from checking on Jane. How's she doing?"

"She's asleep snuggled up with her fingers laced in the fringe of that shawl Abe found in the barn. That filthy cord with the journal on it, is again around her neck. I tried to lift it off, but she's got a death grip on the thing."

"The crocheted garment's dear to her for some reason. I can't help but wonder what's in that journal that causes her to protect it so." Sarah said as she sliced bread for supper.

Doc reached over and popped a piece of crust, that had fallen to the side, in his mouth. "I'm glad you got her to eat some broth and bread before she fell asleep. If we can get her to take nourishment again this evening, her strength should start to come back."

"Should I wake her to eat with us?"

"No, let's let her sleep a bit longer, Doc said. "She looks like she's been near starved to death. It'd be best if she goes easy with food. Just broth for now, or something gentle on her stomach like oatmeal. I think she'll be able to eat regular by tomorrow, but in small portions."

"What about her eye? Any change with it?"

"Yes, the swelling has gone down considerable. The bruising is starting to change color so I'm guessing whatever caused it happened day before yesterday.

"The condition of her feet is still concerning. I don't know how far she traveled to get here but it's obvious it was across some rough terrain. It's going to take a week or better for those cuts and scrapes to heal. The bottoms of her feet are bruised and swollen. I expect she's in a good bit of discomfort."

"Should we give her some Laudanum?" Sarah asked.

"No. Her sleep appears to be peaceful. If she can rest through the pain, I'd rather let her tough it out than give her something that will deaden her senses. I'm hoping that when she awakens, she'll tell us what's happened to her."

"Me too." Sarah said as she carried the platter of roast beef to the table.

The kitchen door opened. As the boys entered Luke was in the lead with Abe close behind. Josh and his ever-present canine companion Lancy brought up the rear.

Luke drew in a deep breath as he hung up his jacket. "Is that roast beef I smell?"

"Yes," Sarah said. "We've got roasted potatoes and carrots to go with it and peach cobbler for dessert."

"Boy howdy. My favorite meal." Luke said.

Zeke was picking up his farm animals and putting them in their storage box. "Luke, you say that ever evenin' when you come through that door. How come you got so many favorite meals?"

"They're all my favorite 'cause our Ma's the best cook in all of Wabash County." The boy said as he took his place at the table next to Josh.

Josh gave Luke a playful elbow to the ribs. "Ma, your cookin' is really good but you know Luke's just throwin' them compliments so he can get an extra big helpin' of cobbler, don't ya." Lancy whined. Josh reached down and patted the dog's head. "Don't worry, boy, I'll make sure we get our share."

Sarah smiled. "I'm quite sure Luke is sincere about everything he said. Now let's say grace and eat before this food gets cold. Abe, I believe it's your turn."

"Yes Ma'am," Abe said. "Father in heaven. Thank you for the food we're about to eat and bless it to the nourishments of our bodies. And please help Jane get well. Amen."

As platters and bowls were being passed around, the bedroom door opened, and Joy gingerly walked into the kitchen. Although Sarah had given the girl a clean gown when she put her to bed, Joy had changed back in to her dirty tattered dress. She had her mother's shawl tied tightly around her shoulders. The frail child hesitated, clutching the journal that lay beneath the wrap's thread-bare façade.

Sarah saw her first. "Jane, you're awake. Come join us."

Abe jumped to his feet. "I'll get another chair."

Joy stared at her bare feet when she spoke. "Thank you kindly but I've been enough of a bother. I'll be on my way."

Zeke forked a hunk of roast from the platter and held it out to the girl. "Get yourself some of this good meat afore you go. We got us a plenty."

Joy didn't look up as she started for the door. Sarah spoke in a voice she hoped would support her plea. "Jane, please don't leave."

Ben stood. "Jane, it'll be dark soon. You're not dressed warmly enough for the night's chill. We'd planned for you to spend a few days with us. Your feet need to heal."

Joy stopped, the shawl slipped down exposing her hunched shoulders as she faced the door that would provide her exit. Her near skeletal thinness accentuated her bones giving the appearance of wings ready for flight.

Sarah walked over and stood facing the girl, blocking her exit. She placed her right hand on her arm and cupped Joy's chin in her left. She raised the child's face so she could look in her eyes. "We sincerely do want you to stay with us for a few days. We won't keep you here against your will, but I want you to know that if you leave now, I'll be awake all night worrying about you."

Joy's shoulders relaxed. "Thanks, Ma'am. I am still a bit tired. I'll stay tonight and leave tomorrow." She reached around Sarah and took ahold of the door knob.

Abe called out. "Where're you goin'? I thought you just said you'd spend the night here."

Joy kept her hand on the knob. "I am staying. I'm going to the bed in the barn."

Sarah placed her hand over Joy's, took it from the knob and intertwined fingers with her. "If you sleep in the barn, I'll still worry about you. I need you to stay here in the house."

"But that bed I was in belongs to you and your mister." Joy said. "I could tell from the clothes hanging on the wall hooks. I can't take your bed from you."

"Nor would we want you to." Ben interjected. "We've got a cot set up for you in the parlor. You'll be sharing the room with the twins. For now, both of their cribs are in there."

Henry and Naomi appeared to know that they were being talked about and started jabbering and banging their spoons on their high chair trays. Joy turned and looked at them. A tear ran down her cheek. "Babies always smell so sweet."

"Well don't get your hopes up with these two." Zeke said, pointing to the twins. "They smell, but ya won't catch me callin' it sweet."

***

Joy lay on her cot listening to the happy chatter coming from the kitchen. She'd eaten oatmeal and drank a glass of milk. Her stomach was content. She raised her arm and sniffed the sleeve of the night gown Sarah had given her to wear. It smelled of pine and freshness. Her feet were sore, but no longer throbbing with pain. Ben had insisted she wear a pair of his socks to bed to keep them warm. *Warm, I'd forgotten how delicious it feels.*

The cot she slept on was near the babies' cribs. They were both asleep but occasionally made tiny murmurs as if deep in a happy dream. Joy got up and walked to them, reached out, wanted to touch, but stopped for fear she'd cause them to wake. She bent low over each bed and drew in their scent. *No matter what that brother of yours said, your smell is sweet to me.*

Joy scurried back to her warm bed. If only for this one night, she'd enjoy the comforts around her. The girl put her hand to her face. She savored the memory of Sarah's gentle touch. Tears threatened. *I'm a stranger but that woman's eyes showed concern.*

A whine at the door disrupted her thoughts. Joy saw a black paw intruding through the crack between the bottom of the door and the floor. *The dog. He wants in.*

A boy's voice yelled, "Lancy, get away from that door and let Jane get some sleep."

Joy pulled the covers up over her head to muffle a giggle. *I giggled! I didn't think I'd ever so much as smile again. Oh, how wonderful it would be to belong to a family like the one living in this house.*

Chapter 5

Ben sat at the table sipping his night time cup of chamomile tea and reading a medical journal when Sarah came down the stairs and into the kitchen. "I didn't wait for you," he said smiling. "I've got yours steeping."

"Thank you. I'll take a quick peek at the twins and our house guest then come join you," Sarah said as she padded in her stocking feet to the parlor. The hinges on the room's door creaked slightly when she opened it. *Got to get those greased.* Sarah tiptoed to the cribs where she found Henry and Naomi sawing baby sized logs.

Sarah moved to Joy's make-shift bed and stood for a moment listening to the rhythm of her breathing. A lock of hair had fallen across her face, Sarah lifted it away. *She's such a beautiful girl. Heavenly Father, she's so frail. She reminds me of a frightened doe, ready to bolt, not sure in which direction.*

Lord, hold her in the grip of your love and grace. Calm her fears so she can think clearly. Father in Heaven, you know the painful story she's holding in tight, we don't. My guess is you had a hand in guiding her to our farm. If we're supposed to be privy to her troubles, give her the courage to tell us soon. Like your promise in Isaiah 43:19, let there be a new day for Jane. Make a way for her to find peace and feel whole. Amen. Sarah leaned down and kissed the girl's forehead before leaving the room.

"Everyone down and out for the night?" Ben asked.

Sarah took the chair opposite him. "Yes, sound asleep, all eight of them." Sarah removed the saucer off the top of her cup of tea and placed it underneath before taking a sip. "Tastes just right. I'll be eternally grateful to the doctor that introduced me to the wonders of chamomile tea."

"And he's eternally grateful to you for accepting his offer to share a cup each evening until death do us part."

Sarah locked eyes with her husband, raised her cup and blew on the rising vapors so that they wafted across the table toward him. For the second time that evening Ben blushed.

Ben attempted to copy the flirtatious gesture. He locked eyes with Sarah and blew, but too timidly. Instead of the steamy essence floating across the table, it maintained its upward spiral and fogged Doc's reading glasses. Sarah put her hand over her mouth but was unable to stifle a full-on chuckle.

Ben took off his glasses and wiped the lenses with the edge of the linen tablecloth. "Sorry, you'd think I'd learn to stick to what I know."

For a time, they sipped and savored the relaxing brew. Eventually Sarah picked up the book Doc had been reading. "*Dr. F. Hollick's Complete Works – marriage guide, diseases, midwifery and child birth, the origin of life and the process of reproduction.* Well that certainly promises a book full of information. What part interests you most?"

"They're all subjects beneficial to me as this area's only doctor. Hollick died in 1900 but his beliefs, while considered controversial for some, continue to make sense to me."

"Controversial? Which ones?"

"Primarily his view about straight talking to patients."

"Straight talking? Do you mean not mincing words, telling folks plain out what he thinks they need to hear?"

"Yes, that's it exactly. I'm guilty of being shy to do it with some I treat, but I'm trying to overcome that. I believe it's important that we in the doctoring profession not feel skittish about discussing functions of the human body with our patients and that includes the subject of marital relations."

"I couldn't agree with you more. After all, it is 1905 and a new century. I'd venture to say that most women never have been skittish and want to be told what's what by their doctor. But, if my mother comes to see you, I'd give that last subject a wide berth."

Doc blushed yet again. "Sarah, you beat all. Don't worry, if your mother comes to my office, I'll put *Hollick's Complete Works* clean out of sight."

After a time of just enjoying one another's company and the quiet of the house, Ben reached over and patted Sarah's hand. "So, what are we going to do about Jane?"

"First we've got to get her to trust us enough to tell us who hurt her and if she has any family we can notify to come and get her."

"It might be that it's family she ran from."

"Oh Ben, I hope that isn't the case. I can't imagine, even at my age, coping without the love of family."

Ben ran a hand through his thick dark hair. "One can learn to cope if they're old enough to fend for themselves, but it's hard to find joy in it."

"Tomorrow's Sunday," Sarah said. "What would you say to us skipping church? We could make it a true day of rest for all of us. After a leisurely breakfast you and the boys might go fishing while Hathaway, the twins and I stay here with Jane. I'd use the time to alter one of my dresses for her to wear and set her up with some proper under garments. If time allows, I could help her wash and style her hair."

"That sounds like a lot of work for you, Sarah. What about your day of rest?"

"Well when I said rest, what I really meant was for us all to do something we'd enjoy a lot. It would give me pleasure to do for Jane. I'm hoping the time we share will draw her in close enough to open up and talk about her troubles."

Doc ventured an opinion. "I know I'm wasting my breath but, I think that's too much to put on yourself on top of cooking a supper for this big family."

"I'll throw on some ham and beans when I first get up. They'll cook slow for several hours and won't require much tending. If I get time, I'll make corn bread. If not, I'll slice some bread to eat with them. I baked extra pies today to cover for any drop-by Sunday visitors. Assuming no one comes, we're all set for a dessert."

Ben half stood, leaned across the table and gave Sarah a peck on the cheek. "You're a wise and most capable woman, Sarah Adams. Whatever the outcome from your day with Jane, I think we should let Jeb Carter know she's here at the farm."

"I guess you're right. Before this is all settled, we might find we need the town Marshal's help."

"I'll be ready to do morning chores when the boys wake up tomorrow. Sunday being Gerald's day off I'm sure they could use an extra pair of hands. That way we can collect our fishing gear and get on our way faster."

"I'll pack a picnic basket for all of you."

"We'd appreciate that. Having a picnic will make the outing even more fun."

"Ben," Sarah said.

"What, Sarah," Ben said tilting his head. "You know it makes me nervous when you look at me like that."

Sarah smiled. "Do you really think you should help with morning chores? Remember what happened the last time."

Doc threw his hands up in defense. "Look, I hadn't had my hands around teats in a long, long time. I still think it was pretty unfriendly of Moon Blossom to put up such a fuss about my milking her."

"That might be but, just to stay on the safe side, leave the milking to Abe and Josh. We've got an extra child to feed and we don't need Moon Blossom kicking over tomorrow morning's bucket of milk. You can muck the stalls."

Doc folded his arms and stuck out his lower lip. "I think we need to reconsider letting the hired hand have Sundays off."

Sarah stood, walked around the table and put her arm across Ben's shoulders. "I know it's been a long day, but I wondered if you might have enough energy left to *talk* about those other marriage concerns you had. Maybe you could share some of that knowledge you've gained from reading Dr. Hollick's book."

Ben stood, took Sarah by the hand and led her to their bedroom. "I believe I can muster up the strength needed for a good *talk,* but I'm not sure I can handle it if *you* gain any more knowledge in certain subjects.

***

"Ed, hey, Ed!" Getting no response, the bartender walked over to the table where Edward J. Humes slept and gave him a smack on the head. "Get up. It's ten o'clock. You're the last one here and I want to close."

Humes grunted but didn't move.

"Dammit, Ed. I'm gettin' sick of cleanin' up your drool every night. Ya need to get on home and sleep it off."

The drunk responded with slurred speech as he tried to rally and get to his feet. "My cabin's too quiet, no one there."

"What do you mean there's no one there? When you first started comin' in here you told me you were a widower with a thirteen-year-old daughter. That was two, no more than three years ago. She can't be old enough to have married and gone off."

"Not married. Ran off." Ed said, standing but wobbly.

"I'm not surprised. You can't be beat when it comes to playin' the banjo, I'll grant you that. But you ain't worth a tick on a flea's back when it comes to workin'."

Ed took ahold of the table's edge to steady himself and made a deliberate show of pulling back his shoulders. "I'm a professional musician, that's my job."

"Ed," the bartender said. "You ain't played anywhere but this tavern since you came to town. We had us a deal. I've held up my half of the bargain but I'm a gettin' the short end of the stick from you."

"Now you hold on," Ed lost his balance and plopped down on the chair. "I've been playing here nearly every night you've been open."

"I ain't sayin' you haven't been here. Our deal was that I'd pay you two-bits every two weeks for playin' Monday night through Saturday night. I sweetened the pot with one, on-the-house drink per night. I even fronted you a two Morgan poker stake. I got my stake back, you were good on your word for that, but of late you ain't played the banjo enough to count for much."

"You lyin' piece of cow dung." Ed pointed to the room's designated entertainment area. "After I down my free shot of whiskey, I take a seat on that stool every night."

"Yes, but instead of playin' the six to eight songs we agreed to, you've taken to fizzlin' out after one or two. The last couple of days you've been so drunk you slid off the stool before you even finished one."

"Since you've cut me off from running a bar tab, how do you figure that one free drink makes me drunk?" Humes asked.

"Ed, you're drunk before you get here. I can smell rotgut sweat comin' off you when you come through the door. You reek of it so bad the men don't want you playin' poker with them, even if you could get someone to stake you."

"Their loss," Ed said. "I'm considered one of the best poker players this side of the Ohio river."

"Good for you. Now pay your bar bill, settle up on your outstanding markers and take your sorry ass on down the road. The town of LaFontaine's just seven miles over yonder." The bartender pointed at an angle west and a bit south of where they were. "They've got a tavern and a hotel. Try your skills on some of their town folk. We here in Banquo are done with you."

***

Back at the shack Ed lay on his filthy pallet and waited for sleep to come. He'd been the same as run out of town. If he was no longer welcome at the local tavern, there was no place left for him to even try to ply his skills.

When he and Joy first moved to the area, he'd been able to make a grand entrance, measured on Banquo's small-town scale. He had a horse; a new suit of clothes and he was well spoken. His handsome face, winning ways, and banjo playing had worked to his advantage. He'd even made a few eyes water telling his sad tale of being a widower with a young girl to care for. He'd easily settled in with a group of folks, that like him, enjoyed the seedy side of life.

The two-dollar poker stake, along with his skill at slight-of-hand, netted him a steady income of pocket change. When the demon broke through Ed's façade and once again consumed him, his card playing got sloppy and his string fingers turned clumsy.

Ed cut a look at his jacket that hung on a peg. *Sleeve's ripped, it's covered with dirt.* He held his arm up and took a sniff. *I do smell like I've been sleeping with pigs. I can't move on to a new town in this condition. Got to get dried out and cleaned up. It'll be rougher this time without the girl to tend to me.* "Joy, you worthless seed of my loin. You had no money, no shoes, you can't have traveled far."

Ed got up, took a few steps to where his banjo was leaning and picked it up. He traced a finger over the three letters in her name that Joy had carved in its once beautiful veneer. With the instrument still in his hand he stomped out on the porch, lifted his arms and yelled to the moon bright sky. "Wherever you are, Joy, don't get too comfortable. I'm coming for you. It might take me a few weeks, but I'll find you. You'll pay, mark my word, you'll pay for this."

It started with the scolding chant of squirrels, followed by the hoot of an owl. Ed tracked the hoot and saw two huge eyes, eerily aglow, staring at him through foliage on the tree adjacent to the mulberry bush. From near the tree chipmunks began to chatter. A multitude of insects and other woodland creatures followed, creating a high pitched, frenzied chorus that assaulted the night's quiet.

Ed put his hands over his ears and yelled, "Shut up."

Branches broke, twigs snapped, the ground trembled, when a twelve-point buck broke through the tree line. The bull skidded to a stop and held his head so that his eyes locked with the beast on the porch.

Humes stumbled backward, managed to get into the cabin, and closed the door. After securing the wooden latch he ran to the shack's only window and drew the make-shift flour sack curtain across the glass.

The buck snorted and pawed at the ground before eventually retreating to the cloak of the forest's foliage. The deer's departure signaled an end to the raucous chorus and the night grew still.

With trembling hands Ed stripped off his clothes and laid down on his pallet. He hoped sleep would come. He knew from past experiences that in a few hours the misery called withdrawal would overtake him and there'd be no rest.

After an hour of tossing and turning his eye locked onto the jug of moonshine he'd picked up on his way home. He got up, crossed the room and picked up the jug. After pulling the cork he looped his forefinger through the handle and slug it back. As he let the rotgut burn his throat and smolder in his stomach he thought, n*o point in letting this go to waste. I'll start the drying out tomorrow.*

Chapter 6

From the fence post just outside the bedroom window, the rooster crowed in sync with the kitchen's Regulator clock. It struck six times, sounding the arrival of another Sabbath dawn. Sarah's eyes fluttered open. While remaining nestled under the bed's cloak of warmth she perked her ears and listened for sounds from the adjacent room where the twins slept. Hearing none, she spooned Ben and drifted into a thirty-minute snooze.

When the clock signaled half past six Sarah bolted to a sitting position and swung her legs to the side of the bed. She trained her ear listening to the muffled sounds that were seeping through the shared wall of the adjacent room. *It's the twins, they're chuckling and giggling. Hope they aren't disturbing Jane's sleep.*

Sarah put on her robe and slippers before tiptoeing the short distance from her bedroom to theirs. She quietly cracked the door, enough to peek in. Naomi was standing beside Henry in his crib, both were holding on to its side rail. Joy, still in her nightgown, stood in front of the pair with only one sock on. The other sock covered her right hand and forearm. The heel of the sock was tucked in the valley between her thumb and forefinger creating the appearance of a head and mouth. Alternating between the babies she was using the makeshift puppet to feign plucking and eating their noses. With each pass their laughter grew louder morphing to squeals of delight.

"What's got the twins so stirred up this early in the morning?" Ben whispered as he slipped up behind Sarah and wrapped his arms around her waist.

Whispering back to him and stepping aside she said, "Take a look."

Ben stifled a chuckle. "It looks as if the room sharing is going well."

"I'll say," Sarah said as she lightly knocked on the door before swinging it fully open. "Good morning, everyone. Giggles and laughs, what a wonderful way to start the day."

"Oh, good morning," Joy said nodding first to Sarah then to Ben. I hope our fun didn't wake you."

"Not at all. The rooster and kitchen clock get the credit for that. Besides, it's time to get this glorious day started." Sarah said as she crossed the room and picked up a squealing Naomi.

Ben said good morning to the girl then took Henry out of his crib. After patting the baby's behind he said, "Dry britches, now that's a surprise."

"Naomi's are dry too." Sarah said turning a smiling face to Joy.

"The wet diapers are over yonder. I didn't know where to put them." Joy responded with a blush to her face.

Sarah let Naomi straddle her left hip while she put her right arm around Joy's shoulders and pulled her close. "Changing their diapers, what a kind thing to do. Come, I'll show you where I keep the bucket for soaking between washings."

"I can't go out in my nightgown. May I get dressed first?" Joy said.

"Of course, you can." Sarah responded. "I sponged out your dress last night and hung it to dry. Give me minute to put Naomi in her highchair then I'll fetch it for you."

***

By nine o'clock the farm's male inhabitants, minus one, were off for a day of fishing. In the corner of the kitchen designated for play, Henry was pulling wooden blocks from the toy box and gnawing on their corners before tossing them aside. Naomi was nestled between Joy's legs as she sat on the floor. Hathaway was on her knees in front of the pair demonstrating how to play Wind, Wind, Wind the Thread.

Sarah walked into the room with several garments slung across her arm. "Jane, when you're done there, I'd like to show you some dresses and undergarments I thought we might make over to fit you. It's nice to have a change of clothing on hand in readiness for eventualities."

Hathaway jumped to her feet. "We'se done. Me see too."

Joy carried Naomi on her hip to the kitchen table where Sarah had placed the articles of clothing. "Ma'am, Naomi keeps yawning. I think she's sleepy," the girl said.

Sarah reached out and took the baby from the girl. "Yes, I'm sure you're right. She and Henry usually take a morning nap about this time each day." Sarah walked to where Henry was playing, squatted down and in a practiced move used her free arm to encircle his waist then scoop him up. He offered no resistance as she carried the two to their cribs.

When Sarah came back into the kitchen, she found Joy with tears streaming down her cheeks as she gently stroked the fabric on one of the dresses. Hathaway was attempting to comfort her. "Don't cry Jane. Big girls not haffa sleep now."

In a soft voice Sarah spoke. "Hathaway dear, I don't think Jane is worried about having to take a nap."

Joy kept her head lowered as she swiped at her eyes. Sarah pulled a handkerchief from her apron pocket and handed it to the girl. "Jane, would you like to talk about what's making you sad?"

When Joy lifted her head to look at Sarah her voice came out in sobs. "My, my mother ha-had a dress made of this same fa-fabric."

Sarah opened her arms wide and Joy allowed herself to be enfolded in the comfort. "Sorry, Ma'am," she said when she'd gained composure.

"No need to apologize." Sarah said. "Sometimes a good cry is just what we women need."

Hathaway grasped Joy's hand. "Me cry when I gets a boo boo. Henry and Omi cry 'bout lots a stuff."

Sarah took the clothing from the table top and draped it over the back of a chair. "After a good cry I like to have a cup of hot tea. Hathaway show Jane where we keep the cookies and the two of you can put a few on a plate. I'll get the tea."

Hathaway clapped her chubby hands and giggled. "Tea party, tea party." In a sing-song voice the toddler said, "'Member Ma, me gets lots a milk in mine."

After a time of sipping tea and munching on cookies Sarah nodded toward the dress that had captured Joy's attention. "Jane, you said your mother *had* a dress similar to that one. Were you implying that she's no longer living?"

"Yes, she died when I was eleven years old." Joy fingered the shawl that was ever present around her shoulders. "This shawl was hers. It's all I have left to remember her by."

"I'm so sorry to hear about your loss, Jane. I'm fortunate that my mother is still living. Although I can't relate exactly to your situation, I do understand the grief of losing someone you love. My husband, the children's father, died a couple of years ago. He was young and it was unexpected. My heart still has an empty spot that only he could fill."

"Oh, that's sad," Joy replied. "Then you met Doctor Adams. He seems like a kind man."

"Kind, yes, that describes our Ben."

Hathaway spewed cookie crumbs as she spoke. "He my pa."

"Was your first mister your boy's pa?"

"Yes," Sarah explained. "My first husband's name was Henry Whitcome and he was the father of all of my children. I was expecting the twins when he died. About a year after his death I married Ben Adams. I'm now Sarah Adams but the children still go by Whitcome.

"Ben has been our town's doctor and a good family friend for years. His wife and newborn baby girl died a few years before my Henry."

"You all seem so happy together," Joy said.

"Thank you, Joy," Sarah responded. "Yes, we are a very happy family and Ben and I love one another. I give God the glory for that.

"Zeke and Hathaway were so young when their father died that they don't remember him, and as I said, the twins weren't yet born. To the four of them, Ben is their father. The older boys have good memories of their pa. They have however accepted Ben and recognize him as their stepfather." After a few minutes of silence Sarah asked, "What about your father, Jane? Is he still living?"

"I don't like to talk about him."

"You've told us that your given name is Jane, what about your last name? What's it?"

"I'm not ready to say."

"Can you tell me where you came from and if you have any other family, aunts, uncles, grandparents?"

Joy's eyes filled and a tear trickled down her cheek. Sarah patted her hand and stood. "I'll stop asking questions. I do hope that in time you'll come to trust me enough to tell me. Now let's get the table cleared and look at those dresses and undergarments."

"Ma'am, I can't take any of your dresses. That just wouldn't seem right." Joy said.

Sarah smiled. "You won't be taking them. I'm giving them to you. After birthing seven children they've gotten a bit too tight in the waist for me to comfortably wear them. In truth I doubt there's enough seam allowance to let them out more. For you we'll be taking them in a good bit."

Joy ran her hand across the tattered and torn dress she was wearing. "If you say so. I haven't had anything but this one dress to wear for more than a year."

"Then it's settled," Sarah said getting to her feet.

Joy ran a hand through her hair. "Ma'am, would it be alright if I washed my hair?"

"Certainly. With all the men gone for the day we have the house to ourselves. I'll fix you a hot bath and you can wash your hair and soak a bit.

"While you do that, I'll tackle the alterations. I'm sure I can get one dress fixed before the troops come home for supper. Which is your first choice?" Sarah asked.

Joy picked up the frock with the familiar blue and lavender floral pattern. "I'd be much obliged if you did this one first."

***

It was nearly supper time when a wagon load of dirty-faced fishermen came up the lane. At the cut off to the barn Abe pulled the team of horses to a halt. "Josh, Luke and me will get off here and tackle the milkin'. We should have evenin' chores done in about twenty minutes."

Ben Adams held up a string of trout. "What about the fish? Don't you boys want to be present when we show them to your ma?"

Abe responded, "As for me, you and Zeke can have the honors. I'm starvin'. The sooner we get the chores done, the sooner we can eat supper."

Josh and Luke nodded in agreement and all three boys jumped down from the wagon and took off racing toward the barn.

While Doc tethered the team, Zeke barreled through the door, the day's catch in hand. It was heavy and fish tails dragged on the kitchen linoleum. "Hey Ma, look at this."

"Well my goodness," Sarah said. "That's just about the prettiest string of trout I've seen in a long time. I do believe you've brought home enough for two suppers."

Ben came through the door beaming. "Guess who caught the biggest one?"

"Zeke." Sarah said with a twinkle in her eye.

"No guess again," Ben said.

"Abe." Sarah teased as a second-choice answer.

Ben threw his arms open wide. "No, it was me. Where's the yard stick. I want to take its measure. I'm guessing a foot long."

Joy knew where the measuring stick was since they'd used it during the dress alteration. She fetched it and handed it to Hathaway who eagerly took it to Ben. "Here, Pa." The toddler wrapped her arms around Ben's leg as he measured his prized catch.

"Eleven and three-quarters inch." Ben reported.

With a rare show of benevolence, Zeke said, "Close enough to call 'er a foot." Then with his characteristic bravado he turned to Joy and said, "I generally catch the most and the biggest ones. Today I thought I'd let Pa have a turn."

Joy smiled. "They're lovely."

"Lovely, but smelly," Sarah said with her nose in a wrinkle."

"I'll go out to the ice house, chip some, cover them up so they'll keep," Ben said.

Sarah ruffled Zeke's hair and patted Ben on the chest, "You fellows see to it they're cleaned before you leave in the morning and I'll fry up a mess for tomorrow's supper."

"Boy howdy!" Zeke hollered. "Ma, you got a deal."

"Sarah, do we have time to get the fish handled before tonight's supper is ready?" Ben asked.

"Yes, I think so. I'll have it on the table in about an hour," Sarah responded.

The boys were washed up and starving when they entered the kitchen after completing evening chores. "Smells great," Josh complimented.

"I'm hungry as a bear." Luke offered.

Abe hung up his jacket and turned to add his two-cents worth, but his words got stuck. Joy was at the table, standing behind a chair with her hands resting on its back. Her hair was golden and glistening. The sides were pulled back from her face and held in place by a large blue bow. The rest of her mane cascaded down her back, stopping just short of her waist line.

The flowered dress she wore appeared to be tailor made. Its bodice tucked in at the appropriate places, just enough to modestly accentuate her budding figure. The glow on the girl's face, flawless except for her black eye, counteracted the shape of her herb book, hanging around her neck and showing under the form-fitting frock.

Joy smiled at the awe-stricken Abe. The corners of his mouth attempted to respond in kind but couldn't. It was obvious that the fourteen-year-old was struggling to swallow the lump that had formed in his throat.

Chapter 7

Ben blew on the hot brew before taking his first sip of morning coffee. "I find it hard to believe that it was only two weeks ago today that we found Jane sleeping in our barn. Somehow it seems longer than that."

Sarah, coffee mug in hand, pulled out a chair and sat down across from Ben. "I know what you mean. I marvel how easily she's blended into our family. It's almost as if she's kin."

"Now, Sarah, don't go getting too attached," Ben cautioned. "She isn't kin and she can't stay here forever."

Sarah's head was bowed while she traced her finger around the rim of her cup. "Why not?"

With palms splayed outward Ben blurted, "Sarah! We don't know the whole story of Jane's circumstances. We haven't even heard her half of it. She might have a loving family that's worried and looking for her this very minute."

Sarah's back stiffened. "If she's got a loving family looking for her, they've been at it a long time and doing a poor job of it. Noticeable injuries aside, she was emaciated and obviously neglected when we found her. I'll not turn her out, Ben, I won't."

Ben reached across the table and cupped his hand over Sarah's. "Nor will I. But, can you agree with me that the longer she stays the more we'll get attached to her. If, or when she does have to leave it might be really hard for everyone to let her go."

Sarah leaned down and kissed the back of Ben's hand. "I agree. When it's just Jane and me alone with the babies, her shoulders aren't hunched. Each day she seems to relax more. She freely talks to the babies. A time or two she and I have come close to having a real conversation."

"Sarah," Ben said in a soft voice. "If one of our children were missing, we'd be beside ourselves with worry. I can't in good conscience wait beyond midweek to talk to the town marshal about this situation. Jeb's a loving father and a good man. He'll not let the outcome of finding Jane's family bring her to any harm."

"I know you're right," Sarah responded. "Today I'll start pressing her to share her story. Jane reads to Hathaway and she's well spoken. It's obvious she's had some schooling. She should have the opportunity to learn more. Can we agree that a week from today, next Monday, we'll send her to school if she's willing to go?" Sarah said.

"Sounds like a good plan to me," Ben said rising from the table along with Sarah. He went to refill his coffee cup and she to finish cooking breakfast.

***

Sarah pulled Zeke's wagon loaded with the twins and Joy held Hathaway's hand as they strolled in the warm September afternoon's sun. Their destination was the pumpkin patch to check on the crop growth. All five were silent. Alternately their faces tilted skyward, soaking up the golden rays that showered down on them.

A large black crow broke the tranquility when it called "Caw, Caw, Caw." He appeared to be in a snit over his failed attempt at sweeping down and snatching a field mouse. The mouse had evaded him by hiding under a leafy pumpkin vine. The predatory bird looked as if it were plotting a second attack as it perched on a nearby fence post and stalked its prey.

Joy had watched the nature interplay. "Stay hidden," she whispered.

"What did you say, Dear?" Sarah asked Joy.

"I watched a mouse run and hide from that crow," the girl said pointing to the feathered predator. "I understand the mouse's fear, I was telling it to stay hidden."

"Nature can at times seem harsh, but we can trust that God has provided a balance which reveals to us the wonder of His grace."

"I don't understand," Joy responded.

"I saw the mouse run too," Sarah said, then pointed, "Look at what's perched on top of the pumpkin under whose leaves the mouse is hiding?"

"It's a dove with its wings spread open wide," Joy replied.

"When I see that," Sarah said, "I see the dove as an agent of God providing protection for the mouse."

"How do you know that's why the dove is there?" Joy asked.

Sarah put her hand over her heart, "I believe that wherever evil or harm lurks, God is near to provide comfort and protection. A few years ago, I prayed for God's guidance with a very difficult decision I had to make. I asked God for a sign that what I thought was the right thing to do, would be. In that moment, God sent a dove that landed on our kitchen windowsill and I knew it was the sign I'd prayed for. Since then, whenever I see a dove, I know God is near."

"I hope you're right," Joy said, "but while I'm here, I'm going to keep an eye on that crow and hope the mouse stays hidden."

Hathaway broke free of Joy's hand, ran to the fence surrounding the patch and climbed through the rails. The wee girl scurried from one orange orb to the next finally resting her fanny on a mid-sized one. "This one mine," she hollered to the approaching foursome.

"Well okay," Sarah called back. "We'll pick it in about three weeks." Sarah lifted Henry out of the wagon and placed him on her hip. Joy picked up Naomi and did likewise, wincing a bit when the baby rested on the frail girl's bruised, boney hip.

Sarah noticed. *When we get back to the house, I'll offer her a piece of pie. Need to get some meat on her bones.* "Jane, don't carry Naomi if it makes your hip hurt."

Joy kissed the top of the baby girl's head. "It's okay, I like carrying her." Naomi snuggled in. Joy responded with an all-embracing hug. "She's so warm and cuddly."

"Jane, does your family carve jack-o-lanterns for Halloween?" Sarah asked.

"Before my mother died, we used to do that when we lived on the farm," Joy replied.

"Where is your farm?" Sarah asked.

"It was in Howard County, but we don't have it anymore," Joy said with a note of sadness.

"Why did you leave the farm?" Sarah inquired.

"We had to, Pa lost it in a gambling game." Joy's voice was barely audible when she continued. "My mother grew up on that farm. After her parents died it was hers and we moved there."

"Did you like living on a farm?" Sarah asked.

"I loved it. Ma and I walked to school on days when weather permitted. I miss that."

"I'm sure you do. I have fond memories of walking Abe to school the fall of his first year."

"Ma didn't just walk me for fun," Joy said. "She was one of the school's teachers."

"Was it a big school?"

"Yes, it had grades one through twelve. When Ma got in a family way with my sister, she had to quit."

"Where's your sister now?" Sarah asked, anxious to continue the conversation.

"Ruthie died a week after we buried my mother. Pa said it was my fault. She and Ma were down sick with pneumonia. Neighbors came to take care of us but when Ma died, Pa wouldn't let them, or the doctor come anymore. He said that with Ma gone, Ruthie was my responsibility."

"How old were you then?"

"Eleven. I tried to tend to her as I'd seen the doctor do. I sat and held her with a blanket over our heads and a pot of steaming water. It helped some, but she needed a doctor's care. I would have spoon-fed her cherry bark tea, but Pa had thrown it out." Joy clutched at the pouch under her dress bodice. *I'll not let that happen again.*

"Ruthie had just learned how to sit up. I was looking forward to taking walks with her. She didn't live long enough for that."

"Oh, Jane, I'm so sorry for your loss," Sarah said, her eyes welled with tears. "Death can be a terrible painful experience. Your father's harshness likely came from his grief over losing his wife and child."

Joy took a quick swipe at her eyes with the back of her free hand. "My pa was harsh with my mother before she got sick and died.

"I wanted to die when Ma did. I knew I couldn't because Ruthie needed me. After Ruthie died too, I had no reason to live. Until I came to your farm a couple of weeks ago, I wished every day I had died."

Sarah wrapped her free arm around the girl and pulled her close. "My dear child, life is a wonderful gift from God. He intends for it to be a joyous experience for all of us."

Hathaway saw her mother hugging Joy and came running. The toddler wrapped her chubby right arm around her mother's leg and the left around Joy's leg. Henry finding himself near his twin, reached over, put her head in an arm-lock and her ear in his mouth. The group huddle was short-lived; Naomi didn't appreciate the nibbling.

"Someone's getting cranky," Sarah said. "We'll have to inspect the pumpkin patch another day. It's nap time."

"Me not sleepy." Hathaway said as she rubbed at her eyes and yawned.

"I am," Joy said as she attempted to stifle a yawn. "Sometimes the remembering makes me really tired. Hathaway, when we get to the house would you lay down with me until I fall asleep?"

"Ok, but me not gonna sleep," the toddler said as she took Joy's hand and turned a smiling face to her new friend.

On the walk back to the house Sarah attempted to continue her conversation with Joy.

"Jane, you said your farm was in Howard County. What was the name of the town where you went to school?"

"I let the name of the county we lived in slip out. It wouldn't be safe to tell you more," the girl replied. "I don't want to bring trouble to your home."

"Who would cause us trouble, Jane?"

Joy turned her face from Sarah's view and said nothing. The cohorts walked on in silence. Eventually Sarah spoke. "I'm sure you were a very good student, Jane. Ben and I commented on your reading skills and how well-spoken you are."

"My mother taught English. She taught me how to read and use good grammar at an early age."

"My older boys read well enough and Zeke's learning. I should insist that they use better grammar. Boys are rambunctious and mischievous. As a result, there always seems to be something I need to call one or the other of them on. I guess I've just resisted adding poor grammar to the list. Ben's been after me about it. He thinks being well spoken is important as an adult and I have to say, so do I. Maybe your good use of the English language will rub off on them." Sarah held back mentioning that she and Ben had discussed sending Jane to school. She didn't want to push too quickly.

After walking a bit in silence Sarah asked, "Jane, are you ready to tell me your father's name?"

"No, Ma'am."

Sarah took Joy's hand and they stopped walking. "Jane, are you afraid of your father? Are you afraid that if we find out his name, we'll locate him, and he'll come for you?"

Joy stood with her head bowed. Large tear drops fell to the tops of her bare feet creating voids in the dust that coated them.

Sarah cupped her hand under Joy's chin and raised the child's face so she could look in her eyes. "Jane, was it your father who physically harmed you?"

"Yes," Joy whispered.

"Jane, you're safe while you're with us. Thank you for telling me a bit about yourself and your family. Perhaps another day soon you'll feel comfortable enough to tell me the rest of your story."

"I feel safe here, but this isn't my home. I don't want to be a burden, I should be moving on," Joy said as she wiped her eyes on the edge of the apron Sarah had given her to wear.

"Jane, if the time comes that it would be best for you to move on, the Lord will reveal that to all of us. In the meantime, please know that you aren't a burden. In fact, you're pure joy."

Although not comfortable with using her mother's name, hearing Sarah say that she was pure joy brought a smile to the girl's face. Joy clung to the awareness that Sarah had said, "if" the time came for her to move on, not "when" the time came. Dare she hope that she might be allowed to stay with this wonderful family?

They didn't talk the remainder of the walk. Grief over what the girl had shared swept over Sarah and she felt the need to silently pray. *Father in heaven, comfort this child. She's known more heartache than most at this point in her life. Place her in the shelter of your wings, protect and nourish her with your love and grace. Amen.*

Sarah focused her thoughts on the information she'd gathered during the walk. *The girl lived on a farm in Howard County. Her mother was a teacher and her father a gambler. He was abusive to her and she's on the run from him. I hope to learn more, but this is a good start.*

Sarah looked behind her to the twins in the wagon. Naomi was out cold and had fallen back and was resting against Henry. Henry was nodding in and out of sleep and didn't seem to care. Hathaway was still holding Joy's hand, but her feet were dragging. Sarah smiled to herself. *An hour of quiet, coming up. That will be a good time to bake and fill the cookie jar.*

***

Later that afternoon, about two o'clock, Sarah heard a rig approaching the house and looked out the window to see Elmo Jones, their postman, tethering his horse. The nosey, neighborhood gossip's jaw sported his trademark chaw of tobacco, and she could see that he was looking for a place to spit. She'd fussed at him more than once about doing it in the dirt pile where the children dug and played.

She cringed when she saw him shoot a stream toward her flower bed, coating her bright yellow mums with the disgusting brown liquid.

"Special delivery," Elmo called through the screen door.

Sarah responded with, "shush", as she opened the door. "Elmo, the babies are sleeping. You could have left the mail in our box and saved yourself a trip up the lane."

"I'm a deliverin' spankin' new Sears and Roebuck catalogues today. If that don't call for a special, to your door, delivery, I don't know what would." The quirky little man made a show of wiping his bearded mouth across his shirt sleeve to remove Mail Pouch drool, then sniffing the air. "Are those ginger snap cookies I smell a bakin'?" Elmo asked, stepping in uninvited.

"Yes, but this isn't a good time to come in for a visit. I'll wrap up a few for you to take along on your route." As Sarah went to fetch the cookies she thought, *so far, we've kept Elmo from knowing that Jane's here. I want to keep it that way until we talk to the town's Marshal. Her black eye and scrapes are healed but I don't want Elmo's gossip mill to contain talk about Jane.*

"I see ya got yourselves a house guest," Elmo said in a tone of approval.

Sarah turned to see Joy standing just inside the kitchen. "Yes, we do," she said.

"Pleased to meet you, Ma'am, I'm Elmo, the postman," he said tipping his hat. Joy made a quick half curtsey and scurried back to her bed.

Sarah handed Elmo three cookies wrapped in brown paper. "Here you go, cookies for eating later."

"Uh, I didn't catch me the name of your guest," Elmo said.

Sarah took Elmo by the elbow, opened the screen door and ushered him out. "Thanks for the special delivery. Hope you enjoy the cookies." She then closed both the screen and wooden doors.

Sarah took a batch of cookies out of the oven and as she turned to set them on the table to cool, her peripheral vision caught a movement at the window. Turning for a better look she saw Elmo with his hands cupped at his temples, nose pressed up against the glass. With intention Sarah put one hand on her hip, stomped her foot while gesturing with the other hand for Elmo to leave. "Scat," she called out.

Sarah's aggressiveness so startled Elmo that he swallowed tobacco juice. As he drove his rig down the lane to the main road, it wasn't a blush of embarrassment on his face, it was a mask of green.

Chapter 8

Ben hung his "Doctor Is In" sign then went to the kitchen to see if their hired hand had left any coffee. Having Gerald live at Doc's house in town was a good arrangement. When Sarah and Ben married, he moved to the farm and the hired hand, who'd been sleeping in Sarah's parlor, moved to Doc's old house.

Ben's doctor office, with an adjacent convalescent room, still occupied the front of the house as it always had. The small parlor that Ben once used when he lived in the home was turned into a waiting area for patients. The kitchen became shared space and the two bedrooms were designated as living quarters for Gerald.

With Sarah's parlor freed, the twins were transferred from Sarah's bedroom to that room. The hired hand having a kitchen in his quarters in town at his disposal, as well as the nearby hotel restaurant, eliminated the need for him to eat meals with Sarah's family. To Gerald, the inconvenience of the trip to and from the farm was off-set by the gain of the quiet and privacy he gained. He was now able to have friends come stay the night.

Doc often thought about that two-mile buggy ride he now made twice during the week. He'd dreamed about it and hoped for it long before he won Sarah's hand in marriage. He'd known that if they wed, he'd be the one to make the move. His house in town was too small for her brood and even if it wasn't, Sarah would never leave her farm. Not even once had he felt the miles were a burden to him or his horse.

Weekdays when Ben traveled America road to the Rudicel road turn-off that provided a straight shot into town, he often counted his blessings. He was thankful for his new life on the farm and the continued opportunity to help others through his practice of medicine. At the end of each day when his trip home followed the reverse of the same route, his thoughts were filled love and joyful anticipation for what awaited him at the farm.

When Ben went to the shared kitchen, he found that Gerald had left a pot of coffee on the cookstove's back burner. He poured a cup. *Still hot.* His attention was drawn to a plate of biscuits setting on the table. He grabbed one and took a bite. *Light as a feather inside, just the right amount of crust on the outside. Wonder where these came from?*

He looked around, turning full circle to inspect the kitchen. *Clean as a whistle. As clean as my former housekeeper kept it. Wonder if Gerald's got a lady friend?*

Ben finished off the biscuit he'd been holding and brushed the crumbs from his waistcoat. *Now why did I eat that?* Doc patted his midsection. *I was still full, from breakfast. Got to cut back. Sarah's good cooking is taking a toll on my waistline. Besides, Gerald might appreciate it if I didn't swipe his leftover food.* Ben ran his hand through his thick head of hair. *How rude of me to eat the man's biscuit.* Ben dashed to his office, jotted a quick note of apology, then took it to the kitchen and laid it by the plate of remaining biscuits.

A knock at the front door brought Ben out of his regrets. It was his first patient of the day. The man's name was Gus Albertson, claimed he'd come to town on banking business and was on his way up north. Gus said he'd spent the night at the hotel. "Doc, I went to bed feeling poorly and woke up this morning feeling down right puny. I've got the chills and I haven't been able to hold down a bit of food since noon yesterday. If I was at home, I'd just ride 'er out, but I've got business on up the road and need to get movin'."

"I'm sorry for your troubles Gus." Ben said as he gestured toward his exam room. "Come in here and hop up on the table." Ben extracted his metal tongue depressor from its vial of alcohol and shook it off. "Open wide, let me take a look in your throat."

"I'll, I'll oblige ya, but first I need to use your privy," the man said as he jumped off the exam table, held his backside and started prancing.

Ben pointed. "Out that side door and to the left."

After a time, the man came back in, started to again climb up on the table but halted. "Privy!" Gus yelled as he clinched his buttocks and took off at a brisk pace. "Guess I've got me a case of the trots," he called out over his shoulder. The dash to the outhouse repeated three more times before the exam got underway.

While looking down the man's throat Doc made a mental note to check the privy's Sears Roebuck catalogue page supply first chance he got. Ben put the tongue depressor away and got out the thermometer. "Open your mouth so I can stick this under your tongue. You feel a bit warm to the touch, let's see if you have a temperature."

After a five-minute wait Doc removed the thermometer and checked the mercury level. "One hundred and one degrees. Yes, you've got a fever." Ben returned the six-inch glass instrument to the vial of rubbing alcohol where it rested alongside the tongue depressor.

"So, Doc, what do you think is ailing me?" Albertson asked.

"You don't seem to have a rash and your throat doesn't look irritated. With your intestinal problems and a fever, it could be the beginning of something, or pan out to be a minor stomach upset. Whatever, you need to rest. I suggest you stay on at the hotel another day at least."

"It isn't the grippe is it. Doc?"

"I certainly hope not. Have you been around anyone that's been ill like this recently?"

"No, but I did hear about a sickness." Gus said. "I come through a little burg east of here called Banquo. There was talk at the local tavern about a sickness a spreadin' around. Folks said several men in town was mighty sick a pukin' and crapin'. A few women too. Tavern's proprietor said the town's preacher was awful worried about his wife. I guess them sayin' the ailment was a spreadin' is what caused me to think of the grippe."

"Time will tell," Doc said patting Gus on the back. "Let's not get overly concerned at this point. You rest. I'll come to the hotel and look in on you tomorrow."

"Is there medicine I can take? I really need to get on up north."

"There's nothing available that I hold much store in," Ben said. "Drink plenty of water, eat chicken broth with dry bread and rest. Use cold wet compresses on your brow and chest if you continue to feel feverish tonight. I'm hoping that with rest your ailment will run its course in a day or two."

Gus reached in his pants pocket. "Thanks, Doc, how much do I owe ya?"

"Twenty-five cents will cover it."

"Much obliged," the man said as he placed a quarter in Ben's hand.

Ben escorted the man outside and watched as he made his way toward the hotel. Before Ben went back inside, he glanced toward the Marshal's office. *That looks like Jeb's horse. Think I'll go over and tell him about our houseguest.* Doc grabbed his jacket, flipped his sign to "Doctor Is Out" and walked the short distance to the Marshal's office.

***

Sarah looked around the kitchen as she wiped her hands on a dish towel. *I guess that was everything that needed washing. Not much to noon meal clean up during the week. The four oldest boys are off at school and Ben eats in town. More days than not Gerald carries a knapsack when he arrives of a morning. That just leaves Hathaway, the twins, Jane and me to eat together.*

"The twins went right to sleep when I put them down for their nap," Joy said when she entered the kitchen. "Hathaway's upstairs lying on her bed, telling her rag doll the story of *Little Red Riding Hood.* Lancy is on the bed with her. His tail is wagging so I guess he doesn't mind that she's pretending he's the big bad wolf."

"Jane, you're such a help with the babies." Sarah said motioning for the girl to take a seat, along with her, at the table.

"Ma'am, they're pure pleasure to me. I'm happy to be of help."

"And I so appreciate everything you do. But Ben, and I have been talking and we think that while you're staying with us, you should go to school along with the boys. Since our America road country school closed, they go into town to the big school where grades one through twelve are available. Several subjects other than the three r's are being taught."

"Oh, Ma'am, I want to be a help to you. I need to earn my keep."

"Jane, like our four oldest, you'd still have assigned chores even though you're in school. In a family everyone pulls together to get the work done. No one needs to feel as if they must earn their keep."

Joy's eyes threatened to spill tears and she bowed her head. "But I'm not a member of this family."

Sarah reached across the table and took the girl's hand in hers. "Jane, we consider you one of us. Even if you do eventually move on, I suspect we'll continue to feel that way about you."

Tears fell freely, but Joy had no words. Sarah took a handkerchief from her apron pocket and handed it to the girl. "Would you like to go to school, work toward getting a graduation certificate?"

Joy wiped her nose. "Yes, ma'am, I want that with all my heart."

"It's settled. Come Monday you can go to school with the boys. You're going to need some shoes. I'll fetch my Sunday pair, they might work for you to wear into town tomorrow. We'll go see if Parker's Store has something that you like and will fit. If not, there might be a pair in the catalogue that we could order," Sarah said as she rose from the table, picked up the new Sears Roebuck catalogue and handed it to the, girl.

"Sarah, I don't feel right about letting you spend money on me. I don't know how I'll be able to repay you?"

"We don't expect to be repaid. Someday, when you're grown, have means of your own, you likely will have an opportunity to help someone in need. That's when you can give back."

***

"Good mornin', Doc," Jeb greeted when Ben walked into his office. "What ya up to? I don't generally see you out of your office until noon time. Are ya short on customers today?"

"Actually no, I've already seen a patient, a paying one I might add. I've come on a kind of delicate matter."

Jeb Carter took his feet off his desk and sat straight up in his chair. "Delicate matter you say? I'm all ears."

"About two weeks ago we found a young girl. Actually, she's more like a young woman, in our barn sleeping. She'd been beaten and she was near starved to death. We took her in, and we've been nursing her back to health."

"Who is she?"

"That's the thing, she won't tell us who she is or where she came from. Sarah is gradually gaining her trust. Day before yesterday the girl divulged that her family used to live on a farm over in Howard County. Her mother, who's now deceased, taught school. Apparently, it was her father who beat her and she's on the run from him."

"Well, now you're sheddin' some light on a yarn Elmo Jones was spinnin'. He told about seein' a girl out at your place. Said she was real skittish and that Sarah was actin' strange about who she was. According to Elmo, Sarah got peeved when he delivered the mail to your door and tried to make conversation. Said Sarah ran him off the property."

"That doesn't sound like Sarah. She didn't say anything to me about an incident with Elmo, but likely there's more to the story than he's telling. You and I both know Elmo's a nosey cuss and not above meddling where he has no business."

"A nosey cuss, that he is," Jeb said.

"Sarah has taken the girl under her wing. She was just trying to protect her. Even though her injuries are nearly healed, she's still thin and frail. She can read and write quite well. We're thinking about sending her to school come Monday. Thought she might as well be advancing her education while she's with us."

"So," Jeb said, "do you want me to go lookin' for her father?"

"Jeb, the girl has evidence of long-term neglect. You'll have a fight on your hands if you try to get Sarah to release her back to her father. Same goes for me."

"Then I'm not sure why you told me about her."

"She'll be out and about with the family. As the town's law, we wanted you to know the particulars about her situation and how she's come to be with us."

"Well I do appreciate knowin'. I'd have been amongst the best of 'em trying to find out who she was and why she's a livin' with you out at the farm."

"Let's keep her circumstances between you, Sarah and me for now. Her life's been a sad, sad story and it's hers to tell, not ours. The girl knows she's free to leave when she wants to, but we've encouraged her to stay with us until she works something out."

"Does she have any other kin?"

"None she's told us about. She said that her mother's parents were dead. No mention of her father's side of the family."

"What'd you say her name is?"

"I didn't. She told us her first name is Jane. She's too afraid to tell us her last name."

"If you take her out, what will you say when folks ask who she is?" Jeb asked.

"We plan to have her participate as a member of our family. For now, I'll tell folks she's my niece, Jane Adams," Doc replied.

Jeb slapped his hands down on his knees and positioned himself to stand. "Ben, I can leave it be, or go diggin' – call the Howard county Sheriff and so on. You decide."

"Leave it be for now. If someone comes asking about her, let us know."

"That works for me," Jeb said. "If someone does come, I'll size 'em up first – make sure I don't send any harm your direction. How old is she anyway?" Jeb asked.

"I'd guess fifteen maybe sixteen from the looks of her. She's a pretty girl, that is once Sarah got her cleaned up and in something to wear other than rags."

"Elmo said she was a looker."

"Jeb, she's still a child. Elmo needs to watch his mouth."

"I hear ya, Doc. You know ol' Elmo is harmless."

"Yeah but, talk stirs up interest. We don't need any young men trying to come to court her. We've got enough on our hands with Abe being smitten. He fumbles, stumbles and gawks at her every chance he gets."

"Abe's fourteen, now isn't he?" Jeb said. "Likely he's just a startin' to feel his oats."

Ben chuckled, "I wish harvest wasn't over. It'd be good to have him tired and worn out come an evening. Well, I've taken up enough of your time. I need to get back to my office."

Jeb leaned back in his chair and put his feet back up on his desk and his arms behind his head, fingers locked. "I'll keep my ears open and my eyes peeled. Close the door when you leave. I've got me some serious contemplatin' to do."

Chapter 9

His eyes fluttered and Edward Humes woke. His head was throbbing, the light in his eyes made the pain worse. He felt disoriented. Squinting he looked around the room to get his bearings. *I'm in the cabin. What day is this? Hot, I'm so hot.* Ed placed his hand on his brow. *Fever must have a fever.* He tried swallowing, it was difficult. *Thirsty, need water.*

Humes had trouble getting to his feet. He was dizzy and staggered to the bucket he used for carrying water from the creek to the house. *Empty.* He stumbled back to the pallet on the floor and picked up his jug before he collapsed to his knees. When he raised the vessel to take a swallow the smell stopped him. *It's gone bad.* He grabbed at his stomach. *I'm going to lurch.* He leaned to his side to avoid soiling his blanket. He needn't have bothered. His intestines wrenched so convulsively that the emesis projected nearly three feet.

His relief was momentary. His nausea returned, building at a rapid pace. Along with it came a cramping in his lower intestines. Ed got to his feet and as quickly as his wobbly legs would carry him, he headed for the door. He made it out and off to the side of shack where he managed to shed his trousers, but not his long-johns, before his bowels let loose. He got his shirt off and eventually his soiled union suit. He hunched naked as several more bouts of elimination and vomiting passed through him.

Eventually he was able to crawl back inside where he inched his way across the floor to his pallet and collapsed. As Ed lay there disoriented, dehydrated and shivering, remnants of past events churned in his mind. One separated from the others. A smile came to the man's emaciated face as a surreal panoramic view began to play out before him.

I'm opening the door. I smell bread baking. A woman, with a raven black braid cascading down her spine is standing at a table. It's my wife, Jane. She's so beautiful.

There's a cradle at Jane's side. I see a young girl with golden hair standing next to her. A frown replaces Ed's smile. *Joy, the girl is Joy. They're giggling. She's the reason I had to marry Jane. I wanted Jane, but not marriage. I didn't want Joy, wanted the one in the cradle even less. The two of them soaking up*

Jane's attention, taking her away from me. Me, I'm the one she should be doting over.

A wrinkle appeared between Ed's brows at the bridge of his nose. *What are, Jane and Joy doing? They're sorting plants and tree bark! So, this is what they do when I'm gone. They were warned before about dabbling in that nonsense.* Humes' breathing became rapid.

I see broken glass and debris flying. I hear screaming and crying. Ed's hands twitched, his eyes squinted. *My hands hurt, knuckles are bleeding.* Ed's fingers flexed. *Fingers are getting stiff.* His mouth took a downturn and his nostrils flared. *If this effect my banjo playing, there'll be hell to pay.*

Humes' mind quieted and the events stopped turning. Momentarily another onslaught of nausea hit him. Naked, Ed slithered to the door. He managed to reach the porch and hang his head over the edge before he regurgitated. The last thought that crossed Ed's mind before he lost consciousness was, *I'm going to die. Joy, where are you. I'll let you brew me some of that tea you and your ma took such stock in.*

***

"Ma," Zeke yelled. "Henry just leaned over the side of his high chair and snatched my bacon right out of my hand. Look at him, he's gnawin' on it and hummin'. I think he likes bacon pert near as much as I do."

"Zeke!" Sarah scolded. "How many times have I told you not to take a piece of bacon before I'm ready to serve it. Now Henry's swiped it from you. He's too young to eat it, he might choke on the gristle. Sarah laid down her cooking fork and started toward the baby.

Ben was entering the kitchen and overheard the exchange. "I'll take care of it, Sarah." In two long strides he was at Henry's side. He held his hand out to the baby. "Give me the bacon, Henry. You need a few more teeth before you can handle chewing it."

Henry shook his little head and proceeded to stuff the entire strip of bacon in his mouth. Ben cupped the baby's face in one hand and used his forefinger on the other to extract the meat from Henry's mouth. "Ouch." Ben yelled. "He bit me."

Henry puckered up and cried. Doc bent over and kissed the boy's wet cheek. Naomi's high chair was setting in proximity. She grabbed a handful of Ben's hairs and pulled hard enough to make him yell ouch again.

"Well for heaven's sake," Sarah said as she came to the rescue by placing bowls of oatmeal and a spoon in front of each baby. The twins happily held their spoon in one hand while they, hand to mouth, shoveled in their cereal.

Ben was rubbing the sore spot on his scalp when he took his seat at the table. Hathaway and Joy entered the kitchen hand in hand. Joy helped the toddler get in her chair next to Ben. Abe, Josh and Luke came in from doing morning chores and took their seats. Joy poured milk for everyone while Sarah set the food on the table.

For several minutes the only sound in the room was the clanking of eating utensils against plates. Doc was the first to break the silence. "There's a fellow staying at the hotel that I need to make a call on this morning. He came to the office yesterday sick as a dog. I told him he needed to take a day to rest before traveling on. I'm hoping his bout with the ailment was short-lived."

Sarah wiped her mouth with her napkin. "I'm sure the man does too. Later this morning we homebodies are coming to town to shop for shoes for Jane and to take care of some other business. I thought we'd drop by your office to see you, perhaps bring a picnic lunch the six of us could share."

Ben leaned over and kissed Hathaway on her head. "A picnic with four beautiful girls and one sharp toothed baby boy. I like the sound of that."

Luke addressed Joy. "So, you're goin' to buy some shoes. If I didn't need them for school, you wouldn't catch me wearin' shoes until snow falls."

"Now that we're on the subject of school," Sarah said. "Starting this coming Monday, Jane is going to school along with you. While we're in town today we'll go by and get her enrolled."

"What grade will you be in, Jane?" Josh asked.

"I, I don't know." Joy replied. "I finished fifth grade, but, didn't get to go to school after that."

Luke chimed in. "Jane, you're a lot bigger than any sixth grader LaFontaine school has. Ma, they's gonna laugh at her if ya make her go to sixth grade. She's tall enough for the tenth or eleventh. Why not stick her in with them? They's more her size."

Sarah reached over and patted Joy's hand. "The grade, a child is placed in, is determined by what the student already knows and what they are mature enough to learn. I'm expecting that Mr. Hornblower, the school's principal, will have Jane take a written exam to determine her appropriate grade level."

Zeke slapped his knee and cackled. "Hornblower. I gotta have me a laugh ever time I hear that name. Last week he was a blowin' that big nose of his to beat the band. He just about caught me a laughin' at him. I had to fake like I was a havin' me a coughin' spell to cover it up."

"Zeke!" Doc and Sarah said in unison.

Ben was the first to continue. "He has hay fever and every fall it flairs up and makes his nose run and his eyes water. Mr. Hornblower can't help all the nose blowing he has to do."

Sarah chimed in. "I don't want to hear tell of any of my children being unkind to others. The man didn't choose the size of his nose. God gave it to him, and He thinks it's just perfect for Mr. Hornblower." Sarah looked at Doc who was staring at her with his eyebrows arched. They both struggled to hold back a grin.

"Yeah, Zeke." Abe said as he grabbed the hair that stood like a shock of wheat atop his brother's head. "We can't all be as pretty as you are, brother."

Zeke slapped Abe's hand away. "Cut it out, Abe. You know my head got licked by a cow when I was little. It ain't my fault that part of my hair won't lay down."

"It's called a cowlick, Son." Sarah said. "That's just an expression for a spot on one's head where the hair won't lay down smooth. That doesn't mean that a cow actually licked your head."

"Now, you tell me." Zeke folded his arms across his chest. "A feller can't hardly take more than one piece of hair a shootin' to the sky. I've been a gettin' the 'gee-willies' ever time I see a cow stick out its tongue. I been scared I'd get licked some more." With lower lip protruding he dropped his head, chin resting on his chest.

"Forget worrin' about a cow's tongue and a shootin' up clump of hair. Gettin' brother licked is more dangerous. It can cause you to grow a pig's tail." Josh stuck his tongue out as far as it would go and leaned into Zeke.

Zeke jumped up screaming and Josh took off chasing him. Sarah clapped her hands and called out, "No time for that now. Get your jackets on and get down the lane. The school hack will be coming along directly. You don't want to miss it."

Abe thoroughly wiped his mouth, then laid his napkin atop his plate. "Have a good day, Jane. I hope you can find yourself a right pretty pair of shoes."

"Thank you, Abe." Joy said to the now crimson faced boy.

***

Ben arrived at his office and set about his morning routine of helping himself to a cup of Gerald's leftover coffee. Today, instead of the remains of breakfast being biscuits, setting on the table was a plate of apple turnovers. The pastries were baked to a golden brown, filling oozing from their seamed edges. A crisscross of white icing adorned the appetizing confections. "Lord, help me." Doc's mouth salivated but he restrained from taking one.

For the second day in a row Ben's morning began with a pounding at his office door. Cup of coffee in hand, he scurried to answer the knock. It was Frank Mitchner, the clerk at the LaFontaine Bank. "Doc, grab your bag and come with me." Frank turned and ran off the porch.

Doc sloshed coffee on his shirt in his haste to put his cup down. He grabbed his jacket, snatched up his bag and called out to Frank as he ran to catch up with him. "What's got you in a panic? Where're we going?"

Frank slowed his pace, turned to face Doc and walked backward. "It's Cleavold. He didn't show up this morning for the Bank's meeting. I went to his house to check on him and found him in an awful mess. He looks like he's dying. From the smell of him he might already be gone. I shook him but didn't get a response."

"Cleavold." Doc stopped dead in his tracks.

Frank stopped too. "Now Doc, it's no secret that you don't like Cleavold. Truth be told hardly anyone does. Still, the man's sick. Don't your types have some oath you have to follow?"

Doc held disdain for the bank's president Cleavold Anubis. Cleavold had been a topic of discussion after Doc and Sarah met with him about investing inheritance money Doc received from an uncle. During their meeting Ben noticed that Cleavold was terribly uncomfortable in Sarah's presence, wouldn't make eye contact with her and so forth. Later that evening Ben brought it up. After considerable coaxing Sarah told him that a couple of years before, Cleavold had propositioned her to get sexual favors as a condition to approving her crop loan. She'd rebuffed him and given him a piece of her mind. Sarah said the man hadn't looked her in the eye since.

Ben was furious and hell-bent to avenge Sarah's honor. Sarah said that she'd forgiven the man and had put the memory behind her. That didn't dissuade Ben's desire to confront Cleavold.

Sarah was adamant that since it happened before she and Ben were married it was her business and she considered it settled. Sarah had told Ben that she'd given the situation over to the Lord. If any retribution was owed, it was up to the Lord to dish it out.

Sometime back, Ben had surrendered his life to Christ. He knew that he was saved by God's grace. He understood that as a Christian he was to extend that same grace to others. How the concept of grace could apply to a despicable man like Cleavold Anubis was beyond Ben's understanding. He'd tried, but just couldn't comprehend. Ultimately Ben had agreed to abide by Sarah's wishes, but he'd developed a severe dislike for Cleavold.

Because of Sarah's family association on the bank's board of directors, Ben continued a financial relationship with the bank but avoided Cleavold. Ben's abhorrence was obvious to others. Doc deliberately shunned the banker and insisted on working with one of the tellers when he had business to conduct.

Frank yelled at Ben again. "Well…, didn't you take an oath?"

"I'm coming." Ben yelled back as he started running toward Cleavold's house. As he ran, he mentally chanted, *do no harm, do no harm, do no harm.*

Ben found Cleavold murmuring and incoherent. He was dehydrated and had a weak pulse. He'd soiled himself and the bed and it appeared there'd been multiple episodes of elimination.

"I told you it was bad, Doc," Frank proffered.

"Frank, I'm going to need you to help me get him cleaned up." Doc said as he laid his jacket aside and started rolling up his sleeves.

Frank pulled a handkerchief from his vest pocket and tied it over his nose. "I'm ready, tell me what to do."

Doc ran into the kitchen while barking orders. "Go get a bucket of water and some rags. I'll try to get some drinking water down him." Doc came back holding a cup of water and a spoon. He gently raised Cleavold's head and tried to get him to sip from the spoon.

When Frank came back with the cleaning supplies the pair lifted Cleavold from the bed onto a sheet on the floor. From there they worked together to sponge-bathe his body and put a fresh night shirt on him.

Frank went to work replacing the soiled bed linens while Doc cradled Cleavold's head and spoon-fed him water. Cleavold didn't rally. At times Doc had to massage the man's throat to get him to swallow. Ben's hand trembled when he placed it around the banker's neck. He whispered, "Do no harm, do no harm."

"What, Doc? Speak up, I didn't hear you." Frank said as he plumped the pillow, the last step in his task of changing the soiled bedding.

Doc deflected the question. "Help me get him in bed."

Once they had Cleavold in bed again they padded him so any future clean up wouldn't be as cumbersome. As they were clearing away the mess, Frank found a jug and held it up. "Doc looks like he's been partaking heavily from this. It's near empty."

Doc took the jug, pulled the cork and sniffed the contents. "Whew, might have once been moonshine. Whatever it is, it's gone bad. Frank, I had a patient yesterday sick like Cleavold, but not as bad. He's staying at the hotel and I need to go pay him a visit. Change those cold compresses every few minutes. Keep on spooning water into him. Even though he's not alert, he's reflectively swallowing the water. Take it slow. If you catch him holding it in his cheek, gently massage his throat and that should get him to take it on down." Ben started to leave then reluctantly turned back. "Frank, tilt his head when you give him the water. Otherwise he might choke."

"You're comin' back aren't you, Doc?" Frank asked.

"Yes, it might be a while, but I'll be back. I'll see if I can find someone to come get the soiled linens for washing," Ben said as he left and headed to the hotel.

Ben inquired at the registration desk and got the room number for the Gus Albertson. After getting no response to his knock he entered the room unannounced. There he found the man in as bad a condition as he'd found Cleavold. The only difference was that the traveler still had his finger looped through the handle on the jug by his bed. Ben extracted it and took a sniff. "Putrid."

Eliciting help from hotel staff Ben got the traveler cleaned up and situated back in bed. After being spoon fed a considerable amount of water he came to enough to whisper. "Where am I? What's happened?"

"You're in a hotel in LaFontaine, Indiana. I'm Ben Adams the town's doctor. You came to see me yesterday. You were vomiting and had diarrhea." Doc put a fresh cold compress on the man's brow.

"Oh, I remember now," Gus said.

"I gave you instructions for bedrest and to drink a lot of water." Ben pointed to the jug. "I found that in your hand."

"Ran out of water. Weak, drank what I had."

"I smelled it. The stuff's gone bad. This morning we found our bank's president sick with symptoms like yours. He too had a jug of moonshine that was putrid. Any idea where he might have gotten it?" Doc asked.

"Cleavold. Cleavold's sick?" The man tried to sit up but didn't have the strength and fell back. "Cleavold's my cousin, I brought him that jug yesterday. The brew's gone bad?"

"Where'd you get the swill?" Doc asked.

"Feller in Banquo," Gus faintly whispered.

With a tone of incredulousness Doc said. "They sell this stuff in town?"

"No. Got from a man–edge of town."

"Where does he get the water to make the moonshine, do you know?" Ben inquired.

"Creek by cabin."

"Does he have a privy?" Doc asked.

Gus's eyes flew open wide. "A privy?" He said, "I'm sick and you're asking if the moonshiner had a privy!"

"It's important because if he doesn't, he likely defecates in the creek." Ben speculated.

"Defecates?"

"Takes a dump."

"No privy. I asked to use his and he sent me to the creek.

Doc shook his head. "Just as I suspected. I'm guessing that the moonshine is contaminated with e-coli. That's bacteria that forms from animal or human waste. When the creek water was used to make the moonshine, it transferred the bacteria to the brew." Doc explained.

"Is eke-oli poison?"

"It's poisonous to the human body," Doc said as he gave the man another spoonful of water.

"Am I dying?"

"I'll be honest with you," Doc said. "You're dangerously dehydrated. If we can't stop this vomiting and diarrhea, you could die. If a body loses more fluids than it can maintain it could result in death."

As in disbelief the man chuckled. "Kilt by shit putrefied moonshine. Put that on my tombstone, Doc." Gus moaned and signaled for Ben to help him lean over the side of the bed where he vomited up what little water, he'd taken in.

The door opened and the hotel clerk entered. "How's it goin', Doc? Thought I'd check to see if you needed any help."

Doc shook his head. "This man is gravely ill. Can you find someone to come and sit with him? I want to go to my office and read my medical journals. I need to see if I can come up with anything to stop his purging." Ben picked up the moonshine jug. "I'm taking this with me. It's contaminated, and I'm pretty sure I know the cause of his sickness."

"Doc," said the clerk, "on your way out would you stick your head in the kitchen and tell the staff I need one of them to come up here. I'll stay with the fellow until someone relieves me."

"Certainly." As Doc opened the door, he said, "Thanks for your help. I've got another sick patient so it might be a while before I return." He paused. "Gus, do you want me to send the preacher over to see you?"

"Wouldn't hurt," Gus whispered.

Chapter 10

With Henry resting on her hip, Sarah opened the door to Ben's office. Hathaway burst across the threshold calling out in a sing-song voice, "Pa, we'se here. We gonna take you on a picnic."

Naomi struggled in Joy's arms until she put her down. Henry seeing his sister free to walk wanted down too. Sarah obliged and the twins meandered about. Doc paused from reading in a medical journal to greet his guests. "Oh, my goodness, is it lunch time already?"

"Yes, it's time to eat our picnic," Hathaway said clapping her dimpled hands.

"Ben, you look stressed," Sarah said as she moved to his side.

"I guess I'll have to admit that I am," Ben said finger combing his hair.

"Anything I can help with?" Sarah asked.

"Not unless you've got a remedy to stop diarrhea." Ben responded. "Just a few minutes after I arrived this morning Frank Mitchner came pounding on my door. Cleavold Anubis hadn't showed up at the bank and Frank went to his house to check on him. He found Cleavold in an awful mess and came running to get me."

"What kind of mess?" Sarah asked.

"The kind that comes with a severe case of dysentery. He was dehydrated and had slipped into a state of semi consciousness. Frank and I got him, and his bed cleaned up. I left Frank to spoon-feed water to Cleavold while I went to the hotel to check on the sick traveler, I mentioned at dinner last night."

Hathaway wiggled her way between Ben's legs and got as close to him as she could. She bent her head backward to an angle that gave her a direct line of sight up Doc's hairy nostrils. Tilting her head right, then left, she said, "Pa, we gots hard eggs, fried chicken and biscuits to eat."

"Oh Ben, Cleavold of all people." Sarah interrupted. "Was it hard for you to tend to him?"

"Yes." Ben responded. "I still consider him despicable. But I was able to see him as a sick man who needed a doctor's help."

Hathaway patted Ben on his arm, "Pa, Pa, did ya hear me? I said we brought hard eggs."

Ben picked Hathaway up and put her on his knee. "Wonderful! They're our favorite picnic food aren't they, little one?" Hathaway snuggled back against Doc's chest and with a smile on her face, folded her chubby arms.

"What about the traveler?" Sarah asked. "Was his condition improved this morning?"

"He was in about the same shape as Cleavold," Ben said. They've both got the worst cases of dysentery I've ever seen. Cleavold and Gus, the traveler, are cousin. It turns out he bought a couple of jugs of moonshine on his way here and he and Cleavold both drank heavily of the stuff. The swill in both jugs smelled contaminated. I'd lay bank that it's the moonshine that's given them dysentery. Gus couldn't hold down what little water I was able to get into him. I don't know yet if Cleavold was able to keep any down. I need to get back to his house and see how he's doing."

"My goodness, Ben. You didn't have to come back to the office to meet us. If we hadn't found you here, we'd have assumed you got called out." Sarah said as she walked to her husband's side and put an arm around his shoulders.

Ben looked up at Sarah. "Truth be told; I didn't remember our picnic plans until I saw you come in through the door. I came back here to read up on dysentery in hopes of finding something that might stop the men from purging."

"Did you find anything?" Sarah inquired.

Ben picked up his medical journal. "Nothing I haven't already tried. Recommendations are to get the patient to drink water to replace the body's lost fluids. Vomiting and diarrhea can quickly result in dehydration. If the body can't take in replacement and keeps purging, it could mean the end."

"You mean d-e-a-t-h?" Sarah spelled out the word rather than say it in front of Hathaway.

"Yes, that's where this is heading for both men if I can't get things turned around. The fellow at the hotel took me up on my offer to send the preacher over to him. Pastor Sloan was leaving the post office just as I passed it on my way here. He said he'd go straight over to the hotel. I told him about Cleavold, and he said he'd go see about him after he visited Cleavold's cousin."

Joy was sitting in a chair listening to the conversation between Ben and Sarah. As she took it all in, she laid her hand on her dress where the herb guide was hiding. *Should I share a remedy that might help? If I offer it, would Doctor Adams make fun of me? If I don't offer and the men die, will I feel to blame?*

With trembling hands Joy pulled the guide from its hiding place. Walking over to Ben's desk she held it out to him. "There's something in here that might help."

Doc took the herb guide. "Is this the book you carry with you around your neck?"

"Yes."

"Where did you get it, Dear?" Sarah asked.

"It was my mother's."

Doc started thumbing through the text. "It's documentation of remedies for common ailments. It's meticulously detailed. Illnesses are listed alphabetically in the back of the journal with reference to the page where nature's remedy is outlined. Sarah, look at these various trees, plants and berries."

Sarah leaned in for a closer look. "They're beautiful, Jane, so intricate. Did your mother draw theses illustrations?"

Joy blushed when she responded. "I drew the illustrations. My mother told me what to draw and on which page. She penned the information."

Sarah walked to the girl and gave her a hug. "I can see why this journal is so precious to you."

"I don't want to ever lose it. That's why I carry it around my neck." Joy said.

Sarah draped an arm across the girl's shoulders. "I think we can find you a safe place to keep your journal, so you don't have to wear it."

Joy shook her head. "I can't chance not having it on me. If I have to run and hide, I might not have time to grab my things."

Sarah locked eyes with Ben. "We'll do our best to see that you never again feel the need to run and hide."

Ben had turned to the referenced page for dysentery. "This recommends a tea made from blackberry roots. Says boil the roots in water for approximately thirty minutes. Drain the liquid and cool. Says to drink one cup of tea every hour until the purging stops."

"Well, Ben?" Sarah questioned. "What do you think? Are you going to try it?"

"Jane, how did your mother come to have all of this knowledge about earth's natural remedies?" Ben asked.

Joy pulled her shoulder back and stood up straight. "They came from my grandmother, on my mother's side. She was a Delaware Indian and an herb healer. My grandmother's mother was one too."

"So, I'm guessing these are proven remedies, passed down through several generations." Ben remarked.

"Yes, they've been used many times to help the sick." Joy responded.

"I can't see any harm in trying the tea," Ben said. "It might contain something that settles the intestines enough to keep them from rejecting sustenance. Yes, let's give it a try. Where can we get some blackberry roots?"

"The fence row …," Sarah stopped mid-sentence when Henry toddled up to Ben and wiped his hands-on Ben's trousers.

Doc grabbed the baby's hands in an attempt to minimize the damage. "What is this? Oh, I'll bet they've found the apple turnovers Gerald left on the kitchen table." Not deterred by his hands being held, Henry leaned over and wiped his mouth on Ben's lap.

"I'm sorry." Joy exclaimed as she dashed to the kitchen to grab a towel.

"You've nothing to apologize for, Jane." Sarah called to the girl. "The children are my responsibility."

Joy came back with a wet towel and started washing Henry's hands. Sarah took a hold of Doc's arm. "If you've got that under control, Jane, I'll take Ben into the kitchen and sponge off his pants."

Henry's partner in crime toddled over to Joy and held out her hands. Their state of stickiness confirmed Naomi's culpability in the messy deed. "Oh, my goodness," Joy said when she saw the approaching hands. "Hathaway, please take hold of your sister's wrists and hold them until I get Henry cleaned and can work on her." Hathaway's compliance resulted in a rolling-on-the-floor, tussle between the toddler and baby girl.

Upon entering the kitchen Sarah found a plate teetering on the edge of the table. It held a single turnover. "Well, at least they didn't break the plate." She surveyed the floor. "Ben, watch your step. There's pastry filling everywhere." She pointed to a blob on the floor, "This turnover's been stomped on until it's flat as paper."

Sarah called out to Joy, "Check the bottoms of their shoes too." Sarah bent and picked up a chunk of crust. She inspected it. "This looks wonderful, it's light and flaky. Did Gerald bake these?"

"I don't know," Ben said. "Yesterday I found a plate of biscuits. I'm embarrassed to say I ate one. They were delicious. I guess Gerald's the one doing the baking, who else?"

"I'll have to ask him for his turnover recipe," Sarah commented. "I'll bake something to replace what the babies took." She walked to the sink and dampened a towel. "Come here, let me see what I can do about your pants."

After a time of Sarah rubbing the legs and fly of Ben's pants, he said, "I, I, uh, that'll be good enough, Sarah. Now, uh, where did you say I could find some blackberry roots?"

"The church, Sarah replied. "Ben, there's still goo on the buttons of your fly."

"I can manage," Ben said taking the rag from Sarah. "Where at church? I don't recall seeing any blackberry bushes there."

"They're along the fencerow of the church's backyard," Sarah said. "Ben, I'm going to need to work on that fly more when you get home."

"Yes, Ma'am, Ben said with a sigh. "I'll need a shovel to dig up the roots. I should still have one in the shed out back."

"Ben, you go on and see to your patients. I'll get the tea made and bring it to Cleavold's house."

"I hate for you to have to dig up the roots."

Sarah gave a back-hand wave. "Don't give it another thought, it won't be hard to do."

Sarah and Doc returned to his office to find all occupants with clean hands, faces and shoes. Ben kissed Hathaway on her cheek. "Sorry, little one. I can't have that picnic with you today. We'll try for another soon."

"Pa," Hathaway said with tears welling in her eyes, "can I have your hard egg?"

"Yes, you may eat my hardboiled egg, Hathaway. Jane, I'd very much like to look at your journal some more."

"I don't like to let it out of my sight." The girl responded. "Maybe we could look at it together."

"I'd like that," Ben said as he closed the door and left.

"Joy," Sarah said, "do you think you can handle the children while I go dig up some blackberry roots? I can move a lot faster if I go alone."

"Yes Ma'am."

Sarah reached in the basket she'd brought and took out a red and white checked tablecloth. "Hathaway, why don't you spread this out on the floor. You, Jane and the twins have a picnic while I go dig some roots."

Hathaway tugged on the skirt of Joy's dress. "Jane, 'member, me gets two hard egg."

"Jane," Sarah said, "if you get a chance will you put a large pot of water on to heat. It might take it a bit to come to a boil and it'd get the tea made faster if the water's ready when I come back with the roots."

Joy knelt to help Hathaway spread out the tablecloth. "I'll have it ready. Hey, Henry, you can sit on top of the cloth, but not under it. Naomi, wait, let me help you get that chicken out of the basket."

When Sarah returned with the blackberry roots, she found the twins and Hathaway stretched out on the floor sleeping. Joy was in the kitchen by the stove. "Looks like you've got everything under control, Jane."

"Yes, Ma'am. The water's ready. Did you get the roots?"

Sarah held out the basket so the girl could see. "Yes, I dug up quite a few. I didn't know how many we'd need."

Joy deftly took charge. "First we thoroughly wash the roots. Then we'll cut off any runners and chop the stems into small pieces."

Sarah poured water into a grey speckled wash pan. "I shook a lot of the soil off the roots, but they still need a good cleaning."

Joy smiled, "My, mother always said a little bit of dirt never hurts. What can we use to put the tea in? Carrying this large pan would be awkward."

Sarah pointed to her right. "Check in the pantry, see if you can find some canning jars and lids."

As Joy went to find the jars she said, "We'll have to let the tea cool before we pour it into the jars, otherwise they might crack." When Joy started across the room with the jars, she saw that Sarah had a smile on her face.

"Oh, Ma'am, I didn't mean to be bossy. Of course, you'd know about hot liquid breaking glass."

"You're not being bossy. It sounds as if you've done some canning before."

"Yes, my mother and I canned green beans and tomatoes every year. I always thought the canning jars looked beautiful lined up in rows of red and green."

"Me too. I wipe the jars until they sparkle before I put them on the shelves in the cellar. Of course, it doesn't take long for them to collect dust.

***

Ben stopped by the hotel before going to Cleavold's house. He found Gus sleeping. The young fellow sitting bedside said the traveler hadn't been able to hold down any water.

"My wife will bring by some tea in a couple of hours," Ben said. "Get some in him. Go for a half a cup, wait fifteen minutes then give him the other half. Wait an hour, then do the same again."

Ben took Gus's temperature and applied a fresh compress. "The compress I took off was quite warm. These need to be changed every ten minutes. He's still got a fever."

"I didn't hire on to be no nursemaid," the young man said. "I'm supposed to be pealin' spuds and cleanin' tables."

"I'm sure you didn't. I'll be back in a couple of hours to check on things. I'll see if I can bring someone more suited to sitting bedside to replace you."

"Thanks, Doc. I'd be much obliged," the man said.

The report Ben got from Frank Mitchner wasn't good. Like his cousin, Cleavold hadn't been able to tolerate any drink. Ben sent Frank to take a break and get something to eat. Doc was sitting at Cleavold's bedside when Sarah arrived with the blackberry tea.

"Any change?" Sarah asked.

"No. I just spoon fed him a little water. He's feverish. I've been sponging him down. I think if we can get him to hold liquids the fever will leave."

"I'll go get a cup to put some of this tea in," Sarah said heading to the kitchen.

"Did you take tea to the hotel?" Ben called out.

"Yes," Sarah called back. "I stayed long enough to see the traveler take some in. The tea was warm, likely it felt comforting to his intestines."

Ben was wiping Cleavold's mouth when Sarah returned with the cup. "Sarah, he just now vomited the water I gave him," Ben said, worry in his voice.

"Elevate his head, Ben, I'll see if I can get him to take some tea." Sarah crooned to Cleavold as she tried to get him to open his mouth to receive her offering. "Cleavold, open your mouth. I've got some warm tea for you. It's blackberry. You drink this, it'll help you get well. If you do, I'll make you a blackberry pie. Would you like that?"

Cleavold nodded his head and opened his mouth. Sarah had spooned in about half a cup of the tea when Doc suggested she stop. "Let's see if he can tolerate that much. If he does, we'll give him more in about fifteen minutes."

Doc lowered Cleavold's head to his pillow. Sarah knelt beside the bed in readiness to pray. She laid her hand on the banker's arm. Doc stiffened at the sight. "How can you pray for this man after he disrespected you? Sarah, his vile actions when you were grieving and vulnerable were despicable."

Sarah gave Ben a stern look. "I learned a long time ago that it's hard to hold resentment against someone when you lift them up in prayer. This won't be the first time I've prayed for Cleavold Anubis and it won't be the last. If I held what happened against Cleavold it wouldn't hurt him, but it would hurt me. I think you're holding a grudge against him on my behalf and if you're honest with yourself, you'd see that it is causing you pain.

"Give it up Ben. Don't let ill feelings occupy a space in your heart that could be given to the glory of the Lord. You were able to exercise God's grace and come take care of Cleavold even though you don't like him. Might God be calling you to take it a step further?"

Ben held Sarah's gaze, he didn't speak.

Sarah prayed, "Almighty God, I come to you today asking for healing for Cleavold. Father, I ask that you touch his body in a powerful way and let the tea we've given him soothe his stomach and bring him comfort. Lord, I know you're watching and waiting for Cleavold to come to you. I pray that this near-death experience will cause him to feel you knocking at the door of his heart. Father, I pray that he will open that door and let you in. I leave him in your hands. "Amen."

Sarah rose and kissed Ben on the cheek. "I've got to go to your office and pick up the children. We bought Jane's shoes before we came to see you, but we haven't yet been to the school. I'm hoping it's not too late to get her registered this afternoon."

Ben's voice was husky when he spoke. "Thank you for bringing the tea. I hope all goes well at the school."

"Do you think you'll be home by supper time?" Sarah asked.

"If both men can keep the tea down, I'll feel comfortable to leave them with someone sitting bedside. I'm hoping I'll be home before it gets too late."

"I'll save a plate for you if you're delayed." Sarah blew Doc a kiss and left.

Cleavold's body tolerated the tea. He was able to take in two more servings during the next hour. Instead of feeling relief, Ben felt overwhelmed by guilt. His heart grew heavier with each passing minute. Eventually he could bear it no longer.

Doc's knees trembled as he knelt by the bed and took Cleavold's limp hand in his. "Father in heaven, I come to you on bended knee confessing that I haven't wanted to forgive Cleavold for the way he treated Sarah. I thought I was justified in holding a grudge against him. I've openly snubbed Cleavold and felt superior for doing it. I wanted him to know that I found him despicable.

"Lord, I now see the wrong in that. I ask for Your forgiveness. If Cleavold rallies enough to hear me, I'll apologize to him. I know that You and You alone are man's judge. Not on my own, but through Your grace, I can forgive. Father, I release my resentment for this man and ask for his healing. Amen."

Chapter 11

During the morning quiet time, before Joy and the little ones got up for breakfast and the three oldest were doing chores, Ben sat in the kitchen enjoying a Sunday morning cup of coffee. When Sarah walked in, he asked, "What's that you're holding?"

"It's a box I'm giving to Jane. I thought she could use it as a place to keep things she wants to safeguard, like the herb guide. The booklet shows through the bodice of her dresses. I'm concerned someone at school might make a comment, ask what she's hiding or the like. I don't want her to feel embarrassed or the need to explain."

"So, are you going to give it to her this morning?" Ben asked.

"Yes. She'll have the whole day to consider the matter, decide if she's comfortable leaving the guide here at the house while she's gone." Sarah poured herself a cup of coffee and took a seat next to Ben at the table.

"Speaking of that herb guide," Ben said, "I want to look at it again today. I'm not adverse to trying more of those remedies since the blackberry tea worked as well as it did. When I checked on them last evening, Cleavold and his cousin Gus, had improved significantly. Neither of them has had further purging after drinking the tea. I'm hopeful that after a couple of days of rest and taking in food, they might be ready to go on about their business."

"After such a bad experience from drinking moonshine and the success with Jane's brew, they might just become teetotalers," Sarah teased. "No telling how many folks got sick from drinking that rotgut."

Ben got up and poured himself another cup of coffee. "Gus said several folks in Banquo, the town where he got the swill, were sick but no one knew the cause. I used Jeb's phone at the Marshal's office to call and let the town's doctor know I'd had a couple of cases of dysentery and had connected the cause to moonshine from their area."

"Does Banquo's doctor have a phone in his office?"

"No, but Jeb knew that their marshal, a man named Hickman, had one. Hickman took the message and said he'd pass it on. He thought he knew where the hooch might have come from. He said he'd go tell the fellow what had happened and shut him down if need be."

"If need be?" Sarah responded. "Isn't having a still against the law?"

"Yes, it is, but in small towns like Banquo the law usually looks the other way when they come onto one. If it's causing trouble, they'll take action but otherwise they don't do anything."

"I hope he thinks selling moonshine that makes people sick is causing trouble," Sarah said.

Ben responded, "I asked him if they'd had any deaths due to dysentery."

Sarah abruptly set her cup down. "What'd he say?"

"One elderly man died. Another fellow escaped death by the skin of his teeth," Ben responded.

"Escaped by the skin of his teeth, how so?" Sarah asked.

"Apparently there was a local guy who frequented the tavern and played the banjo but hadn't been seen in several days. The tavern owner wasn't too surprised 'cause he'd run the guy off. After regular clientele complained about lack of entertainment the barkeep went out to the man's cabin to tell him he could come back. He found him near death, hauled him back to town and to the doctor. The marshal said the doctor told him he'd never seen a human live that was so near death."

"I'd say that rather than by the skin of his teeth, he was saved by the grace of God. Did you tell the marshal to relay your recommendation for using blackberry tea to treat dysentery?" Sarah asked.

"Yes, I think it helped with my two cases and I don't think it will do any harm even if it doesn't work for others. Maybe tonight Jane and I can a look at her pictured guide," Doc said, "I'd like to study it some more."

"Speaking of those drawings in the booklet," Sarah said, "I recall Jane saying that she drew them."

Doc interjected, "Yes, that's what she told us."

"The thing is," Sarah said, "the illustrations were signed with the name Joy, not Jane."

"They were? I didn't catch that. Let's ask her for clarification," Ben said.

"Jane doesn't seem like a prideful girl, Sarah commented, "one who would take credit for something she didn't do." The kitchen clock struck. "Six-thirty, the boys will be coming in from chores at seven. I'd better go wake Jane to come help me with breakfast and give her this box. If we don't watch the time, we'll find ourselves late for church."

Sarah opened the door to the parlor and tiptoed in. Joy lay sleeping so near the edge of her bed that her long hair cascaded, touching the floor. Sarah bent and whispered in the girl's ear. "Jane, wake up dear."

Startled, Joy woke and jumped out of bed. "Am I late?"

"No, Dear," Sarah whispered, motioning for Joy to follow her out in the hall.

Joy grabbed her robe. Once they were out of the room Sarah said, "I didn't want to wake the twins. Before we start making breakfast, I have something I'd like to give to you." Sarah handed Joy a twelve-by eight inches, hinged wooden box with a hasp.

Joy took it and ran a hand across its fine-grained, polished surface. "Ma'am, this is beautiful." When Joy lifted the lid, a distinctive aroma wafted to her nose. "It's made of cedar. I love the smell. Why are you giving me this?"

Sarah reached in her apron pocket and extracted a padlock with the key inserted in its eye. "I wanted you to have a secure place to put things that are dear to you. Your mother's shawl might not fit but your herbal medicine guide will." Sarah handed the device to Joy along with a length of string. "You could carry the key around your neck instead of the guide. We achieved such a nice makeover on your dresses that I'm sure their custom fit makes it uncomfortable to carry the booklet beneath your bodice."

Joy clutched the guide under her nightgown.

"If you don't feel comfortable being without the guide," Sarah said, "I've got an across the shoulder pouch you can put it in. You decide."

Joy's voice was hoarse with emotion when she spoke, "Thank you, Ma'am."

***

Sunday evening the family lounged around. Sarah was in her rocker by the fireplace crocheting. Josh was lying on the floor next to her reading *Swiss Family Robinson*. Lancy was snuggled at Josh's side snoozing. Occasionally the Lab moved his legs as if chasing a rabbit in a dream. Abe and Luke were nearby playing a game of checkers. Zeke and Henry were repeatedly building and demolishing wooden block towers while Hathaway tried to have a tea party with Naomi. Naomi refused to grasp the concept of sipping from her tiny tin cup. Instead she enjoyed, to her big sister's consternation, tossing it and giggling as Hathaway, again and again, fetched it and brought it back to their make-believe table. The picture of hearth and home was complete when Ben and Joy took side by side seats at the table to look through the herb guide.

"Wait, don't turn the page so fast," Ben said. "I want to read the dedication to the booklet."

Joy reluctantly relinquished her hold, sitting with her head hung low while Doc read.

A Practical Guide to Nature's Cures
Illustrations drawn by Joy Humes, beloved daughter
of
Jane Anderson Humes, Author

This book is proudly dedicated to
Onida Anderson, Medicine Woman,
mother of Jane, grandmother of Joy.

Nature's, God-provided, remedies herein are tried and proven,
having been passed down through generations of
Delaware Indian Medicine Women.

When he was finished Ben closed the book, took off his glasses, laid them on the table and folded his hands. In a soft voice he said, "Dear girl, by now you must recognize that we cherish you and will do all we can to keep you from harm. The time has come for you to tell us your real name."

Sarah, who'd been listening to the exchange between Ben and Joy, got up and joined them at the table. Sarah put her arm around the girl. "You're starting school tomorrow. You'll be making new friends. Don't you want to be known by your rightful name?"

Tears streamed down Joy's cheeks.

In a whisper Sarah said, "Your name is Joy, isn't it?"

"Jane was your mother's name wasn't it?" Ben asked.

"Yes," Joy whispered, "when you asked my name the day you discovered me sleeping in your barn, I was afraid to tell you. I feared my father might come looking for me and ask if anyone had seen a girl named Joy. Jane was the first name that popped into my head."

"It's been nearly three weeks since you came to us." Sarah tightened her shoulder hug on the girl. "Are you still afraid your father might come looking for you?"

"Yes. He won't give up until he's found me. I left a message for him that I'm sure he didn't like. His desire to make me pay for leaving the message will keep him on the hunt."

Sarah withdrew her arm from around the girl. "Oh my, what a predicament," she said, finger rubbing her temples. "I don't hold with lying but if using your mother's name makes you feel safer, maybe you should continue. When I registered you at school, I had to give a full name for you. I lied and told Principal Hornblower that your last name was Adams and that you were our niece."

Joy covered her face with her hands. "I saw you filling out that registration application, but I didn't even think about you needing to give a last name for me. I've caused you to lie, I'm so sorry."

"Don't be. You didn't cause me to lie, I chose to. At the time, I did think your first name was Jane, but I knew your last name wasn't Adams and that you aren't our niece," Sarah responded.

"There's a story in the Bible about a woman named Rahab who lived in a town called Jericho," Sarah began. "The short of it is that she met spies sent by God, gave them a place to hide and lied to protect them. Although God eventually destroyed Jericho, Rahab and her family were spared because God knew that she believed in Him. I've talked to the Lord about your situation. I have faith that He's in agreement with us helping to protect you. What do you think, Ben?"

"I think she should go by her own first name, keep Adams as her last name for now. Joy, going to school will give you an opportunity to make friends. A person's name is important, and you have the right to be identified by it," Ben said. "You're with us now, you aren't alone. If your father does come looking for you, we won't let him harm you."

"Joy, I think Ben is right. Your name is beautiful, your mother gave it to you. You should use it," Sarah said.

"But you've already registered me as Jane at the school," Joy said.

"Yes, but only Mr. Hornblower knows that at this point," Sarah said. "I'll think of something to tell him and I'll get the correction made on your enrollment records. That way you can be introduced on your first day as Joy Adams."

"Joy, we now know that your last name is Humes. I need you to tell me your father's whole name."

Sarah clasped Joy's hand and felt the girl's body tremble when she spoke. "His name is Edward J. Humes. He goes by Ed."

Ben gave the girl's arm a reassuring squeeze. "Thank you. Now, let's call Abe over here and fill him in on all of this. He's old enough to know that Joy is hiding from her father and why. He needs to know the man's name and Joy you need to give us a general description of him."

Joy's voice quivered a bit when she spoke. "He has dark brown hair, a mustache and is about your height, Doctor Adams."

"I'm six feet tall," Ben interjected.

Joy continued. "He likes to dress like a 'dandy', wants his clothes to be just so. Some folks have said that he's a handsome man. Maybe he is when he isn't drunk, I wouldn't know. He wears a belt with a large silver buckle." Joy's tone of voice became foreboding, "He hit my mother and me with that buckle. I wouldn't have let him hurt my baby sister if she'd lived."

Doc's eyes welled with tears. "Is there anything else important to his description?"

"Yes," Joy responded, "he's never without his banjo. He loves it more than anything."

"Joy, this is all very helpful. I'll give Jeb Carter his name, description and the particulars about the banjo."

Sarah shook her head, "I'm not sure we should. Won't Jeb be obliged by law to tell Joy's father where she is if he comes to the Marshal's office asking about her?"

"Sarah, I told Jeb about Joy's condition when she came to us. If Ed Humes comes looking for her, Jeb will do whatever is needed to keep her safe."

Sarah reached across Joy and grasped Ben's hand. "You're right. I've known Jeb a long time. Law or not, he won't side with a man who would abuse his child."

Ben raised Sarah's hand and gave it a kiss. "I suggest we tell the other children that we're introducing our girl here, to the community as Joy Adams, our niece. They've already accepted her as part of this family. I don't think they'll even question the niece association. Now let's get Abe over here, fill him in, then tell the others. It's getting late and the children all need to get to bed."

"I'll go get Abe," Joy said rising from the table.

Ben moved over and took Joy's vacated seat, placing himself next to Sarah. He leaned in and in a teasing tone whispered in her ear. "So, you compare yourself to Rahab do you. As I recall she got around Jericho a lot, so to speak. Wasn't she referred to as a prostitute?"

"Leave it to you to remember that piece of the story," Sarah responded. "The point was that God justified Rahab's lying because she did it for the greater good."

"I see, I see," Ben said.

"I'm not so sure you do see it clearly," Sarah quipped, then leaned in to whisper in Ben's ear. "I'm no Rahab but when I get you in bed, I think I can 'clarify' a few things for you."

Ben's eyebrows shot up and he swallowed hard. "Let's get this talk done."

***

Josh, Luke and Zeke took off running to the end of the farm's lane to stand in wait for the hack to pick them up and carry them to school. Abe and Joy followed at an easy pace. For this first day Joy had chosen to wear the dress with the blue and lavender floral pattern that matched one her mother had once had. Sarah had braided the sides of the girl's hair. The braids were secured at the back of her head with a blue ribbon while the rest of her mane fell in soft waves down her back, stopping just short of her waistline. The tips of Joy's new shoes peeked from beneath the hem of her dress. She'd buffed them that morning until they shined.

"Joy, that there pouch you got slung across your shoulders is somethin' new, ain't it?"

"It's your mother's. She loaned it to me to carry my herb guide so I could keep it with me without wearing it around my neck."

"Well, it looks a lot better than havin' your dress a stickin' out on your chest where it shouldn't." Thinking he might have spoken inappropriately Abe said, "Sorry, I didn't mean no disrespect."

"Thank you, Abe. Are you mad at me for not telling you my real name from the start?" Joy asked.

"Not at all. You didn't have no one to look out for you so you did the best you could to protect yourself. That's all changed. Now you've got a big new family to depend on. If that man, I ain't gonna call him your pa, 'cause he don't deserve the title, comes a lookin' for you, we'll give him what for and send him hightailin' it on down the road."

Joy reached over and briefly took Abe's hand in hers. "Abe Whitcome, I'm glad you're on my side."

Abe turned three shades of red before he found his voice. "Are you excited about goin' to school?"

"I'm more nervous than excited. Mr. Hornblower asked me a lot of history and geography related questions on Friday and I answered them all correctly. My score on cyphering the arithmetic problems he gave me was a hundred percent. Still, it's been a really long time since I've been to school."

"He put you in my class," Abe said with a big grin. "I can help you get settled in."

Joy tried to smile back. "I hope I can keep up with grade eight studies, I don't want anyone to look at me and think I'm stupid."

The pair had reached the end of the lane just as the hack, driven by Julib Carter, pulled up. The younger boys hopped on and Abe motioned for Joy to climb the steps ahead of him. The twenty-year-old's customary morning greeting got hung up in his throat when he saw Joy.

"Julib, this here's Joy. She's our kin and she'll be goin' to school with us ever' day now."

Julib tipped his hat, tried to speak, but his hello came out as a croak. Abe had a disconcerting frown on his face when he took a seat next to Joy. *Just what I figured. Ain't nobody gonna be lookin' at Joy and thinkin' she's anythin' but pretty.*

Chapter 12

The school bell rang in synchronization with LaFontaine's noon whistle. Joy waited for Abe to come from the back and join her before exiting the classroom.

"How'd ya like settin' in the front row seat, Joy?" Abe asked as side-by-side they made the trek down a long corridor, then descended two flights of stairs before arriving at the dining hall.

"I'd much prefer sitting in the back with you," Joy said.

"Miss Messner put ya front and center 'cause you're new," Abe responded. "She might let ya move after you've been here a while and she finds out ya don't need special help."

The pair entered the room where Abe directed Joy to a long, two-bench table at the rear. "Why don't we sit by the window so we can enjoy the sunlight?" Joy asked.

"'Cause back here is where the eighth-grade sets," Abe responded placing his lunch pail at the end seat and motioning for Joy to take the one opposite him.

Joy asked for clarification, "So there's assigned seating by class?"

Abe's lips took a downward turn, "Well, it ain't official but ya abide by it unless ya want a fight." The boy launched into a detailed description of the seating hierarchy. "Grade twelve gets the near window seats. Eleventh, then tenth grades take the next two rows of tables. The middle is for ninth grade and us eighth graders get this long table back here at the rear of the room."

Ernie Brown, a known bully and Abe's longtime arch nemesis sidled up to the table. He listened in on Abe and Joy's conversation as he wedged his man-sized bulk between two of his classmates.

Ernie's and Abe's near hatred for one another was born from a run-in they'd had a couple of years back. Ernie, a fourteen-year-old upper classman at the time, had made hateful remarks about Abe's mother. Abe fought the boy in defense of Sarah's honor. Despite Ernie being older and larger, Abe held his own, returning punch for punch until the teacher intervened. Both boys had been sent home from school bloody and bruised.

Sarah had asked Abe to promise he would never again fight with Ernie Brown. What Abe promised was to never again fight him on school grounds. The *never on school grounds* was inserted as a loophole should the need to defend his family's honor come again.

Each boy had given the other a wide berth since that day, but their mutual disdain remained. It took two years for Ernie to get through the seventh grade and he was now doing his second year of eighth grade. He was sixteen and legally old enough to quit school. He wanted to quit, he preferred the heavy lifting of farm work. He was repeating the eighth grade at his father's insistence.

Directing his comment to Joy, Ernie said, "*Men* call it the butt section, the rear of the room…butt, get it?" With an exaggerated laugh, he slapped the table.

The mixture of boys and girls who had filled the seats at the table gave a collective gasp and turned to look at Abe.

Abe's chin thrust outward and upward accentuating his fine chiseled jawline. The veins in his neck bulged as he moved his lunch pail from his right-hand side to his left. Slowly, with deliberation he turned his head and leaned in so he could make eye contact with Ernie. "Brown! Watch your mouth. They's ladies present." The wide berth had shrunk.

In a tone that indicated mock contrition Ernie responded, "Well, pardon me. I didn't think any cousin of yours would be the delicate lady-like type. Is it okay to call her Joy like Miss Messner introduced her, or do ya expect me to address her as Miss la dee da Adams?"

Abe brought his arms into view and laid them, hands fisted, on top of the table.

Joy nudged Abe's shin with her foot causing him to abruptly turn and look at her. With lips in a thin line she slightly shook her head. The message to *let it go* was clear.

"Oooh," Ernie taunted, "better do what the lady wants."

Abe locked eyes with Ernie as he slowly placed his arms back under the table where his fists remained clenched. In a near growl, he said, "Brown, you'd best watch your step."

A girl sitting at the opposite end of the table spoke up. "Ernie Brown, Abe wasn't just referrin' to his cousin, Joy, he was tellin' you that all us girls at this table deserve to be treated like ladies." Heads nodded in agreement as she continued. "Oh, I forgot, you flunked last year. Perhaps you're too dumb to know how to act mannerly."

Ernie rose from the table, his face crimson. As he departed the room, he passed near enough behind Abe to let his elbow graze the back of the boy's head. Abe's shoulders visibly tensed.

The school's principal, who with his hands locked behind his back had been sauntering around the dining hall, came up to the eighth-grade table. "Everything okay over here?"

With mouths locked in solidarity no one responded. Hornblower's voice raised an octave, "Eighth graders, I ask…is everything okay at this table?"

Abe's focus was concentrated on the handle of his lunch pail when he drew in a deep breath, held it, then slowly exhaled. "Yes, Sir, everythin's just fine and dandy."

Hornblower patted Abe's back. "Good to hear young man. Good to hear." The bulbous-nosed educator strolled away, continuing his room monitoring.

The class burst into a buzz of conversation, much of it was speculation over who'd make the next move in the continuing feud between Abe Whitcome and Ernie Brown. The girl sitting next to Joy leaned over and, in a rush of words, said, "My name's Breanna Johnson. I moved to the area this summer to live with my mother's cousins. Their farm is just a half-mile down from yours. I'm new to this school, too. Would you like to get acquainted? We could help one another settle in."

Joy's face beamed, "I'd like that very much."

The table fell silent when the ten-minute warning bell sounded. Heads bent, eating in a rush to allow time for a stop by one of the outhouses before returning to their classroom.

***

The Mississinewa River snaked through some of the farms west of LaFontaine, Indiana, the Brown's homestead being one. Ernie had his pant legs rolled up and was sitting on its bank, cooling his heels, literally as well as figuratively. The boy stretched out his long legs then leaned back, letting his body rest on his arms. His muscles bulged threatening to break through their shirt-sleeve restraints as he lifted his face to the sun and soaked in the comforting warmth.

He was at his *thinking place*, the name he'd dubbed the spot. A great northern loon made an ungainly landing, then floated downriver, breaking the silence with its mournful wail.

Ernie sat up and folded into a cross-legged position. He spied an errant stock of lavender that was within reaching distance. After plucking it he held the long-stemmed plant under his nose and drew in the fragrance, thought by some to be calming. It didn't work for the boy. His mind continued to be filled with thoughts of revenge and hatred for Abe Whitcome.

A grey cloud floated in and eclipsed the sun such that a shadow spread over Ernie. He tossed the stock of lavender aside. The shadow suited the boy, it matched his gloomy thoughts.

That dad-burned Whitcome, tryin' to make a fool outta' me. He thinks he's so special. Just 'cause he's smart and has a pretty ma. That don't mean nothin'. My ma might be pretty too if she smiled all the time like Mrs. Whitcome...uh, Adams. Pa's real hard on Ma, he ain't friendly like the doc. Guess Ma ain't got nothin' to smile about. Me neither.

I felt like smilin' at Abe's cousin when I saw her today. Weren't no use, a fine lookin' girl like her ain't gonna pay me no never mind.

I'm sick of goin' to school, tryin' to learn. Pa thinks I'm just bein' lazy about book learnin'. That ain't it. I can't read half them words I'm 'sposed to. I'd like to make Ma proud, that might bring a smile to her face. Fat chance of that happenin', I ain't good at nothin' 'cept fightin'."

A ray of sunlight hit the metal guard on the hunting knife he'd unstrapped from his right ankle and laid to his side. The glint caught Ernie's attention. He reached over, picked up the leather sheath and extracted the knife.

Ernie rubbed his thumb up and down the deer antler that was the handle of the homemade knife. "Grandpa, I sure wish you hadn't died," the boy said out loud. His thoughts traveled back six years to the day he and his grandfather had made the knife. Again, the boy spoke with none other than himself. "I reckon us making this knife together is my best memory."

Ernie dug a plug of dirt from a deep grove in the horn and heard his grandpa's deep voice. He chuckled as he conjured up a pleasant scene from his past. *"First, we set this piece of a buck's rack to soakin' in that bucket of creek water over yonder. Now it's gonna take quite a spell afore it's ready."*

I weren't figurin' on it taken a whole month for the pithy core to get soft enough to shove in the tine. Grandpa, I can still hear ya tellin' me, real gentle like, "Hold your britches boy, hold your britches. I said it'd take a spell." I 'spect ya tolt me that near a hundret times.

The boy's eyes welled, and he used the back of his hand to swipe away a tear. A mother duck with three ducklings trailing turned his direction. They started quacking as they paddled to the shore line. They stopped in front of Ernie where they remained, treading water as if they'd come to listen. Ernie raised his voice in response to the overture. "I'm settin' here rememberin' my grandpa Brown. Him and me was easy together. I guess I miss that the most. I don't have me no one to talk to now. Least ways no one that cares enough to listen to what I got to say."

The duck entourage gave a few consolatory quacks before resuming their course and swimming on downstream. Ernie selected a stone from the river's rocky bank. Using smooth repeated motion, he ran the knife's blade across the stone's surface. After a time, he used his thumb to test for sharpness. A bright red line appeared oozing blood. Ernie wiped the blade on his pants then held the knife up for close inspection. Satisfied with his effort, he stood.

Near the bank of the river Ernie saw a large swarm of water striders hovering. He assumed a swashbuckler's stance and lunged his knife at the insects. "I ain't never been in a knife fight. I recon if I were, this here one would do me good."

Chapter 13

Cleavold Anubis responded to the knock at his door, "Come in."

Doc Adams entered carrying his medical satchel. "How's it going today?"

"I feel stronger than yesterday," Cleavold responded as he sat down on the edge of his bed. "I fixed myself a couple of eggs for breakfast and ate them along with a slice of bread. Stomach feels calm so, fingers crossed."

Ben took out his stethoscope and listened to Cleavold's chest. "I just came from looking in on your cousin," Doc said. "He, too, is much improved and anxious to get on the road. I gave Gus the go ahead to travel, as long as he takes time out of the saddle to rest and drink water."

"That's good news. I'd like to get back to work myself. Do you think I'm up to it?"

Doc stuck a thermometer in Cleavold's mouth, "You're holding down solid food, your color's good," Doc said. "Let's see what your temperature reads."

After a few minutes wait, Ben extracted the thermometer and examined the mercury reading. "No fever, that's a blessing. I'd suggest continued rest today. Go on back to the bank tomorrow. If you're feeling tired by noon, come home and nap for a couple of hours. Force yourself to eat three squares a day and drink as much water as you can hold. This being Monday, I'd be willing to speculate that you'll feel near normal by week's end."

Cleavold stood and Ben shook his outreached hand. In a voice choked with emotion the banker said, "I know you've held contempt for me over the way I handled your wife's loan request a couple of years back when she was still Mrs. Whitcome. I've never apologized to her for my actions and yet, instead of shunning me, your wife has always treated me with cordiality."

"Sarah's a wonder," Ben said. "She used your illness as an opportunity to show me an example of grace. I watched her wipe your fevered brow and spoon feed you. She knelt by your bedside and prayed for your healing. When I asked her how she could do that after the deplorable way you'd treated her, she said that she'd left the incident in the past. She told me that when she looked at you as you lay sick and weak, she saw you as Jesus does, a cherished life."

"I heard a woman praying but I was too weak to respond. When I woke, I remembered it and decided it had been in my imagination because I didn't know any woman who would pray for me."

Doc returned his medical instruments to his bag. "Now you do," he said as he unlatched the door.

***

"Pass them taters," Zeke said to anyone who'd listen.

"Zeke mind your manners," Sarah admonished.

"Sorry, Ma. Ever since we got home from school, I've been a countin' me the minutes 'til supper was on the table."

"What about that glass of milk and three cookies you ate when we got home?" Joy asked.

"You're new to bein' around a growin' boy so I guess ya don't know," Zeke said patting his stomach, "it takes a lot more than three cookies and a glass of milk to fill this tummy."

"Joy," Sarah said, "I know that you and your mother walked to school. What did you think of riding in a hack?"

"I enjoyed it very much," Joy responded.

"Speakin' of the hack," Luke interrupted, "they was something wrong with our driver this mornin'."

"Are you talking about Julib Carter?" Ben asked.

"Yeah," Luke said, "the Marshal's boy."

"Pa," Zeke said with a scrunched brow, "I've knowed Julib all my life, I thought you had too."

"Yes, Son, I know who Julib *is*, it's just that I saw him this afternoon and he didn't look ill or say anything about feeling sick," Ben responded.

"I didn't mean he looked sick," Luke continued. "It's just that he generally is talkative while he's a drivin' us to school. Today when he stopped for us, me and Josh was the first ones to climb in the buggy. He said good mornin', real regular like, but after Abe introduced him to Joy, his voice got all clogged up. When he tried to speak, it came out squawky and then he didn't say nothin' the rest of the way into town. Weren't much better when he came to fetch us home."

Ben spoke, "How curious, might be he got stricken by something he saw." Ben looked at Sarah and twitched his eyebrows.

"I don't know what it could have been," Luke responded. "He weren't lookin' at nothin' but Joy."

"Joy," Ben asked as he spooned a helping of mashed potatoes onto Hathaway's plate, "what did you think of the school and your first day?"

A smile spread across Joy's face and talking fast she responded. "The school is really huge. It's so much larger than the one I attended. I'd been in the administration area when Sarah took me to enroll. I thought that space was big with the principal having a private office, but I hadn't seen the rest of the school until today.

The classrooms are spread out over three stories and grades one through eight each have their own teacher. Grades nine through twelve have a teacher for each subject and they change classrooms accordingly. There's even a large study hall for doing homework."

Joy took a break from her description to grab a gulp of milk. Ben and Sarah made eye contact and smiled.

The girl continued, "We didn't eat at our desks. The school has a separate dining hall. It's enormous and seating was sectioned off by grade. I would have gotten into trouble if Abe hadn't been with me to show me where the eighth graders are supposed to sit."

"Lunch room hierarchy," Ben said, "I remember it well from my medical school days, it existed there as well."

"That was a lot for you to take in," Sarah said. "Despite all of that, did you enjoy your first day?"

"Oh, yes, Ma'am." Joy responded. "It was good, and I made a friend."

"That's wonderful," Sarah said. "Who is it?"

"Her name is Breanna Johnson." Joy said. "She lives down the road with her mother's cousins, Josephine and William Johnson. They're brother and sister. Breanna moved here to live with them late this summer so she's new to the school too."

"Praise be to God," Sarah said. "Josephine Johnson and I have been good friends since we were in school together. We know her brother William quite well too."

"So, do you already know Breanna?" Joy asked.

"I did meet her about a month ago, when she first arrived. She seemed like a sweet girl, but I haven't had the pleasure of getting acquainted with her."

"I don't know about sweet," Abe said, "but I do like it that she ain't all giggly like most of the girls in my class. She's kinda quiet like you, Joy."

"Joy," Sarah said, "I think you'll find that you and Breanna have a lot in common. It did cross my mind to introduce you to her. Then things got busy around here and time went fast. I'm so pleased you'll be getting to know one another."

"I haven't had an opportunity to meet Breanna," Ben said. "Sarah, one day soon do you think we could invite the Johnsons over for supper?"

"Let's have them over for dinner after church on Sunday," Sarah suggested. The little ones and I can take a stroll over to their farm tomorrow and make the invite."

"Ask Josephine iffin' she can bring one of her chocolate cakes," Zeke interjected, then turned to Joy to explain the request. "Ma's pies are the best you can get but, every now and then, a feller gets a hankerin' for cake. Generally, we only get one when it's someone's birthday and they ain't none comin' up in this family any time soon."

"Well," Ben interjected, "actually we don't know that for sure. Joy, we haven't asked. When is your birthday?"

"It was last week, October 15th." Joy responded.

"Last week!" Sarah exclaimed. "I wish you'd have told us. Oh, we should have thought to ask."

"Ma'am, no need to take on about it," Joy said softly. I haven't had a birthday celebration since my mother died."

"Better late than never," Josh piped up.

"Yeah, better late than never," Zeke repeated. "Ma, now you got a reason to bake us a cake. If you don't want to, then you can just tell your friend Josephine she has to bring one of her chocolate ones."

"No need for anyone to worry about a cake. It will be my pleasure to see that we have one on the table next Sunday when we celebrate Joy's birthday," Sarah said.

"Joy, did ya just turn fourteen or are ya already fifteen?" Abe asked as he shoveled in a spoonful of corn. A kernel fell out and down on his plate when he spoke before properly chewing. Zeke giggled, Abe apologized and continued. "I'll be fifteen come March, and I'm thinkin' we's about the same age."

Joy hung her head. "I'd be embarrassed for anyone to know my age."

"Ain't no reason to be embarrassed," nine-year-old Luke said. "What if ya was sixteen and still in the eighth grade like Ernie Brown. Talk about embarassin', I don't know how he can show his face at school."

"Luke," Sarah scolded. "I don't like to hear you talk that way about Ernie Brown. Book learning is hard for the boy. Ernie's doing the best he can and that's all that can be asked of any of us."

Joy's head still hung low and she brought her napkin up to cover her eyes as tears spilled and trickled down her cheeks. Hathaway who was sitting next to Joy was quick to notice. With a lilt in her voice she said, "Don't cry, Joy." The toddler shoved a biscuit under Joy's napkin. "Here, you's can have my biscuit."

Ben, who was seated on the other side of Hathaway reached over the toddler and patted Joy on the shoulder. "We're sorry if we've upset you, Joy. Has all of this birthday talk got you thinking about your mother?"

"Yes," Joy said dabbing tears with her napkin, "but, I'm upset," Joy dropped her hands, looked up and blurted, "because I just turned sixteen." Up went the napkin.

Abe shouted, "Sixteen." Henry's highchair was next to Abe, the baby flinched and dropped his piece of meat. Abe retrieved it from the floor and handed it to Henry who popped it into his mouth. Lowering his voice, Abe said, "I never figured you to be older than me."

In a voice still tearful Joy said. "I knew you'd be shocked. Now you'll make fun of me like you do Ernie Brown."

Abe's face flushed red. Joy's words stung as truth revealed often does. *I reckon I have been a makin' fun of Ernie. I never thought it hurt his feelin's none. Didn't figure a lunkhead like him had any.*

"Joy," Sarah interjected, "Ben and I won't tolerate our children making fun of you, or anyone. You've got nothing to be ashamed of. The fact that you've been kept from going to school is not your fault. Mister Hornblower said, if all goes well, he'd be willing to test you for higher grade placement, maybe on to tenth grade."

Using her napkin, Joy wiped her eyes then blew her nose. Thank you, Ma'am, I'll work hard toward that."

Josh brought to halt the emotional exchange when he blurted out, "Let's get back to talkin' about school today. I heard that noon meal break didn't go so well."

"Oh," Sarah said, "what happened at noon meal?"

Abe was still looking at Joy with an awe-struck expression when he interjected, "Nothin'. Didn't nothin' worth tellin' happen."

Luke's arm shot in the air and he propped it with his other hand and arm, elbow resting on the table.

"Luke, you don't have to raise your hand for permission to speak here at home," Sarah said. "What is it, Dear?"

With a tone that comes from being the one that knows, Luke said, "On the hack ride home, some kids were whisperin' about what happened."

"Let's hear it," Zeke said.

Abe turned from looking at Joy to give his brother the stink eye. "Luke, no," Abe warned. "I said it weren't worth repeatin'."

With composure restored Joy said, "It was a chivalrous thing you did, Abe. I think your mother would be proud to hear it."

Sarah leaned in, eyes wide, "Now I've got to know."

Luke blurted out, "Ernie Brown said something disrespectful in front of Joy and Abe told him to watch his mouth."

"I ain't surprised," Zeke said as he shoveled in a spoonful of corn. "Ernie's a donkey's behind and always will be."

"Language, Zeke Whitcome!" Sarah admonished.

"What's wrong with sayin' donkey's behind? I thought it was jackass I weren't supposed to say."

Baby Henry chuckled, kicked his chubby legs and jabbered, "ja a, ja a."

Naomi, seated in her high chair next to Henry, looked at him and giggled. In unison, the seventeen-month-old twins chanted, "ja a, ja a, ja a."

Hathaway's eyes grew large. The rest at the table, except for Zeke, placed napkins over mouths to stifle snickers. Zeke burst into tears and ran to his mother. "I'm sorry, Ma, I done turned the babies into sinners."

Chapter 14

Sarah's back ached from spending the morning bent over the laundry tub. Pleasant memories floated through her mind as she stretched. *Thank goodness, the babies and Hathaway went down for their naps without fussing. Guess they were tuckered out from playing in the dirt pile while I washed diapers.*

She smiled as she pictured Henry digging with a spoon, throwing dirt over his baby-sized shoulder. *He caught on after his first fistful that dirt wasn't something to eat. Naomi's more gullible.* Sarah chuckled out loud as she recalled the baby repeatedly spitting to rid herself of the bite of dirt pie her big sister had offered. *Hathaway seemed surprised when Naomi leaned in and put the spoon in her mouth. She showed good instincts by using the hem of her dress to clean off her sister's tongue. She's going to make a fine mother one day.* Sarah whispered, "Thank you, Lord for the precious blessing of watching the babies play."

After pouring herself a cup of coffee Sarah grabbed the calendar from the wall and took a seat at the kitchen table. The LaFontaine Bank distributed a calendar annually as a means for advertising. On the cover the Board of Directors were listed under a picture of the bank. Sarah's eyes were drawn to the size of the type used to print the names. *Wonder why I never noticed before, Cleavold Anubis' name is in larger print than the other names. Like his shoe lifts, it might be another attempt to make himself appear larger than he is. I need to ask Ben if he's seen Cleavold recently. Wonder if he's fully recovered from his moonshine poisoning?*

While sipping her coffee, Sarah studied the calendar. She flipped back and reviewed the two previous months then returned to October. *No mistake about it, I'm a week past my monthly time.* Sarah patted her waistline. *I've no symptoms. I'll wait a few more days before jumping to conclusions.* A knock at the door took Sarah out of her thoughts. She got up to see who'd come calling. Elmo Jones with his signature, tobacco induced, cheek bulge stood on her stoop.

"Hello Elmo. What brings you to my door?"

"Howdy, Miss Sarah, I got a letter for ya. Looks like it's from your old hired hand, Sam Hartman."

Sarah opened the screen door, "We've been good at keeping in touch with Sam."

Elmo swung the letter behind his back. "How's about I trade this letter for a cup of coffee and a plate of your cookies. That is if you've got a minute to shoot the breeze with me."

"Come on in. But don't be making a habit of this." Sarah jokingly warned as she stepped aside to let the quirky mailman enter.

"I've been deliverin' your mail neigh on to fifteen years, Miss Sarah. You'd think you'd know my habits by now."

Smiling, Sarah said, "Elmo, you're right. After fifteen years, you'd think I'd be smart enough to get my mail from you without giving up baked goods. Now have a seat and keep your voice down. The three littlest are napping."

After fetching a cup of coffee and a saucer with three cookies, Sarah set them on the table and asked, "Elmo, I'm curious, why is it you've taken to calling me Miss Sarah?"

The mailman leaned over the saucer, dropped his chaw and grabbed up a cookie. Sarah's stomach churned as she watched the black blob ooze juice. The juice created a pool that grew, eventually breaching the space on the saucer occupied by the snicker doodles. To her horror, the cookies' delicate, porous edge soaked it up like a sponge.

Seemingly oblivious, Elmo munched a few bites of the cookie in his hand before he answered Sarah's question. "Ma'am, it's strange you're just now a sayin' somethin' about it. I been a callin' you Miss Sarah ever since you married Doc. I tried callin' ya Mrs. Adams, but it reminded me of how I weren't quick enough on the draw."

"Quick enough on the draw? What in the world does that mean?" Sarah asked.

"Ma'am, after your husband, Henry, died and you bein' in a family way and all, I was just a bidin' the respectful amount of time afore I asked ya if I might come a callin' on ya. Next thing I knowed the church bell was a ringin' and you and Doc was gettin' pelted with rice."

"Elmo, Doc Adams and I are approaching two years of marriage. I'd think you'd be long past thinking about a lost opportunity, not that there ever was one."

With an obvious tongue-in-cheek tone, he responded, "Well, I'm a sensitive man. When it comes to matters of the heart, the pain of loss lingers, don't ya know." The mailman took in a deep breath of air followed by a long stretched out sigh. With a sly smile on his face Elmo leaned over toward Sarah. "I think a half a dozen of these cookies for me to tote home might ease the pain some."

"Now you're getting greedy old friend and besides, I know you're joshing me."

"You're right. I knowed where we stood when you laid me low that night I offered to come and keep you company. Your Henry was still alive but livin' in that mental institution. You let me know right quick that I was out of line."

"I'd forgotten we had that dust up."

"I gotta admit I was afeard of ya for a while after that. You threatened to sick your big brother Jack on me."

"You'll get no apology from me," Sarah said.

"None needed, I had it comin'. Ma'am," Elmo said hanging his head low, "I'm real glad you didn't shun me over that and that we've become friends."

"Me too, Elmo," Sarah said as she patted his arm. "Now tell me, what's really behind your claim of unrequited love? Is there something you'd like to discuss with me?"

"I'm lonely, Miss Sarah. Yes, they's no two ways about it, I'm just plain lonely."

"But you do know that you're not alone, don't you?" Sarah said.

"Yes. Ever since that night at that tent meetin' in Wabash when I ran down the aisle, knelt, and evangelist, Billy Sunday, prayed over me, I haven't felt alone." Elmo placed his hand at his chest. "I let the Lord into my heart that night and he's a been livin' here ever since."

"You left that revival a changed man," Sarah said. "It's the spirit of the Lord, that lives in both you and me that has paved the way for our friendship. It's that spirit that gives us a common bond."

"Yes, Ma'am, that's a fact."

"Elmo, I've never known you to live other than alone. What's changed? Why do you feel lonely after all this time?"

"Well Ma'am, after I got saved, I did like a good Christian ought, I stopped my uh, uh, galivantin'. I used to make a regular visit to Wabash to one of them…"

"Whoa," Sarah held her hands up, palms out, "no need to give me chapter and verse Elmo."

"Okay, okay, but Lordy, Lordy, Lordy, I'm just gonna say it right plain, it's been nearly two years since I ran down that aisle and I need me a woman."

"Elmo, if you're telling me you would like some female companionship, I have a suggestion in that area. But, if all you're looking for is someone to *galivant* with, I feel obliged to remind you of the Apostle Paul's words, "And he said unto me, 'My grace is sufficient for thee: for my strength is made perfect in weakness.' Most gladly therefore will I rather glory in my infirmities, that the power of Christ may rest upon me."

Elmo reared back in his chair and crossed his arms. "Well Ma'am, they's no denyin' that I'm a gettin' older but I ain't got me no infirmities that would keep me from enjoyin' a trip to Wabash don't ya know. That is, if I took a mind to. And if I did have me an infirmity in that area I sure as shootin' wouldn't be takin' glory over it."

"Oh, my goodness Elmo," Sarah said, "this conversation is brushing up against unseemly and you're missing the meaning of that scripture. The Bible doesn't tell us what the Apostle Paul's infirmities were. But, when he says that he will glory in them, he's saying that his inner knowing, that through God's power living in him, he can have victory over his infirmities, allows him to live a joyous life despite them. The fact that God's power is displayed in Paul's weaknesses gives him courage and hope.

"Tell me, are you seeking a wife?" Sarah asked.

"Yes! I've been a bachelor long enough. I have a hankerin' for havin' someone by my side. I got me a mind's eye picture of me sittin' by my hearth of an evenin', I got me a fresh chaw in my mouth. I'm content, a whittlin' away on somethin' or 'nother. My woman's next to me, a darnin' my socks or a knittin' me a new cap. The 'what' don't matter. What's so pleasin' about the picture is that she's happy cause she's busy doin' one of them things you women like to do to please your man.

"You know I ain't a selfish man, Sarah. That's plain to see in my picture of my woman bein' kept happy."

Sarah shook her head, “Elmo, that vision of blissful matrimony that you’ve got in your head could benefit by an adjustment or two. Although the Lord knows that I’m itching to enlighten you, I think you’d find a discussion with Ben about what pleases a woman to be more beneficial.

“Besides, you’re getting the cart before the horse,” Sarah said with a smile. “Courting comes before marriage. Have you found someone you’d like to court?”

Elmo took a sip of his coffee then leaned in, resting his arms on the table. “Well, they’s a new woman in town that I’ve got my eye on.”

“Do tell,” Sarah said eyebrows raised.

“Yep. Her name is Penelope Peterson. She’s a lady’s hatmaker that Parker’s Dry Goods done hired. She’s lives out the edge of town on the Bickel farm. Word is that she’s a distant cousin of Clara Bickel’s.”

“That might explain the new hat Clara wore to church last Sunday,” Sarah said. “I must say it’s feathers were opulent and complemented Clara’s style beautifully.”

“Clara ain’t so young any more but still she’s a strappin’ woman and they ain’t no denyin’ that she’s got herself a penchant for feathers. I ‘spect she had her niece make that hat, specifyin’ tall feathers. One of ‘em looked to be near twelve inches long, had her a duckin’ to clear the sanctuary’s entrance.

“Clara sets in the amen section don’t ya know. Third row back, directly in front of Jeb Carter. Jeb’s near six foot, five inches tall and he was a scootin’ left then right to get shed of that feather a blockin’ his view,” Elmo said.

“How special to have a hat tailor made.” Sarah reached up and tucked in a wisp of hair that had escaped her topknot. “I’m sure she appreciates having her niece live with her.”

“Hat makin’ aside, I was happy to see that Miss Penelope ain’t on the tall side like Clara. She’s a little bit of a thing, considerable shorter than me. I’m 5’ 8” tall and I don’t think that, even with that pile of hair atop her head, she’d stand more than shoulder height to me.”

“How old is she, Elmo?” Sarah inquired.

“I ain’t much good with you women’s ages. She’s not young, I’d say she’s about your age. Old enough to be tagged an old maid, her not bein’ married don’t you know.”

"Describe Penelope to me," Sarah said.

"She's not purdy like you Miss Sarah, but she's got a right pleasant face. Whilst she's quick with a smile, she carries herself dignified and proper like. Her hair is light brown and her nose is small and turned up a bit. I ain't had me a chance to look close enough to be sure but I think her eyes are either hazel or brown."

A clanking sound came from the direction of the parlor, now nursery. Sarah turned her head to listen. *They're jerking on their crib side rails.* "It sounds as if my two youngest monkeys are awake and want out of their cages. I need to tend to them. We can continue this conversation at another time."

"Darn the luck. I was wantin' to hear me those suggestions you had about me gettin' a relationship with a woman."

Sarah scooted her chair back and stood. "You and I will talk again soon, Elmo, I promise. I encourage you to talk to Ben as well. He's a wise man when it comes to the development of a lasting mid-life relationship."

Elmo stood. "I best get on out of your hair then." He started toward the door, stopped, came back to the table, snatched the remaining, albeit soggy, cookies from his saucer, grabbed up his tobacco chaw and pocketed it in the valley between his teeth and cheek.

"Elmo," Sarah said, "getting shed of that tobacco chewing habit of yours would likely help a lot if you're serious about finding someone to court."

"Get shed of tobacco chewin'!" Elmo's mouth hung open in disbelief of what he'd heard. With his hand that was free of cookies he pulled a large plug of tobacco from his shirt pocket and held it up. "Back in Kentucky my family made a livin' from this. I started chewin' when I was knee high to a grasshopper. My grand pappy chewed.

Ma mostly smoked a pipe but even she enjoyed herself a chaw ever now and then." He slid the plug back into his shirt pocket. "I'd feel naked as a jaybird if I didn't have this with me."

"Elmo, you've described Miss Peterson as dignified and proper. Do you think she'll be accepting of an invitation to be courted by a man with tobacco stains around his mouth and an ever-present cheek bulge?"

Elmo didn't have a ready response. "Pray about it Elmo," Sarah urged. "God might reveal the habit as an affliction for which He wants to provide the hope and grace for you to shed."

The rattle of baby bed rails persisted and the cries to be freed grew louder. Hathaway walked into the kitchen rubbing nap sized sleep from her eyes. "Ma, 'Omi and Henry is makin' a fuss. Cain't you hear 'em? I think they're tryin' to tell you they's hungry for milk and cookies."

Sarah gathered the three-year-old into her arms. "I'm sure you're right. Mr. Jones was just leaving."

"Bye, Mr. Mo," Hathaway said.

"Goodbye, little one," the mailman said.

Elmo climbed up on his rig. Before leaving he placed his chaw on the small shelf he'd installed in the buggy, a spot he'd dubbed, *The Holdin' Space*. Then he crammed a whole cookie in his mouth and took the reins. "Trot on, Clementine" he called to his horse. The mare assumed an easy gait.

They'd gone about a half mile toward town when Elmo said, "Clementine, I'm gonna do it. I'm gonna ask that new gal workin' at Parkers if I can come a courtin'. I don't need me no advice from Miss Sarah or Doc." Elmo snatched up his chaw of tobacco from the resting place and stuck it in his mouth. "Listen to this, Clementine, I've got it all worked out in my mind."

"I'll walk into Parker's store and sidle up to the haberdashery counter.

Penelope Peterson will turn and give me a sweet smile. *"Hello, kind sir, how might I help you today?"*

I'll tip my hat. *"My name's Elmo Jones, I'm the mail carrier here in LaFontaine."*

Her cheeks will flush. *"Oh my! I've heard so many wonderful things about you Mr. Jones. You're even more handsome than I had you pictured. I was hoping for an opportunity to meet you."*

I'll say, *"Ma'am, would you like to have dinner with me over at the hotel on Saturday night."*

She'll say, *"I'd be delighted. You may call on me at 5:00. I board at the Bickel farm."* With my hat in hand I'll bow low and say, *"I know the farm of which you speak. Until we meet again, good day, Ma'am."*

"So, Clementine, what do you think?"

The mare turned her head and looked back at Elmo. "Heewh" she neighed as she raised her tail and dropped a load.

Elmo took his hat off and finger combed his hair. After donning it again he extracted the tobacco wad from his mouth and placed it back on the holding shelf. "I guess a word or two of advice won't hurt me none."

Chapter 15

Tuesday morning, the second day for Joy at school was promising at the start. While most students lingered in the hall, waiting until the bell rang to indicate the start of class, she'd gone on in to get situated. Joy wasn't surprised to find Miss Messner sitting at her teacher's desk, but she was surprised when she saw Breanna sitting up front.

"Good morning, Joy," Miss Messner greeted. "Welcome to your second day at LaFontaine school."

Joy's return greeting came out in a drawl as she looked from Breanna to Miss Messner and back to Breanna again.

Breanna gave Joy a huge smile. "I told Miss Messner that I thought I could see the blackboard better if I sat up front. Since this desk next to yours wasn't assigned, she let me move."

Joy laid her books down on her desk and slid into its seat. "Yes, sitting up front does make it much easier to see."

With a twinkle in her eye the teacher interjected, "Of course, sitting next to a friend also has advantages." Both girls blushed. "I was pleased to see that you two girls were getting acquainted yesterday. I'm happy to let you sit next to one another, but I won't tolerate whispering in my classroom. So, mind your "P's" and "Q's" and this will work out just fine."

The girls reached out and grasped hands. "Yes, Ma'am."

The bell sounded and the room flooded with students scurrying to get to their seats. Miss Messner rapped her ruler on her desk, "Quiet, class," she said. Getting only partial compliance she brought the ruler down hard and took her voice up a few decibels. "I said get quiet!"

All voices went mute. "I expect every one of you to be in your seats and quiet by the time that morning bell stops ringing. Those who aren't, are at risk of being sent to the principal's office. Do I make myself understood?"

Ernie Brown came shuffling into the room just as the class responded in unison, "Yes, Ma'am."

"Ernie, you're late," the teacher said. The boy gave the her a sullen look. "I was just telling the class that I won't tolerate tardiness. Consider yourself forewarned. Now please take your seat."

All students watched as Ernie diverted from the direct path to his desk so he could pass by Abe. As he did, he gave Abe's upper arm a punch. Eyes immediately swung to the front of the room to see if Miss Messner would react. Her back was turned, she was writing on the blackboard and hadn't seen.

When the teacher turned to face her students, it was evident that the room's collective mood had changed. Some children had heads bowed, others appeared nervous, eyes darting about as if looking for a means of escape. "What! What's happened?" she asked.

No one spoke. Harmonious Beechwood, the class brown noser, couldn't resist making eye contact with the teacher. "Harmonious," she called out, "can you tell me what's caused the change in everyone's mood?"

Beechwood's prominent proboscis grew a shade lighter in the eyes of his fellow eighth graders that day when he responded, "No, Ma'am, I can't."

After giving the classroom a careful eye sweep, the teacher instructed, "Turn to page 10 in your math books."

***

It was a sunny afternoon and Ben had decided to make a house call on foot. He was making his way back toward his office when he came upon a stretch of brick walkway in front of the widow Barlow's house. It had been invaded by a snarl of hickory tree roots.

Those roots are a death trap to someone Mrs. Barlow's age, Ben surmised. Simultaneous to that thought Ben stepped down on a cluster of hickory nuts. His arms failed as he successfully prevented falling.

"My apologies, Doc Adams," Leona Barlow called from her porch. "I'm afraid those roots have taken over since Russell died. I guess I'm not doing a very good job of keeping this place up to snuff like he did."

A white picket fence framed the Barlow's tidy home. Ben grasped on to it for balance while he removed a twig that'd gotten stuck in the lace of his shoe. "Ma'am," Ben said as he made a backward hand sweep across the home's front yard view, "You've still got the prettiest place in town. You should be proud of yourself for keeping things up like you do."

"Thanks for the compliment, Dr. Adams." Concern clouded Leona's face. "As much as I hate to lose the tree and the shade it provides, I don't see any remedy but to saw it down. If we hack the roots back as much as needed to clear the walkway, the tree might die."

Ben interjected, "I'm concerned you might trip and fall, maybe break a hip. Why don't I talk to the town's council and see if I can get them to come take care of this for you."

A smile spread across Leona's aged, yet still beautiful, face. "Doc, I'd be much obliged if you'd do that."

Both Doc and Leona turned to look when they heard the fast-paced clip-clop of an approaching horse and buggy. Elmo Jones pulled Clementine to a halt next to where Ben stood. "Doc, catch," Elmo called out, tossing the reins to Ben. Mail in hand he jumped down.

Elmo waved an envelope high above his head as he walked fast, dodging roots as he made his way to Leona's gate. "Got a letter here for you, Mrs. Barlow. It's postmarked Cincinnati. 'Spect it's from that son of yours."

Elmo opened the fence gate and like a squirrel rushing to deposit a nut, scurried to the porch where he handed the mail to the eagerly waiting mother.

Leona's words of thanks bounced off Elmo's back as he scampered back to his rig, grabbed the reins from Ben, and in a near whisper said, "Doc, your missus said that you and I need to have us a talk."

"About what?" Ben responded.

"Shushhhhhhh," Elmo said placing his pointer finger at his lips, "Not so loud." Tobacco juice dripped from the corner of the man's mouth as he leaned into Doc's space. The droplets landed on the toe of Ben's shoe. "It's of a personal nature," he whispered while twitching his eyebrows.

Doc took a handkerchief from his inside jacket pocket, bent over to wiped off the top of his shoe. "Elmo, I'd appreciate it if you wouldn't drool on my shoes."

"My apologies, Doc. The chewin's one of the things your wife said I ought to talk to you about," Elmo said as he climbed up on his rig.

Ben stuffed the soiled linen in his pants pocket. "I'm headed back to my office. I'll be there until five o'clock. Stop by if you want to talk."

Wasting no time, Elmo called out to Clementine, "Trot on." Wheels were turning and dust was flying when he yelled over his shoulder to Ben. "I'll finish up deliverin' this here mail and then I'll come to your office."

The tail end of his call out, "This is important, Doc…," got muffled by the noise of the rig's wire rimmed wheels grating against the brick pavement.

I missed that last part, guess I'll find out what he said when he stops by to talk. "Good day," Ben said tipping his hat to Mrs. Barlow. "I'll see what can be done about the tree and get back to you." Waves of goodbye were exchanged, and Doc continued the three block's walk back to Main Street and his office.

***

The noon meal break came and went, albeit not without emotional stress. Abe sat at one end of the eight-grade table while Ernie sat catty-cornered at the far opposite end, neither talking. Students positioned between and across from the two foes ate in silence, eyes darted from Whitcome to Brown, then back again. The smell of hatred filled the air and overpowered the usual pleasant aromas home-packed lunches brought to the table.

When the ten-minute warning bell rang, the only sound that came from the table was the clunk of lunch pails being closed. Bench seats were vacated and the grating of boots and shoes against the wooden floor began. Students' faces were glum, and their shuffle produced a sound akin to a funeral dirge, as the mournful group trudged back for the last half of the school day. Vibrations of hostility darted between Abe and Ernie, creating anxiety for the entire eighth grade class.

The afternoon hours passed slowly for Joy who watched the Regulator clock that hung on the wall behind the teacher's desk. The clock was in her direct line of sight. She not only heard its tick, tick, ticking, she saw the minute hand advancing. Joy had the lap section of her dress wadded in her hand as she struggled to curb her mounting apprehension. Beads of sweat formed at the nape of her neck and trickled down her back. *It's going to happen, I know. Anger, fighting, hitting…ran from Pa to get away from it.*

At the close of school, the bell rang and most of the class made an immediate exit. Joy's stomach threatened to lurch, she clasped both hands over her mouth.

Breanna jumped to her feet. "What is it Joy, are you sick?"

Joy took a couple of deep breaths, then stood. "They're going to fight as soon as they get outside. I know, I can feel it."

Breanna patted her friends back. "No, they won't, at least not here at school. Luke told me that Abe promised their ma that he'd never fight on school grounds. He won't break his word."

Miss Messner came from behind her desk. "Who's going to fight?"

"Ernie Brown and Abe Whitcome," Breanna responded.

"Why are they going to fight?" the teacher asked.

Breanna gathered up her books. "They've got a pick at one another that goes way back, before they came to this new school."

"What's the pick about?" the teacher asked.

Joy responded, "Neither Breanna nor I know the particulars. We've only been told that there's bad blood between the two of them."

Miss Messner walked to the window and saw Abe trotting across the schoolyard toward the gate and waiting hack. Ernie was in hot pursuit with several children who'd gathered, following. When she turned back, she noticed that Harmonious Beechwood hadn't left the room. "Harmonious, high-tail it to the principal's office and tell him there's a fight brewing between Ernie and Abe."

Upon getting the teacher's message, Principal Hornblower picked up the telephone and asked the operator to ring up the Marshal's office.

"Marshal's office," Jeb Carter answered.

"Marshal Carter, this is Principal Hornblower. Ernie Brown and Abe Whitcome are fixing to have a fight. There's been noticeable animosity between the two of them since the start of school. Ernie has a dark spirit and twenty pounds on Abe. I'm concerned things could get out of hand."

"Animosity don't begin to cover it. Those two have a grudge against one another that goes way back," Jeb said. "I'm on my way."

As Abe ran, his mind raced. *Ernie's gonna think I'm runnin' scared. No matter, I can't break my promise to Ma, ta not fight at school. It's gonna happen Brown, just not here, not now. I'm gonna wipe that smirk so clean off your face not even your own ma will recognize ya.* The vicious thought gave Abe pause. *I never even tried to settle things with Ernie by talkin' it out. Pa always said a smart man would do that, he said any fool can fist fight.*

Abe was reaching for the gate's latch when Ernie jumped him from behind. Abe fell to the ground and Ernie piled on top of him. The pair started to wrestle in a tangle of arms and legs.

By now, a crowd had gathered. They formed in a semicircle a few yards back from the boys. Josh and Luke were wedged near the front where they had a clear view of the action.

They boys separated and stood. Despite his large bulk, Ernie moved quick. He got Abe in a choke-hold pulling tight enough to cut off the boy's air supply. Abe's face grew as red as a ripe tomato. He was starting to black out when Principal Hornblower grabbed Ernie's arm. "Boys…"

With a reflex motion, Ernie elbowed the little man releasing the pressure on Abe's neck. Hornblower grunted, "oooph" as he tumbled and fell on his back. He was out cold.

Miss Messner saw it happen. When the principal didn't get up, she took off running to him. Her large bosom swayed to and fro as she labored to cover the distance.

With the choke-hold released, Abe fell to the ground holding his neck, gasping for air.

Showing no mercy, Ernie lunged at Abe. Abe rolled. Ernie missed his target, hit the ground and did a humiliating belly skid.

Abe stood, legs wobbling as he backed up a few feet. Ernie rolled to his side and looked over at Abe, hatred in his eyes. Speckles of blood popped out on a large abrasion on Ernie's cheek. While never losing eye contact with Abe, Ernie cupped the injury with his work calloused hand and slowly got to his feet. Ernie spit dirt and gave his head a shake before resuming a fighting stance.

Zeke attempted to wheedle his way to the front of the crowd, found it difficult, dropped to his knees and started crawling between pant legs and under long skirts. He left a trail of shrieks and screams as he burrowed his way to the front where he crawled to a position next to Joy.

Abe and Ernie started circling, fists clenched. Ernie struck out with a right that caught Abe on the mouth, splitting his lip. Abe shot back with a punch, Ernie dodged. The hard, no contact swing, knocked Abe off balance. He stumbled and went to one knee. Ernie took the advantage hitting Abe with a one-two punch that caused a cut at Abe's right brow line.

"That's fightin' dirty, Brown," one of the boys yelled. "Give Whitcome a chance to get to his feet."

Joy saw the blood, she understood the pain and it sickened her. This time when her stomach lurched, she couldn't prevent it from emptying.

Just as Abe managed to get to his feet, Ernie swung and connected with Abe's midsection, he collapsed again, this time to both knees. He stayed down to let his head clear and his equilibrium return.

"Givin' in so quick, Abe?" Ernie taunted. "Or is it that you prefer fightin' women. Afterall, your pa did beat up on your ma a couple of years back."

Abe heard a roaring in his ears. In one seamless motion the boy jumped to his feet, charged Ernie and landed a midsection uppercut that hit his opponent in the solar plexus. With his wind knocked out, Ernie folded to the ground where he lay, gasping for breath.

Abe paced back and forth, swiping with the back of his hand at the blood dripping off his lip and oozing from his brow line. "You, worthless piece of cow dung," he screamed, "don't you ever mention my Ma or Pa again."

Ernie now on his side, pulled his legs up to his chest. He lay there, waiting for the spasms in his abdomen to subside. While Abe continued to pace, the crowd began to chant, "Brown, stay down. Brown, stay down."

Principle Hornblower was now awake but his vision was blurred. Miss Messner tried to help him, and he fell again.

He stumbled and Miss Messner caught his arm, preventing him from falling. "You've had quite the jolt. Give yourself a minute to recover before you wade back into that fracas."

Abe let a few moments pass before walking to Ernie's balled-up form. "I guess this means you've had enough." Ernie didn't speak, instead he waved Abe off.

Abe stood looking down at his enemy's curled body. In a low tone he said, "Ernie, you've had a gripe with me since we were in second grade together. For a long time that grieved me, I wanted us to be friends. The wantin' left a long time ago. It's clear that you hate me and my family, and I don't rightly know why."

Abe's shoulders lost their hunch and he unclenched his fists. "You've been wantin' a fight. Today you got one. I'm done with you. You're no longer my enemy. Now you're absolutely *nothin'* to me." With his guard relaxed, Abe turned his back to Ernie and started walking away.

Someone in the crowd yelled, "Knife." Abe turned in time to see Ernie running toward him, knife in hand. Ernie lunged and Abe dodged. The pair started circling again, Abe with fists clenched, Ernie brandishing his long-blade knife.

"Ernie, let it go," Abe pleaded. "Let's not do somethin' that one or both of us can't walk away from."

Doc was coming down Wabash street and was about a half a block from the school when he looked over toward the playground. He saw a gaggle of students and two males faced off, one with fists raised, one holding a large knife. A man on the ground was trying to get up and a woman was helping him. Ben sprinted toward the scene.

As he drew closer, he saw that it was Abe and Ernie Brown who were fighting, Abe wasn't the one holding the knife. Ben pushed his limit in an all-out, heart-pounding run. *Dear God in heaven, protect our boy.*

"Whitcome," Ernie yelled, "you're gonna be sorry for makin' me look bad in front of your cousin."

Ernie's words pierced Joy's heart. *Is this about me?* Joy took off running. *I can't let this happen.* The girl leapt into the space between Ernie and Abe just as Ernie lunged with his knife. Blood gushed from Joy's arm as the blade sliced a near six-inch gash.

Abe screamed, "No!" and pushed Joy off to the side. The realization of what had happened shocked Ernie and he froze. Abe bent forward and like a raging bull charged. The head butt knocked Ernie down, he hit his head and was momentarily stunned, he relaxed his grip on the knife.

Zeke had followed Joy into the action and was fast closing ground when he saw Joy get cut. Maintaining his momentum Zeke reached the scene, catapulted himself through the air and landed on top of Ernie. The first grader began pummeling the sixteen-year-old in the face.

Ernie belly bucked Zeke off, tightened his grip on the knife and started to get up. A man's dress shoe came down on Ernie's chest and flattened him again. Before the boy could get the knife raised, a work boot stomped on his wrist causing his fist to splay and release the knife.

"It's over boy," the man said as he bent and picked up the weapon.

From his pinned down position, Ernie looked up to see Marshal Carter on the other end of the boot and Doc Adams wearing the shoe.

"Ben," Abe yelled, "Joy's been hurt!"

Doc looked at Jeb, "Go," the marshal said, "I've got this handled."

Luke and Josh reached Joy first. When Doc ran up Luke had his arm around Joy's shoulder, her head was resting on his chest. Josh was patting her hand.

Ben knelt and gently began unwinding the skirt of Joy's dress that she'd used to stem the bleeding. It had worked, the wound was long and gaping, but the blood had reduced to a seeping flow. "This will need several stitches," Ben said as he pulled out his handkerchief to bind the wound, saw that it was soiled with tobacco juice and stuffed it back in his pocket.

A large figure casting a wide shadow came up alongside Ben. "Here, use mine, its clean."

Ben raised his head and found Julib Carter towering over them. "Julib, thanks," Ben said as he pinched the cut closed and bound it with the large piece of linen. "I've got to get her to my office."

Julib pointed toward the street-side fence row. "My rig's parked close." Julib knelt and scooped Joy up in his arms. "I'll get her settled, you best go see to the rest of them."

"The rest of them? You mean Abe and Ernie."

"Those two plus Zeke and the principal. They all got hurt."

"It's all my fault," Joy cried out.

"No need to take on, girl, nobody's dead or dyin', Julib crooned. Joy nestled her head on Julib's shoulder as he carried her to the hack.

Doc turned and spotted Abe with his battered face, turned more and saw Ernie, an angry looking scrape showing atop his puffed-out cheek. He turned again and spotted Zeke laying on the ground with Principal Hornblower and Miss Messner knelt beside him. *Zeke first, then Abe, Ernie and Hornblower.*

Ben yelled for the crowd of students to move back as he ran to Zeke, knelt and gently brushed damp strands of hair from his step son's brow. "Zeke, its Pa, can you hear me? Zeke, Zeke!"

"He was out when we got to him, Doc," Miss Messner said. "He landed hard when Ernie bucked him off."

Zeke's eyes fluttered open. He looked at his step father, then Miss Messner. When he turned his head to his right, all he could see was the principal's large nose with huge nostrils. The boy flinched and bolted to a sitting position. "How'd I get over here?" He thrusted out his arms. "Out of my way, where's Ernie Brown, I've got to help Abe."

"Steady, Son, the fight's over," Ben said. "You fell and hit your head. You might have a concussion, let me look at you."

"Don't worry Pa," Zeke said. "My head does hurt some but not enough to cause me to take to cussin'."

Doc picked Zeke up and cradled him close. The child's face was streaked with dirt and he smelled of boy sweat. Still, Ben kissed his forehead. "Just the same, you're coming along with Joy and me to my office."

Josh and Luke ran up to them. "Here," Luke said holding out his arms, "I'll take him while you see to Abe."

Abe walked over to Doc, his head hung low. Ben gently cupped the boy's chin and raised his head so he could inspect his injuries. "I'm guessing there's a story behind your actions today."

"Yes, Sir," was Abe's reply.

"It'll keep, you can tell me and your ma when we're all together. Go climb in the hack with the others. I want to check on Ernie and Principal Hornblower before I join you."

Principal Hornblower interjected. "I'm fine. I was seeing double for a short time, but that's cleared up." The petite man rubbed at the back of his head. "I've got a knot back here that's tender to the touch. I'm sure I'll mend in time."

Doc was a full head taller than the school master. He had to bend a bit to get a good look at the head injury. "You've got yourself an egg-sized knot that will take a week or so to heal. I expect you'll have a headache for a couple of days."

"He was unconscious for a short spell," Miss Messner interjected.

"You need to stay awake for the next eight hours. Apply cold compresses to the knot. Have you got someone to stay with you?"

"No, I live alone, I'm a bachelor," the principal replied.

"We live close to one another, I'll keep a check on him," Miss Messner said.

Jeb walked up, Ernie in tow. "This one's next. I'm not sure if it's his cheek or his pride that's hurt the most."

"Ernie, may I look at your cheek?" Doc asked. The boy was sullen and didn't speak. After palpating Ernie's cheekbone Ben said, "It seems like a tissue injury. It'll scab over in a couple of days. Ernie, I expect you'll have a black eye by morning. Tell your mother to keep a cold compress on your cheek. That should help with the soreness."

Jeb turned the boy so Ben could see his handcuffs. "Mrs. Brown's gonna have to come to the jail to apply them cold presses." In his peripheral vision Jeb saw Abe headed for the hack. "Abe," he yelled. I need you over here!"

"Jeb," Doc said, "I'm taking him to my office so I can tend to his injuries," Doc said.

"He need stichin' or bandagin'?" asked Jeb.

"No, just cleaned up," was Doc's response.

Abe walked up just as Jeb said, "Then he's stayin' with me 'til we get this sorted out."

"Ben," Abe pleaded.

"Do what you've been told, Abe. I'll come find you after I tend to Joy and Zeke." Doc took off on a trot to join Julib and his cargo.

"Hornblower," Jeb called out, "let's take these two lunkheads down to my office where we can interrogate them, official."

"Good idea," the principal responded. Cupping his hands at his mouth he yelled, "Everyone go home, the show's over."

Marshal Carter yelled to his son, "Julib, drop Doc and his brood off then hightail it back here to pick up these children." Jeb gestured toward the group that had formed for their hack ride home. "Let Sarah and the Brown's know I'm takin' their boys over to the jailhouse.

"Abe, hold out your wrists. I'm cuffin' you too."

"Is that really necessary Marshal Carter?" the principal asked. "Ernie was the only one with a weapon."

"No matter," the Marshal responded. "This was more than two boys knocking each other around to settle a scrap," he jerked on Ernie's cuffs. "This has the stink of something truly nefarious. Until we get it sorted out, they're both gettin' locked up."

"What manner of malfeasance are you charging them with?" Hornblower asked.

"I got to think on this some before I make a final decision," the Marshal responded. "For now, the charge is disturbin' *my* peace. I'd just settled in for a nap when you called."

Chapter 16

The afternoon sun slipped behind a cloud casting a shadow over Sarah's house. It was Tuesday, Sarah's day for baking their weekly cookie supply. Three dozen snickerdoodles and three dozen ginger snaps lay on the sideboard cooling. Sarah was at her baking table working flour into a batch of sugar cookie dough. Her rolling pin and a three-inch diameter drinking glass lay at the ready. The tumbler would serve as a round shaped cutter that would produce the remainder of the eleven dozen confections needed to carry them through the week. Sarah's heirloom, Hedding and Covalt four-gallon lidded crock, served as the family cookie jar. The prized possession would be brimming by afternoon's end. Come the following Tuesday morning it would be picked clean of every morsel and crumb.

A smile spread across Sarah's face as she gazed at the peaceful panorama before her. Henry was in the corner bent over the toy chest. Only his bottom and dangling legs could be seen. His head and arms were immersed in the depths of the box searching.

The toy chest was placed in the kitchen on Abe's first birthday and had graced the same corner ever since. Years of little Whitcomes foraging likewise had worn the box's edges smooth as glass.

Naomi was sitting on the floor between Hathaway's outstretched legs. Her cheeks glowed while her dimpled hands lay motionless on her lap. She appeared to be basking in the pleasure of having her big sister brush her flighty crop of hair. "Ma," Hathaway called out. "'Omi's hair is a stickin' up worser than afore I started brushin' it."

"Worse than before, Dear, not worser," Sarah corrected in her uphill battle to introduce proper grammar to her daughter's still malleable vocabulary. "Likely your brushing has caused static to form."

Pausing mid-stroke Hathaway asked, "What's attic?"

"It's static, not attic. It's a reaction that brushing can cause with fine hair like Naomi's. It's nothing to be concerned about."

"I ain't 'serned about it. Me jest want her to look purdy," the girl responded.

"You aren't concerned, not ain't concerned," Sarah said, using the back of her hand to swipe away a damp strand of hair from her forehead. "It's near time for the hack to drop Joy and your brothers at the end of the lane. Why don't you watch out the window for them?"

"When I see Joy can I run to meet her?" Hathaway pleaded, holding the brush close to her chest, fingers intertwined.

Sarah gave her daughter a wistful look. *She's growing up too fast.* "Yes, you may go out to meet her."

Hathaway tossed the brush, abandoned her sister and positioned herself in front of the window. The small girl reached the windowsill collarbone high. She rested her chin on the ledge.

Henry stopped his hunting efforts and scurried to stand by her side. Naomi toddled over and joined them. The twins could grasp the windowsill with their fingertips, but their height fell short of being able to look out. The pair started whining in unison.

Sarah was transferring a batch of sugar cookies from the baking sheet to their cooling spot when Hathaway clapped her hands and yelled, "Ma, the hack's a comin' up the lane, real fast." Hathaway ran to the door and started to pull it open, "Me go meet Joy".

A sense of alarm swept over Sarah. *Why would Julib drive the hack to the house?* She dropped the baking sheet, dashed to the door and grabbed Hathaway's wrist. "You must always stay clear of a trotting horse."

Julib had his horse on a run as he barreled up the lane and approached the Y that provided a path to the barn on the right and an approach to the house on the left. The wheels on the school hack spewed dirt and groaned as he maneuvered the left turn and sprinted the remaining yards to Sarah's door. "Woah," he called to his mare. In a cloud of dust Julib jumped down from the rig and ran to the house.

Sarah had opened the door and she and Hathaway were standing in the threshold. Sarah called out, her voice frantic, "What's happened?"

"Pa sent me to tell you that he was takin' Abe to the jail along with Ernie Brown." Julib sucked in air and spewed out details. "The pair got in a fight in the school yard. Zeke and Joy got caught up in the fracas. Zeke got knocked out cold. Ernie had a knife and Joy got cut."

"Did Zeke come to?" Sarah asked putting her arm around Hathaway and pulling her in close. "How bad was Joy cut? Did someone fetch Ben? Did you say Abe was arrested?"

"Doc was there," Julib responded. "He and Pa stopped the fight. I took Joy, Zeke, Josh, Luke and Doc to his office then went back to the school to pick up the children for their delivery home."

"Did Zeke regain consciousness? Where was Joy cut? And, why was my boy arrested?", Sarah barked.

"Yes, Zeke came to," Julib said. "Joy's arm was cut bad, Doc said it'd need stichin'." Julib held up his hands, palms out. "I'm just bringin' you the message, you'll have to ask Pa about the arrestin' Abe part."

"Was Abe hurt?" Sarah asked.

"Abe's beat up considerable and so is Ernie. Doc said they didn't need no stitchin', so Pa took 'em both straight to jail."

Sarah heaved a sigh of relief. "Praise be to God, no one's dead or dying. I'm sorry I barked at you Julib, I'm upset. Thank you for coming to tell me."

Julib took off his hat and reached for his handkerchief. Remembering he'd given it to Doc to use as a bandage for Joy, he used the sleeve of his jacket to wipe the dust off his brow, "No apology needed, Ma'am, I've been pretty upset myself. Seein' boys fight ain't new to me, but that brawl today was somethin' else. I gotta join ya at praisin' God ain't nobody dyin'"

"Julib," Sarah said, "I need to get into town. Could I impose on you to hitch up our wagon while I gather the little ones?"

"Ma'am, Breanna Johnson was real upset over Joy gettin' hurt. She was a blubberin' so bad I took her up to the house instead of droppin' her off at the end of the lane. After hearin' the news, Miss Johnson said to tell ya that she and Breanna would be over to tend the babies. She figured you'd be wantin' to get into town to see what's what."

"Josephine knows me well."

"I'm headed back to town," Julib said. "I can wait 'til Miss Johnson gets here then you can ride in with me if you want."

"Then ride home with Ben and the children. Yes, thank you," Sarah said stepping aside and gesturing for Julib to come in the house. "It'll take a bit for Josephine and Breanna to get here and I need to gather up some things and change the twin's diapers.

"Have a seat," Sarah said gesturing to the table, "I'll get you a cup of coffee and some warm cookies to enjoy while we wait."

The Johnson women arrived in short order and Josephine assured her friend that they could stay as late as needed. Sarah pelted Julib with questions as they made the fast-paced trek to LaFontaine. By the time they arrived at Ben's office she had the gist of what had occurred, but not the why.

***

With the short hand on four and the long one on three, the clock in Ben's office chimed. "Luke, darn it, stop wakin' me up!" Zeke growled. "Pa said seein' Joy get cut and Abe beat up done give me 'motional drama. I need me some sleep."

"Zeke, I said you experienced head trauma and are emotionally destressed. Don't be mad at your brother," Doc said while bent over Joy's wounded arm. "I asked Luke to wake you up every fifteen minutes. It's important to make sure you don't go into a deep sleep for at least another hour. I know you're tired. Once you're home you can sleep as long as you want."

Josh was holding Joy's hand. In a low tone he said, "Maybe he'll go to bed and sleep 'til mornin'. In case he does, I'm callin' first dibs on his pork chop. Ma said were havin' them for supper tonight."

Zeke yelled and threw a shoe at Josh, "I heard that. Ain't nobody gettin' my meat."

"Boys," Doc admonished, "this is no time for roughhousing. I've got a few more stitches to go before this wound is completely closed."

With watery eyes Zeke looked at Luke and held out his little finger. "I need me a pinky promise that you'll wake me when supper's on the table." Luke ruffled Zeke's hair and locked fingers.

I hope this length of catgut is long enough to finish," Doc said. "I prefer a continuous line of suturing over having to knot it twice."

"How many stitches will I have?" Joy asked from her laudanum induced haze.

"I've counted fifteen so far," Josh interjected. "Doc, how many more do you reckon it'll take?"

"Five more should be enough," Ben paused and gave Joy a reassuring smile. "I've made the stitches small and close together. If you do have a scar it shouldn't be more than a thin line. It'll be red at first but will fade over time."

Luke walked to the exam table and glanced at Joy's arm, "When Abe sees them stitches, Ernie's gonna be in for another beatin'."

From across the room Zeke chimed in, "Marshal Carter might not let 'em fight while they's behind bars. We ought to break 'em out of jail."

"There will be no more fighting, period!" Sarah said bolting through the office door. She rushed to Zeke's side and knelt. Stroking his brow, she said, "How do you feel, Son?"

"I'm 'motional but I think I'll be over it by supper time. You're still cookin' pork chops ain't you?" Zeke asked.

"I'll be cooking your supper tonight," Mary Riley answered for her daughter. "I was thinking corn mush and fried eggs."

Tom Riley agreed, "Sounds good to me."

Surprised to see her parents there Sarah asked, "Ma, Pa, how'd you know to come?"

"The town crier, Elmo, of course," Tom said as he came up alongside Sarah. "He stopped by the farm and told us what'd happened. We hightailed it to town, but just got here ourselves. Thought we'd come to see if we could be of any help…wanted to know how the children were doing."

Ben knotted the last stitch and snipped the catgut. "Elmo came by. I asked him to go tell you that we could use your help this evening. Thanks for getting here so quickly."

"When family is in need, we come running," Mary said.

Ben washed and dried his hands then joined Sarah at Zeke's side. He gently turned the boy, removed the cold compress and palpated the knot at the base of his skull. "Zeke fell and his head struck the ground really hard. After this goose egg goes away, I think he'll be just fine."

Sarah leaned down and kissed Zeke's forehead. "That's good news to hear. Zeke, you catch your grandfather up on what happed. I want to go see how Joy's doing."

Josh placed a chair beside Joy's bed for his mother. Sarah brushed stray curls from Joy's face, "How do you feel? Is your arm giving you pain?"

Joy burst into tears, "Ma'am, I think the fight had something to do with me. I heard Ernie say that Abe made him look bad in front of me. I'm so sorry, I didn't know this was going to happen."

Sarah pulled an embroidered hanky from beneath the cuff of her dress sleeve and wiped Joy's eyes. "You've nothing to apologize for. The embers of discourse have been smoldering between those two for a couple of years. Likely they used you as an excuse to fan up a flame."

Josh placed his hand at the nape of his mother's neck. "It wasn't Abe's fault, Ma. Abe was headed for the hack and Ernie come at him from behind."

"That may be," Sarah said, "but a round of fisticuffs takes two and Abe gave me a promise that he wouldn't fight Ernie at school again."

Josh leaned down and kissed his mother's cheek. In a croon he said, "Ma, I'm sure Abe's promise meant he wouldn't *pick* a fight with Ernie at school and he didn't. When a feller gets jumped, seems like even his Ma ought to understand he has to defend himself. We Whitcome boys ain't no lily livers."

Sarah felt a tug at her heart. Her nine-year-old's hold on her apron strings was beginning to slip. "I agree, there isn't a lily liver among you. This has been a lot for me to take in and there's a lot more for me to find out. It's only fair that I reserve making judgement."

Tom Riley walked to Sarah and patted her on the back. "Your Ma and I need to take the children out to the farm, get them cleaned up and fed." With a jerk, he looked around the room. "Where are the twins and Hathaway?"

"Josephine and Breanna Johnson are at the house tending to them," Sarah said. "I'm sure by now their eyes are glued to the lane watching for someone to come to their rescue."

"No doubt," Mary said. "You and Ben need to get on over to the jail and get Abe's troubles sorted out. We'll save plates of food for the three of you to eat when you get home."

"Three of them if Jeb lets Abe leave lock up," Tom quipped.

Sarah bolted to her feet. "From what I've heard about the incident, Jeb had no call to arrest Abe in the first place. I'll hold my tongue until I hear his reasoning, but it better be good. One thing's for sure, unless something more dire than I've been told took place, my boy's not spending the night behind bars."

Chapter 17

Jeb Carter was reared back in his chair, his feet propped on his desk, ankles crossed. The Marshal had a nightstick in his right hand, taping it on the palm of his left. His stomach growled and he glanced at the clock. *Tonight, we're havin' pot roast.* He closed his eyes and drew in a breath. *I can pert near smell them onions and taters simmerin' in rich brown broth.* Jeb licked his lips. His hunger was eating through what was left in his patience reserve.

During the first half hour of Abe Whitecome's and Ernie Brown's incarceration, Marshal Carter and Principal Hornblower had attempted to get them to discuss their schoolyard fight. They'd failed, to the extreme consternation of the principal. Jeb had sent the little guy home so Miss Messner could nurse his head injury. A picture of the petite man with his head resting on her ample bosom gave him a chuckle. His smile lingered.

The wall clock chimed five-o'clock. The smile disappeared and Jeb got to his feet. He walked center room and took a stand facing the twin cells. With legs parted slightly, left hand on his hip, right one still holding the night stick, his tall figure cast a long shadow as the setting sun filtered through the side window. "Gal-dern-it," he boomed. The boys took notice, Abe sat up on the edge of his bed. Ernie rolled to his side and propped his head on an elbow stand.

"I took it in stride when your brawl cost me my afternoon nap. Considered it a hazard of the job don't you know. It ain't afternoon any more, it's evenin'. And every evenin' at five-thirty sharp, my missus has supper on the table. And every evenin' I'm settin' in my chair, fork in hand, when the clock chimes half-past."

Jeb's voice took on a menacing tone, "Do you know what will happen if I'm not there at the appointed time tonight?" He cut a look at Abe, then Ernie. "I'll tell you what, I'll be eatin' warmed over pot roast and cold biscuits. Now that's somethin' I *ain't* gonna take in stride.

"Time's up boys, I'm done bein' nice, done tryin' to get you two lunkheads to tell the cause for your fight and talk out your differences. I'm goin' home to my supper and my soft warm bed. You'll be spendin' the night in a damp cell on a lumpy cot with nothin' but hardtack to gnaw on."

Abe's eyes started to well, Ernie gave a snort and Ernestine Brown came charging through the jailhouse entrance. She flung the door open with enough force for it to swing back and hit the wall. The glass shattered. "Jeb Carter, Abe Whitcome can spend the night but I'm takin' my boy home. Now unlock that cell."

Jeb stood slack-jawed, looking at Ernestine then at the door's broken glass. Ernestine scolded, "If you had a proper stop on that door your glass wouldn't have got broken."

Jeb couldn't take his eyes from the broken glass. The door pane had been installed just the week before. The town council had ordered it special with *LaFontaine Jail, Jeb Carter, Marshal,* embossed on it in gold lettering.

"Stop gawkin' and unlock that cell," Ernestine screeched.

"Ma don't make things worse," Ernie called from his cell. "Where's Pa?"

"Ernie, put your boots on," Ernestine ordered as she paced like a lioness ready to pounce. "You're goin' home."

Jeb gathered his wits and pointed the nightstick at Ernestine. "Get aholt of yourself woman! I'm the one that gives the orders in this jailhouse."

"Don't you point that club at me, you two-bit excuse for the law," Ernestine said with furry.

"Mrs. Brown," the Marshal cautioned, "I've had me enough excitement for one day, I don't need a hysterical woman addin' to my misery."

"Misery, I'll show you misery," Ernestine said as she lunged at Jeb's chest.

Jeb dropped the nightstick and grabbed Ernestine's wrists. The petite woman stood chest high to the six-foot five, marshal. When Jeb grabbed her wrists, she hopped up atop his boots. At first glance, their gyrations might have been mistaken for a father and daughter attempting to dance.

Their struggle got ugly when Ernestine thrust her knee upward toward Jeb's groin. The Marshal's evasive action caused the pair to fall against the heating stove. The smoke stack dislodged, and soot rained down on them. The pair looked like a vaudeville act in black face, and no one was laughing.

Jeb transferred Ernestine to a one-handed hold, grabbed the keys, unlocked the cell and deposited her alongside her son. Abe ran forward and grabbed the bars. He winced when the skin around his knuckle cuts stretched but he persevered and pulled his head in close so he could see it all. Ernie tried to comfort his mother. She pushed him away leaving black handprints on the boy's shirt.

Jeb was standing hands on hips, surveying the carnage when Jasper Brown walked in. "What in the blazes?" He said as he took it all in. His eyes landed on his wife. She was clutching the bars of the cell while her tears flowed like mud on the Mississippi down her cheeks.

"Ernestine, I dropped you off," Jasper said, his tone incredulous, "then drove the team two buildings down, tied them to the hitching post, then came directly here. It couldn't have taken more than five minutes! You beat all woman, you know that!" Jasper shook his head, "Lord, have mercy, you do beat all."

Doc and Sarah came through the door and everyone momentarily froze. The scene thawed when Ernestine swiped the nasal mucus from under her nose with the back of her hand, then reached up and straightened her lop sided hat.

"Sarah Adams," Ernestine spewed with venom, "I wondered if you'd show your face." She pointed to Abe, "Take a good look at your boy behind bars. I hope he stays there. That's where he belongs."

Ben reached out and took ahold of Sarah's arm. She jerked it away. Ernestine continued, "Your Abe's been nothing but a thorn in my boy's side, always pickin' on him, tryin' to show him up…." Ernestine's mouth clamped shut when Sarah started toward her. She let go of the bars and took a few steps backward.

Sarah didn't walk directly to the cells. Instead she went to the stand that held a large bowl and pitcher of water. She pulled a towel from the bar on the stand's side, wetted and rung it out. Then she lifted the ring of keys from their adjacent nail hook. She walked first to Ernestine and handed the towel through the bars. Ernie accepted it for his mother. Sarah then stepped over to Abe's cell, stuck a key in the lock and opened the door.

She walked in and took Abe's hand. "Jeb, I'm taking my boy home. Doc and I will bring him back in the morning. We'll talk then and get this situation sorted out."

Together Sarah and Abe walked to the door. Before leaving she turned to Jeb. "I hope you'll send the Brown's home too. With everyone cleaned up and rested, I'm sure cooler heads will prevail tomorrow."

Doc looked from Ernestine to Jasper and then to Jeb, but, said nothing. He tipped his hat and followed Sarah and Abe.

Jeb, looking more like a raccoon than the town's marshal called out to Sarah's back, "Abe can go home, but not Ernie." The Marshal turned to Jasper Brown, "Your boy drew his huntin' knife and a girl got cut bad. That changed what I would have been willin' to consider a schoolyard scuffle, into something sinister. He's stayin' locked up 'til we get to the bottom of this. If charges get filed against him, he may be facin' extended jail time."

"That's not fair, Jeb," Jasper said. "If you let the Whitcome boy go home then we should be able to take Ernie home too."

"Abe Whitcome didn't draw a weapon," the Marshal said. "If Doc and I hadn't broken up the fight, no tellin' how much damage Ernie might have caused with that knife of his."

"What about my wife? You keepin' her too?" Jasper asked.

"No, sorry to have to tell ya. I'm sendin' her home with you. I'll expect you back here in the mornin'. Thus far, the boys haven't been willin' to tell me what the fight was about. Tomorrow I'll be open to listenin' to any *ex-ten-u-waitin'* circumstance behind your son's behavior."

"You can't do this," Ernestine whined. "I won't stand for bein' treated differently than the high and mighty Sarah Whitcome." She shook the bars, "Unlock this door! Unlock this door! You can't leave my boy here alone tonight!"

"Mrs. Brown," the Marshal said in an irritated drawl, "Red Buttman sets vigil of a night when we got someone in lockup. He'll fetch supper for the boy and keep him company 'til I get here in the mornin'."

Ernestine started to object, "I'm not let….".

Jeb held up his hands, palms out. "Ma'am, I done already told you that I'm the one that gives the orders around here. Now, I'm askin' as polite as my growlin' gut can muster. Please-shut-your-trap! If you don't, I'll tell Red to bring two plates of supper and you can stay and keep Ernie company your own self."

Jasper interjected, "She's shuttin' it or I'll shut it for her."

Jeb unlocked the cell and let Ernestine out. He then gave Jasper a stern look. "Now, Jasper, you'd best watch your tongue too. I ain't sure what you meant by sayin' you'd 'shut it for her. But just so you know, I don't hold with wife beatin', not even when a feller has got one that it might benefit."

Jasper didn't respond as he escorted his wife out the door. Instead of locking the cell door, Jeb held it open for Ernie. "Come on out boy and get yourself cleaned up for supper. They's water in that pitcher yonder. Your ma used my towel, but I got an old shirt in my desk drawer you can use for dryin'.

"You like chicken and dumplin's?"

"Yes, Sir," Ernie responded in a low tone.

"The billboard over at the hotel said they was servin' 'em as tonight's special. I'll tell Red to get you a double helpin'. Get some rest, clear your head. Tomorrow let's talk this *shitiation* out. They's always two sides to a story and I'm meanin' to hear me both."

Chapter 18

Sarah greeted Ben with a kiss and a cup of coffee when he walked into the kitchen. "You look exhausted, Dear. I'm guessing you didn't get much sleep."

"No, I didn't. I couldn't put yesterday's turmoil aside. Between thinking on that, what could have happened, and checking in on Zeke, I just didn't rest." Ben set his cup on the table and pulled Sarah into a hug. "You were out cold as soon as your head hit the pillow."

"Yes, I guess I was. I feel rested. Thank you for offering to be the one to check on Zeke during the night. I looked in on him first thing this morning. He was sleeping, breathing softly with a goofy grin on his face. I guess his head wasn't damaged enough to keep him from dreaming up his usual mischief."

"The little dickens does have a hard head. In my opinion, he's out of the woods as far as concern over a concussion goes. You…," Ben held his wife at arms-length, "you I'm still wondering about. How you can fall asleep so quickly after you've had such a stressful day?"

"Trial and error," Sarah said. "I learned years ago that when something as troubling as yesterday's fight happens, there's no use wasting time trying to figure it out on my own.

"Your coffee's going to get cold," she said, releasing herself.

Ben took his seat at the table. Sarah joined him after fetching her Bible. "There's a scripture that I hung my bonnet on when Henry had his stroke." She'd rested her Bible on its spine. When she let go, it fell open. "The book of James, just the one I wanted," she chuckled.

"It's chapter 1, verses 5 through 8 that sustained me then and continues to calm me now. 'If you need wisdom, ask our generous God, and he will give it to you. …but when you ask him, be sure that your faith is in God alone. …a person with divided loyalty is as unsettled as a wave of the sea.... Their loyalty is divided between God and the world, and they are unstable in everything they do'."

"That says it plain and simple, doesn't it?" Ben said. "Guess my mulling over and over ways to deal with the situation didn't gain me anything except a sleepless night. So, did you wake up with a plan?"

"Nope, I'm just going to let God lead," Sarah said. "I've no doubt that Jeb will leave it to us to decide if Abe needs to be punished for his role in the incident. By all accounts he didn't start it, he wasn't the one who brought a knife to a fist fight. Joy got cut, Mr. Hornblower was injured, Zeke got knocked out cold… it's Ernie I'm most concerned about. He's already sixteen years old. We know he isn't going to get good counsel from his parents. Jeb likely knows that too. If Jeb sends it to a judge to decide, the court will treat him like an adult rather than the confused boy he still is. He likely will spend some length of time behind bars. That might cause him to turn even darker than he already is. I hope to keep that from happening."

Sarah leaned in for another kiss, then squeezed her husband's hand. "I'm sorry you woke up tired. When I checked in on Joy, she was asleep and looked peaceful."

"That's good," Doc replied. "I checked in on her about midnight. She was asleep, but restless. I saw her wince when she rolled to her side. "I want to look at her wound and change the dressing before I leave this morning."

"What do you think about her tending to the little ones while I take Abe back to jail?" Sarah asked?

"It would be best if we had someone come in to help with the twins while you're gone. I'm concerned that lifting or holding the babies might put too much strain on her wound this early in the healing process. The stitches need to stay in for about ten days." Doc responded.

"I'll have Luke go by the Johnson's when he leaves for the egg run. I'll take Josephine up on her offer to help us again this morning," Sarah said.

Ben drained his coffee cup, fetched the pot and poured a second cup for himself and Sarah. "I've got a couple of home visits to make before I come into town. What time are you taking Abe to the Marshal's office?"

"We'll leave here around seven-thirty, arrive by eight" Sarah said. "I'm hoping to get Abe and Ernie to talk, see if they can sort things out before the Browns arrive."

"Good luck on that," Ben said. "From what Abe told us last night, he wasn't surprised that Ernie wanted to fight. He was honest about the long-held hostility between them. What seems to be puzzling him is Ernie's level of anger."

"Anger doesn't give rise to pulling a hunting knife in a fist fight," Sarah said. "I'd say the boy had worked himself into a state of rage."

"You're right, rage describes it better. When rage enters the picture, there's a risk that reason will walk out."

***

Josephine came to care for Hathaway, Henry and Naomi while Sarah was in town. Breanna had asked to come along so she could say hi to Joy before leaving for school. After a brief, heads together with Joy, Breanna boarded the hack along with Luke, Josh, and Zeke. The four were jabbering like magpies in speculation of the questions they'd be bombarded with once they arrived at school. Julib interrupted them to make what seemed to be an obvious, very sincere, inquiry about Joy's condition. After getting seated, the entourage made eye contact and arched their eye brows. That brought on giggling.

***

Sarah and Abe arrived at the jail before the Browns or the Marshal. They were greeted by Red Buttman. "Mornin' Mrs. Adams, Abe."

Abe did a double take while taking off his hat. Red looked like a rung-out raccoon. "Uh, g-good mornin' Mr. Buttman," Abe mumbled.

"Such as it is," was the man's reply.

"Good morning, Red," Sarah said with a chuckle. "Red, I apologize for laughing, but I'm guessing you haven't looked in a mirror."

"I don't doubt I look a mess," Red responded as he took out his handkerchief and covered his nose. His forceful blow left two evenly spaced black circles on the linen in its wake. "It won't be news to you that I come on duty last evenin' to find this place in a mess. I spent half the night cleanin' up soot." He drew his forefinger across the board that was the make-shift repair to the door's broken glass. Holding up a now black digit he said, "My back wore out before I got to cleanin' this and the winders. These bones of mine are hollerin' for a stretch out on my feather tick."

"Red, I'm so sorry you were left with such a mess to tackle. I feel partially responsible. My boy was involved in the beforehand circumstances that led to the ruckus that dislodged the stove pipe. If that hadn't happened, there wouldn't have been soot to clean up."

Red gave a dismissive wave to Sarah. "Ma'am, from what I heard, you weren't the one behavin' like a screemin' banshee."

"That aside, I feel bad about you doing all this work," Sarah lamented as she looked around the office. "Don't you have a daytime job over at the hotel to get to? When will you rest?"

Red responded, "I appreciate your concern, Ma'am, but no need to take on. Once the Marshal gets here, I should be able to go get me a few hours of shut-eye before I go to the hotel and my mop and broom that's a waitin'."

As Sarah walked toward the cells she said, "I'll send an apple pie in with Doc this next week for you. It won't make up for what you've been out, but it's the least I can do."

"I'll look forward to it," Red replied.

Sarah opened the door to the cell adjoining the one that held Ernie captive. "Red," Sarah said, "I'm putting Abe in here while we wait on Marshal Carter, Ben and Ernie's parents to arrive."

"Ma," Abe whined as she took his arm and steered him in and closed the door. The boy flinched when the latch clicked.

"I won't leave you here, Son," Sarah reassured. "I want you boys to be on equal footing and talk this situation out. See if you can't come to some sort of resolution. Marshal Carter's a good man. I suspect a promise from the both of you that you're done fighting will hold sway when he decides what to do next."

Awake, but still lying in bed, Ernie listened in on Sarah's conversation with Abe. When she crossed the room and took a seat, Ernie sat up on the edge of his cot. He rubbed his face and stretched, drawing Sarah's attention. "Good morning, Ernie," Sarah called out as she picked up the basket, she'd brought with her and walked to his cell. "I brought you some breakfast.

"Red, would you unlock Ernie's door so I can give this to him?" Sarah asked, holding up the tote.

"Sure thing, Ma'am. That's real nice of you to feed the boy. That'll save me from a trip to fetch his breakfast and get me to my bed quicker." The cell was unlocked, the meal handed to Ernie, then locked again.

Sarah found a tin mug and poured a cup of coffee in it. "Ernie, do you take sugar in your coffee?" she asked. "Sorry, I can't offer you any cream, there doesn't seem to be any here."

"Black's fine Ma'am," Ernie responded.

Sarah handed the mug of coffee through the bars to Ernie, then left him alone to enjoy the breakfast of biscuits and gravy, a side of sausage and a huge slab of rhubarb pie. Abe laid down on the cot in his cell, locked his arms behind his head and stared at the ceiling. Sarah passed the time with Red, getting song and verse on his mother's latest bout with rheumatism. She ended their conversation when she saw Ernie place the basket, now empty, on the floor.

"Abe, sit up please," she called out as she approached the cells. "Ernie, could I have your attention, too, please."

Keeping his head hung low, Abe swung his legs to the side of the cot and sat up. Ernie put full eyes on Sarah, belched, then farted. His face flushed as he mumbled, "Sorry, Ma'am."

Lowering his head more, Abe covered his face with his hands while his shoulders slightly jostled. Any discerning soul could have read the boy's mind. Sarah cut a look from Abe to Ernie, sending up a mental *praise be* that Ernie hadn't noticed Abe's reaction.

"You're excused," she said. All eyes went to the clock when it struck a quarter past eight. "Mr. Buttman told me that Marshal Carter arrives at eight-thirty sharp. Ernie, your parents won't be far behind." Sarah looked from Ernie to Abe and back again. "Before they get here, I want the two of you to talk."

Both boys responded with a sullen stare.

Sarah continued with her advice. "You need to get to the root cause of your feud. My prayer will be that you can mend the friendship that you once had. If not, then at least agree to lay down your swords. LaFontaine is a small town. Your paths will cross often, intended or not. No one can *keep* you from harboring your bad feelings, your anger for one another. If you choose to do that, to keep it bottled up, you run the risk of the cork popping and the anger spilling out again, maybe lead to another fight.

"The Bible, 1 Corinthians 10:13, has guidance for avoiding trouble. I'm going to share it with you. Take it to heart or not." Working from rote memory Sarah began, "'There hath no temptation taken you but such as is common to man, … but God is faithful, who will not suffer you to be tempted above that ye are able; but will with the temptation also make a way to escape, that ye may be able to bear it.' Boys, that includes fist fighting."

"Think back to yesterday before the fight. It started after school was out. Ernie, you jumped Abe. Something must have been said or done during the day that you let fester to the point that you got angry enough to strike out.

"Abe, Ernie attacking you had a reason behind it. What transpired between the two of you while at school yesterday? Did you say or do something that was demeaning or offensive to Ernie?

"The law *can and* will take control if you two don't. If you're going to continue to live in this town, you'll have to do it peacefully. Talk, see if you can resolve this enough to be able to promise the Marshal that you won't fight again. As I said earlier, that promise may have an impact on the Marshal's decision about what will happen next. He can wash his hands of the mess, turn you over for a judge to deal out your penalty. I surely do hope that you boys aren't stubborn enough to let that happen."

Sarah returned to her chair where she unabashedly knelt and started silently praying.

When Abe saw what his mother was doing, not in privacy by the side of her bed, but openly where all could see, his resolved softened. He got up and walked toward Ernie. The cuts on his knuckles stretched when he grasped the bars between their cells. He winced, sucked in a deep breath and blew it out. "Ernie, let's agree to tell the Marshal that we won't fight again." Abe stuck his hand through the bars for Ernie to grasp.

"When we was havin' lunch yesterday, you called me out in front of the others," Ernie snarled. "You made me look the fool to your, cousin. If you do somethin' like that again to me I ain't gonna let it slide. I don't make promises I know aforehand I can't keep."

Abe withdrew his hand. "I know that made you mad. I suppose I could have waited until we were alone to do it."

"If I hadn't let it simmer all afternoon, I might have been able to hold off and jump ya when we was alone somewheres," Ernie offered.

"That would have been smarter," Abe said.

Ernie clinched his fists. "Are you sayin' I'm dumb."

"Awe gee-whiz, Ernie, I didn't mean it that way."

"Yes, you did, you think you're smarter than me. Truth be told, you think your smarter than everyone."

Abe put his hands on his hips and moved to within an inch of the bars and hissed, "Are you sayin' I put on airs. I don't do no such …?

The clock struck half past eight, the door opened and in strolled Jeb Carter. Jeb made the perfunctory greetings to Red, then Sarah who'd stopped praying when he entered. He walked center room, faced the bars, took the stance, and patted his side arm. "What's it gonna be boys," he growled.

Abe eased his hand through the bars and reached out to Ernie. "Me and him was just fixin' to shake on our agreement to never fight again. Weren't we, Ernie?"

After a couple of beats, Ernie shuffled forward and gripped Abe's hand. "Yeah, we was just a fixin' to do that, Marshal." The grip on still sore knuckles was fierce, beads of sweat popped out on both boy's foreheads and blood seeped from their wounds.

Chapter 19

"Joy, thanks for helping set the dinner table," Sarah said. "Do you think you can pour milk one handed too?"

"Yes, Ma'am, I can handle that," Joy responded. "My sling helps remind me to not use my cut arm."

Henry toddled to Joy and tugged on the hem of her dress. "Up," he pleaded. Joy leaned down and kissed his head. "Sorry, I can't pick you up today." She knelt so she could face the baby boy. "Your papa said I have to let my stitches heal a few days before I can lift things." She handed the child a crust of dried bread. "After supper I'll hold you and we'll rock, would you like that?" Henry nodded as he took the crust from her.

The door flew open and Zeke came in, Lancy at his heels and accompanied by a gust of chilly air. "Shuta the door, Zekek," Hathaway yelled. "'Omi and me's a gettin' cold." The pair were on the floor under the window playing with dolls.

Henry ran to greet his big brother. He gave the bread to the dog then tugged on Zeke's pant leg, "Up," he pleaded.

"You want to play blocks," Zeke said in a sing-song voice as he shut the door and picked Henry up. The toddler was a hefty load for the six-year-old. The baby's toes dragged along the floor as Zeke jockeyed him to the corner of the kitchen where he plopped him down next to a pile of wooden blocks.

***

The family was seated at the supper table waiting for Luke. It was five o'clock and the clock started chiming. The boy entered the kitchen on a run, slid in his stocking feet to his chair and took his seat just as the fifth strike sounded.

"You're cuttin' it a little close ain't ya, brother," Josh teased, poking Luke with his elbow. "You know I don't like cold mashed taters."

"Luke," Sarah said. "It's your turn to say the blessing."

"Yes, Ma'am." The boy clasped his hands steeple style and sucked in a breath of air, "Dear Jesus, thank you for this food we's about to eat. And, for answerin' Ma's prayers that Abe not get jail time. I didn't hear her prayin' but I knowed she did 'cause she prays about everthin'. I was thinkin' about prayin' for Abe too, but I had my mornin' chores to do, then, when I got to school, I just plum forgot. When noon break came, I was meanin' to pray to ya, but Tommy asked me to shoot marbles and…"

"And, Amen!" Zeke boomed.

"Zeke Whitcome mind your manners," Sarah scolded. "It's rude for you to finish your brother's prayer."

"I did it for Josh, Ma," Zeke defended. "I had my eyes closed but I could see through the cracks that the steam had stopped comin' off the tater bowl. Josh done said he don't like 'em cold."

Ben picked up the bowl, served himself then after spooning a small helping onto Hathaway's plate reached past her and handed it to Joy. "How's the arm doing Joy?" He asked.

"It still hurts a bit, but not as bad as yesterday," the girl replied.

"Two to three days from now it likely won't pain you much," Doc said.

Joy passed the bowl to Sarah who gave herself a modest helping. Sarah gave a dab to Naomi then Henry and on it went to Luke who took a large scoop. "Is Ernie goin' to prison?" he asked.

"Praise God, no." Sarah replied. "Abe and Ernie told Marshal Carter they wouldn't fight again. Jeb saw them shake on their agreement and he decided that sentencing them to a good deed would be their penalty."

The potatoes were passed from Luke to Josh who took a portion of the vegetable so large it covered two-thirds of his plate. He had a spoon in his right hand creating a center reservoir for gravy in the volcanic like mound, while he used his left, to pass Abe a now empty bowl. Abe having little appetite didn't react.

With a mouth full of food Zeke said, "Ma, you'se always tellin' us that doin' a good deed would bring us happiness. That don't sound like no punishment to me."

Ben interjected, "The good deed will require physical labor. They'll be working side-by-side chopping out the roots that have invaded the sidewalk in front of the widow Barlow's picket fence."

Josh's eyes were big as saucers when he said, "Are you tellin' us that Abe will be workin' alongside Ernie, whilst Ernie is swingin' an axe?"

"As I've already said," Sarah reiterated with a sigh, "Ernie and Abe gave their word that they won't fight one another again. I expect them to get along working together because a man that breaks his word, sullies his name and loses his reputation."

"Ernie will be swingin' an axe," Zeke said shaking his head. "It ain't his reputation I'm afraid Abe might lose. Word or no word, I'm a volunteerin' to set on Mrs. Barlow's porch and keep watch whilst they work. Besides, Mrs. Barlow's the one that hands out real big oatmeal cookies when we come a trick-or-treatin'. Halloween's gettin' close. I'm bettin' she has a jar full of 'em ready and waitin'."

"Could we please change the subject? No more talking about my punishment, pleeeese." Abe asked with his head bowed low over his empty plate.

Sarah gave Abe a knowing look. "I think that's a very good suggestion, Son. Ben did Elmo Jones come see you today to discuss his situation?" she asked.

Hathaway had already helped herself to a biscuit when Ben took one and passed the platter to make the round. "Yes, Ma'am, he certainly did. However, I don't think a remedy for him will be in my medical journals." Ben held top and bottom of an opened biscuit in the palm of one hand. His knife in his other paused mid-air, a blob of creamy butter in balance. "I'm still considering how I might return the favor of you sending him my way."

Sarah gave him a teasing smile, "No need to thank me, Dear. No need at all."

Chapter 20

"Yeowww! Sarah, your feet are cold," Ben said as his wife crawled into bed and snuggled close to him.

Sarah put her arm across Ben's chest and pulled him to her. "I'd get up and put some socks on but I'm too exhausted to move."

Ben swallowed hard, "Your feet are fine, they've already warmed up considerably." His breathing quickened, he put his arm around Sarah and held her tight. "Are you *really* exhausted?"

Sarah kissed Ben on the cheek and scooted to her side of the bed. "Yes, Dear, back to back stressful days have been draining. I'm physically and emotionally tired."

"Amen to that. I think Abe is stressed too. He was quiet at the supper table tonight," Ben said.

Sarah patted Ben on his chest, "Yes, he was. You know, as I think on it, I don't recall him eating."

Ben took Sarah's hand in his and kissed it, "The boy's got a lot to think about and sort out. After the last couple of days, he probably doesn't have much of an appetite."

"You're likely right," Sarah agreed. "I'm thinking that he's of an age that we need to give him time to, as you said, sort it out. He's fourteen. If he doesn't know the right and wrong of his actions by now, us telling him will probably fall on deaf ears."

"Do you think Abe and Ernie were being sincere when they promised Jeb that they wouldn't fight again?" Ben asked.

"I hope so. But, if I were a betting woman, I wouldn't lay any odds on it. They said the right words, but I felt as if their faces told another story."

"I guess we'll find out soon enough," Ben said. "Since they're both expelled from school for a week, I thought I'd get them started on chopping out the widow Barlow's tree roots on Monday."

Sarah's voice trailed off. "That's good Dear…"

"I'll hush," Ben whispered. "I can see you're drifting to sleep."

Sarah struggled to open her eyes, "Wait, can't sleep before I hear what you told Elmo…."

Ben kissed his wife on the forehead. "In the morning, over coffee."

***

"Ernestine, enough! I'm done listenin' to you complain. Marshal Carter was more than fair with Ernie. One night in jail didn't do the boy no harm. Ernie pulled a knife and a girl got cut real bad. A week chopping out tree roots, is better than hard labor at Michigan City by a long shot. Get your head on straight, woman."

"But, Jasper, Ernie's been expelled from school for a whole week. He's sixteen and repeating the eighth grade. You've insisted he stay in school. I thought that was important to you."

"I had to quite school to work the farm. I wanted Ernie to get the chance to graduate," Jasper said.

"As I said, he's sixteen and in the eighth grade, he can't afford to miss…"

Jasper gave his wife the hush signal. "Ernestine, last week when I was in Parker's, I ran into Principal Hornblower. He pulled me aside to talk about Ernie's schoolin'. He's of a mind that Ernie's likely learnt all he's gonna learn at LaFontaine's school. Hornblower says it's clear the boy's frustrated over book learnin' and embarrassed to be in class with children so much younger than him. He said probably Ernie didn't get a tight hold on the basics his early years and that's a givin' him trouble now."

"Basics?" Ernestine questioned.

"Yeah, basics, Readin' Ritin' and Rithmatic. To get through to graduation, you gotta have 'em set to mind."

"What did you say to Principal Hornblower?"

"Nothin'. What he told me hard to hear, I got mad and walked off. Still, Hornblower gave me somethin' to think on. Maybe book learnin' just ain't in the cards for our boy."

"Are you saying you think Abe Whitcome is smarter than Ernie?"

"You beat all, woman. What I just said ain't got nothin' to do with the Whitcome boy."

Well, did you see that smug look on Sarah's face when Doc Adams suggested that the boys' punishment be chopping roots and the Marshal agreed? She thinks she's so …"

"Shut up! God Almighty, Ernestine, just shut up. Why do you have such a pick at that woman? I ain't never seen her without a smile on her face and she ain't never been nothin' but cordial to us."

"Jasper, there're things a man just wouldn't understand. Besides, what's so special about a woman smiling."

"Try puttin' one on *your* puss once in a while and you might find out." Jasper blew out the kerosene lamp, turned his back to his wife and pulled the covers up around his neck. "I'm done talkin'."

"Well, I never," Ernestine said in a huff.

"Now there's somethin' you got right," Jasper Brown mumbled.

***

The sky above Sarah's farm was clear, except for a few stringy clouds. The moon was full, and the clouds hovered over its surface creating the appearance of an unhappy face frowning down at the house. Moonbeams poured through the windows on the home's north side. A flock of crows, some nearly the size of a large laying hen, was perched on the fence rail that stood about eight feet from Sarah and Ben's bedroom window.

The kitchen clock chimed half-past eleven and Sarah's eyes fluttered. *It's just the clock, no need to get ...* She drifted back to sleep.

The clock struck midnight and Sarah bolted from sleep to a sitting position. *It's just the clock.* She brushed errant strands of hair from her eyes then gathered and tucked them in the braid that cascaded down her back, falling into a coil at the base of her spine. *Why did the clock wake me?* Her attention was drawn to the window and the ensemble of dust motes that danced in the moonbeams. Sarah swung her legs to the side of the bed and rubbed sleep from her eyes.

While sitting there, groggy, she began to feel as if someone was watching her. She squinted as she struggled to focus through the swirl of particulates and out the window. Her body gave a slight jerk when she saw pair after pair of little, beady, black orbs staring back at her. She tracked the birds to the far left, then the far right. As far as she could see their feathered heads were turned in unison as if watching her. *Crows, roosting on a fence line rather than in a tree...never saw that before.*

The clock was finishing its chain of twelve strikes. A shiver ran down Sarah's spine. *Midnight, the witching hour.* Sarah rubbed her face again.

Sorry Lord, that just popped to mind. Guess it's 'cause Halloween is near. You know I don't really believe in such.

Sarah's ears perked. *Someone's crying? Not one of the babies. Must be Joy.* Sarah put on her robe and slippers and quietly slipped out of the bedroom. She tiptoed to the parlor, now bedroom and placed her ear against the door. The crying was muted, but unmistakable. It was Joy.

Sarah eased the door open a crack and peeked in. The girl's thin frame was silhouetted by the light of the moon. She was sitting on the floor with her head lying on her arm that was propped up on the window sill. Her injured arm was out of its sling and wrapped around Lancy who had his head lying in her lap.

Lancy whined, when Sarah approached his tail began to thump against the wooden floor. "Hush," Sarah whispered as she knelt beside the pair.

Joy turned a tear stained face, "Sorry, Ma'am, I didn't mean to wake anyone."

"You didn't. It was the clock striking midnight that woke me. What's troubling you Dear," Sarah asked as she sandwiched the girl's hand between hers.

"I was dreaming about the fight between Ernie and Abe. Except, in my dream it was my father, not Ernie, holding the knife."

"Oh, Joy. I'm so sorry. Ben and I were focused on the trouble the boys were in for fighting. We didn't think about the impact on you beyond, getting cut. Of course, the violence has brought back memories, I'm sure."

"The memories will always be with me, but since coming here, starting school, they were beginning to fade a little. I know you said I wasn't to blame, but I can't help feeling that if I hadn't been at school yesterday, the fight wouldn't have happened."

"Yes, it would have," Sarah said. "If not yesterday, then one day soon. I'm just grateful that it happened where Ben and Marshal Carter were available to intervene. If they'd fought in some remote area, the outcome could have been much worse. Them getting taken to jail was a good thing. Now they both know that there are consequences to actions. I hope they can come to be friends again, like they were when they first started school, but if not, then at least be able to act reasonable when they encounter one another."

A crow called out, "Caw, caw, caw." Several others joined in. The cacophony of caws reached a chilling crescendo before growing quiet. Henry, then Hannah whimpered. Sarah held her breath, expelling a sigh of relief when the baby's breathing returned to sleep pace.

Joy separated her hand from Sarah's and pointed out the window. "The fence is lined with crows. They scare me. They're staring at me, they look evil."

"I saw them out my window and thought they were looking at *me*," Sarah shared.

"I wonder if my father sent them to find me, spy on me. If so, are they going to fly back to him and tell him where I am?" Joy said.

Sarah patted the girl's slender shoulder. "Joy, we're letting our imaginations carry us away tonight."

"Sarah," Joy said, "do you remember a few weeks back when we took a walk out to the pumpkin patch?"

"Yes, I remember," Sarah said.

"You told me that day that you believed that whenever evil or harm lurked, God was near to provide protection. You told me that the dove in the pumpkin patch that day was a sign of God's nearness."

"Yes, I remember telling you that," Sarah responded.

"Sarah," Joy said, choking on her tears, "I can't see the dove."

"We don't always see The Dove, Joy," Sarah said in a tone that supported her firm belief, "but, I assure you, He is always near."

Joy reached over, took Sarah's hand in hers and squeezed hard. "I hope you're right."

"I know I'm right," Sarah said then kissed the back of the girl's hand. Then, doing what came second nature to Sarah, she prayed. "Heavenly Father, Joy and I both have gotten a bit rattled by the crows. Please fill us with peace. Father, I know that you are near. Wrap your arms around Joy so that she may feel your healing presence."

Sarah kissed Joy on the cheek. "You and I both need to climb back in bed, see if we can get a few more hours of sleep. Try not to worry about your father coming. The family, Marshal Carter, we're all looking out for you. Ed Humes has likely decided to move on, not look for you."

After Sarah left the room Joy said to Lancy, "No, he'll come. He'll never let me be until he gets revenge for me scratching my name on his banjo." The girl clenched her fists. "He won't take me without a fight," she whispered. The dog showed his solidarity by giving a low menacing growl and Joy pulled him closer.

***

The next morning, Sarah was standing at the cook stove when Ben slipped up and hugged her from behind. "Good morning," he said before kissing her on the neck. "Sorry yesterday was so exhausting for you. This being Saturday and with no house calls I need to make, I'll be home to help. We need to get you rested up."

Sarah moved the coffee pot to the back burner, then turned and gave her husband a full on-the-mouth, lingering kiss. "So, *we,* need to get *me* some rest, do *we*?"

Ben's voice was husky when he responded. "I'm hoping *we* do."

"We do," Sarah said giving him a quick peck on the cheek. "But, right now, let's sit down and drink our coffee while you tell me about the romance advice you gave Elmo yesterday."

They each carried a cup of morning brew to the table. "So?" Sarah asked while adding sugar to her coffee.

Ben poured cream in his, "As you already know, Elmo has his sights set on courting Penelope Peterson who runs the haberdashery corner at Parker's store."

"Yes, I knew who he had his eye on. I'm concerned though that with his habits and curiosities, he'd have a more likely chance of becoming our next United States President than he would getting an acceptance to come to court."

"Wow, that was uncharacteristically harsh, coming from you."

"I know it was, I shouldn't have said it, even if it was just to you. I know that through Christ all things are possible and that includes finding our quirky mailman a sweetheart. So, tell me, what did the doctor order?"

Ben patted Sarah's hand, "While my medical journals didn't have a cure for what ails our postman, I did share a few home remedies with him.

"For starters, I gave Elmo a toothbrush. Told him to stop chewing Mail Pouch and start brushing his teeth with baking soda. I suggested morning, noon and night. That should get some of the tobacco stains off his enamel."

"When he approached me for advice," Sarah interjected, "I too, told him he should stop chewing if he wanted to go courting. I've known Elmo for fifteen years or more, I don't think I've ever seen him without a chaw in his mouth. Do you think he can give it up?"

"If he's determined enough, he might be able to quit chewing. I doubt he can go without some tobacco consumption. Doctors have known since the 1860s that tobacco can have a potent effect on humans. In 1828 nicotine was isolated from tobacco and identified as the component that causes craving for the darn stuff.

"I suggested to Elmo that he wean himself off the chew and take up the pipe. I'd like to see him get shed of tobacco altogether, but I doubt that'll happen. The tobacco from the pipe won't stain his teeth as much as the chewing does. Elmo's pooched out cheek distorts his face and the man wasn't blessed with any noticeable good looks to begin with. There's no spitting with a pipe, so Miss Peterson won't have to guard the hem of her dress when she's with him."

"Did you talk to him about overall grooming?" Sarah asked.

"Yes. I pressed the importance of a weekly bath and daily toilette. I suggested he shave his mustache and beard since they're tobacco stained."

"Both good suggestions," Sarah said leaning in close. "What else?"

"I urged him to change underwear and clothing more often, put on a clean shirt when he's out and about."

"Good suggestion, they're all good. What if we were to invite Elmo to supper, here? After that, one of us could have lunch with him at the hotel. We could instruct him in table manners and let him practice making conversation. A brush up on general etiquette couldn't hurt and might help give him confidence to approach Penelope Peterson and pop the question."

"Pop the question!" Ben exclaimed. "Aren't you getting the cart before the horse?"

"Oh, Ben, of course I mean ask her if he can come courting."

"Well, okay then. Inviting him to supper and eating at the hotel are both good ideas." Ben said. "I also suggested he cut back on his bean consumption. He needs to get his digestive system on an even keel before he makes an approach."

Sarah's eyes took on a twinkle, "I can see you were quite thorough with your advice."

"If memory serves, and it hasn't been that long since I came courting you, that's an important aspect when keeping polite company with a female."

"That it is," Sarah said as she patted Ben's hand. "It would be appreciated if you'd also share some of that wisdom with Zeke. My explaining social decorum, like not breaking wind in public, doesn't seem to be sinking in with him."

"I'll work on that too, I promise," Ben said. "Elmo needs help with putting together some suitable clothing."

"You're right. He does look like a ragamuffin most days."

"I'm sure Samuel Parker would accommodate me bringing Elmo in after store hours some evening," Ben said. "Samuel could help Elmo pick out new shoes, other needed ready-to-wear purchases. Since Parker's tailor shop is across the street from the dry goods store, Elmo can slip in and get measured for a suit of clothing without being noticed by Miss Peterson."

"Do you think Elmo can afford to buy new clothes?" Sarah asked.

"I expect he can. If not, I'll give him a stake. If the clothes help *mine* him a female companion, I'll consider it a *strike* worth backing."

Sarah fetched the coffee pot and poured Ben a second cup. You know, Dear, I found the mother lode when you came courting. You're pure 14K, every ounce of you." Sarah bent and pressed her cheek to Ben's, "When Elmo accepted the Lord at the Billy Sunday revival a couple of years back, God cleansed his heart, white as snow. Now God's using you to spiff up his outside."

Chapter 21

When the spinning eventually stopped, Ed Humes rubbed the sleep from his eyes. Aided by ambient moonlight he could see that a few feet to his left was a wall of steel grey bars. *Jail! How'd I get here?* "Hello," he yelled. "Anyone here?" There was no response, just the rhythmic ticking of a clock hanging on the wall outside his cell. He squinted.

With effort, Ed swung his legs to the side of the cot. Using a trembling arm, he pushed himself to a sitting position and rested his pounding head in his hands.

Humes got to his feet. *Legs feel like cotton.* He staggered toward the bars grasping hold just in time to prevent falling. He felt them move. Instinctively he pulled backward. The resulting click sounded loudly in the stillness.

"Dammit," he cried out. "The dang door wasn't locked. But now it is." He pushed outward a few times hoping to prove himself wrong.

He looked at the clock again. *Not enough light can't make it out.* Holding the bars, he let himself slide to the floor. While he lay there trying to piece together his muddled thoughts the clock struck five times. *Morning or evening?* Humes perked his ears to see if he could hear sounds from the street. *Nothing. It can get dark by five in the evening, but there'd still be activity on the streets. It's morning. Wonder how long I've been here?* He glanced toward the cell's window. *What's out there?*

Using the bars, he pulled himself up. Too weak to walk on his own he held fast and side-stepped to the cell's outside wall. From there he got down on his knees and crawled to the window. By holding on to a chair that set beneath it, he pulled himself to a standing position. *Window's too high.* Ed collapsed to the chair. Adjacent to it was a small table with two large jars of water on top. Ed had gone through this enough times before to know that his body needed water. He drained one of the jars then leaned his head against the wall and waited. After half-an-hour nature's cure began to work its magic. His thinking started to clear, and his arms didn't feel so limp. He stretched them out. *Still trembling, but not as bad.* Ed rested a few more minutes then again used the chair as a prop to stand.

By getting on his knees first, then reaching up and grasping the window's ledge he was able to stand on the seat of the chair and look out the window. There was a full moon. Ed held on to the bars as he surveyed the street. The only movement he saw was an animal. *Can't make it out, walks like a possum.* He looked to the east and saw that the horizon held a faint hue of light. *Dawn's beginning.* A mere whisper of breeze wafted through the chinks in the chipped caulking around the pane of glass. Ed laid his cheek on the window's cool sill. Inhaling deeply, he sucked in fresh air.

After a time in that position his muddled memory began to sort itself out. *I was at the cabin, lying on the floor. My gut was killing me, I was thirsty. Tried to take a drink of hooch, jug was empty. Where was Joy?* Ed's thinking reverted to a swirling jumble of disconnected thoughts. He put his face against the bars then stretched his tongue out, letting the tip touch the glass. The cold was soothing to his parched mouth. His arms and legs began to tremble. *Need more water.*

Ed got down and sat on the chair. When he reached for the second jar of water a piece of paper was stuck to the bottom. He pealed it off. It was a note addressed to him. Moonbeams streamed through the bars, Humes leaned into them to read.

Mr. Humes,

The bartender found you at your cabin unconscious and in a bad way. He brought you back to town to my office.

You were poisoned from rotgut bought down by the river. I tended to you until you were able to hold down liquids, then the sheriff took you in for a few more days of rest. He'll see that you get food and water. I'll stop by tomorrow to check on you.

Sincerely,
Dr. Dillard

Ed downed the second jar of water. After a few minutes the pounding in his head subsided considerably and some of his memory began to return.

The note said I'm here for rest. That explains the unlocked cell door. Either the deputy or the sheriff should be here by 7 o'clock. He looked at the empty jar in his hand. *Need more water.*

Still weak, Ed got down on his knees and crawled to his cot. He was drifting off when a memory surfaced. *Joy! That girl damaged my banjo and went on the run.* Tears filled Ed's eyes.

The banjo was Ed's identity. His childhood had been bleak, and it still pained him to think of those years. *Nothing but heartache and hand-me-downs. Father never gave me anything except the back of his hand. Unless you count him demanding proper English as something. The early years when he taught school were bearable. He started drinking, let that take over, lost his job. Mother ran off, took my sister. Left me to rot.*

When Ed was fourteen, he'd heard a banjo being played. The notes it produced, the music it made, spoke to him and transported him out of his misery. His banjo was the first new thing Ed had ever owned. *Wore blisters on my hands earning money to buy it.* Humes loved his banjo, he felt taller when he held it. He craved the adulation his playing brought from listeners. When words eluded, the instrument spoke for him. Through the music he played he could express love and joy, compassion and sorrow. When he held the banjo, he felt whole. It was an extension to his being and when he ran his fingers across its polished surface, he was able to feel proud, less flawed. *If Joy had carved her name in my flesh, it wouldn't have hurt as bad. The booze long ago scarred me for life. The banjo was the only part of me that was unblemished.*

Humes' feelings for his daughter fueled his emotions until he worked up a blaze of hatred. *Got to get out of here and find her, make her pay. Where could she have gone? Couldn't have been far. Lincoln Ville? Treaty? Not Roann or Wabash, they're both twelve miles or more from here. Joy's scrawny body couldn't walk that far.*

His eyelids grew heavy again. As he was about to succumb to sleep a cry of *caw, caw* and the flapping of wings jolted him wide awake. He looked toward the window. Sitting on the sill, making a silhouette against a backdrop of a now red sky, were four large crows. He called out, "It's awful early for you yahoos to be out and about." *Can't make out their eyes but it feels like they're staring at me.*

Ed lie with his arms folded behind his head. Random, seemingly disconnected thoughts flitted about in his mind. *Odd to see crows at this hour…as the crow flies, wonder if they're locals or just passing by?… So, I nearly kicked the bucket. … Cheated the grim reaper.*

The emaciated man stared at the ceiling's plank boards. *"Guess my times not up yet." … Got to figure out where that girl went. She might be lying dead somewhere…as the crow flies. …* With a flash of clarity, he thrust forward an arm, his pointer finger directed at the window. "LaFontaine," he said with a menacing chuckle. I'd forgotten about that two-bit town. *As the crow flies, just a skip, hop, and a jump from here.* "Much obliged," Ed called out to the birds with a salute. Ed tugged at the blanket wadded up at his feet and pulled it up to his neck. *Now that my mind's cleared, I need a plan.*

Got to look presentable. Folks in hick towns are close-knit. Can't make inquires the way I look now, I'd be shunned. Ed finger-combed his oily hair and ran a hand across his scruffy face. *Need a bath and shave.* He lifted the blanket to look at the condition of his shirt and pants. "Whew," he blurted. *When you can smell your own stench, it's real bad.* Ed picked at a crusted patch on his soiled shirt. *Puke. It'll wash off.* He lifted one leg, then the other, to inspect his trousers. *Can't see any rips or tears, just dirt.* Ed used the sleeve of his shirt to polish his silver belt buckle. *It's a bit tarnished.* Humes ran his fingers across the large silver buckle. *Just the sight of this always could make the girl tremble.* He polished it some more. *I want this thing shining bright so when I find her, she can see it.*

He patted it. *You've served me well in many a fight.* A picture of him using it on Joy flitted through his mind. He winced, then shoved the thought into the corner of his mind where his darkest deeds were buried. Ed's jacket lay on the floor in a heap, the back-seam split. *I need money. Not many options here in Banquo. Pickin' pockets that are empty is useless.*

The bartender found me at the cabin. Bet he's changed his mind about letting me play at the tavern. Should be able to wheedle my way back in. Play a few tunes – get enough money to rent a horse and make my way over to Wabash. Plenty of deep pockets there.

I'll pilfer until I have a decent wad. Get my jacket repaired or buy a new one. I can hang out at the Wabash Hotel lounge, make some connections. Word is that on Saturday nights there's a high stakes poker game in a back room at Gackenheimer's Pharmacy. It's likely play for a selected few. I'll need a reference to get a seat at the table. Wabash is a money town and I plan to free a few of its residents from the burden of carrying theirs.

When I go to LaFontaine, it will be in style. I'll have enough money to grease a few palms if that's what it takes to find Joy. Edward J. Humes yawned and stretched. *For now, sleep, then solid food. In a few days execute my plan. Joy, you can run, but you can't hide.*

Chapter 22

The screen banged and the glass in the kitchen door rattled when Abe slammed them. Sarah was at the stove cooking oatmeal. Abe saw her stern look and said, "What?"

"You just made a rude entrance into *my* kitchen, that's what."

Abe gave his mother a sullen look but didn't respond.

Sarah opened the oven to check on the breakfast biscuits, determined they needed another couple of minutes and closed it. "It's Monday, I'm surprised to see you in from egg deliveries already. Did you and Josh trade days for making the deliveries?"

"Since I'm the one that come in the kitchen, I'd think that'd be obvious," the boy snapped.

Sarah's brow furrowed, "You act as if something is bothering you, Son. What is it?"

"It's Monday, I'd think it would be obvious."

Sarah stopped stirring the oatmeal, her large wooden spoon suspended mid-air. She took a deep breath and pointed the spoon at Abe. "Abraham Whitcome, that's the second time you've told me that a response to a question I asked you should be obvious to me.

"I'll tell you what's obvious to me. It's obvious that you've forgotten your manners and it's obvious that you've forgotten to whom who you're speaking. It's further obvious that if you don't apologize to me for being disrespectful *and* make an immediate attitude adjustment, you'll find yourself suffering the consequences."

Abe had taken a seat at the table. He remained mute, his head hung low. Sarah's voice lowered a few octaves, near to a growl, "*Abraham*?"

Abe kept his head down, refusing to make eye contact, "Sorry, Ma," he said. "I'm out of sorts 'cause I have to chop out the Widow Barlow's roots with Ernie today."

Sarah said, "Why would that trouble you, Son? You and Ernie told Marshal Carter that you'd made peace with one another. You even shook hands."

Abe didn't respond.

"Son, you have the look of a fox caught in a chicken coop. I'm thinking that you and Ernie were insincere with Jeb," Sarah said as she took the biscuits from the oven.

Ben entered the kitchen carrying Henry and holding Hathaway's hand. He looked from Sarah to Abe and back again. "Who's being insincere?"

Sarah took the biscuits from the oven and gave Ben the, *we'll talk later*, look.

Hathaway jerked on Ben's hand, he looked down. "It ain't me, Pa," the toddler said. "I ain't bein' insarear."

"Me neither," Luke said, as he came into the kitchen carrying Naomi. "I'm starving and I'm bein' sincere as a heart-attack."

Naomi reached out, placed her baby hands on her big brother's cheeks and turned his face to look at her. "Hungie," she said nodding her head. Luke put her into her high chair and kissed the top of her head. As if choreographed, Sarah split a biscuit, blew to cool it, then, put one half on Naomi's tray and the other on Henry's. Henry grabbed the biscuit and started chewing on it before Ben got him secured in his high chair.

Zeke ran down the stairs and nearly collided with Joy who was coming down the hall. They entered the kitchen together. "Somethin' sure smells good, Ma," Zeke said as he took his seat at the table and Joy took the one next to him.

"Thank you, Son." Sarah said as she set two platters on the table, one bacon, the other biscuits. Ben carried the pot of oatmeal to the table and placed it alongside. Josh came in from the egg run to the sound of chair legs scraping the wooden floor. He rushed to the vacant seat next to his mother and bellied-up with the rest of the family.

"Perfect timing, Josh," Ben said.

Leaning into Josh, Sarah kissed his cheek and grasped his hand. "Abraham," Sarah said with a tone that clarified her authority, "I think it would be good if you gave thanks for our food this morning. I suggest you also pray for the Lord's guidance to handle the work you and Ernie will start today." Sarah reached across the twin's high chairs and took Luke's waiting hand initiating the family's morning chain of hand holding in preparation for grace.

Abe's tone was meek when he replied. "Yes, Ma'am."

Zeke leaned over and whispered in Joy's ear, "She called him Abraham. That ain't good."

***

"Whoa," Marshal Carter called to his team when at 8:00 a.m. he pulled it to a stop in front of Mrs. Barlow's house and the offending tree. "Abe, hop down and start unloading the tools. Ernie should be here directly. His Pa's bringin' him and a fellin' ax. The shovels, hoe, wood ax and fellin' ax should do the trick."

"What's a fellin' ax?" Abe asked.

"It's got two blades, used mainly for loggin'. If you ain't familiar with one, let Ernie use it. A fellow needs to catch on to the knack of twistin' the handle on the back swing so the down swing falls on the opposite blade. They's good to have but can be more dangerous to use than a one blade."

Abe surveyed the tree bottom to top, "This tree is huge. Look at the size of these roots," he said as he kicked at one.

Jeb jumped down from the wagon and nudged his boot at a couple of the displaced bricks. "I'm sure you're right. They's no denyin' that you boys have a couple of days of hard work ahead of ya."

A rig pulled up. Jasper Brown was at the reins with a scowl on his face. Ernie was sitting beside him and made no attempt to move. "Get down," Jasper growled. "Had to get you here by 8:00 a.m. and I missed my second cup of coffee. I need to get back to the farm." Ernie sat as if frozen in place.

Jasper took off his hat and started slapping Ernie's head with it. "Get – your – sorry – keister – off – my – wagon."

Ernie moved as if in slow motion and climbed down. Jasper barked, "Grab the ax and the tote your ma sent. It's got your lunch in it."

The man-sized boy looked like he'd had more than just the fight wrung out of him. "Dimwit," Jasper spewed at his son. "I've seen a turtle move faster than you."

Abe stood staring, his mouth agape. Marshal Carter stepped forward. "Good morning, Ernie," he said patting the boy on his back while conspicuously eliminating Jasper from the greeting. "Put the ax over there." Jeb pointed to the pile of tools Abe had placed near the tree.

Gesturing to a spot about ten yards away, the Marshal said, "Set your lunch over yonder under that lilac bush alongside Abe's." Jeb turned up the collar on his jacket while he surveyed the sky. "Ya got your expected October mornin' nip, but no clouds. When the sun's directly overhead, it'll warm up considerable. The lilac bush is dormant, but it'll provide enough shade to keep your food from turnin'."

When Jeb had picked Abe up at the Doc's office that morning, the boy was carrying a lunch basket mounded past the brim. Although the contents were covered with a blue calico towel, the escaping aromas got the Marshal's mouth salivating as they made the short trek to the work site.

Ernie set his puny tote down next to Abe's basket. Jeb noticed the disparity in sizes. Jasper noticed too. The Marshal gave Jasper a questioning look. "Don't look at me," was Jasper's terse response. "I ain't the one that packed the numb scull's lunch."

Jeb shook his head as he stared at Jasper. He took in the whole of Ernie's father and the message the boy's mother was conveying by sending a lunch so small it wouldn't give a mouse enough sustenance to make it through a day.

When the Marshal turned to address the boys, his eyes held a hint of moisture. And, his heart ached with compassion for the young man left wanting, that stood slouching next to a boy, standing tall that had come equipped with a basket full of love.

Jeb took out his handkerchief and blew his nose. "Must be tryin' to catch a cold." With deliberation he folded the linen and put it back into his pocket. He squared his shoulders, put his hands on his hips, and spread his legs, assuming his signature stance. "You two ex-jailbirds need to work hard but pace yourselves. You ain't gonna get it done in one day.

"You can take a mid-morning fifteen-minute break. Stop when the noon whistle blows. Take a half-hour lunch. At 2:00 p.m. take an afternoon fifteen-minute break. I know you both have evenin' chores so quittin' time is 4:30 p.m.

"Tidy up the work site, don't leave the shovel layin' where someone could trip over it. Take the axes over to Rutherford's place. The blacksmith knows you'll be comin' by. He has a grindstone you can use to sharpen the blades, so they'll be ready for your use tomorrow. Don't dally. Be at my office by 5:00 p.m., your folks will be pickin' you up then. No fightin'. When I took your word that you wouldn't fight again, I treated you two with the respect I would have given growed men. I aim to hold you to it. A man who breaks his word ain't worth sickum."

He started to leave, then turned back. "Either of you got a watch?"

"Abe pulled a pocket watch out of his pants and flipped the lid open. "I got my Pa's watch."

Jeb tapped his pointer and middle finger to the brim of his hat. "I best leave you to it then."

Jasper Brown had taken his leave and was hightailing it down the road leaving a trail of dust behind him. The pavement on Wabash Street from the Barlow house, past LaFontaine's school, to the jail at the intersection of Wabash and Branson streets, then left on Branson street through the heart of town, had been removed and was awaiting replacement. Jeb knew he and his team would be eating Jasper Brown's dust all the way back to his office. Jeb yelled, "Brown, you dad-burned ignoramus."

Jasper was too far ahead to hear. Jeb mumbled to himself, "It ain't rained in a fortnight. Any fool would know you can't move a team faster than a walk on a dry dirt road without causin' ramifications."

With that in mind, and with the clarity of a gypsy fortune teller, the Marshal began mentally playing out the remainder of his morning. *The dirt's done billowed into a cloud that will continue to grow. If Brown turns left and travels down Branson the cloud will pass in front of Parker's Dry Goods. Lord, help me if that happens. Sure, as shootin' it will filter in around the door and winders.*

First it will cover them black Bowler hats at the haberdashery counter in the front to the left. Miss Penelope will be there workin' on a bonnet. She'll commence to hackin' and coffin'.

The vision gained clarity, Jeb's mouth took on a sneer and his head began to bobble. *Next, the dirt will descend on them la-de-da women's petticoats and lace drawers. Mrs. Parker will be standin' there tendin' to them. She'll grab her bosom and screech. Samuel Parker, or the missus, one or the other, maybe even both, will come marchin' to my office to make a complaint.*

Jeb's mind was quiet for a couple of beats, then another thought struck him. *And, I ain't gonna get my mornin' nap!*

Jeb took off his hat, slapped it against his leg and yelled into the wind. "Jasper, do that again when you come back at five o'clock and I'll lock you up!"

The Marshal's outburst jolted his team and they sprinted into a fast trot creating their own dust cloud. The team refused to respond to Jeb's commands. They slowed down when Wabash street intersected with Branson, and on their own volition, made a left-hand turn, trotted down Branson, past the hotel, past the barber shop and stopped directly in front of Parker's store.

The dust cloud Jeb had created swept over the wagon, Jeb, then the team. The Marshal's shoulders went slack. He felt thirsty, licked his lips and found them dirty with grit. He jumped down to inspect his horses and their harness.

Jeb didn't have to worry about angry merchants knocking on his office door to lodge a complaint. Not only did Mr. and Mrs. Parker come out to give him a piece of their mind, Noble Simon, the barber was standing on his stoop shaking a fist at the Marshal. The scripture about removing the log from one's own eye before complaining about a speck in another's flitted into the embarrassed Marshal's mind.

Back at the work site, Abe had grabbed the ax and was chopping on a large root at the base of the tree. Ernie stood off to the side holding the felling ax, studying the tree, then the bricks. Across the street and down a few yards the school hack arrived. The door flew open and Zeke Whitcome jumped out. The six-year-old took off running like his shirttail was on fire. He made a beeline to the fence that bordered the street. From that vantage point he could clearly see the Barlow house. He saw Abe chopping at the base of a tree. Ernie was standing nearby, holding an ax. Zeke stuck his face as far through the fence rails as space would allow and yelled, "Abe, watch your back. Ernie's got an ax."

Abe heard him, stopped chopping and leaned his ax against the tree. He cupped his hands around his mouth and yelled to Zeke. "Ever'thin' is fine over here. Get yourself on into the school before the bell rings. I don't need you gettin' in trouble on my account."

Zeke hollered back, "Okay. I'll come check on you again when I get my mornin' recess."

Abe was touched by his little brother's concern. He smiled, then reached for the ax.

"That brother of yours reminds me of a banty rooster," Ernie said, "always ready for a fight."

"Mind your own business, Brown, "Abe snapped. "You gonna help do this work or just stand there watchin' me?"

Ernie's muscles flinched. He reached up and rubbed his still swollen cheek. He shook his head as if to clear his mind. His voice sounded tired when he responded. "I'd like to talk it out first."

Abe folded his arms across his chest and faced Ernie. "Talk out what?"

"If you keep choppin' on that big root at the base of the tree," Ernie said, "you'll run the chance of killin' it."

"Oh! I suppose you think you've got a better idea?"

"Well, I've been studyin' the situation. Looks to me like we should tear out these buckled bricks and take a look. Likely they's feeder roots under 'em that's causin' the problem. They'll be smaller and easier to chop out. If we don't disturb none but the stragglin' offenders, the tree should stay healthy."

Abe knew a good suggestion when he heard one. It would cost him considerable pride to take Ernie up on it, but his already aching back convinced him it would be worth it. "Okay, let's give that a try." Abe put the ax aside. "You could have told me about your idea before I started choppin'"

Ernie growled in response, "You started in a choppin' before I thunk it up. Let's toss the bricks in a pile, it'll make 'em easier to load for haulin' away."

"That'll work for the broke ones," Abe said. "The ones that are up rooted, but ain't broke, we should stack. They could be used again."

"I would have come up with that idea, too, if I'd had me more time to think on it," Ernie spewed back.

Abe reached up and touched his still tender black eye. He drew in a deep breath, held it, then slowly exhaled, "Let's just get to it. I'm gonna start a pile with the good bricks."

"I'll start stacking the ones that's broke," Ernie proffered.

By ten o'clock they'd made noticeable progress. "My goodness, you boys work fast," Mrs. Barlow called out from her porch, while holding a plate of cookies. "It's time you two took yourselves a break."

The boys looked at one another and nodded. Abe went through the gate and to the porch to accept the goodies. "Thank you, Ma'am. This is real nice of you."

"You're welcome to come sit on the porch while you rest," Mrs. Barlow said.

"We appreciate the offer, Ma'am, but we're both dirty. We'll just set a spell and enjoy these," he said, slightly raising the plate as a substitute tip-of-the-hat.

The boys picked a resting spot that faced street side. They sat with their backs against the fence and a three-foot distance between them. Abe positioned the plate of cookies midway, so they could both reach it. It held six cookies. Ernie grabbed up three. Abe took the remaining three. They munched in silence.

The peal of a bell caused their heads to turn toward the school. They saw a swarm of squealing children rushing out on to the playground. "Must be mornin' recess for the lower grades," Ernie said. The comment was made more to himself than to engage conversation.

In short order a familiar voice yelled, "Abe, you all right?" It was Zeke.

Cookie in hand, Abe waved at him. "I'm fine. We're takin' our mornin' break."

"Is that a cookie you got in your hand?" The first grader called back.

"Yeh," Abe responded.

"Is it one of Mrs. Barlow's oatmeal cookies?" Zeke questioned.

"Yes." Abe said, gesturing with a now half-eaten cookie.

"Bring me one," Zeke hollered. "I'm needin' me somethin' sweet to eat."

"Sorry," Abe said as he popped the half cookie in his mouth. "Mine are all gone." He held his hands out, palms splayed.

Not to be deterred Zeke tried again, this time in a sweet, sing-song tone, "Ernie, oh, Ernie. How about you? Can I have me one of your cookies?"

"Nope," Ernie bellowed as he gobbled his last bite of cookie and wiped his hands on his pants.

Zeke took another tack. "Abe, can you please ask Mrs. Barlow for more cookies. Tell her your next to littlest brother, is hankerin' for some."

Abe scolded, "Go play, Zeke. "Leave us in peace. Our break's almost over."

Zeke's hangdog look was noticeable when he left to join his friends.

"Gee willikers," Ernie said. "Is he always that annoyin'?"

"Not all the time," Abe responded. "Zeke started talkin' about the size of Mrs. Barlow's cookies when he heard we were comin' here to work."

"They were big. Near as big as a cow pie."

"Yes, but a lot tastier."

"Whitcome, I knowed you was full of shit, but I never thought you'd admit to eatin' it."

Abe threw a clump of dirt at Ernie. "You're the one that's full of it," he quipped." The smile on the fourteen-year-old's face conveyed that it wasn't a sincere retaliation.

Ernie chuckled and said, "Let's get this done." Both boys got up and returned to moving bricks.

The boys' separate focus, Ernie piling broken bricks, Abe stacking those that were reusable, worked well throughout the morning and after lunch. They'd made considerable progress by three o'clock. The pile was big and the stack high. What had been a decent distance between the heaps, was now a narrow divide. "Ernie," Abe said, "I'm puttin' one more layer on my stack, then I'm gonna start a new one over yonder. If I let it get too high, it might topple over."

"You stacked 'em four to a layer," Ernie said. "Start your next stack with six-eight as your base, continue that count as you layer up."

"Good suggestion," Abe said, "I'll do that. Ernie you ought to start a new pile. Somewhere away from my stack. The one you're usin' is too close. If your throw is off one of them broke chunks might hit my stack and break some of the good bricks or knock it over.

"Mind your own business, Whitcome," Ernie growled. "If I think I need to start a new pile I'll do it. I don't need you bossin' me around."

"Gee, Ernie, I was just givin' you a suggestion back."

Abe was reaching up placing a finishing brick on his stack when Ernie said, "'I'm good at pitchin'. My chunks land right where I'm aimin' 'em." He let one fly. The broken brick hit its mark at the peak of the pile. The chunk at the pinnacle had become wedged in a crevice. It didn't shift, and the incoming one couldn't find purchase. It ricocheted off, became airborn, and hit Abe in the head.

Abe grabbed the base of his skull and dropped to his knees. The creatures occupying their tree top gallery, saw the incident play out. The squirrels cut their chatter and the birds ceased their singing. Ernie slapped his hand over his mouth stifling a gasp. The deafening silence was broken by Mrs. Barlow who screeched, "Abe, Abe, are you hurt?" She launched herself from her porch rocker and scurried to the fence.

Abe withdrew his hand, saw blood, then put it back. Ernie, now at Abe's side, took ahold of his elbow, jerked him to his feet and answered for him. "He ain't hardly bleedin'." With a scared look Ernie mounted his defense. "The piece of brick landed on the pile where I aimed but bounced off and hit him. It was an accident."

Mrs. Barlow looked from Ernie to Abe and back again. "I wouldn't know. What I saw was Abe collapsing to his knees. Let me get to the gate and come look at that wound," she said nodding to Abe's head.

Abe found his voice. "Please, Ma'am, don't do that. They's stuff to trip on everwhere. You might fall."

"Then come over to the fence, I'll take a look from here," the Widow said motioning to Abe. Abe complied, and Mrs. Barlow tut-tutted. "You've got yourself a hefty sized goose egg. The skin's broken but the bleeding seems to have stopped. Maybe you should go to the Doc's office, let him have a look."

Ernie sounded defensive when he piped in, "No need to do that. You saw for yourself that the bleedin's stopped." He slapped Abe on the back. "No harm, no foul. Come on Abe, let's get to work."

Abe turned his back to the Widow and gave Ernie a look that would shrivel a gopher's liver, then turned again. "Thanks for your concern, Ma'am. If it needs tendin', Doc can do it when I see him at supper time."

Mrs. Barlow's brow furrowed. "Well, I guess that'll be okay," she said, "I best get in the house and start cooking. It'll be supper time directly. It's just me, but a body has got to eat." The boys were in a stare down when she called over her shoulder, "You need to put some distance between that pile of rubble and brick stack. It'll be safer."

Abe's fists clenched. His breath rate intensified, his nostrils flared, and his lips thinned as the stare down, turned to standoff. Maintaining a defensive stance but allowing his countenance to soften, Ernie broke the silence. "It *was* an accident. The chunk *did* bounce off the pile before it hit you."

At that same moment a team and wagon pulled up to the work site and stopped. "Boys," a stern voice drawled out. The pair immediately dropped their stares and relaxed their stances. "Is there a problem?" Marshal Carter asked. Neither boy spoke.

When Abe saw Jeb start to climb down, he replied, "Ain't nothin' wrong we can't handle between us."

Ernie interjected, "No need to get down if you was just, uh, uh, comin' by to check on us."

Jeb jumped down and tethered his team. As he was approaching Abe and Ernie, a female voice rang out, "Marshal Carter." Jeb looked toward the Barlow house and saw the Widow standing on her porch drying her hands on a dish towel.

"Howdy," Mrs. Barlow. Are these boys stayin' out of trouble?"

"Lands a Goshen don't know when they'd have time to get into any. They've worked themselves to the bone today. Abe, how's your head doing, honey? I expect it's still throbbing some."

"Head?" Jeb addressed the question to all. "What's wrong with Abe's head?"

Mrs. Barlow waved her towel dismissively as she spoke. "Oh, we had us a minor accident. Ernie was tossing a chunk of brick and somehow it missed the pile and hit Abe in the back of the head."

"An accident was it?" The Marshal quizzed, as he faced the boys. "Abe, is that right? Did you get hit in the head by accident?"

There was a strained control to Abe's tone when he responded. "Ernie said the chunk ricocheted off the pile and come my way by accident."

"I ain't asked for Ernie's version yet," Jeb said. "What do *you* think? Was it an accident?"

Abe turned so the Marshal could see the lump on his head. "It hit me in the back of the head. I didn't see it comin'."

"Mrs. Barlow, did you see what happened?" Jeb called out.

"I saw Abe go to his knees," she responded. "I wasn't watching when Ernie made the toss."

Jeb took off his hat and finger combed his hair. "This job is gonna be the death of me," he said as he surveyed the results of their day's work. With hat in clasped hands that hung relaxed below his waist, he said, "By the look of the progress you two have made, they couldn't have been much in the way of shenanigans goin' on."

Jeb donned his hat and pulled it down snug. "Boys, what I come by for was to call quittin' time for the day. Jasper Brown sent word through Elmo Jones that he's got a mare that's close to foalin'. He needs Ernie back at the farm.

"Abe, you'll have to clean up and get the axes sharpened by your lonesome." Jeb took ahold of Abe's shoulders and turned him, so he could inspect the back of his head. The Marshal sucked air through his teeth, "That's a big one. It's turnin' purple, looks ugly.

"Dad burn it, your Ma's gonna have my hide. Have Doc look at it before you go home. Maybe he's got some salve or somethin' that might cover it up some." He patted Abe's back then climbed up on his wagon.

"Come on, Ernie, I best get you out to your farm. Abe, get yourself some rest. See you at 8:00 tomorrow mornin'." Jeb gave the command and his team started forward. The Marshal's voice trailed out of hearing range as he called out a last-ditch suggestion, "If the salve don't work, wear a haaa…"

Chapter 23

Sarah's day had been clouded with anxiety. She was concerned about Abe and Ernie working together on Mrs. Barlow's sidewalk repair. The fight they'd had was on Friday. Their schoolmates, their parents and the whole town had likely been discussing it all weekend. When the morning passed and there'd been no, to-the-door mail delivery from Elmo, Sarah had lifted a *praise God* for being spared from hearing the town's gossip about her family.

She was eager for the children to get home and to find out how their first day back at school hand gone. The kitchen clock chimed, Sarah noted the time was a quarter to four.

School let out at three thirty. The children are probably getting on the hack about now and will be home directly. Hope Joy coped all right with the chatter about her cut arm and the fight. No doubt Josh, Luke and Zeke bantered with friends about it every chance they got. Jeb's working Ernie and Abe until 4:30. Abe will ride home with Ben. It'll be after five before I see them. There will be a lot of stories told at the supper table tonight. By bedtime, we're all going to be emotionally drained.

"Heavenly Father," Sarah whispered, "It's me again. I know you heard me the four other times I prayed today for my children, Joy and Ernie. I gave the situation over to you to handle, but I'm struggling with anxiety just the same. Lord, give Ben and me wisdom to know how to respond when the children tell us about their day. And, Lord, forgive my weakness. Amen."

The house was peaceful. The three little ones were up from their afternoon naps and playing quietly. Henry was in the toy corner stacking wooden blocks. Hathaway and Naomi were sitting together on the floor. The baby girl's eyes held a glaze of pure pleasure as Hathaway ran a brush through her wispy fine hair.

Supper was on the back burner simmering and the aroma of freshly baked apple pie filled the air. *I'm ahead of schedule, think I'll stop for a rest before everyone gets home.* Sarah sat down in her chair and started rocking and humming. The dog's ears perked up and Lancy left his warm spot by the cookstove to come and curl up at Sarah's feet. Sarah ceased humming and broke into song. "Some glad morning when this life is o'er, I'll fly away, to a home on God's celestial shore, I'll fly away."

Hathaway had heard her mother sing the song many times and knew the refrain, her favorite part, was next. She jumped to her feet and pulled Naomi to hers. "Do like this 'Omi," Hathaway demonstrated, jutting her elbows out and cupping her hands in her armpits. "See, wings, we'se birds now." Sarah helped her youngest daughter assume the position before starting the refrain.

Sarah clapped her hands, Lancy thumped his tail, and the girls flapped their wings as Sarah sang, "I'll fly away, O glory, I'll fly away. When I die, hallelujah, by and by, I'll fly away."

Hathaway called out, "Again, again." The singing and dancing continued through several choruses, abruptly stopping when Lancy yelped. Sarah looked down. The dog had placed a paw on the top of his head and a wooden block laid at his side. Before Sarah could absorb what had happened, a second block and then a third flew at the dog, one missing, one connecting. Sarah jumped up, Lancy too. The dog stood facing the culprit. Lancy's head leaned to the right and then to the left. Rather than growl, he barked once, as if to say, "Why?"

With hands on her hips, Sarah scolded, "Henry, no, no. You must not throw blocks." Her voice turned from stern to soothing, "You hurt Lancy," she said, kneeling and stroking the dog's back.

Lancy's tail was hanging. He made eye contact with Sarah and whined. "I'm sorry, Boy," Sarah said, "Henry's still a baby. We have to teach him how to behave."

Henry was holding a block in each hand. He banged them together several times and giggled. "Henry," Sarah said, "you come over here and tell Lancy you're sorry." The baby didn't budge. Sarah went to her son, extracted the blocks and tossed them in the toy box. She took his chubby hand, walked him to the dog and helped the baby stroke their pet's head. "We must be gentle with Lancy. He's our family. Can you tell him you're sorry?"

The toddler nodded, then threw his arms around the dog's neck and squeezed. "Okay, okay, that's enough hugging," Sarah said as she pried the baby's arms away. "Let's let Lancy have some peace for a while."

The dog barked, ran to the door and whined to be let out. The sound of a buggy coming up the lane could be heard by everyone in the house. Hathaway ran to the window. "It's Pa," she called out.

"Are you sure?" said Sarah. "It's time for the hack, but not your Pa." She joined Hathaway and confirmed that it was Ben with a load of children. "Wonder why he's bringing the children home?"

Hathaway called out names as one by one the buggy's passengers jumped down. "I see Joy," she sang with glee while clapping her hands. "I see Zeke, Luke, Josh, and Abe, our family's all home."

"Abe? Wonder why he's home so early?" Sarah questioned as she opened the door. Lancy ran out and jumped up on Josh. Zeke flew past his mother, grabbed Henry's hand and took him to the toy box. Joy entered and after receiving a hug from Sarah she picked up Naomi and grasped Hathaway's extended hand. Abe walked in at a slow pace and sat down in the nearest chair. Luke ran up the stairs to change clothes. Josh tossed a stick for Lancy to chase, but, abandoned the dog and followed Luke. Ben gave Sarah a quick hug then headed at a fast pace toward their bedroom. He slowed when Sarah said, "You're home early."

Talking fast, Ben responded, "Jeb let Ernie and Abe off early. I flagged the hack down and had the children come with me. Thought we'd save Julib a stop. I'm in a rush to change my clothes, I'll be doing Abe's chores tonight and I want to get them done and come back for supper, I'm starving." As Ben was closing the bedroom door he added, "I'd like for Abe to lay down and rest. Please put a cold compress on his head."

"Rest?" Sarah questioned turning toward her son. "Abe, was the work that hard today?" Before he could answer she pivoted and yelled at the closed bedroom door. "Ben, did you say put a cold compress on Abe's head?" Turning back to Abe, "Are you hurt? Did something happen? Is that why you were let go early?"

"Ma," Abe said in a soothing voice, "Ain't no need to get yourself upset. We're here early 'cause Ernie had to get home. The Browns have a mare that's foalin'."

"What about your head, did you get injured?"

Ben came from the bedroom buttoning his shirt. "Abe got a knock on the head. I think he should be excused from chores and take it easy the rest of this evening."

Sarah reached for Abe's hat, "Knocked on the head, let me see."

"It ain't much," Abe said, trying to duck away.

"Abe Whitcome, you sit still." She pulled his hat off exposing a purple knot near the size of a walnut. "Dear Lord in Heaven, what happened?"

Josh and Luke rushed through the kitchen and started out the door. Ben called out. "Hold up, boys, I'm going with you to the barn. I'll do Abe's chores tonight."

Josh and Luke stopped dead in their tracks then looked at one another, eyes open wide. Luke spoke first, "Ben, Abe generally does the milkin'."

Josh interjected, "We don't mean no offense Doc, but you still ain't got a handle on how to pull on them teats."

Ben cut a look at Sarah, she was struggling to hold back a grin. Doc defended, "I think I've got a better handle on the situation than I did when I first came to the farm."

"You'se some better," Luke offered, "but you still get Moonblossom to bawlin'. How about I do the milkin' and you take my job of muckin' out the stalls? After Abe milks, he checks on the chickens and gets them settled in for the night. You can go ahead and do that."

"You've got a deal," Ben said as he took ahold of the screen door. "Sarah," he paused his exit, "supper smells delicious." He looked outside, back at his wife, then let go of the door and walked to Sarah and gave her a kiss on the cheek. Turning to Abe he said, "Tell your mother about your day, I know she's anxious to hear."

Sarah gave Abe a glass of milk to drink while she prepared a cold compress for his head. Abe lay down on the kitchen daybed and Sarah put the cold cloth on his goose egg and helped him nestle his head on a pillow. As she covered him with a crocheted throw she asked, "Are you comfortable? I want to go talk to Joy, see how her day went."

"Sure, Ma," Abe said closing his eyes.

The three girls were sitting on the floor playing tea party. Sarah joined them mimicking their cross-legged sitting position. "So, Joy, tell me about your day. Were you able to put last night's bad dream out of your head?"

"Yes, once I got to school and saw Breanna, I didn't think of it again. Now that I'm home, it has come to mind some. Those crows really scared me. I don't understand why. I've never been afraid of birds or creatures."

"As I told you last night," Sarah said, "they caught my attention too. Seeing them sitting on the fence row in the dark of night was a curious thing. So, how's your arm, did it trouble you any today?"

"No, Breanna helped me carry my books." Joy lightly touched her bandage. "I can feel the stitches pulling. Doc said that means the wound is healing. After supper he's going to change my bandage and put some ointment on the stiches. He said that'd soften them, so they won't pull as much."

Sarah accepted an imaginary cup of tea from Hathaway and feigned sipping. "Was there a lot of talk today about the fight?"

"Oh, yes." Joy responded with big eyes. "One of the teachers must have complained to Principal Hornblower about all of it. He came to our class, went to all the others too, I heard, asking that we put what happened aside and concentrate on our studies."

"Did that work?" Sarah asked.

"The whispering died down, but the note passing was obvious."

"What did Miss Messner do about that?" Sarah asked.

"Nothing. She looked really tired this morning. Breanna said she heard our teacher spent a lot of time at the principal's house this weekend. I guess he needed someone to look after him due to him getting roughed up when he tried to break up the fight. Anyway, Miss Messner seemed to just ignore the note passing."

"In a day or two," Sarah offered, "we can only hope that all of this will be old news."

"Abe was quiet on the ride home," Joy said. "I think something must have happened between him and Ernie over at the Barlow house. A lot of us wanted to go to the fence during lunch break and watch them work, but we were given strict instruction to say clear. Mr. Hornblower stood watch to make sure everyone obeyed." Joy giggled, "I heard that during first grade's morning recess Zeke was seen hanging on the fence, yelling across the street at Ernie and Abe. I think that's what prompted the principal to take up watch."

Sarah shook her head. "I can't say I'm surprised. I'm sure at supper tonight Zeke will have a story to tell." Sarah got to her feet. "Abe's got a big knot on his head, hope it wasn't caused in a fight with Ernie. Ben wants him to rest, but I'm going to ask if he feels up to telling me how that happened."

"I heard Doc say that he was going to cover Abe's chores," Joy said as she accepted a refill of make-believe tea. "Since coming here, I've gotten the impression that Abe doesn't like anyone but himself looking in on the chickens of a night."

"You're right about that. I think his head must be hurting him," Sarah responded.

Sarah pulled her rocker over next to the daybed. Before sitting she brushed a lock of hair, off Abe's forehead. His eyes popped open. "Do you feel like talking, Son?" she asked.

"Sure, Ma. It feels good to lay here, but I ain't sleepin'."

Sarah got comfortable in her chair and started gently rocking. "I want to hear about how it went, working with Ernie today."

"I appreciate that, Ma. I was just a thinkin' I might feel better if I talked to you about it. Do you want me to start at the beginin'?" Abe asked.

"Yes," was Sarah's reply, "I want to hear it all."

"Well, first off, Marshal Carter picked me up at Ben's office and took me to the Widow Barlow's house. We was gettin' tools and such unloaded when Jasper Brown pulled up to deliver Ernie."

"How'd that go, was Mr. Brown cordial?" Sarah asked.

"I don't think Jasper Brown knows much about bein' cordial. Ma, this next is the part I wanted to talk to you about," Abe's voice grew soft and raspy, his eyes filled with tears, "Ernie's Pa treated him real bad."

"Treated him bad, how?" Sarah asked, her voice relaying her concern.

"He yelled at Ernie, called him names, whacked him in the head with his hat."

"Did you see him do that?" Sarah asked.

"Yes, he did it right in front of me and the Marshal."

"Oh my, that must have been embarrassing for Ernie."

"I know it was embarrasin' for me to see it. Why would someone's Pa treat them so mean? I think his ma's mean to him too."

"What makes you think Ernie's mother is mean to him?"

"'Cause alls she packed for his lunch was two pieces of bread with a dab of apple butter spread between. That was it. If it hadn't been for Mrs. Barlow giving us cookies he'd probably starved to death."

"I recon that's why Ernie wouldn't give me one of his cookies," Zeke interjected, coming over and sitting on the floor next to Sarah. "I wouldn't have asked him for one if I'd knowed he was starvin'."

Abe tried to sit up, but Sarah motioned for him to lay back down. "Ma," he said, "do you reckon Ernie gets his meanness from his parents?"

Before Sarah could respond Hathaway tugged on her dress sleeve. "Ma, I think your Afragran is thirsty." The three-year-old was holding a potted plant that had droopy leaves.

"Oh, Hathaway, thank you. I did forget to water it today. Leave it with me and I'll make sure it gets a drink."

Hathaway motioned for Sarah to lean over. The small girl gave her mother a kiss on the cheek. "It ok, Ma. You do better tomorrow."

Sarah held the plant out, so Abe and Zeke could see it. "African violets are very delicate plants. They need water and sunlight every day. They do best if I keep their soil cleared of dead leaves. They even like to be talked to."

"Gee, Ma, that's a lot of work, are you sure it's worth it?" Zeke asked.

"Zeke, they do need a lot of daily nurturing. But, if I give them what they need, they will grow strong and healthy and then produce blooms. If they don't get nurtured, they will begin to wither. If they go neglected for a long time they will dry up and be very sad looking.

"Zeke, you questioned whether this plant is worth the work it takes to care for it. When you care for another living thing it most often gives something back. The pleasure this African violet gives me, the way its blooms brightens our kitchen and blesses this house, makes all the work worth doing. Really, I don't even see it as work. I take care of it the way I do because–I love this plant."

Zeke giggled, "Ma, you can't love a flower, that's silly."

"It might be silly to you Zeke, but it isn't to me," Sarah said with a smile. "People are like this African violet. If you neglect them, don't show them love, don't give them what they need daily, their spirit will shrivel up and die."

Zeke placed his hand to the side of his mouth, leaned in and whispered, "Shriveled up like Joy looked when she first come here? Is that gonna happen to Ernie too?"

Sarah patted Zeke on his head, "I'm sure that the Browns aren't neglectful of Ernie to the degree that Joy's father was to her. Ernie likely got hungry today with only one thin sandwich to eat. He wasn't *truly* starving to death. Joy was. But, you're right, Joy was sad when she came to us and right now, Ernie's sad too."

"What about people who don't even have a family to look out for them, to love them," Abe asked, "does their spirit shrivel up and die too?"

"Not always, and it *never* has to come to that," Sarah responded. "Discovering the love God has for each one of us and accepting the forgiveness by grace that He freely gives, can mend a dried up and dying spirit."

"Grace?" Zeke questioned, "ain't that what we say before we eat?"

"Zeke, in this instance, grace means forgiving and loving someone even if it seems they don't deserve it."

"Well, Ernie Brown's about as mean as a person can get," Zeke proffered, throwing his arms out wide for emphasis. "I don't see me no way anyone would be givin' him some of that kind of grace."

"Well, deserve it or not, God offers that kind of grace to anyone willing to accept it. I'll pray for God to make a way for Ernie to come to know that good news for himself.

"In the meantime, when Ernie acts out, remember he might do it because he's in emotional pain. Maybe his parents don't know how to show him the love he needs, especially when he makes mistakes. That's called unconditional love. Without it, Ernie likely feels that if he messes up, he isn't loved. God's grace, is like unconditional love, it's there no matter how bad we bungle our lives."

"Ma," Abe said, "that's just plain sad to hear that Ernie's parents might not know how to love him that way. I never considered that Ernie might act out mean because he's hurtin' inside."

"Is Ernie the cause of that knot on your head?" Sarah asked.

"Yes," Abe replied, "he was tossin' chunks of broke bricks onto a pile. One of them hit me in the head. Ernie said it was an accident, that the piece ricocheted and came flyin' my way. I don't know, I didn't see it comin'."

"Did the two of you get into it over the incident?" Sarah asked.

"It made me mad, I ain't gonna deny that. We was faced off when the Marshal pulled up with his team and wagon. That cooled me down in a hurry. Truth is, Ernie was tryin' to get me to back off by tellin' me it was an accident. It probably was. I guess I've become used to thinkin' the worst of Ernie. It was at the end of the day and we didn't part on friendly terms. Tomorrow, I'll give him the benefit of doubt. I'll tell him I can accept that it was an accident."

"Abe," Sarah said squeezing the boy's hand, "in doing that, you'll be showing Ernie grace."

Abe's face flushed, he attempted to deflect the personal attention. "I doubt he'll be gettin' a supper tonight that smells as good as the one you got cooked up for us."

"Boy howdy," Zeke chimed in. That smell has got my stomach to growlin'"

"Speaking of supper," Sarah said rising out of her rocker, "I'd best be getting ours on the table."

Abe was still holding his mother's hand. He squeezed tight, "Thank you for lovin' me, Ma, even when I do stupid things."

Sarah leaned down and kissed her oldest son's forehead. "That's grace, you'll always have it from me."

Chapter 24

Ben glanced at the kitchen clock. "Nine o'clock," he said as he stretched and yawned. Extending a hand to Sarah, he asked, "Are you ready to turn in?"

Sarah rose from her rocker and took Ben's hand. "Not yet. I'd like to enjoy the peace and quiet a bit longer."

"Peace and quiet in this house *are* things to savor, I'll grant you that," Ben responded with a smile.

"It's such a clear night," Sarah said. "Let's go outside and gaze at the stars."

"Gaze at the stars?"

"Yes, as in tilt our heads and look at the sky."

"I'll go," Ben said with a wily grin, "but gazing at stars isn't foremost on my mind."

"Perhaps if you hold my hand and gaze at a starlit sky with me, something other than the constellations might be foremost on *my* mind."

Ben was quick to grab their jackets. "Get your jacket on, woman, let's get ta lookin' at them there stars."

Ben's country vernacular had Sarah giggling as they stepped from the warmth of the kitchen into the chill of the night. The maple tree, just outside the door, formed a massive canopy of branches and leaves. It not only covered the stoop area, it stretched out over the woodshed as well. Droplets of moisture sprinkled down on their heads. Sarah squealed and broke into a sprint, pulling Ben along with her. They ran the distance it took to get out from under the dew laden foliage to the open sky.

For a time, they stood with faces lifted heavenward. Ben was behind Sarah with his arms around her holding her in close. "I spy the big dipper," Sarah whispered as she pointed.

Ben whispered back, "And, just to the left of its handle is the little dipper."

"Big and little dippers, my favorite constellations," Sarah said.

"Well, actually my dear," Ben said, "the big dipper is an asterism consisting of seven stars. It's the Ursa Major constellation, the one referred to as the big bear."

"Doctor Benjamin Adams, sometimes the vastness of your knowledge astounds me," Sarah said as she let her head rest on Doc's chest.

"Thank you, Dear. Let's turn in on that high note. I'd like to end the day without you seeing me pull something stupid."

Later, in the afterglow, Ben took Sarah's hand and kissed it. "I'm going to sleep well tonight."

"I hope I do too," Sarah replied. "Are you sure it's okay for Abe to do hard labor tomorrow?"

"Yes," Ben assured, "I watched him throughout the evening. He didn't exhibit any confusion, slurred speech, vision or balance problems. His complaint of an aching head is centered at the wound site. I expect it's an aching along with the soreness. That's to be expected, he took a hard knock. I was comfortable with letting him go to sleep come bedtime. Unless something changes overnight, he can."

"Okay, you're the doctor."

Ben squeezed Sarah's hand, "Are you up to talking about Elmo's love life?"

"Eeeeeks," Sarah squealed, jerking her hand away and using it to fan herself.

Ben was chuckling when he spoke. "Sarah, you squealed like a girl being chased by a boy holding a worm. I've never known you to be squeamish."

Sarah gave Ben's arm a punch. "There, Mister, laugh at that," she retorted. Now giggling herself she continued, "When you said love life, an image of Elmo kissing Penelope Peterson with his tobacco stained teeth and beard popped into my mind."

"I've no doubt that would give a woman pause," was Ben's dry response. "Elmo's coming to the office tomorrow to discuss this situation with me. I'm going to suggest he try substituting peppermint sticks for the tobacco while he works to get shed of the chewing habit. I've got a box of candy canes leftover from last Christmas. I've been using them for the occasional handout. I can donate them to the cause. Chewing licorice would be more satisfying but defeat the clean teeth effort."

"Don't forget tooth brush and tooth cleaning powder," she interjected.

"I've got both waiting for him alongside the peppermint.

"What I meant by love life was, I'd like to continue our talk about teaching Elmo some etiquette and giving him an opportunity to practice his social graces. You'd mentioned having him out for a meal and possibly eating with him in the hotel's dining room."

"I can do both of those," Sarah said, locking arms with Ben and snuggling in close. "Let's invite him here for dinner this coming Sunday, then on Tuesday, next week, if I can get Josephine to watch the three little ones for about an hour, I could come to town then have lunch with you and Elmo at the hotel. That's assuming those plans fit with his schedule."

"That sounds like a good plan," Ben said. "I've made a clandestine arrangement for Elmo to meet late Monday afternoon with Samuel Parker to get fitted for a suit."

"Let's get him to the barber this next week too. If he's clean shaven with hair trimmed when he first puts on his three-piece suit and looks in the mirror, perhaps he can get a vision of himself as a changed man. It should give him some confidence," Sarah said, turning her back to Ben and snuggling under the covers.

Ben patted Sarah's backside, "It might just do that. Goodnight."

"Goodnight, Dear."

***

Abe was stiff and sore when he woke on Tuesday morning. The Barlow project had him using muscles that had lain dormant since September when they'd felled trees and split logs for firewood. At breakfast he didn't complain. He wasn't going to give anyone the satisfaction of telling him what he already knew, that he'd just have to grin and bear it. The goose egg on the back of his head was a topic of discussion. Sarah looked at it, fussed over it a bit.

Doc examined Abe, noted the lump was considerably smaller, albeit still quite tender. He patted Abe on the back, "You're good to go, Son."

Abe flinched. Doc noticed and smiled tenderly at the boy. "Abe, I called you son out of affection, I didn't mean to take liberties."

"No offense taken, Ben. It's just that except for Ma, ain't no one in this house called me that for a long time, guess I was caught off guard. I don't think I can ever call you Pa. There'll only ever be one of him. But you can call me son if you want."

"Thank you, Abe," Ben said.

"Ben," Abe had a catch in his voice when he spoke, "I am proud to tell folks that you're my stepfather."

The extra scrutiny over Abe's health caused him and Doc to leave the farm later than planned. It was a few minutes after eight o'clock when Doc dropped the boy off at the Widow Barlow's house.

Jeb had picked Ernie up at his farm and the pair were already onsite when Abe arrived. "Good morning," Abe called out as he jumped down from Ben's rig. "Sorry I'm a bit late."

"No worry," Jeb responded. "How's the head?"

"Better," Abe replied. "Ernie, how's the mare? Did she deliver?"

"She's fine," Ernie curtly responded.

"Boys," Jeb said, "get yourselves organized, try to get the sidewalk bed cleared and leveled today. Wednesday you'll pour sand, level the bed again, and hopefully start layin' new brick. If all goes well, on Friday you'll be fillin' the grooves with sand. Then tamp the bricks down real good and I'll declare the job done. If not, you'll have to come back here on Saturday. Come Monday you need to be back in school. Any questions?"

"No, Sir," was their synchronized reply.

"Keep a distance between you today," Jeb called out after boarding his wagon. "I don't want any more accidents."

"Yes, Sir," both returned.

Abe and Ernie had been working about an hour and a half, making good progress when Ernie stopped and stretched his muscles. Abe mimicked him. "Ernie," Abe said, "was it your Appaloosa mare that foaled?"

"Yeah. It was her first, but she seemed to know what to do."

"What did she have, filly or colt?" Abe asked.

"We got us another filly," Ernie said, a note of pride in his voice. "She's a pretty little thing. Head and front quarters is solid chestnut. Her rump's full spotted."

Abe looked off into the distance. "You know, your Appaloosa is the only one I've seen in this neck of the woods." After appearing to contemplate further he mused, "And, I ain't *never* seen me an Appaloosa filly."

The pair's attention was drawn back to their work when the school bell rang signaling morning recess. Children came pouring out, spreading across the playground in a flow as smooth as molasses on a stack of hotcakes.

Zeke, risking getting caught, went to the fence, climbed up and yelled, "Hey, you two, how's it goin' over there?"

"We're doin' fine," Abe yelled back to his brother.

Zeke cupped his hands at his mouth and shouted, "Ernie, I got a question for ya." He continued with deliberate intonation, "Does_your_Ma_grow_African_violets?"

Ernie stopped, put his hands on his hips. "African violets?" He yelled back. "She had some once, but they withered and died."

Zeke gave an arm pump and yelled back. "That's jest what I had me figured!"

Ernie watched as Zeke abandoned the fence and joined the other children. "Why on earth would Zeke ask me if my ma has African violets?"

Abe didn't make eye contact when he responded. "Oh, my ma was tellin' us last night about how the plant needs lots of care."

"Gee, Whitcome," Ernie said, "are you takin' up girlie stuff like tendin' houseplants?"

Instead of answering the dig, Abe said, "Ernie, I wanted to tell you that I decided to accept your explanation that the chunk of brick hit my head by accident."

Ernie's face was flush with emotion when he responded, "It *was* an accident. Glad you can see that."

The morning passed quickly. Both boys seemed surprised when the noon whistle blew. They again sat with their backs resting against Mrs. Barlow's fence. Ernie's tote held the same measly lunch his ma had sent the day before. Abe's lunch basket was bigger. So large Abe looked embarrassed when he took out the contents. Sarah had sent two thick meat sandwiches, a side of potato salad, a slab of apple pie and a big container of sweet tea and two tin cups. That was just the first layer. The second was covered with a tea towel and a note that read, *For Ernie from Mrs. Adams.*

Abe handed the basket to Ernie, "The rest in here is for you."

"For me?" Ernie questioned, taking the basket and reading the note. He lifted the tea towel to find the same generous meal Sarah had packed for Abe. "Did you tell your Ma to do this?" Ernie said with a scowl. "I ain't no charity case."

Abe held up his hands, palms out. "I might have mentioned that all you had to eat yesterday was one sandwich, but I didn't say nothin' more.

Ernie, I didn't even know she packed food for ya. My Ma is always givin' food and stuff to people. She's just like that. It don't mean nothin' more than her sayin' 'Howdy'."

Ernie continued to give Abe the squint eye as he sucked in and snorted out short puffs of air.

"Look," Abe said, "eat it or leave it. It don't make me no never mind. Abe looked up at the midday's full sun. "But, if you don't eat it, it'll go bad by quittin' time."

Ernie picked up one of the hefty sandwiches. "I guess it'd be a sin if a feller was to waste good food." He took a big bite.

For a time, the boys sat quietly eating. Abe was ready for his pie. He picked up the slab, then laid it back down. "Ernie, when we were in third grade, at the school out on America Road, you and me was friends. But after the night you slept over at my house you turned mean and I took to stayin' clear of ya. Over the years your meanness turned to hate. Why did you start hatin' me so much?"

Ernie was on his last bite of potato salad. The fork he'd been using made a loud clink when he tossed it with force into the now empty glass jar. "I started hatin' you, Whitcome, 'cause I saw you had everthin' and I didn't have nothin'. You still do, and I still don't."

Abe's response was measured, "I don't know what you mean. We're farmers just like you."

Ernie's shoulders slumped. "We're both farmers but we ain't nothin' alike."

"No, come to think on it," Abe said defensively, "we ain't. You still got your pa, mine's dead. You don't have to share with no one, and I got me a pack of brothers and sisters that figure in when it comes to split ups. Oh, and a cousin to boot. If a feller thought on it, he might feel he's the one that's come up short."

"You know, Whitcome, for as smart as you think you are, you're really dumb," Ernie said with a sigh.

"Are you sayin' I put on airs?"

"Nah, it ain't that. It's, it's…well take that day when we was fightin'. That runt brother of yours jumped on me and started poundin' even though I'm four times Zeke's size. Everyone was cheerin' you on. All I got was jeers.

After the fight, I saw Doc put his hands on your shoulders and look at your face. He weren't just lookin' at your cuts, he was lookin' at *you*."

"Well…ain't nothin' wrong with havin' friends," Abe responded. "Zeke and Doc, they's family. We care about one another."

"Now do you see the difference?" Ernie said with a tone of exasperation. "You got people that care about you. I ain't felt anything even akin to that since my grandpa died. My pa is always mad, and my ma never smiles. I can't do nothin' to please 'em.

"When I slept over at your house that night, I saw what you had. You all was a laughin' and talkin'. Ya took turns settin' on your pa's knee. Your ma's face looked like she was smilin' even when she weren't. She was givin' out hugs right and left, for no reason at all. I saw it that night, Whitcome. You had everthin', everthin' that really counts. You had it a plenty and I had none.

"Your pa had a stroke and lost his mind. He hurt your ma and was put in that mental hospital, then he died. All that and I thought, now Abe will know what it's like to live with sadness. It didn't seem that ever happened. Your ma just kept on smilin'. For years and years, I held hope that one day I'd get just a little of what you had. I don't no more. You saw how my ma acted out at the jail. I know you saw my pa givin' me heck when he dropped me off yesterday. I ain't never had your family's kind of carin' and I ain't never gonna have it."

The boys held a prolonged stare. Abe swiped his shirt sleeve across his eyes before he spoke. "I'm sorry, Ernie. You're right, when a feller has family that loves him and a ma that always smiles, he's got pert near the best there is to have."

"I ain't never been good at book learnin'," Ernie said.

"But you're good at other stuff," Abe interjected gesturing around the work site.

Ernie shook his head. "That's just common work know-how. Book learnin' is somethin' special.

"When I discovered I was good at fightin', I felt that was somethin' special, at least I had me that. I thought I could bring you down a peg by beatin' you in a fight. When you knocked me flat and I looked the fool in front of your cousin and everyone, I lost reason. I'd one time mulled over what it'd be like to pull my knife, but I hadn't planned on using it. I didn't even know I could get as mad as I did the other day. I'm sorry your cousin got cut and I'm glad that the Marshal and Doc held me down, so I couldn't do more. I wanted to best you in a fist fight, but I didn't want to cause you or no one real harm."

"Ernie, I'm sorry for dumpin' you as a friend years back. We should have talked things out then. Like you said, I've got a plenty of what really counts. My ma would box my ears if she thought I weren't willin' to share it." Abe reached a hand out to Ernie.

Ernie didn't respond. After a time, Abe let his hand fall to his side. He didn't pick up his pie, he'd lost his appetite.

After several minutes of both boys staring ahead, Ernie tossing twigs and dirt clumps, he stretched out his hand to Abe. "I'm willin'."

Abe cautiously accepted Ernie's hand, "Deal," he said pumping once.

"Deal," Ernie repeated back.

The boys picked up their slabs of apple pie and ate with abandon. Eventually Ernie spoke. "Since you ain't never seen an Appaloosa filly, come Saturday you could ride over and see ours, if you want."

Abe couldn't hold back, he smiled so big that nearly every tooth in his mouth showed. "Boy howdy! I'll take you up on the offer. Could I bring my brothers with me, all but the baby one? I'll catch heck if I get to see it and they don't."

"Yeah."

"Ernie," Abe timidly spoke, "what about Joy. Could she come too?"

Ernie swiped his mouth with his shirt sleeve then picked up a clod of dirt and aimed it at the pile of broken bricks. "If she wants to come, I reckon that'd be okay," he said as he tossed the clump, watched it hit the target and break apart.

Chapter 25

It was Wednesday evening when Josh pronounced, "Amen," ending his weekly turn at saying grace. As if synchronized, he shoveled a mound of mashed potatoes onto his plate and passed the bowl to Zeke with his left hand while ladling gravy on the creamy white mound with his right hand. Luke snagged a chicken breast and off handed the platter to Joy. Ben spooned green beans onto Hathaway's plate, then his and sent the side dish to make the round. Zeke's hands now free, grabbed a biscuit and stuck it in his mouth. Instead of passing the bread basket he used both of his hands and started lobbing the golden fluffs to his table companions.

"Zeke Whitcome, where in heaven's name are your table manners?" Sarah scolded, her tone incredulous.

"Ma, I'm jest tryin' to save some time, I've got me things to tell."

"That's no excuse, Zeke," Sarah told him. "Don't do that again. It's rude and besides, folks don't want you fingering their food."

"This might be a good time for us to tell you that we're going to have a guest for this coming Sunday's dinner," Ben announced.

Sarah looked at her husband. "I take it that Elmo accepted our invitation."

"Yes, he was pleased that we invited him, "Ben replied. "Family, Elmo Jones is coming for Sunday dinner and we're going to help him improve his table manners by showing him how it's done."

"Children," Sarah interjected. "This is important to Elmo for personal reasons. He's a good friend to this family and I hope you'll all take this opportunity to help him out."

"Ma," Zeke said with a look of concern on his face. "You ain't gonna make us drink our milk out of tea cups with our pinkies pointin' to the sky are ya?"

"No, Dear," but, I do expect to see napkins being used and to hear plenty of please and thank you being spoken. Now, what were you so anxious to tell us?"

Zeke scooted back in his chair, his spine ram-rod straight. "I wanted to tell ya that it's official, I done found out today."

"What's official?" Sarah questioned.

"Ernie's ma done kilt all of her African violets, she ain't got a one a livin'."

Sarah's eyes grew large as she struggled to hold back a chuckle. "Oh, my goodness," was all she could manage. Zeke took his mother's comment as praise for his detective work and dug into his supper, a look of satisfaction on his face.

"Dead African violets?" Ben questioned, eyebrows raised.

Sarah responded, "Later, Dear," as she exchanged a sly smile with her husband.

"Abe," Ben interjected, "why don't you tell the family your exciting news?"

All turned to Abe whose face sported a broad smile. "The Brown's Appaloosa had a little filly yesterday and Ernie said we could come see it on Saturday. That is if he and I get the Widow's sidewalk finished on Friday."

"Boy howdy," Luke, Josh, and Zeke yelled in unison. Hathaway echoed a single "howdy" and the twins banged their spoons on their wooden high chair trays.

"Well, praise the Lord, Abe," Sarah said clapping her hands. "I take it that you and Ernie made some progress toward mending fences between the two of you."

"Ya, Ma, we did." Abe responded. "I told him I accepted his explanation that my hit on the head was an accident. He said he appreciated that and then invited us to come see the filly."

"What about Joy?" Luke asked. "Is she invited too?" The family all looked at Joy who had her head hung low.

Abe reached around Josh to pat Joy on the back. "He said he was sorry that Joy got hurt, that he hadn't intended for that to happen. He said that she should come, if she wants to."

Joy lifted her head. "I've never seen an Appaloosa filly. I think I'd like to go."

"Me not see one, I want to go," Hathaway said.

"I don't know about that Hathaway," Sarah responded. "You have to be very careful around horses, especially one that's a new momma."

"I hold Joy's hand, promise, Ma." The three-year-old responded.

Joy looked at Sarah then Ben. "I'll take responsibility for her, see that she doesn't get hurt, if you'll let her go."

"Yeah, Ma," Abe chimed in. "We boys will help look after her. Please let her go."

"It isn't that I don't trust all of you to look out for Hathaway," Sarah explained, "it's that she's too young to appreciate the danger and she can be quick to bolt off on her own when she gets excited."

"What if we put her on a leash, like we do Lancy sometimes?" Zeke suggested.

"Sarah," Ben said, "that's not a bad idea. A rope could be tied, one end around Hathaway's waist, the other around Abe's or Joy's. Make the tether short enough that she can't get in harm's way when they're near the horses."

"Hathaway," Sarah said, "would you be willing to wear the rope when you're near the horses?"

The small girl nodded her head several times, an anxious look on her face. "Then, yes," Sarah said. "You may go too."

Hathaway jumped out of her seat and ran to Joy who lifted the girl up on her lap and wrapped her in a hug. Sarah's eyes weren't the only ones that were watery when she said, "Who wants apple pie?"

Chapter 26

Friday afternoon the bell on the door to Ben's office tinkled. He left his desk to see who had come in. Standing, hat in hand, just inside the door was Cleavold Anubis. "Cleavold, hello," Doc greeted. "It's good to see you out and about. Nice weather today isn't it?"

"It's a beautiful day," Cleavold said. "When I passed Mrs. Barlow's house this morning, I saw Abe and Ernie Brown working hard. It looks as if they're about finished with the widow's sidewalk repairs.

"Yes, they've been at it since Monday," Ben responded. "We anticipated it would be a five-day job, so they're right on schedule. Cleavold, what brings you here, how are you feeling?"

"I'm fair-to-middling, constitution wise. Thank you again for all you and your wife did to nurse me. That's the sickest I've ever been."

"Well, you were one of sickest *I've* ever treated," Doc responded.

Cleavold shook his head. "You know, Doc, I could feel myself edging closer and closer to the other side. If you hadn't sat by my bed and spoon fed me, I've no doubt I'd be dead."

"Caring for the sick is my calling," Doc said. "I'm pleased to see that you're doing much better. I thought you were going to go back to work."

"I did, but I left early to come here," Cleavold said, his head hung low.

"That's good to hear," Doc responded. "What is it you wanted to see me about today?"

"It's late, near your closing time I expect. I don't want to make you late for your supper. I was hoping I could make an appointment to come back and talk to you."

"You're here now," Doc said putting an arm around Cleavold's shoulders, "come into my office. I'll get us a cup of coffee and we can talk."

"Thank you, Doc, I'd appreciate that," Cleavold said as he took a seat, the toe of his shoe just barely touching the floor.

In short order Ben was back with a tray holding two cups of coffee, a sugar bowl, cream pitcher, and a plate, sporting two sticky buns. "Enjoy," Ben said pointing to the confections. "Our hired hand, Gerald, who you know lives here in my old quarters, has a friend who's a baker. Some days

I find something special like these two beauties left on the kitchen table for me."

Ben stayed quiet while Cleavold sipped his coffee and nibbled on the pastry. "Doc," Cleavold said, "When I was sick, and you were at my house, I told you I'd heard a woman praying for me and you told me that it was Sarah."

"Yes," Ben said. "I did tell you that."

"When I asked you why she prayed for me after I'd treated her so poorly, you said that she told you she was able to see me through the eyes of Jesus. She said that when she did, she saw me as a life He cherished."

"That's right."

"My cousin, the one you doctored at the same time as me, he and I have maintained a family connection over the years. We care enough about one another to keep in touch now and again. But, other than that, I've never had anyone express a caring for me. The thought that Jesus, God's son, saw me as a cherished life when I was near death…well, I can't stop thinking about that."

"Cleavold, I'm glad you came to talk," Doc said. "Jesus saw you as a cherished life before you were sick, during your illness, does now, and will continue, here on out, to see you that way."

"That's a lot to take in," Cleavold said, "I heard a man praying at my bedside too. Was that you, or did I dream it?"

"It was me," Doc softly said.

"Why? I know you held me in contempt because I propositioned Sarah when she asked for that crop loan after her husband died and before you two married. Men don't forget it when someone does something untoward to a person they love. Feeling that way, how could you pray for me?"

"Sarah helped me realize that my holding a grudge against you was creating a wedge between me and my relationship with God. She reminded me that as a Christian, God expects me to show love and grace to everyone, not just to those I like. That grudge was holding a place in my heart that God wanted to occupy. As I prayed, I felt my resentment toward you peel away. I entered your house that day with the notion that my praying for you was unthinkable. I left feeling blessed by the act."

Cleavold's eyes were at the brink of spilling, "You and your missus have a faith that I just don't understand. I'm grateful for your kindness but the concept of grace eludes me. I know who I am and what I've done. I can't accept the notion that God or Jesus gives a tinker's damn about me. I've crossed that line into what I'm sure They consider depravity. And, I've done it more than once. I don't see any way of making restitution."

Ben set his coffee cup down and leaned in toward Cleavold. "That's the beauty of it Cleavold. God doesn't require us to make restitution before we come to Him. We couldn't on our own, even if we tried. God bestows on us unmerited favor. We can't earn God's love, we already have it. That's grace.

"What He wants is for us to surrender to Him our will, our drive to live according to our own desires. He wants to fill us with His spirit so that we become like minded with Him.

"Your proclivities that led you to what you referred to as depravity, will be gone if you let Him in. They'll be gone because they aren't compatible with God's desire for you. You literally become a new being."

"What if those, uh, proclivities, pop into my head again. What if I can't stay on the straight and narrow."

"You don't have to. God stays with us through all the twists and turns we make in life. No one walks the straight and narrow as you put it. We all have our unique path in life to travel. Along the way, when we're tempted, God provides us with a way to overcome that temptation, a means of escape in the moment so we don't surrender to it."

Ben picked up his Bible that he kept on his desk. "I want to share a scripture with you, John 15:1-10." Ben had read the passage so often his Bible fell open to the page. "These are Jesus' words," he said. They explain how and why we should have a relationship with our Heavenly Father." Ben read and Cleavold listened.

"I've never heard that before," Cleavold said. "Truth be told, I've heard very little Bible reading or preaching in my life time. That scripture you just read, it sounded like Jesus was emphasizing the word abide. He kept repeating it. Abide in me as I abide in you. The branch cannot bear fruit unless it abides in the vine. If we cut ourselves off from the vine we wither and die."

"Yes, yes, Cleavold, you've captured the essence of this scripture," Ben said smiling broadly.

"Would you read that first part again to me?" Cleavold asked.

"Certainly," Ben replied. "*I am the true vine, and my Father is the vine grower. He removes every branch in me that bears no fruit. Every branch that bears fruit he prunes to make it bear more fruit.*"

"So, is that removing branches, referencing taking away our sin?" Cleavold asked.

"Yes," Ben said. "God takes away all of the garbage that keeps us from growing in His love, bearing fruit. Along that winding path we walk we sometimes gather a bit of dust and dirt. Garbage if you will. If we continue to abide in Him, stay connected to the vine, He will keep that debris pruned away, so we are clean and clear to produce fruit. Fruit meaning good deeds, doing whatever it is that God leads us to do. If we let our lives get cluttered with worldly thoughts, our view of the Heavenly Father leading us gets obstructed and we veer off into the brambles."

"I'm sick of wallowing in the brambles, of living the way I have. When I stared death in the face, my life to this point played out in my mind. I was ashamed of what I saw. I made a vow that if I didn't die, I'd change my wicked ways? I know I'm going to need help."

"Cleavold, help is available just for the asking."

"Doc, can you tell me how to ask? What do I have to do to get connected to, the vine, to God?"

"All you have to do is open your heart's door to Jesus and say, welcome, come on in."

Doc prayed with Cleavold and Cleavold opened his heart to let God abide in him. The short man had come to Doc's office that day with his feet dragging and his head hung low. He left standing tall, head held high, his countenance aglow. He was a man changed by accepting love through grace.

"Good afternoon, Cleavold," Elmo said when he encountered the banker coming off Doc Adam's porch.

"Good afternoon," was Cleavold's perfunctory replay.

"Cleavold, it's me, Elmo Jones."

"Elmo, I didn't recognize you. You're all spiffed up. You look like a new man."

"You do too, Cleavold. You must be over the rotgut poisonin' and feelin' better."

"Yes, Elmo, I feel worlds better. I can honestly say that I feel better than I ever have. I feel healed, inside and out."

Chapter 27

When Jeb Carter approached the Barlow house, he saw a collection of tools laying on the berm behind the widow's large maple tree. Abe and Ernie were standing, backs to the white picket fence, arms folded across their chests. Jeb reined in his team, jumped down and called out, "Did you get 'er done?"

"Yes, Sir," the boys replied in unison.

Jeb took off his hat and ran his fingers through his hair. After putting it back on he stood with his hands on his hips surveying the length of sidewalk that had been the target of the weeklong repair project. "Looks pretty good to the eye," he commented, "let's see how it feels to the feet." Jeb walked the newly bricked section. "Bricks are equally spaced and tamped down firm. Feels level to the walk. I don't see nothin' that might catch the toe of a shoe or boot."

Jeb walked a circle around the huge tree inspecting the ground where the offending roots had been removed. "Dirt's packed down firm. What's this?" he said squatting down for a closer look. "Grass seed! You boys planted grass where the earth's been turned?"

"Yes, Sir, Ernie said. "Abe brought it from his farm."

"It weren't nothin'," Abe said, his face flushing, "didn't take but a couple of handfuls to seed it right good. 'Sides, it weren't my idea, it was Ernie's."

Ernie interjected, "More than likely it won't take root this late in the fall. If not, come spring, I'll seed it again."

"Marshal, oh, Marshal Carter," Mrs. Barlow called out as she stepped off her porch and hobbled across her yard toward the trio.

"Evenin', Ma'am," Jeb called back, "watch your step now, your yard has got a lot of dips and mounds."

"Yes," the widow responded taking a gulp of air when she reached the picket fence, "and, these arthritic hips of mine," she paused for another gulp, "feel every one of them. Whew," she said as she rested an arm on a fence post. "I was rushing because I was afraid, you'd all get away before I got you properly thanked."

She lifted some totes she was holding. "I've baked the three of you, cookies to take home. It's my way of showing you how much I appreciate you fixing my sidewalk." She handed her offering, to Jeb, Ernie and Abe.

"Much obliged, Ma'am," both boys said tipping their hats to the widow, huge smiles on their faces.

Jeb followed in kind then stretched out an arm and used it to sweep the breadth of the work site. "Let's make this official," he said. "Today, Friday, October 20, 1905, I declare this project finished, thus ending the period of punishment," he swung his arm to gesture to the boys, "for these two lunkheads that I hope have learnt how to be civil to one another."

Ernie and Abe were standing tall as they basked in the recognition of a job well done. "Marshal, I can go ya one better than that," Ernie said. "Abe, and me, we've decided to try bein' friends again."

Abe extended a hand to Ernie, "Yes, Sir," he said as his reunited friend clasped it. "Ernie's invited me and mine to come over to his place tomorrow and see his new Appaloosa filly."

The smile on Jeb Carter's face spoke volumes.

Everyone's attention was drawn to the rig that pulled up and stopped. "Howdy," Doc Adams called out. "Abe, you ready to go home?"

"Yes, Sir," I'm ready 'cept for puttin' the tools away."

"If you've time," Mrs. Barlow called out, "come on over here and look at my new sidewalk."

"I'd like nothing better," Doc replied jumping down from his buggy. Ben examined the area much like the Marshal had. "This looks really good. You two should be proud. Mrs. Barlow, no more worrying about you tripping on those roots or broken bricks."

"Dr. Adams," the widow said, "I know you were the one that suggested my work project to the Marshal, thank you."

"It was my pleasure," Doc said tipping his hat. "Ernie, do you need a ride home? Abe and I can drop you off on our way out to the farm."

Jeb interjected, "If you don't mind, I'd like to take Ernie home. I've got somethin' I'd like to discuss with him."

Abe slapped Ernie on the back. "See you in the mornin', about ten o'clock okay with you?"

"Ten o'clock is good. See you then," Ernie replied.

Night began its full descent as Jeb and Ernie made the trek from LaFontaine to the Brown's farm. The pair made a black silhouette against the sky awash with hues of orange and red fueled by the afterglow of the sun that had slipped below the horizon. The musky smell of hard-labor sweat emitted from Ernie. He sniffed at his armpit then rubbed his nose. "I generally take my bath on Saturday night. I smell pretty rank, think I'll do it tonight instead."

Taking notice of the bath reference, Jeb drawled, "So, you've invited friends to come tomorrow mornin' and see your new filly. Is it just the Whitcome children or others too?"

"Well," Ernie responded, "Abe asked could they bring their cousin. I said I reckoned that'd be okay. And when Joy's out and about, Breanna Johnson is generally stuck close to her skirt tail. Likely she'll show up too."

"Have you seen Joy since the fight?" Jeb asked.

"No, I ain't. I told Abe to tell her I was sorry she got cut. I'm thinkin' I ought to tell her my own self. But it'll be hard to do."

"I've no doubt it will be, Ernie," Jeb said in a nurturing tone. "Thing is, apologizin' to her will go a long way towards you and her both puttin' the incident behind you."

Ernie held his head in his hands. "I'm for anythin' that'll help with that. My stomach hurts somethin' awful when I think about goin' back to school come Monday. Makin' things right with Abe helped a lot, apologizin' to Joy will help some more. But, as to them others in my class, the ones that's got opinions and big mouths, I don't know. It'll be terrible hard to hold my temper if they come at me about the fight. I don't want to get in trouble or hurt anyone. I'm scared I won't be able calm myself enough to walk away."

"That's what I wanted to talk to you about," Jeb said. "I've got a proposition for you. Now just hear me out before you respond. Can you do that?"

Ernie sat up straight and looked at Jeb, "I'll try my best."

"I know you've struggled with book learnin' and that you're fed up with tryin'. You're sixteen and of a legal age to quit school if you've a mind to do that."

"My folks won't hear of it, they'll" …

"I know they won't like it, but let me finish," Jeb said placing a hand on the boy's arm. "I've got a brother that has a farm over at the edge of Lincolnville. His son is gettin' married at the end of this month and leavin' to farm on his own. LeRoy, that's my brother's name, he needs some help a runnin' things. He's got a slew of pigs, cows and goats to milk. They'll need tendin' along with winter season repairs that need doin'. Come spring, he's got near forty acre to plant and manage.

"I've bragged about you to LeRoy, told him you'se a hard worker, good with tools, clever at fixin' things. If you've got an interest, I could get you a job workin' for him. Room and board comes with the offer. They'll put you up in my nephew's old room. Frances, that's my brother's wife, can cook as well as the best of 'em. So, you won't go wantin' for good vittles.

"Before you answer, listen to this. Frances retired last spring after teachin' for many years. I've told her about your learnin' struggles. She's of a mind that a feller that's good at figurin' things out, ain't stupid. She told me that she's taught some that's had trouble catchin' on to readin', writin' and such. She said she's got a few tricks up her sleeves that work real good and she'd be willin' to help you of an evenin'. She'll work with you, get you up to speed. She said she could even arrange for you to sit for a graduation exam when you're ready. You work hard and maybe you can get a high school diploma without havin' to go back to classes. You know, they's more than one way to skin a cat. What do you think?"

Ernie's eyes were as big as saucers and his face was flushed. "Ifin' I didn't have to worry about lookin' the fool in front of others, weren't constantly bein' told how stupid I am, I think I might could catch on to learnin'." Ernie shook his head, "Pa and Ma ain't gonna go for it. There ain't a chance they'll let me get away from the farm."

"If you want to go work for LeRoy, see if Frances can help you finish your schoolin'," Jeb said, "then that's just what you need to do. You tell me yes, and I'll work out gettin' your folks' blessin'."

"I don't see how," Ernie replied his head hung low.

Jeb sounded determined when he responded, "They know how close you come to gettin' jail time for pullin' your knife, cuttin' that girl. You leave it up to me. I'll convince them that for you to stay clear of trouble, you need space between you and LaFontaine folks for a spell. Before long, the locals will move on to somethin' or someone else to yammer about. But, right now, you're the fodder for their gossip."

"When would I go there?" Ernie asked.

"LeRoy, Frances and me was thinkin' that first of November would be good. Work at their farm will be scaled back due to winter. That'll give you more time to work with Frances on your learnin'. Lincolnville ain't so far from here. You could come back at Christmas if you wanted, or for short visits when you get homesick."

"They ain't no chance I'll get homesick. I've been miserable at school and even more miserable at home. If they's any chance to get away from them that's harpin' and yappin' at me, I'll take it."

Jeb made the turn up the Brown's lane. "You sleep on it, boy. I'll come out tomorrow mornin'. I'd like to see your new filly, and you can let me know if you've still got your mind set on takin' the job. If you do, I'll use the opportunity to talk to your parents about it. Ain't but a couple of weeks left in October. No need for you to go back to school here, if you're movin' on come November. I'll suggest that your Pa take advantage of your help for the rest of this month. Get things shored up here on the farm so he can manage without your help."

"That's a good idea, Marshal," Ernie said in an eager tone. "I'll come up with a list of repairs and winter needs that I can get done between now and when I leave. Ifin' Pa sees all I plan to get done in the next couple of weeks, it might help make him more agreeable. But, Marshal, I want the job and I ain't gonna change my mind. If push comes to shove, I'll leave without Ma and Pa's blessin'. You can go ahead and tell your brother that I'm a comin' first of November."

Jeb pulled up to the house and reined the team to a stop. "I hear ya, Son. Just the same, I'll hold off callin' LeRoy until after I've talked with your folks tomorrow."

Ernie turned to Jeb. "Thanks for all you're a doin' for me. I really appreciate you tellin' your kin that I'm good at figurin' things out so's they don't think I'm dumb."

Ernie placed his hand on his midsection. "Here, in my entrails, I know I can catch on to learnin'. It'd mean the world to me ifin' I could get me a diploma."

"We'll make 'er happenin' boy, we'll make 'er happenin'," the Marshal said. "Hop on down, my supper's waitin' and my stomach's a growlin'."

Ernie jumped down, started for the house, then turned back. "Marshal," he called out. "Can I have my knife back?"

"Yes," Jeb said. "But, I'm gonna hold on to it until you leave town."

Chapter 28

"We need to get a move on family," Sarah called out as she removed a hat pin from her black felt, Sunday best bonnet. The bejeweled pin was a cherished gift from her deceased husband Henry. With hat in hand she securely wove the treasure through the band. "Pastor Sloan's sermon went long this morning," Sarah lamented as she brushed dust from the hat's crown and began dispensing orders.

"Abe and Josh, please put two additional leaves in the table. Luke and Zeke work together to cover the table with the white linen cloth draped over the back of the rocking chair. Wash your hands first. I don't want it soiled.

"Joy, I'd appreciate it if you'd take charge of setting the table," Sarah said.

Joy was sitting on a chair letting the twins and Hathaway take turns playing ride the horse. "Sure, I can do that. Little Miss Hathaway, would you help me? You can be in charge of the spoons." Hathaway responded by jumping up and down while she clapped her hands.

"Ben," Sarah said, "please set out the good china for Joy, enough for twelve. It might be difficult for her to reach. It's on the top shelf of the china cabinet."

"Got it," Ben said. "Do I put out your crystal tumblers?"

Sarah took a moment to ponder the question before answering. "No, using them might be risky. The everyday glassware will be fine. No coffee cups needed for Josh, Luke, Zeke and Hathaway." Sarah put a lid on the pot of potatoes she had placed on the stove to boil and walked over to Ben. "Sorry if I sounded bossy. I know we'll be eating with friends that are used to our family chaos, but with the added emphasis of helping Elmo with his table manners and general social decorum, I want things to be just right."

Ben leaned down and kissed Sarah's forehead. "You didn't sound bossy, but just so you know, it would be okay if you had. Knowing all that you accomplish is still a wonder to me."

Sarah went back to her cooking. Zeke, with freshly washed hands walked to Ben. "Pa, I heard Ma tell you to set up for twelve. That ain't the right count. They's ten in our family. Add Elmo and you're up to eleven."

"Don't count the twins," Sarah called out, "they won't be eating off my good china."

"Oh, of course," Zeke said. "Eleven take away two leaves nine. The count's nine Pa."

"Zeke," Ben said, "we've three other guests coming; Jeb, Judith and Julib Carter. Add three to your count of nine and you'll get what?"

"Twelve," Zeke responded with a smile. "The counts at twelve, Pa."

"Yes," Sarah called out, "twelve. Isn't the count of twelve what I said originally?"

Ben smiled and responded in a placating tone, "Yes, Dear." He patted Zeke on the back. "You're really good at arithmetic. I'm impressed with how quickly you did the cyphering."

Zeke stood tall, his chest puffed out. His stance belied the bluster in his voice. "I would've had me the answer right off if I'd knowed the particulars." The six-year-old's countenance took on a worried look, "Gee, Ma," he called toward the kitchen, "have you figured on how much food Jeb and Julib might eat? We'se already got Elmo to share with. Them men is all big eaters. I've seen 'em go at it at church dinners. What if we run short on food? If you is expectin' me to show good manners, I'm gonna need to have me enough to eat. A feller can't hardly be polite if his belly is a growlin'."

Sarah didn't answer. "Your Ma's busy, Zeke," Ben said. "Don't you worry. She always cooks plenty of food. Today won't be any different. But if the table starts to look like slim pickin's I'll share some of my helpings with you."

Joy and Hathaway, hand in hand, approached Sarah. "Would it be all right," Joy asked, "if Hathaway and I made a centerpiece for the table?"

Sarah smiled. "Yes, a touch of fall color is just what we need to make our table festive."

Sarah called out, "Thanks for all of your help getting ready for our guests. The food is ready, and the table looks splendid. Girls, the yellow and orange maple leaves and milkweed pods are the crowning glory."

Hathaway stood with her nose pressed against the window pane. Henry and Naomi, both barefooted, stood tiptoe on either side of their sister. Not tall enough to see out the window, the twins were instead gnawing on the windowsill. Their gums were swollen from the impending arrival of new teeth.

"Hey, everbody," Hathaway excitedly yelled. "I gots two fhings to tell ya." She held up her pointer and middle fingers on her right hand. "The letterman's horse and buggy just come up the lane, but he ain't drivin' it. That's fhing one." The small girl folded down her pointer finger then turned her hand, palm side in, leaving her middle digit jutted upward. "Fhing two is, 'Omi and Henry is eatin' the wood off the window."

Abe and Joy bolted to the rescue, each scooping up a baby. Abe glanced out the window. "Ma, Hathaway's right. It's Elmo's rig, but it ain't Elmo that's comin' up to the door. Do you reckon somethin's happened to him and this man's come to fetch Doc?"

Sarah dried her hands on her apron. She and Ben went to the door together. Ben opened it on their visitor's first knock. "Come in, come in." Ben eagerly invited.

Sarah smiled, curtseyed and teasingly said, "Welcome to our home, kind sir."

The clean-shaven man entered and doffed his hat revealing a full head of hair that was neatly cut with a razor-sharp part down the middle. He smiled showing pearly whites with a missing, right-side lateral incisor. "Thank you kindly for invitin' me."

Recognizing the man's voice, Zeke blurted, "It's Elmo Jones. He has lips. I ain't never seen his lips afore."

With a bow and a right-handed sweep of his hat Elmo said, "Elmo Jones, United States of America mail-carrier and gentleman extraordinaire, at your service."

A speechless Josh and Luke stepped forward and shook hands with Elmo. Abe, holding Henry, offered his hand and said, "Elmo, you clean up real good. You look twenty years younger." Joy, carrying Naomi, moved closer, smiled and nodded. Both babies hid their heads as they often did when meeting a stranger. Hathaway attempted to mimic her mother's curtsey, got her feet tangled and fell on her bottom. Looking up from the pine board floor the three-year-old said, "Hello, Mr. Mo. You look purdy."

Shortly thereafter the Carters arrived. Greetings were exchanged and expressions of awe over Elmo's transformation were given. Jeb Carter quipped, "Elmo, you look good enough to get buried."

Judith Carter said, "Elmo, I was expecting to see you here but didn't recognize you." She raised her hand but stopped short of touching his smooth-shaven cheek. "No tobacco bulge," Judith cut her eyes to her husband. "I'm guessing there's more to this story than simply having one of Sarah's Sunday dinners. Whatever the occasion, you look mighty handsome today, Elmo." Absent the facial hair, Elmo's blush was evident.

Sarah announced seating assignments at the round table. "Joy, you take your regular seat," Sarah pointed, "Julib, please take the one next to Joy. Jeb and Ben, you're here," she gestured. Judith, you're next to Jeb and beside Hathaway." Sarah took hold of the back of the chair next to hers. Elmo, you're here, between Hathaway and me." Zeke, Josh, Luke and Abe take your usual seats. Sarah swept her arms out over the table in a welcoming gesture. "There are no guarantees out here on the farm, but fingers crossed," she demonstrated, "that should place all of you guests out of the line of fire should the twins start a food fight."

Jeb chuckled, "Does that happen often?"

"Yes," Sarah responded, "more than we'd like to admit. Naomi eats faster than Henry. If she calls for a second helping and we aren't quick enough to serve her, she steals Henry's food. Henry gets mad, retaliates and…we'll, let's just say, it isn't pretty."

Zeke was sitting next to Henry. He leaned in and patted the baby's arm. "A food fight wouldn't be good manners," he whispered. "Don't worry, I'll keep an extry biscuit handy. If Naomi goes for your food, I'll toss it to her." The baby boy grasped a handful of Zeke's red hair and giggled. Zeke pulled it free and gave the dimpled hand a kiss.

Ben prayed the blessing. At his pronouncement of Amen, Elmo cut a look at Sarah. Sarah picked up her napkin and began to unfold it. Elmo snatched his, unfolded it and before tucking it in his shirt collar gave the linen an air fluff hard enough to make a cracking sound. Sarah gave him a slight, under the table, kick. They made eye contact and she motioned that he should put the napkin on his lap.

With the table top full, Sarah had placed the breadbasket atop her plate. She took a biscuit then passed them to her left. Ben, the children, and guests served themselves from side dishes setting in front of them and then passed them on to their left. A large platter of ham, bowls of mashed potatoes, gravy, squash, collard greens-wilted with red-eye gravy, butter, and corn relish made the rounds. The compote of raspberry jam was in front of Elmo. He served himself but didn't pass it on.

"Elmo, please pass the raspberry jam," Zeke said. Elmo was intent on buttering and slathering jam on his biscuit and didn't respond. Sarah and the others were engaged in conversation and didn't hear. Zeke's second and third request again went ignored. Fearing that his biscuit would go cold before he got to eat it with jam, Zeke raised his voice and in a near shout, requested a fourth time. "Elmo Jones. Pleezzee paasse the dad-burned raspberry jam!"

Elmo picked up the compote and handed it to Sarah who passed it to Zeke. "Zeke," Elmo said in an incensed tone, "I cleaned my ears out real good. You don't have to yell." He looked to Sarah, "That ain't polite manners is it, Sarah?"

"No, it isn't," Sarah replied, giving Zeke a scowl.

Zeke held his hands out palms up and arched his shoulders. "Ma, I had my reasons."

Sarah had seated Julib, so he'd be between Ben and Joy. She was aware that Joy had caught Julib's eye. She was beautiful, sweet and intelligent. What young man wouldn't notice her. What Sarah was watching was to see if Joy had noticed Julib.

Joy has matured without the guidance of her mother. I may need to have a talk with her, make sure she knows how to handle a man's romantic advances. Sarah turned to look at Abe. *I'm pleased to see that Abe is taking Julib's attention to Joy in stride. When Joy first arrived, I could tell the boy was smitten. Over the past several weeks he seems to have eased into a familial relationship with her. She needs a brother big enough to look out for her and Abe can benefit from an older sister.* Sarah glanced at Joy and the reality of her feelings for the girl hit her bringing her eyes near to tears. *Lord, help me, I've come to see her as one of my own.* Sarah was brought out of her reverie when she heard Ernie Brown's name being mentioned.

Jeb was talking. "…so, I told the boy I could get him a job workin' for my brother, helpin' him handle his livestock and farmin'. He was keen to accept the idea of movin' away."

"Did you say Ernie Brown is moving?" Sarah asked.

"Ernie's quittin' school, Ma," Abe interjected. "He's leavin' town at the end of the month. He told me yesterday."

"I know the Lord has a plan for Ernie," Sarah said. "I've been praying that it would be revealed soon. Have his parents agreed to this?"

"They was powerful against it, at first," Jeb said. "The thing was, Ernie told me he was takin' the job and leavin' whether they liked it or not. I didn't want a family break, so I kept at 'em. It took me some wranglin', but Jasper eventually gave his consent."

"What about his education?" Sarah asked. "I'd so hoped he'd be able to graduate high school."

"Well, that's the beauty of this plan, Sarah," Jeb said. "My brother's wife has retired from teachin'. She's gonna work with Ernie, continue his learnin'. She thinks she can help the boy, might even get him learnt up enough to set for the graduation exam. He might could get a diploma without havin' to be in a classroom."

While Jeb continued with talk of Ernie's future, Julib started a side conversation with Joy. "Pa said he saw you and the Whitcomes over at the Brown's place yesterday. Did you go to see their Appaloosa filly?"

"Yes, we did," Joy responded. "She was beautiful."

"Do you like horses?" Julib asked.

"Yes, although I don't have much experience with them." Joy shared.

"Do you ride?" Julib asked.

"No, but I'd like to learn," Joy's eyes sparkled. "I'd really like to learn."

"We've got a mare that's real gentle. I could teach you to ride," Julib offered.

"I'd like that," Joy said, lifting her eyes to contact Julib's. A warm blush spread over her face. "I'd have to ask permission," she said, nodding toward Ben.

Julib's face grew red and he swallowed hard before he spoke. "We'll ask him together."

With their aside conversation at a lull, Joy and Julib turned their attention to Jeb's continued story about Ernie Brown. "…so, I say, Jasper, your boy's gonna end up in the calaboose, sure as shootin' if you don't let him get some space between him and this town." Jeb took a bite of ham and let his fork dangle. "Ernestine raised a ruckus," Jeb shook his head. "Woo-ee, did she make a ruckus. It made her act-out in my office week before last look like it'd been a tea party." Jeb hunkered down over his plate and began loading his fork again, "Jasper saw the right of what was bein' offered to Ernie and told Ernestine to hush. She stopped breathin', turned purple. I thought I was gonna have to whack her on the back. She finally took in a draw, but kept her trap shut."

"Jeb Carter," Judith said, elbowing him in the rib.

"What!" was the Marshal's startled reply.

"Kept her trap shut? Think on it, Jeb. If it doesn't come to you," Judith said, "later I'll make sure you get my point."

Jeb hunched his shoulders and raised his eyebrows but continued. "Jasper said if they was anyway Ernie might finish his schoolin', he'd make the sacrifice of farmin' without the boy's help."

"I'm heartened to hear that, Jeb," Ben said. "Push comes to shove, even a rascal like Jasper Brown can show a father's love.

"That makes me think of the heartfelt sermon the Pastor gave this morning," Ben said as he took another helping of mashed potatoes.

Out of the corner of his eye, Zeke saw Naomi pop her last morsel of food into her mouth. Just as she started to reach for a piece of Henry's meat, Zeke lobbed a biscuit her way. It landed neatly on Naomi's high chair tray. The baby girl picked it up, examined it and took a bite. With a look of triumph, Zeke made a fist pump.

"Yes, I agree, Ben," Judith Carter interjected. "You could have knocked me over with a feather when Cleavold Anubis responded to the altar call." Judith made eye contact with Sarah and arched her brows. "I never thought I'd see the day-him with his ways and all, don't you know."

Sarah caught the nuance the arched brows brought to Judith's statement. *I'm guessing I haven't been the only woman in town to fall victim to Cleavold's advances."*

"Ben, Cleavold gave you credit for his decision to surrender to the Lord," Jeb said.

Ben's face colored. "It was my honor to share the story of God's love and grace with him. To God be the glory for the decision Cleavold made."

Sarah, knowing that Ben felt uncomfortable with the attention stood and announced. "We've peach pie for dessert. Joy, would you please help me clear the table."

Aside from spearing a hunk of meat with his fork, holding it mid-air and biting off a piece, Elmo had maneuvered the main course in good form. However, when Joy started clearing the table and she reached for

Elmo's plate, he grabbed it up and slurped the broth that lingered. When he handed it to Joy, he saw the grimace on her face. "I weren't supposed to do that was I?" He said.

Joy whispered in response, "I don't think so."

When Sarah served Elmo his piece of pie she whispered. "You're doing fine, Elmo. During dessert, try to initiate a topic of conversation. It'll give you practice in social discourse."

Elmo took a bite of pie and chewed it thoroughly before swallowing. Oblivious to the conversations taking place between others, he wiped his mouth on his napkin, raised his voice above the din and said, "I've got me half a dozen hogs that's a needin' castrated." Conversations halted mid-sentence. "I was wonderin' if any of you men would have time to come help me do that?" Mis-interpreting the look on Joy's face, Elmo's brow furrowed. "No offense intended Miss Joy," he said. "Ifin' you're good at castratin' I'd be right proud to have your help too. You'll want to wear some work clothes. I'm sure you've heard the expression, 'bleedin' like a stuck pig'. Ya don't want to be wearin' your Sunday best."

Sarah was stunned speechless. As she looked at her quirky little friend a thought that fit him came to her mind. *You can't make a silk purse out of a sow's ear.*

Chapter 29

"Ma'am," the man wheeling a dolly said, "this crate was just delivered at the back dock. Mr. Parker said to bring it directly to you."

Penelope Peterson was on her knees in Parker's Dry Goods double window storefront, right side, arranging an array of hats. "Oh, good, that might be my delivery from Fort Wayne."

She stopped her work, stood, then hopped down and checked the label on the crate. "Roseberg's Millinery, yes, I was hoping this would arrive today, thank you."

The stock handler pulled a short crowbar from his back pocket. "Do you want it opened now?"

"Yes, please," she said as she ran her finger down the bill-of-lading's itemization of contents. "It's a delivery of some much-needed ribbon, notions and the like."

"Miss Penelope, let me know when you've got it unloaded and I'll come and take the crate out of your way."

"I will," she said gesturing around the immediate area. "It's close quarters here in the haberdashery corner. I'm going to finish setting up this window display, then I'll get busy unpacking and putting away these new supplies."

A figure passed the store's window and caught Penelope's attention. She craned her neck to catch a glimpse of the man's back. "Do you know that man who just walked past?"

"No ma'am, it weren't anyone I've ever seen before. Curious, ain't it. He was carrying what looked like a mail pouch. Wonder if somethin' happened to Elmo Jones. Elmo's been deliverin' the mail here and around LaFontaine for," the man counted with his ten fingers, glanced down at his feet, then up at Penelope, "well, I can't cypher the exact number, but I been workin' here at Parker's for more than ten year and all that time it's been Elmo bringin' in the daily mail."

"Oh, it isn't important. It's just that he's walked by here several times today and I didn't recognize him. He was smoking a pipe. My father smoked one, I always thought it was a pleasant aroma. Maybe that's what caught my attention."

"Well, it weren't straggle-faced, tobacco chewin', Elmo Jones, I can tell you that for sure."

Elmo was later than usual delivering Monday mail to the town marshal's office. He'd amended his normally efficient foot delivery route, so he could repeatedly walk past Parker's Store. He was catching glimpses of Penelope Peterson behind the haberdashery counter. With each passing he tried to focus on a different aspect of his heartthrob's person.

"Lordy, Lordy, Lordy, that woman's easy on the eyes," Elmo mumbled as he entered the next door jail-house.

Jeb Carter took his feet off his desk and sat up in his chair. "What woman's easy on the eyes?" he asked accepting the proffered mail and sorting it.

"Miss Penelope Peterson, that's who," Elmo snapped. "I've been tryin' to fix her in my mind's eye. I need me her image to remind me that givin' up my chew is worth the torment I'm goin' through." Elmo opened the door to the potbellied stove and tapped his pipe, dislodging the burnt tobacco.

"No need to snap at me, Elmo," Jeb said. "Don't that pipe help your cravin'?"

"Maybe a titch, but it ain't hardly worth the bother," Elmo said as he filled the pipe's bowl with fresh blend. "It's kinda like takin' a parin' knife to a sword fight. It ain't cuttin' the muster."

"Stop sufferin', ask Miss Peterson if you can take her to the hotel for dinner this Saturday night." Jeb said. "If she don't take you up on the offer, you can go back to your Mail Pouch and get shed of your misery."

"You got a point, Jeb. You saw me in action, so to speak, when we ate Sunday dinner out at Sarah and Doc's yesterday. Sarah wants me to meet her and Doc at the hotel for noon meal tomorrow. She thinks I need more practice with my table manners. I think I got 'em nailed down. What do you think?"

"You used your fork and knife proper," Jeb said while rubbing his chin and staring off in the distance. "Got your napkin situated-after some help. When you put sweetener in your coffee you returned the spoon to the sugar bowl real polite like. You did stir your coffee with your knife. Seemed okay to me, but I saw my Judith cut you one of them 'looks'. I will say Elmo, you bringin' up castratin' hogs weren't the best table topic for mixed company."

Elmo, oblivious to Jeb's feedback, walked to Reinhold Hatchery's wall calendar. "This here's Monday," he said placing his finger on the date. "I'm a thinkin' that I get me past Wednesday," Elmo held out his hand and watched it tremble. "See if I'm shed of this shakin'. Doc said it should go away once my body gets used to takin' in less *nicrophen*."

"It's nicotine, not *nicrophen* and why is gettin' past Wednesday important?" Jeb said as he tacked a wanted poster to the wall and scanned the caption under the sketch of a middle-aged man with dark hair and a mustache. *Edward J. Humes, wanted in Wabash for skipping out on paying hotel fees and gambling debt.*

"'Cause, Sarah told me a lady needs at least three days advance to an invitation to supper. I guess they need the extry time to get beautified."

"I've no doubt that's right," Jeb drawled.

"I'll follow Sarah's advice more practice can't hurt. But, if Miss Penelope makes herself any more fetchin', I'll be worrin' about more than the fear of shakin' and clangin' my fork on my plate whilst eatin' with her." Elmo situated his mail bag on his shoulder and headed for the door.

"I think I'll close up early and get myself on home to Judith," Jeb said. "I ought to be thankin' the Lord I don't have to worry about goin' courtin'."

When Jeb put his key in the lock a niggling thought that he'd missed something caused him to take a glance through the door's glass. His eyes landed on the newly hung wanted poster. *Edward J. Humes, where have I heard that name*...the bell rang.

Jeb looked across the street and down a few buildings to Doc Adam's office. He could see that Ben's rig was gone. *Doc must have left for the day. I'll leave him a note to come see me first thing in the mornin'. Need to alert him that Joy's father might be in the area. That son of a gun ain't gonna get to that girl on my watch. 'Forgive me, Lord, but I find myself wishin' he'd try.'*

Elmo made one last pass by Parker's Dry Goods. He wasn't prepared to see Penelope Peterson, on her knees in the display window, the edge of her petticoat showing. He dropped the bag of mail, spilled the contents, and for a few moments, stared, frozen in place.

Penelope looked up, saw him and wiggled her fingers in a wave. Elmo came to, stuffed the strewn mail into the pouch and took off running. His hat blew off, but he didn't stop until he reached the safety of his rig and his beloved Clementine.

Penelope Peterson came out to the sidewalk. She watched Elmo's back until he was out of view. Bending down she picked up his hat and brushed it off. With a smile on her face she went back inside taking it with her.

Chapter 30

Sarah stood at the kitchen window watching as the children walked down the lane to wait for the school hack. She pursed her lips and blew on the hot coffee in her cup. *Hate to see them walking in the dark.*

The kitchen's Regulator clock struck a quarter till eight. *It's gonna be like this for the next six months. A* glint of light caught her attention. She looked toward the east and saw the sun edging above the horizon. A smile over took her face. Her focus stayed on the orange orb as it slowly inched skyward. "Always a blessing, praise be," she whispered.

From behind, arms wrapped around Sarah and pulled her close. "What was that you whispered?" Ben asked as he nuzzled her neck.

"Praise," was her prayerful response.

Together they stood, watching and waiting. There was a slight catch in Sarah's breath when the fence row that framed the farm became visible, silhouetted against a sky now aglow with brilliant hues of orange and yellow. The darkness was pushed away, the day had come.

Ben understood Sarah's reaction. "It is a wonder to behold. I feel compelled to give thanks for another day to live and love the woman I'm holding in my arms," he said.

A baby's cry invaded their reverence. "It sounds like Henry," Ben said as he stepped away from Sarah. "I'll go…it's not like him to wake up crying. I expect his gums are hurting."

"I'm sure you're right," Sarah responded. "I don't remember any of the others having this much trouble with teething. Naomi seems to be tolerating it better than Henry."

"We all have different levels of pain tolerance," Ben said. "Henry's might be low, or, he may actually be having more pain than is common."

"If you're going to go get him…and, change his diaper," Sarah said with a teasing tone, I'll get a cool wet rag for him to chew on."

Sarah and Ben sat at the table discussing their plans for the day. Henry and Naomi were in their high chairs and Hathaway was at the table atop her booster crate. All three were intent on eating their breakfast. "I've made arrangements with Josephine to watch the little ones while I come in to town today to have lunch at the hotel with you and Elmo," Sarah informed

Ben. "Hopefully today's practice with manners in a public social setting will be helpful to him."

"I'll be out this morning making home visits," Ben responded. "I'll plan on meeting you at my office at noon."

"How many visits do you have?" Sarah asked. "I'd like to have you join Elmo and me, but don't let it be a burden if you're too busy."

"I'll go by the office, pick up some supplies," Ben said, then drained his coffee cup. "My first visit will be to the Jordan farm. Then I'll swing by the Gordon's, look at Rupert's stitches. Then on to the Alvarado place, drop off some medicine for Elmer's rheumatism. Then, as I come into town, my last stop will be to check on Mrs. Barlow – see if that salve, I gave her is working on her poison ivy."

"My goodness, Ben, that's a busy morning for you. Sometimes I don't know how you keep up," Sarah said.

"Yes, I work hard all day while you get to stay home and live the life of leisure," Ben teased as he gestured around the kitchen to the pile of dirty breakfast dishes, two chattering babies and a precocious three-year-old, all with faces and hands sticky with strawberry jam. "If I'm not at the office when you get into town, go on to the hotel and meet Elmo. I'll come directly to the restaurant to join you."

Sarah fetched a damp towel and began cleaning the children's mouths and hands. "You're a good man, Ben Adams. Not many would take time out of their busy day to eat lunch at the hotel with a forty-five-year-old man, for no other reason than to help him work on his social skills."

"I'm happy to do it. Elmo really stepped up to his challenge to get cleaned up in support of romantic pursuits. Truth be told, he's moved far beyond what I thought he was capable of. His desire to court Penelope Peterson must be powerful. I hope he isn't setting himself up for a big let-down." Ben reached out and took Sarah's hand in his. "Sarah, do you think he has even a ghost of a chance to get her to say yes?"

Sarah leaned down and kissed Ben full on the mouth. "Even an old shoe gets to have a mate. So, yes, I do think there's a chance she might say yes."

Sarah pulled the rig up in front of Ben's office. *I don't see Ben's horse and buggy.* Before getting down to tether the team she flipped open her watch that was pinned to her dress. *Quarter to noon. I'll go on in and wait a bit...tidy up my hair, brush the dust off my skirt. It's not often I get to eat lunch at the hotel.*

Sarah placed her hand on the office door's knob, it wouldn't turn. *Feels like it's locked. Curious, I didn't think Ben locked up, except at the end of the day.*

Sarah retrieved the key Ben kept hidden under a nearby rock. She wondered why he bothered to hide it. Its location was common knowledge to town folk. More than once, after he'd locked up for the day and was called out on an emergency, he'd sent someone to the office to fetch medicine or other supplies.

Sarah unlocked the door and entered bringing with her rays of sunlight that spotlighted a multitude of dust mites doing their dance. *It looks like it's past time to do some dusting and sweeping in here.*

She went to the nearby hall tree. As she was looking in the mirror, primping, she heard a sound coming from the back of the house. Their farmhand, Gerald, used the bedrooms as his living quarters and shared access to the kitchen. *Sounds like someone's back there. Gerald told me he'd be repairing fences in the field near Thompson's pond today. I can't think he'd drive all the way in to town to eat lunch. He usually carries a pail to the farm of a morning.*

With doubt that it was Gerald making the noise Sarah listened more intently. *It sounds like moaning. A sick person? Came looking for Ben – didn't find him, lay down to wait? Door was locked, could be someone who knew where the key's kept.*

Sarah had to pass through the kitchen to reach the bedrooms at the back of the house. A tantalizing aroma drew her attention to a platter of cinnamon buns on the table. *Looks like Gerald's friend has delivered baked goods again.* A fleeting thought to get the man's recipe passed through her mind. *More groaning.* An intuition that she wasn't going to find an ill person filtered into her awareness. Her better judgement told her to leave. With her curiosity fueled, she couldn't halt her momentum to find out. The door to Gerald's bedroom was slightly ajar. Sarah tiptoed to it and peeked in. Gerald and his friend, the baker, were in bed together, their bodies twisted around each other. Sarah clasped her hand over her mouth to stifle a gasp.

Making a quick turnabout, she tiptoed as fast as she could to the front door and left. *I need to sit down.* Sarah crossed the street to the empty bench in front of the marshal's office.

She prided herself on never getting flustered. She didn't want to admit to it now. *I'm not flustered, I'm flummoxed, not that there's a hair's difference. Get ahold of yourself. It's not like you don't know that type of persuasion exists.* She checked her watch. *Nearly noon. Got to get over to the hotel restaurant. Elmo will be waiting, don't want to add to his nervousness.*

Sarah headed for the hotel restaurant just as the town's whistle blew one long blast signaling noon. A familiar voice called her name. She looked, saw Ben, but didn't stop. "Sarah, wait," Ben called out as he used long strides to close the distance between them.

Ben took Sarah's arm in the crook of his. She didn't acknowledge his presence. "Sorry I'm late," he said a bit out of breath. "I was surprised to see you sitting on Jeb's bench. Have you been waiting long?" Sarah didn't respond.

"Hey," Ben sucked in air, "You're not mad at me, are you? I told you this morning to not wait on me, to go on to the restaurant if I was late."

Sarah's intent wasn't to be rude to Ben. She was in a state of oblivion to his presence; her mind was absorbed in prayer. *Lord, Lord, I could have lived my whole life without seeing something like that. But I can't think about it right now. Dear Lord, clear my mind. I want to talk about this, but later this evening…after supper…after the children are in bed. It might be best to wait until I'm in bed and the lamp's turned down. No, no, let's not talk while I'm in bed. Outside, yes, outside would be better….*

Ben jerked on Sarah's arm. "Sarah, stop! What's happened? Are you all right, has one of the children been hurt?"

Ben looked at Sarah, she appeared to be stunned. Ben took ahold of both of her arms and shook her gently. In a soft voice he said, "Sarah, please, talk to me."

Sarah's head made a visible shake. "I saw something," she blurted.

"What? Where?"

"At your office."

Ben turned, looked across the street to his office, then back at Sarah. "Do we need to go there now; does someone need help?"

"No, no, we *can't* go now." Sarah drew in a deep breath and exhaled. "Ben, I'm sorry for losing my composure. No one is hurt, it isn't an urgent matter." Sarah patted Ben's arm. "I'm sorry to have alarmed you. Let's have lunch with Elmo and then we can talk."

"Are you sure it can wait?"

"Yes, it's a private matter, it can and needs to wait."

***

Ben pulled Sarah into a spooning position. "Quite the busy day wasn't it?"

"Yes," Sarah replied. "I was so pleased with Elmo's table conversation, albeit a bit like a lecture. There wasn't much opportunity for a back and forth discussion."

"Who knew," Ben said, "that George Washington was on so many different versions of the postage stamp?"

Mimicking Elmo, Sarah replied. "Now you've got your G.W., that's what we in the business like to call him, with a right sided profile on the two-cent stamp. Came out in 1885. Turn of the century brought a left sided profile of the old boy. Still a two-cent, but in blue, not green like the first one."

Ben jumped in, "And, unbeknownst to those outside the U. S. of A. Postal System, a full-on face of G.W. is coming out soon. Still two-cents, but in red."

The pair giggled. "We should be ashamed of ourselves for mocking Elmo," Sarah said.

"You're right. I'm sure Miss Penelope will appreciate discussion of the postage stamp over castrating hogs."

The couple grew quiet. As was their habit, they'd opened their bedroom's window a few inches. They both enjoyed the smell and feel of the night air. The lace curtains swayed slightly as if in rhythm to the symphony being played by crickets, bullfrogs and other critters. Occasionally there was a hoot of an owl. It was uncertain if it was a hoot of appreciation or one of aggravation. Its monotone prevented discernment.

"So, I guess we're going to have to let Gerald go," Ben said.

"I've been pondering the situation all day," Sarah replied, "as have you, I'm sure. Gerald is a good worker and has been a big help to us. On my way home I drove the team past the field by Thompson's pond. He was working on fence posts, looked like he was nearly done with the repairs."

"He might be a good worker, but how can we sanction his lifestyle?" Ben asked.

"His lifestyle, I think that's an important thing to consider here. Ben, do you agree that for the most part, when we are an adult, we choose our lifestyle?"

"Yes, I do, with the exception of a mental or physical disability that might prevent us from doing so."

"Have you ever seen any indication that Gerald has a mental problem?"

"No, he's articulate, intelligent. He's really quite interesting to talk to."

"How about a physical problem?"

"No, of course not. He's strong as an ox, great with tools."

"Then why in heaven's name would he choose a lifestyle that, if publicly known would cost him his job, cause him to be ostracized. You, said he's good at conversation, smart. I think he's a decent-looking man. I've no doubt he could find a woman to court."

"I'm not sure I'm catching your point here, Sarah."

"My point is, why would a man choose to be with a man to fulfill a yearning for an intimate relationship, when he could easily get that from a woman."

"Are you saying that if Gerald isn't choosing his preference for men, God may have created him that way?" Ben said.

"I'm not qualified to say, I'm just trying to figure out the rationale of someone choosing a deviant lifestyle that could cost them everything," Sarah responded.

"From a medical and spiritual standpoint something popped into my mind," Ben said. "When I was in medical school, we were taught that babies being born Mongoloid just happen. There is no scientific explanation for it.

"From the pulpit we are taught that we are all uniquely created by God, born perfect in His eyes...God doesn't make a mistake, etc. Therefore, children brought into this world Mongoloid are the way God designed them.

"The possibility that God has created Gerald and his friend the way they are is something to ponder."

"Yes, it's complicated," Sarah agreed.

"A common place example is that one person may love peach pie, another thinks it tastes nasty. How is that explained?"

"Peach pie!" Sarah giggled.

"Okay," Ben chuckled, not such a good example for this subject."

"No, it wasn't," Sarah said. "But, the rest of what you said made perfect sense to me. I'm thinking, as long as Gerald upholds his side of our working bargain, his intimacy proclivities might just not be any of our business."

"Proclivities!" Ben took a turn at giggling.

Sarah playfully punched Ben's arm. "I'm saying, who put us in the lofty position of sanctioning how Gerald lives and who he loves? It isn't our place to judge. If he's living in sin, that's between him and God to sort out."

"Okay, but, Sarah, you were really upset to the point of being aghast about this when you told me earlier today. I can't believe you've made such an about face. The man's boarding at my office. This is a small town. I have a reputation to maintain. What would people think if they knew?" Ben questioned.

"I won't deny that I was thrown for a loop when I peeked in that bedroom. Yes, I was still upset about it when we talked after lunch. But, for the most part, I've had to pigeon-hole the issue. I've got too many responsibilities to allow this to take over and occupy a big spot in my mind. You either. We've got Joy to think about. What if her father does come looking for her? That concern should take priority.

"As for what others will think if they know. Well, at first, they'll be tickled pink to have something so titillating to gossip about. Next, they'll come at Gerald with two-barreled judgement," Sarah said. "Gossip and judgement are two things I know beyond all doubt, that God abhors and doesn't want us to participate in."

"What about the Scripture," Ben interjected. "The Bible is pretty clear how God stands on the subject."

"Is it?" Sarah said setting up in bed to lean against the headboard. "Ben today was the first time I've ever seen what I saw. But I knew it occurred. I've never had a need to really think about the subject until now. You know me, Ben, you know how much I revere the Gospel. I've turned to it for answers more times than I can count. I don't pretend to be a Bible scholar, but I do know which scriptures have spoken to me with such clarity that I knew they were meant for me, Sarah Adams, to hear. These are scriptures I've tried to commit to memory, and they can, in an instant, bring me into focus, remind me of God's instructions for treating others."

Ben sat up in bed and joined Sarah in leaning against the headboard. "I'd like to know which scriptures those are."

"The most powerful message given to me is found in the gospels Matthew and Mark," Sarah said. "A Pharisee, who is mentioned as an expert in religious law, asked Jesus what he considered the most important commandment in the law of Moses.

"Matthew and Mark give a near identical accounting of His response. This might not be a perfect quote, but it goes something like, 'You, must love the Lord your God with all your heart, all your soul, and all your mind.' Jesus said this was the first and greatest commandment. But, second, and equally as important, He said, 'we must love our neighbor as ourselves'.

"The thing that struck me the most is that these commandments don't come with examples of exceptions, or a requirement that we like or approve of another or their actions. It just says we must love. Plain and simple, love."

Ben took Sarah's hand in his. She continued. "The second most powerful scripture that God has revealed to me, the one that stays 'stuck' in my head and comes to me when my own nature wants to lash out, is found in 1st Corinthians 13. I find the entire chapter to be a guide for daily living. I read it again this afternoon."

Sarah reached for her Bible that she kept by her side of the bed, "I'll read some of it to you. I know you've heard it many times," she said as she thumbed to the page. "I've got to say, the first time the power of the message sank in, I was awestruck by its clarity. Verse 1, 'If I could speak all the languages of earth and of angels, but didn't love others, I would only be a noisy gong or a clanging cymbal.' Ben, who do we both know that when she speaks, it sounds like a clanging symbol?"

"Ernestine Brown!" Ben blurted. "I agree clanging symbol fists her. But, she's even worse. I put her in the category of a fingernail scraping across a blackboard." Ben shivered.

"The other verse that pierced my heart," Sarah said, "is verse 7, 'Love never gives up, never loses faith, is always hopeful, and endures through every circumstance.' One more, it's a short one she said as she turned to the passage. Written by James, who you know was Jesus' brother. Chapter 4, verse 12, 'There is only one Lawgiver and Judge, the one who can save and destroy. But you – who are you to judge your neighbor?'"

"So, Sarah," Ben said, "let me see if I'm hearing you correctly. You want us to just forget about what we've discovered, go on as if we didn't know, as if everything is all right with having Gerald work for us."

"Yes, Ben. I'd like for us to do just that. It's clear to me that the scripture is saying that we are to love, not judge Gerald. He hasn't done anything untoward to us. Us knowing doesn't have to interfere with him working for us. The scriptures about the right and wrong of men with men relationships, or women with women, for that matter, say what they say. I'm not trying to argue their intent or importance. I believe that the role of those scriptures in Gerald's life is up to God to reveal to him, not for us to use them as a tool to beat him over the head. Why make it complicated. Let's just pray for Gerald and his friend to come to know the Lord personally, as you and I do. When that happens, God will show them the way to be in spirit with Him. Nothing but that matters. God will reveal to them what He wants them to get shed of."

"Explain," Ben said.

"The pile of debris left after God's through trimming us doesn't look the same for everyone. I might get pruned from one thing, yet, you might get to keep it in place. What must go is anything that occupies a place in our life that keeps us from being one in the spirit with Him."

Ben took a deep breath and exhaled, "So, we pray for Gerald and his friend, nothing else?"

"Well, Ben, I don't know what God expects you to do or not do. Ask Him, He'll let you know. As for me, yes, I think He's telling me to just go on as usual and lift Gerald and his friend up in prayer."

"Sarah, you're a wonder, you know that," Ben gave her a kiss then snuggled down under the covers. "Besides, that friend of Gerald's makes the best cinnamon buns this side of heaven. I'd hate to think I'd never have a chance to eat them again."

"See," Sarah said as she too snuggled in for the night, "every cloud has a silver lining and who says it can't be made of cinnamon buns."

Chapter 31

Elmo's hands shook as he placed the day's mail in his delivery pouch. He looked up to see Leo Finkenbinder, the postmaster, staring at him. "Guess you've noticed that I got a case of the shakes today," Elmo said.

"Yup," Finkenbinder responded.

"Ain't you gonna ask me why I've got 'em?" Elmo replied.

"Figured you'd get around to tellin' me," The postmaster said.

"Since you ask," Elmo said as he hitched up his trousers and adjusted his suspenders, "I got me a two-fer that's causin' my nerves to act up."

After a long pause Elmo said, "Ain't you gonna ask me what them two things is?"

Leo's response was dry, "Figured you'd get around to tellin' me."

Elmo took a stance, legs spread apart, hands on his hips, "Leo, that's the second time you've said that. Are you tryin' to imply I do a lot of tellin'? 'Cause if you are, that just ain't true. I share things from time to time to be social, but I don't generally run off at the mouth. Folks around here know me, ask anyone, they'll tell you the same."

Finkenbinder arched his eyebrows.

"All right, if you're gonna insist," Elmo said, "I'll tell you what's troublin' me. First, and you may have noticed, I'm tryin' to kick my chewin' habit. Traded it out for the pipe. That switch-off has been a bumpy road to travel. Second, this bein' Wednesday and my deadline day, 'cause women need notice, I'm gonna ask Miss Penelope Peterson if I can come a courtin' her. She runs the haberdashery over at Parkers, if you didn't know."

Leo Finkenbinder gave Elmo a thumbs-up.

"Thank you kindly," Elmo said as he hitched his bag, chocked full of mail, over his shoulder. "Havin' this talk, tellin' you about my worries, you givin' me encouragement, has helped a lot." Leo's head gave a nearly imperceptible nod as Elmo made his exit.

Elmo's deliveries for the day were complete, except for Parker's Dry Goods. He'd saved it for last and was standing across the street watching Penelope adjust the arrangement of hats in the display window. *You can do this.* Elmo reached up and ran his fingers through his hair. *You lost your hat, you got a legitimate reason to go in the store. Strike up a conversation with her about hats, move the talk to food, ask her if she likes to eat, then pop the question.* Elmo patted his bag of mail, jutted his chin out and crossed the street with purpose.

"Good morning," Penelope Peterson said glancing at her lapel watch. "You're much later than common in delivering the mail today."

Elmo froze. He'd rehearsed him being the one to initiate the conversation, not Penelope. "Ye, yes, Ma'am," Elmo responded reaching up to doff a non-existent hat.

"It looks as if you're missing something," Penelope said nodding toward Elmo's head. "Would it be this?" She asked as she pulled a battered fedora from behind the counter.

"My hat, you found it," Elmo said, dismay in his tone. *Now I don't need to talk about buying a hat, what'll I say?*

"You lost it in front of the store on Monday," Penelope said. "I'd intended to give it to you when you delivered the mail yesterday, but you must have come when I was out for lunch."

Elmo stammered as he reached for his hat. "Th, thank you. Yes, you was out eatin' your lunch when I come by yesterday" After an awkward pause Elmo said, "Uh, uh, I like to eat too. I don't suppose you knew that."

Penelope smiled, "While I assumed that you ate, I wasn't aware that you had a particular affinity for the act."

Elmo was quick to respond, "Oh, it ain't no act for me, Ma'am. When I get me somethin' I like, I generally hunker down and just go to it."

"Oh, my," was Penelope's response.

Elmo fumbled the brim of his hat, diverting his look to his boots. "Miss Penelope, I'd be honored to have you come over to the hotel and do it with me."

***

Sarah was taking apple pies out of the oven when Hathaway yelled from her kitchen window vantage point, "He here, he here."

Sarah glanced at the clock and noticed it was a quarter to two. *Wonder who it is? Might be Elmo, bringing the mail to the door.* "Who is it, Dear," Sarah asked her daughter.

"It's our new purdy mailman," the 3-year-old responded.

Elmo pounded on the kitchen door, "Sarah, Sarah, let me in, I've got good news."

Sarah, who had already started her approach to the door, jerked it open. "Shush, you'll wake the twins," she said as she stepped aside to let Elmo in. "What's got you so excited, Elmo?"

"She said, 'yes'!"

"Glory be," Sarah clasping both hands over her mouth. "I'm assuming you're referring to Miss Peterson."

"The one and only. Me and her is havin' supper at the hotel this Saturday night."

Sarah gestured toward a chair at her kitchen table. "Take a seat, we girls want to hear all of the details, don't we Hathaway," Sarah said as she went to fetch two cups of coffee, a glass of milk and a saucer of cookies.

Hathaway pulled out the chair that held her booster crate, climbed up and folded her chubby hands on the table in front of her. "Mr. Mo, are you scared of somethin'? Your hands are shakin'."

Elmo held out his hands. "You're right, little 'un, I am shakin' and, I'm scared. A bite to eat and some strong coffee will do me good."

When Sarah took a seat at the table, Lancy got up from his spot by the cookstove, waddled over, stood on his hind legs and rested his paws on the table top. "Ma," Hathaway giggled, "Lancy wants to hear the news that's got Mr. Mo scared."

Sarah patted the big dog's head, then called for him to follow her to the door. "Lancy can go chase rabbits while we enjoy our refreshments and hear what Elmo has to say."

Elmo talked fast as he munched cookies and slurped coffee. "…so, like I said Miss Sarah, I owe this all to you and Doc. I can never thank you enough for helping me come this far. A year ago, I would have never imagined I'd be lookin' forward to dinner at the hotel with a beautiful woman, maybe even a future wife."

"Elmo, God answers prayer and this time He did so in an obvious way. I know you're happy, but I caution you to not get too far ahead in your thinking. Dinner at the hotel is just that. Don't go making it anything more than an opportunity to get to know Miss Peterson better. Take it slow, a woman doesn't like to feel rushed. And, you don't want to appear needy."

Elmo took a gulp of coffee. "I guess you're tryin' to tell me to let nature take its course."

"Yes, that's exactly what I'm telling you. You've caught Miss Peterson's eye, or she wouldn't have accepted your invitation to supper. Just be yourself, Elmo and let her do the same. If God intends for the two of you to develop a lasting relationship, it will happen."

A rattling could be heard coming from an adjacent room, followed by a yelling of "out, out". "Sounds like Henry is awake and shakin' the bars on his crib to get out," Hathaway said. "I'll go get him."

"No, I'll go, Dear," Sarah said. "You're growing fast but you still aren't big enough to get him safely out of his bed. Naomi's likely awake too."

Sarah patted Elmo's arm. "You'd best get on your way so I can tend to the babies and get supper started. Elmo, you're excited about this dining engagement, but, please, please don't go telling folks, not yet. Keep your good news between you, me, Ben and maybe Jeb Carter for now."

"And me, me too," Hathaway chimed in.

"Yes, and Hathaway can be in on our little secret too," Sarah said patting her daughter's hand. "The point is, Penelope Peterson might be the private sort who wouldn't appreciate hearing second and third hand that she's accepted an invitation out with the local mail carrier. If word gets out, let her be the one to tell it."

"Yes, Ma'am," Elmo said as he made his way to the door. "You've done right by me with your advice in this romance department thus far and I intend to keep on listenin' to what you've got to say. At least until I feel like I've got 'er nailed down my own self."

Sarah held out her arms and Elmo stepped in. "I'm so proud of you Elmo Jones. Godspeed, my dear friend."

From her lookout perch Hathaway watched Elmo climb up on his rig, wipe his eyes on his handkerchief, then call "giddy-up" to his horse Clementine. "Goodbye, Mr. Mo", the toddler said as she waved.

The girl's attention was diverted to four of her siblings plus one self-adopted sister arriving home from school. Elmo passed them as he went down the lane and they came up. Hathaway darted out the door and skipped the distance to meet them. "Joy, Joy, I got a secret to tell you.

Chapter 32

"Stop your yappin', Abe, and pass them taters," Zeke bellowed.

"Zeke Whitcome," Sarah scolded, "mind your table manners. There's no need to raise your voice at the table and it's rude to interrupt someone who's talking."

Zeke splayed his hands, palm side up, "Ma, I done told this family over and over again that I don't like eatin' cold mashed taters. I want 'em hot on my plate when I put gravy on top."

"Josh," Zeke called out, "stop fiddle-fartin' around and get that gravy started round, I'm gonna need it next." Seeing his mother's arched eyebrows that were her signature piece of *the look*, Zeke quickly added, "Please and thank you, Josh."

"Language," Sarah said to Zeke.

"Language? Oh, fiddle-fartin'. Ain't nothing wrong with saying fartin' everybody does it," was Zeke's retort.

Sarah held a stern gaze on her young son, averting with her last-chance finger wag when she saw a look of contrition mask his sassy countenance. Turning to Abe, Sarah said, "Son, please continue with what you were telling us."

"Like I was sayin'," Abe responded, fork held mid-air, "Marshal Carter came to school today and lectured us on pullin' Halloween pranks this Saturday night after the fall festival."

Luke interrupted, "That's just 'cause, he gets tired of cleanin' up the mess each year when the privy behind the jail gets hauled around to the street and set afire."

"That's happened the last five years in a row." With a bit of tongue-and-cheek, Ben continued, "Jeb never has figured out who was doing the mischief. Last year he threatened to call in the Pinkertons to help suss out the mystery."

"Likely it won't happen this year," Josh said.

"Why don't you think it will happen?" Joy asked.

Cutting a look at Abe, Luke said, 'cause we knowed Ernie Brown was the one a doin' it. Naw, it ain't gonna happen this year."

"Unless...," Abe drawled out, "someone decides to continue the tradition."

"Boy Howdy," Zeke said with an arm pump. "I been a wantin' to get in on one of them Halloween trickditions." He made eye contact with each of his older brothers, "What say we do 'er this year."

"Absolutely not," Sarah snapped. "I want each of you to promise that you won't get involved in any Halloween pranks."

"Don't worry, Ma," Josh said. "I'll keep my brothers in line. I guess you've had your fill of seein' a Whitcome behind bars."

Abe gave Josh the stink eye. "I promise, no pranks," he said to his mother.

"Me neither," Luke offered.

All eyes turned to Zeke who remained mute. "Zeke," Ben said, "we'd like to hear from you. Will you promise to stay out of mischief during the fall festival?"

Zeke slipped his arms under the table and crossed his fore and middle fingers on each hand. "I promise I won't pull the outhouse from behind the jail and set it afire in the middle of the street."

Sarah reached over and patted her seven-year old's head. "Thank you, Son."

"Joy," Hathaway called across the table, "will you dance wiff me at the festible?"

"I would, Hathaway," Joy responded, "but I don't know how to dance."

"I'll show you," Hathaway said jumping down from her chair. The small girl started twirling while holding out the hem of her dress which was only mid-calf length. The combination of holding out the hem and twirling exposed the child's bloomers. Sarah and Ben made eye contact and smiled. Joy, Abe, Josh and Luke giggled.

Zeke's eyes grew big. "Ma, ain't you gonna stop her from showin' her britches to the whole world? If you ask me, that's worser than burnin' an outhouse."

"Hathaway," Sarah called to her daughter. "Hop back up on your chair and finish your supper, Sweetie. After we get the kitchen cleaned up," she cut a look at Josh then Ben, "if we can talk Ben into playing his fiddle and Josh his harmonica, we could all practice our dancing."

"Sounds like a plan," Ben said. "This family hasn't sashayed around the dance floor since last fall's harvest festival. Besides, I could use a brush up on my fiddle playing."

***

Light had succumbed to dark when the dancing began. Outside the walls of the cozy farmhouse the atmosphere was filled with the smell of approaching rain. Dense, rumbling clouds gathered threatening to eclipse the moon and void the stars. The figure of a man on a black horse was silhouetted against the night's landscape as he traveled down the road that passed in front of Sarah's farm.

Supper dishes were done, the twins were down for the night and the dining table and braided rugs had been pushed aside. The family stood ready to choose up partners. "Me gets Joy," Hathaway squealed clapping her chubby hands then grabbing the one the older girl offered.

Sarah took Zeke's hand and linked it with Luke's before grasping Abe's. "Let's start paired up like this, then we can switch. The switching is an important part of social dancing and you boys should be ready to do that if you're dancing with a gal and another fellow taps you on the shoulder."

"Why would a feller tap me on the shoulder?" Zeke asked with a puzzled look.

Ben answered, "It means that the fellow doing the tapping wants you to step aside and let him dance with your partner."

"Ain't gonna h*appen!"* Zeke exclaimed. "If I get me a girl to dance with I ain't lettin' no yay-who take her away from me."

Ben looked at Sarah, "Are you sure this child is only seven-years old?"

The look Sarah returned was one of exasperation. "Let's just get this dance going," she said.

***

Edward J. Humes called "Woah" to his mount bringing it to a halt at the top of a high rise in the road. "Black as a witch's hat and looks like rain," he said to his horse as he reached in his saddlebag and pulled out a slicker.

After donning the garment, he stretched then raised up in the saddle for a clearer view of what lay before him in the distance. "Considerable glow ahead, likely LaFontaine," he said patting his horse on the side of its neck. "If this road cuts a straight line, might be a mile, two at the most to get there."

Something swooped close over Ed's head. He pulled his hat down tight. "Dang bats," he cursed as he looked at the sky. What he saw gave him a start. Although dark, he could make out a huge mass approaching, flying low. He could see that it was a flock of crows rather than bats.

"I'll be damned," he muttered. "It's not like crows to take flight after dark." He turned in his saddle, looked over his shoulder and watched as the formation made winged determination back toward the farm and the two-story house he'd just passed.

"Bats give me the willies," Ed mumbled as he hugged himself under his slicker. "Crows serve a purpose. They're good stalkers and hunters. Handy skills for man as well as *feathered beast.*"

His mind focused again on his travels, Humes pulled back the slicker and sniffed at his coat sleeve. *Smells of campfire.* His stomach growled. A week of hiding out in the woods had left him hungry and stinky. The gambler fumbled the silver dollars he carried in his inside waistcoat pocket. *Board the horse at the livery, get a room, a bath, something to eat.* Ed ran his hand across his scruffy chin, then lifted his hat and finger combed his hair. "*Tomorrow go to the barber for a shave and haircut.* Humes knew he'd need to look the part of someone well-heeled if he was going to get a seat at the high stakes game rumored to occur weekly at LaFontaine's tavern. He fisted his coins. *I'll barely have enough left for a stake, assuming, the rumor is true.* Ed scratched his chin, *I'll ask the barber, they usually know the town's where to's and what for's. It's time for my luck to improve.*

Ed had been bested in a heavy betting game in Wabash. Absent enough collateral, he'd been forced to write a short-term IOU. His plan had been to leave town looking good and stepping high. Instead he'd not only run out on the gambling debt, he'd stiffed the hotel too. Now he was on guard, wondering if the law would bother to track him down. Humes looked up at the dark sky. *Ought to get a move on, try to beat this rain.*

He turned in the saddle and looked behind, then to his right, then left. "I've never been here before, old boy," He said patting his horse, "But there's something that seems familiar about this area."

Unbeknownst to Humes the rise in the road on which he perched was a mere 100 yards from the lane leading up to Sarah's kitchen door.

Feeling inexplicably compelled to linger where he'd stopped, Ed unbuckled the strap that secured his banjo to his saddlebag.

***

Ben and Josh sounded rough when they first started playing their instruments together. However, by the time they'd reached the second chorus of *Buffalo Gal Won't You Come Out Tonight,* they'd achieved harmony.

Sarah motioned to Abe that they should switch partners. She tapped Luke on the shoulder, and he relinquished Zeke. Luke tapped Joy on the shoulder who stepped aside for him to dance with Hathaway. That left Joy and Abe to link as partners. Joy caught on quickly when Abe talked her through the two-step. Being near in height, they soon found their rhythm. Both were smiling when Ben called out for the family to join in the singing.

"As I was walking down the street,
a pretty girl I chanced to meet.
We danced by the light of the moon.
Buffalo gals won't you come out tonight, come out tonight, come out tonight."

Their collective voices, singing with abandon, rang out into the dark foreboding night. Their joyous chorus was assaulted by the cawing of a flock of crows, taking position on the bare branches of the large maple tree that stood outside of Sarah's kitchen window. The cawing was raucous enough to catch Sarah's attention. She strained to listen. When she realized that a flock of crows had again come to roost at the farm, a chill ran down her spine. *They sound taunting and angry.* Sarah mentally lifted a prayer. *Heavenly Father, please don't let Joy hear the crows. Forgive me for allowing their presence to give me a chill. I know when evil comes, You, hover near.*

Sarah put a forced smile on her face and signaled for a partner change. The result was that she became paired with Joy. While the two maneuvered in step around the floor Sarah struggled to block the scolding of the crows.

Another chill ran down her spine. *Lord,* she whispered in her head, *please send the dove.*

***

While Sarah held Joy close, dancing, Humes was pulling his banjo up on his lap. He traced his fingers over Joy's name scratched on its surface. "Times up, Girl," he said into the darkness. He began to strum a soft melody and croon his dark thoughts as he savored the hatred that consumed him.

> "I'm coming for you, Joy, to soothe my pride.
> You can run, but you can't hide.
> Seeking vengeance is my game,
> To make you sorry you scratched your name.
> Girl, soon the clock will stop tickin',
> Marking time to get your lickin'.

***

"I'm calling intermission," Josh said. "My mouth needs a rest and I need a drink of water."

Ben chimed in, "Me too."

With the music stopped and the only sound in the room being that of dancers catching their breath, the crows could be heard by everyone. "Sounds like a murder of crows has descended on the farm," Abe said.

Joy clutched Sarah's hand so tightly that their intertwined knuckles turned white. Zeke shrieked, "Murdering crows, where?"

Ben put his arm around the boy. "A murder of crows is just a term for a flock of crows."

Suddenly the cawing stopped. The abrupt change from intrusive onslaught to silence, brought an earie feeling to the room. Eyes on questioning faces darted from one to another. Abe gathered a whimpering Hathaway into his arms. Josh and Luke moved to stand one on each side of their big brother, placing their shoulders within a whisper's distances of touching his brawny biceps. Sarah released Joy's hand and drew the girl into a hug. No one spoke, no one moved.

Chapter 33

When Ben arrived at work the next morning, he found a note tacked to the door. It was from Jeb Carter asking him to stop by the office, before noon if possible. Ben knew he didn't have any early patients scheduled that morning, so he decided to go then.

"I can see you're hard at it," Ben said as he entered the Marshal's office.

Jeb quickly took his feet from atop his desk and sat up straight in his chair. "'Mornin', Ben. You caught me contemplatin', which is what's required in this business when you've got a dilemma like the one, I wanted to talk to you about.

"What's up?" Ben asked.

Jeb pointed to the wanted poster tacked on the wall behind his desk. "Recognize the name?"

Ben crossed the room for a better look at the posting then read aloud. "Edward J. Humes wanted by Wabash authorities for skipping out on gambling debt and hotel fees." Ben gave Jeb a stunned look. "Don't suppose there could be but one Ed Humes lurking in these parts."

"I reckon not," was Jeb's reply. "At least now, we've got a likeness of the fellow. Might make it easier to identify him should he come here lookin' for Joy."

Ben put a hand to his brow and shook his head. "Do you really think that's possible? Wouldn't he want to stay clear of towns if there's a wanted poster out on him?

"They's a chance he'll think Wabash law won't bother trin' to find him if he's left town. He'd be thinkin' wrong. Word has it the town has been hit with several of his kind recently. Local merchants have demanded better law enforcement. It comin' up on their November elections, the Wabash county sheriff will be watching his P's and Q's which would include bringin' in them that's stiffed the area constabularies."

"I expect you're right about that," Ben responded.

"Even if Humes tries stickin' to the woods, campin' out and such, he'd need to surface for provisions," Jeb said.

"Good thinking." Ben responded. "And, given that Joy has described him as a drinker, he'd be seeking liquor, likely sooner than later."

"I've shut down all the moonshiners in this area, unless one's operatin' that I'm not aware of. He'll not get hooch to satisfy his cravin' so, yes, he'll likely show up here or another town close by for his booze."

"Jeb, I hate this," Ben said. "I guess I'll need to tell Sarah and the older children. If he comes looking for Joy, he could pop up at the farm, the school, Lord only knows where he'd look."

"To complicate things a bit," Jeb said, "I've promised Judith I'd take her on the train to visit her sister over in Kokomo this afternoon. We spend the night then be back here in time for the fall festival tomorrow evenin'. I've deputized our jail attendant, Red Buttman to act on my behalf while I'm gone. I asked Julib to come by the office after this hack run this mornin'. Had him look at the poster, read it. He went back to our farm to tend to chores that can't wait then he'll come back to town about noon. He'll be on the lookout for the man. He plans to tether his hack at the school and keep watch throughout the afternoon until he delivers Joy back to your place after school."

"Thanks, Jeb, sounds like you've given this considerable thought," Ben said.

"Like I told you, my time with my feet propped up on my desk is my contemplatin' time," Jeb said. "I do my best figurin' in that position."

"Jeb," Ben said, "we sincerely appreciate all of your efforts. I'll make a run home at noon to alert Sarah and I'll try to get out to the farm early this evening. Hopefully the man will have sense enough to stay clear of this town, but I won't be banking on it."

Ed Humes sat up in bed and stretched. Having slept rough for the past several days he'd savored the comfort of the feather tic and warm room. He dug in his saddle bag for the single bottle of whisky he'd absconded with when he'd run from Wabash. He tilted it to his mouth but was unable to extract even a droplet from the now empty bottle. *Been nursing that for more than a week.* The parsing out, a little each day, had kept the jitters at bay, but just barely. Humes felt a shiver go down his spine and he scratched at his arms then his legs. *The creepy crawlies are starting, got to get me something to drink.*

The bell rang signaling a morning break at the LaFontaine school. Joy, Breanna and the others in the class scurried to line up at the drinking fountain. Abe came up alongside the girls.

"Hey, Joy, how you doin'?" He asked. "I knowed at breakfast you was still upset over that murder of crows that come to the farm last night. Just wonderin' if you've shed your mind of worry yet?"

"No, I haven't been able to let go of the eerie feeling they gave me," Joy said.

"They's just birds. You've nothin' to fear except bein' pelted with bird shi…, uh, I mean droppin's," Abe said.

"Oh, Abe Whitcome," Breanna said with a giggle. "You say the funniest things."

Abe blushed at the welcomed flirtatious comment. "I will say that findin' 'em still roosted in the maple tree when we left the house this mornin' did give me a touch of the creepy-crawlies. I expected to see they'd moved on come daylight. But they didn't caw at us, so, there's that to be thankful for."

"Maybe they didn't caw," Joy said, "but, I could feel them watching me. I've tried, but I just can't get free of the feeling that something bad is going to happen when crows appear."

Breanna took Joy's hand and held it in hers. "Like Abe said, they're just birds. You've got me and Abe here with you. You've nothing to fear."

"I hope you're right," Joy said with a sigh.

Sarah had just pulled the sixth pan of bread from the oven when she heard a knock at the door. Before going to answer it, she glanced at the kitchen clock. *Two o'clock. Might be Elmo with the mail.* Sure enough, Elmo Jones stood on the stoop, mail in hand. "Elmo, come in. You're running a bit late today, aren't you?"

"Yes, I'm about an hour off my regular delivery time," Elmo responded. "Sarah, I'm tryin' to keep up this clean shavin', teeth brushin' and clothes washin' and changin' you done taught me. But, by gum it, it takes me more than twicest as long to get up and out of the house in the mornin'.

"Your efforts are paying off Elmo," Sarah said. "And, doesn't it make you feel confident when you deliver the mail at Parker's Store each day looking good and smelling nice? I'm sure Miss Peterson notices the effort you're making with your appearance."

"Yes'm," Elmo responded, "My spiffin' up does make it easier for me to make conversation with her when I pop in with the mail. We've gotten comfortable with our quick howdy-dos and such. I've stopped feelin' like

I need to impress her with my knowledge of the postal system and such. We generally just exchange about the weather or what the special is on the menu at the hotel."

"Elmo," Sarah said as she got up and looked out the window and touched the ball bat she'd leaned by the door. It was the tenth time she'd done so since Ben came home and told her about the possibility of Ed Humes being in the vicinity. "It doesn't make a hair's difference to us what time of day you deliver our mail here to the farm. But I suppose it might to the merchants in town and the bank. Have you considered having your laundry done in town?"

"No, I haven't considered doing that. Thanks for the suggestion, I'll check and see what it costs. I've gotta mind my spendin' these days. I ain't never done any regular courtin' before Miss Penelope and it does take a toll on the old do-re-mi."

"You might consider inviting Miss Peterson out to your farm, fix her a home cooked meal," Sarah suggested as she paced the floor and again glanced out the window.

"You lookin' forward to company arrivin', Sarah?" Elmo asked. "You done looked out the window twicest since I been here."

"No, Elmo," Sarah responded. "Actually, it's an uninvited guest I'm watching for."

"Uh, say what?" Elmo asked.

"Never mind, Elmo, let's get back to talking about you inviting Penelope Peterson to your house for dinner."

"Sarah, would that be seemly for us to meet alone, unchaperoned?"

"Elmo, this is 1905. The two of you are adults with a few years under your belts. If your intentions are pure, Penelope won't be offended by your invitation. If she accepts, I'd say she does so without worry over impugning her reputation."

"I trust you when it comes to figurin' social proprieties, Sarah. But I've been a batchin' at my farm for more than twenty years now and I ain't never had invited guests. I'd have to clean the place up first. Wonder if Miss Penelope likes beans and fatback. That's my specialty meal."

"If she accepts an invitation to come to supper at your house, Elmo, she'll be coming to enjoy your company. What you serve to eat won't matter. But, if you do decide to invite her, let me know. I'll toss in a jar of my corn relish and an apple pie to round out your menu."

Elmo got up and headed toward the door. "I'll take you up on that offer, Sarah. When I came down the road with your mail today somethin' just told me to come on up here to the house. Whenever I deliver the mail to your door, I always leave feelin' good about somethin' you've told me. Or, given me," the mailman said as he eyed Sarah's cookie jar.

Sarah caught the hint and fetched three cookies for her quirky friend to take as he left. "Have a good rest of your day, Elmo," Sarah said. "Will we see you and Miss Peterson together at the festival tomorrow night?"

"Yes, ma'am," Elmo responded with a twinkle in his eye. "I ain't got much to impress a lady, but I do know how to dance. I'm hopin' there'll be some lively tunes so I can show Penelope my footwork."

Ed Humes admired himself in the mirror. "Lookin' pretty good," he said to his empty hotel room. He'd had a bath, gotten a shave and haircut and he'd had the change of clothing he maintained for appearances sake cleaned and pressed. The barber had verified that the saloon hosted a high stakes game on Friday nights. Participation was by invitation only. Fortified with several belts of whiskey and with plans to garner favor with his banjo playing, Humes was ready to visit the local watering hole.

Twilight was descending when Abe, Luke and Josh came up from the barn. As they neared the house, they could see Ben standing out by the chicken house. Abe jogged ahead to where he stood. "Somethin' wrong?" he asked.

"No, the chickens seem content. I was just standing out here enjoying the evening air," Ben said.

"Is that my ball bat you're a holdin'? Abe asked.

"Yes, I guess it is," Ben said looking down at his hand. "It was by the back door and I thought I'd hold it while I stood out here."

"Well if you're a wantin' to play some ball, it's gettin' too dark don't you think?" Abe asked.

Ben hefted the bat, judging its weight. "You're right, now's not the time to be outside playing ball."

Zeke stuck his head out the kitchen door. "Suuuper's reaaady," he yelled.

"Why didn't you just ring the dinner bell?" Abe said ruffling Zeke's hair as he passed him.

"I'd have to get the egg crate to stand on to reach the bell and yellin' was faster. Let's get to the table, I'm starvin'," Zeke said.

Joy's eyes were red and puffy when she took her seat at the supper table. She held a handkerchief which she used to frequently dap at the tears rolling down her cheeks.

"Don't cry, Joy," Hathaway said. "Ma, she don't have to eat liver and onions if she don't like 'em, does she."

"Dear, one," Ben said as he took his seat beside Hathaway, "Joy isn't crying over liver and onions for supper. She's gotten some news that's made her sad."

"What news?" Abe asked as he reached beside him and patted Joy on the shoulder.

"Let's say the blessing and get the food started around," Sarah said. Then Ben and I will tell you what's got us troubled."

The clock was striking midnight when Ed Humes left the saloon. The smile that spread across his face was nearly as full as the moon that lighted his way to the hotel. He patted at the bulge in his pocked as he hiked the strap on his banjo more firmly up on his shoulder. *Two-bit excuses for poker players never knew what hit them. Bigger haul than I could have imagined.*

Humes was ending his first full day in LaFontaine with more than just full pockets. He'd entertained with his banjo to the extent that the locals had begged him to join in the band at the dance the next night. The only thing Ed Humes liked better than whiskey and winning at cards was performing in front of an audience. His mind was filled with thoughts of applause and adulation.

The event promised to bring town folk and rural inhabitants together under one roof. Humes opened the door to his hotel room salivating at the prospect of a confined hunt. It had been a good day, he was prepared for a night of blissful sleep.

Chapter 34

Sarah and Ben told the children that Ed Humes might be in the area and looking for Joy. They'd done their best to assure them that although they should be on the lookout, they needn't be afraid. Still, the news had the family on edge.

Saturday morning faces at the breakfast table were glum. Bowls of fried potatoes and scrambled eggs were passed. Platters of hot biscuits and crisp bacon made the round. Requests for the passing of butter and jam were perfunctorily answered. Absent was the usual joyous chatter that accompanied a leisurely breakfast on a weekend day.

In keeping with Sarah's outlook on life and her firm belief that one should maintain a joyous attitude even amongst hardship, she was determined to turn the mood. She wanted her children to not only enjoy themselves at that evening's fall festival, she wanted them to experience the joy of anticipating the fun event.

"Josh," Sarah asked, "Are you excited about performing with Slim Kilty and the others in the band tonight?"

"Yeah, but more than excited, I'm nervous. Ever since you gave me the harmonica three years ago, I knowed I wanted to get good and play in a band," the twelve-year-old said. "It's been my lifelong dream to perform with Slim Kilty and the Boys. They's the best around."

Zeke had a puzzled look on his face after his brother's pronouncement. Under the table he splayed all ten of his fingers and raised the big toe on his left bare foot. First, he lowered his toe, then the thumb and pointer finger on his left hand. Looking down he counted the digits that remained at attention. "Hey," he blurted, "how can playin' in Slim's band be a lifelong dream of yours when you'd already lived nine years afore you even got your harmonica?"

"Zeke, saying something is a lifelong dream can be what's called a figure of speech," Ben said coming to Josh's rescue. "It doesn't generally mean a dream one has had since birth."

Zeke flung back, "It sounded to me like a li…." He stopped mid-sentence when Sarah's pointer finger flew up and threated a wag. She had to stifle a smile when Zeke quickly feigned locking his mouth and throwing away the key.

"Josh, your skill certainly has improved from when I initially heard you play the instrument," Ben said.

"Boy howdy," Luke interjected. "Back when you first got the thing, you sounded like a cat with its tail caught under the rocker of a moving chair. Night before last when you and Ben played while we danced, you sounded like a professional."

Josh beamed at the praise. "I hope to do my family proud tonight," he said.

"Ain't no doubt about it, brother," was Abe's reassuring reply.

The mood at the table now somewhat lifted, Sarah decided to attempt to engage Joy in conversation. "Joy, how about we wash and style your hair for the dance tonight?"

"I don't know," the girl said, head hung low. "I was thinking about asking if I could stay here at the farm while the rest of you go."

"No," Hathaway cried out. "You promised to dance wif me."

Ben, who had slipped from the table re-entered the kitchen with a package in his hand. "Joy," he said, "Your mother, uh, uh, I mean Sarah and I, have something for you." He handed the bundle to the girl.

"Something for me?" Joy asked as she hesitantly accepted the package.

"A present when it ain't even your birthday or Christmas," Josh exclaimed, "them's the best kind."

"Yay," Zeke chimed in. "Do you need me to open it for you?"

"I can do it," Joy said with a timid smile. The wrapping came off and a new dress was revealed. She jumped up and held the garment in front of herself. It was a floral pattern of autumn colors on a medium brown backdrop. The neck and cuffs were trimmed in lace and the ruffle that completed the dress's hem was wide and full. "Why, how? It's beautiful," she sobbed with what appeared to be a mixture of joy, appreciation and emotional release.

"I've been working on it for a couple of weeks," Sarah revealed. "Since you liked that blue flowered dress, we made over for you, I used the same pattern."

"Joy," Hathaway said clapping her chubby hands, "now you go? You'se be the most butiful one at the dance."

"Well, maybe not," Ben said pulling a smaller package from behind his back where he'd kept it hidden. He handed the parcel to Hathaway."

With help from Ben she unwrapped the gift to find a pint-sized version of Joy's dress. "Hope you don't mind the likeness," Sarah said looking at the older girl.

Joy walked over to the now standing, beaming Hathaway and stood at her side. Both held their new dresses out in front. "I not only don't mind, I'm honored," Joy said.

"Now 'Omi needs a dress like ours," Hathaway said to her mother, a squeal of glee in her voice.

Sarah gave the baby girl who was in the high chair next to her a kiss on the cheek. "I'll see if I have enough material to do that."

Sarah lifted a mental prayer, *Thank you, Lord, for your wisdom with this timely gifting of the dresses to the girls. Lord, I know you're watching over this family, for that I give you praise.*

Henry, sitting in his highchair, had managed to grab a piece of half-chewed bacon off Zeke's plate. Zeke had eaten the crispy part and left the grizzle. Attention was diverted from the dresses when Zeke yelled, "Henry's done turned blue".

In one seamless motion Sarah turned to the baby at her side, stuck her pointer finger down his tiny throat and extracted the obstruction. Henry sucked in air, his face turned pink and he again reached over to snatch another piece of grizzle from Zeke's plate.

"I think it's time we cleaned up the breakfast dishes and got on with this day," Sarah said, standing and removing Zeke's plate from the baby's reach.

"Thanks for savin' my brother's life, Ma," Zeke said as he lifted Henry out of his high chair. "Me and Henry is gonna play blocks, that's safer for him than eatin'."

After the table was cleared and the dishes done, Joy went to the room she shared with the babies for some alone time. She tried on the new dress and stood in front of a full-sized mirror. She ran her hand across the bodice and skirt. *I've never had anything this beautiful.* Fingering the locks of hair that cascaded over her shoulder she considered a hairstyle that might complement the dress. *Pull the sides away from my face and up, let the back hang free. Stick in one of Sarah's gold mums.*

Her pleasant thoughts were interrupted when visions of her father invaded. *Sarah says I'll have to accept that I might never know why my father has treated me so bad. I know he hates me. Sarah says it isn't my fault. I want to believe that. Wonder if he saw me in this dress, he'd feel differently, think I might be worth caring about.*

A tear ran down the girl's cheek as she took the dress off and donned an everyday garment. *He might hunt me down, but he'll never take me. If he attempts to, I'll get away, or die trying.* "God in heaven," she whispered, "I mean it, whatever it takes, I won't live with him again."

Ed Humes lay in his bed. It was only midday and multiple empty bottles were scattered about the hotel room's floor. His newly composed rhyme about his daughter floated into his drunken head. *I'm coming for you Joy, need to soothe my pride, you can run, but you can't hide.*

"I hate that girl. Can't help it, I just do,"Humes mumbled to himself. Ed lifted the bottle in his hand and took a swig. *It was me, I was the one that had Jane's attention until Joy came along. She idealized that girl from the moment she put her to her breast. I saw it on Jane's face, Joy would come first from then on. I hate that girl, all she's ever done is take from me.*

Humes stumbled from his bed and picked up his banjo. He began strumming as he sang, "Girl, soon the clock will stop tickin', marking time to get your lickin'. Standing had made Ed's head swim, he gently laid down his banjo. After assuring his bottle of whisky was within easy reach he crawled back into bed and succumbed to another round of sleep.

Sarah was pressing her Sunday dress when Ben came up behind her and kissed her on the neck. "I saw you holding your stomach just now. Noticed you've been doing that the past several days. Are you in pain?"

"Oh! I didn't realize I was doing that. No, I'm not in pain," Sarah responded, reaching back and cupping the back of Ben's head, pulling him nearer.

Ben's voice was gruff with emotion when he spoke, "Is there something we need to talk about?"

"Go, get on in to town, take care of business then hurry back." Sarah turned and patted her husband on his chest. "I promise, you'll be the first to know if I have something to talk about, but nothing today," Sarah reassured.

Ben said good-bye to the children and headed for town. It was the hired hand's day off and Ben wanted to talk to him before the dance that night. Ben and Sarah had discussed it would be a good idea to let Gerald in on the fact that Ed Humes was suspected to be in the area and might come looking for Joy. The man had been aware of the girl's poor condition when she first came to the farm. He hadn't asked any questions, nor had he spread any gossip about the child. Doc greatly respected him for that and felt as if he'd be a good ally.

As Ben climbed up on his horse a thought struck him. *Gerald's been gracious enough to hold my family's business private, not interject, nor pry, I need to return the courtesy to him and his friend.*

Abe stood at the window and watched as Ben mounted his horse and trotted down the lane. The boy glanced to his side to the ball bat that remained leaned up against the wall, then back at the family's father figure leaving the farm.

Abe unconsciously flexed his muscles before calling out to Luke, "Wanna play some ball?"

"Sure," was Luke's reply as he quickly donned his jacket and reached for the bat.

"Best leave my bat by the door. We can just play catch for a while."

"Okay," was Luke's amicable response.

Abe looked at the bat, then at the farm's now empty lane. "Go on and get your bat, Luke. We can lean it by the tree in case we need to hit a few, uh, a few..."

"Hit a few balls?" Is that what you're tryin' to say?" Luke asked.

"Yeah, hit some balls," the teen-aged boy said, fully aware of his double meaning.

Josh sat off to himself practicing his harmonica. Hathaway and Naomi were playing with a tea set and Zeke was building block towers with Henry.

Zeke's thoughts wandered to the evening festivities that lay ahead. *Can't move an outhouse by my own-self even if I hadn't promised not to.* The boy's mind flitted to the woodpile that Jeb Carter kept stocked at the side and toward the front of the jail. *Pile up some wood, add some kindlin'. Take some matches, grab up some paper to use as a starter. One match ought to do 'er.* The boy's eyes took on a glow of excitement as he saw a bonfire roaring in the middle of the street, in front of the jail while those that might thwart his plan danced to the likes of Slim Kilty's band plus one.

Henry tugged on Zeke's arm, "Uh, uh," he said.

Before resuming the block building, Zeke rubbed his hands together. *Gonna start my own Halloween trickdition. I ain't breakin' my promise to Ma and I won't need no help.*

Chapter 35

"Whoa," Ben called to the team as he pulled them to a stop in the lot at McVicker's livery stable.

Zeke, who was itching to get to the town hall and the evening's festivities, complained. "Pa, why didn't you just tie the horses up in front of the building?"

"Because, Zeke," Abe interjected, "there'll be countless other rigs already parked there. Doubt if there's room for one more."

"Mr. McVicker leaves his lot open on festival nights," Ben said. "Lets anyone that wants to, tether their horse or team free of charge."

"Besides", Abe said, "It will be more peaceful for the horses here, away from the band music, ruckus and such."

Zeke's head whipped to look at his brother. His eyes were squinted, and his head tilted to the side when he asked, "What kind of ruckus you talkin' 'bout?" the boy asked as he fingered the wad of paper and fistfull of matches, he had in his pocket. "Who said they might be a ruckus?"

"He's talking about the kind of ruckus caused when a hundred or more folks gather in one building, talking, laughing, dancing," Sarah responded. Sarah's brow furrowed when she took a close look at her precocious son. "What on earth is that bulge in your pocket, Zeke", she asked.

With fingers crossed Zeke responded, "Would you believe I packed me a sandwich in case I get hungry afore we get back home tonight?"

"My goodness, Zeke," Ben said. "Didn't you see us carry out four pies and a platter of fried chicken and load it in the wagon to bring tonight? There'll be enough food at this festival to feed everyone in town and their dogs."

Abe reached over and tussled Zeke's hair. "You beat all, little brother, you beat all."

The smug smile the six-year-old had on his face was lost in the haze of dusk that had spread over the sky and the close-knit town of LaFontaine. Zeke was standing tall and walking with a swagger as he and his family traveled the block-long distance between the livery stable and the town hall.

When they arrived, Josh handed the two pies he'd been carrying to Ben who had just deposited his armload. "I best get up on the stage," Josh said. "I see Slim and most of his band have already gathered there. "Wish me luck," he called out to his family as he left.

"Go get 'em. Do us proud," were the calls returned to the excited boy.

"Good evening," Ben said to their hired hand Gerald and his friend who walked up to the food table.

"That boy's buttons looked like they're near ready to pop off his shirt," Gerald said as he set down a basket chocked full of sticky buns.

"It's my buttons that's likely to pop first," Ben said. "He might not be my blood, but I couldn't love him any more if he were."

"Hope nothin' happens to spoil the boy's big night," Gerald said.

"Me either," Ben responded." "Thanks, Gerald, for agreeing to keep a lookout for Joy's pa."

"Think nothin' of it," Gerald said. We're both glad to help out." The friend tipped his hat.

Jeb Carter and Red Buttman, assisted by Julib Carter, finished making a town walk-around. Nothing untoward had been noticed. As an added measure to guard against the past practice of moving and burning the jail's outhouse, they'd attached two, half-inch anchor chains to the structure securing it to the ground with foot-long spikes driven through the end links.

"It'll take a team of horses to pull out them stakes," Jeb said. "Ain't nobody gonna mess with my outhouse this year." He patted Red, then Julib on their backs. "Thanks for your help boys. Julib, you go on in and enjoy yourself this evening. Red and I will do some more walkin' about. If it don't seem like there's no trouble, we'll come on in, get us a bite to eat. It should be all right for us to socialize for a while. If any mischief is planned, it likely won't happen until much later."

"What about that Humes fellow?" Julib asked. "You still worried he might show up?"

"Yes. I was concerned that might happen while I was out of town," Jeb said. "I asked at the hotel when I got back this afternoon. The day clerk had left and the feller that covers of an evenin' said he hadn't signed in any strangers. I looked at their log book and a man by the name of Smith took a room yesterday. I didn't see anyone named Humes that registered.

The clerk said he hadn't seen any unfamiliar faces go into the hotel's restaurant."

"Did you talk to the barber?" Red asked. "If the feller's been travelin' a spell he might have gone there for a shave. Nobel Simon don't miss nary a thing. He gets up right close don't ya know when he's a shavin' a face. Ain't no one unfamiliar gonna get past him."

"Noble had closed up shop by the time I got back into town. If I see him here tonight, I'll ask if he's had any new customers," Jeb reassured.

"What about at the tavern?" Julib asked. "Did you check there? You said the man is a drinker."

"Yes, and they told me there was a stranger that bought several bottles of whiskey," Jeb responded. "One of the bartenders said he was tall and bald. Another said he was short and fat. Neither description fit the likeness of Humes shown on that wanted poster."

"Well, Boss," Red interjected, "we got us a plan. 'Bout the best we can do is stick to 'er, keep our eyes peeled and be ready if somethin' or someone pops up."

"I'll leave you to it then," Julib said with a wave as he headed toward the town hall.

When Julib entered, the band had just struck the first cords of *Turkey in the Straw.* Initially the dance floor was flooded with many town-folks paired up and dancing to the lively tune. All at once the crowd parted and formed a circle around a single dancer. Julib moved closer to see Elmo Jones at the center of everyone's attention. He was showing off his footwork while the crowd clapped and cheered.

Julib was scanning the crowd looking for the Adams/Whitcome family's cousin Joy, who Julib now knew was no kin to either Ben's or Sarah's sides of the family.

Julib spotted Sarah first. He noticed that instead of watching Elmo dance, her attention was focused on Penelope Peterson, the hat maker at Parker's General Store. The petite woman appeared to be enjoying the performance immensely. At one point she got so excited she gave Elmo a two-finger whistle.

A fellow standing next to Julib commented about Elmo, "That old coot sure is good at pickin' 'em up and layin' 'em down, ain't he."

"That he is," Julib responded in admiration as he glanced down to what he considered his own *two left feet.*

The song ended and the band immediately started playing *Oh, Dem Golden Slippers.* The dancers thinned out, many going for a cool drink or a bite to eat. With fewer people on the dance floor Julib was quickly able to spot Joy. The twenty-year-old doffed his hat as if in reverent respect for what he saw. The young man's Adam's apple moved, then appeared to get stuck mid-throat, as if his mouth had gone dry.

The man at Julib's elbow noticed. "She's a pure beauty ain't she. If I was fifty years younger, I'd be tappin' that little-'un on the shoulder and askin' for a dance."

The little-one he was referencing was Hathaway Whitcome who, wearing a dress identical to Joy's, was showing off some fancy footwork of her own. The older girl held the toddler's dimpled hands and swayed in rhythm to the music. The light from the many kerosene lanterns about the room highlighted Joy's tall, slender figure and set her blond hair aglow.

At six o'clock, the band announced they'd be taking a short break. Josh came down from the stage and was cheered by his immediate family. Standing near were his grandparents, Tom and Mary Riley, Sarah's parents.

Tom was holding baby Henry and his twin, Naomi, was standing between Mary and Hathaway. Naomi struggled to get free while grandmother and sister held her tiny hands. Tom gave Josh a catcall and Mary beamed with pride.

Sarah enveloped Josh in a hug. "I wish your Grandpa and Grandma Whitcome could have been here to hear you play," She said. "But these days, at their age, travel is hard for them. I'll have to write and tell them all about your professional debut."

Breanna Johnson was standing with Abe and Joy. "Josh," Breanna said. "I could tell by the way Mr. Kilty kept looking at you and grinning, he was proud to have you play in his band."

"Thanks for the compliments, everyone," Josh said, "I'm enjoying myself, but I'm glad for a break. Think I'll get me somethin' to eat and drink. Luke, wanna come join me." Luke gave a nod.

"Breanna," Abe said, his face blushing. "Could I get you some punch?"

Breanna's face lit up. "Why, yes, Abe. That would be lovely." When Abe walked off Breanna and Joy put their heads together and giggled.

Their moment was interrupted when a deep voice said, "Miss Joy, I saw that Abe didn't offer to bring a cup of punch for you, may I get you one?" Julib Carter asked.

Joy's cheeks took on a pink glow. "Yes, Julib, that would be nice."

***

A noise woke Edward J. Humes. He rubbed sleep from his eyes and was surprised to find the room dark. It had been daylight, although late afternoon, when he'd last drifted off to sleep. Ed turned to look out the window. Sitting on the sill was a large black crow, pecking on the glass. *A crow, what the…dang-it, it's dark.* Humes bolted up to a sitting position. His head spun and his mouth was dry. *Bet that dance has started.*

He attempted to stand but lost his balance and abruptly sat back down on the edge of the bed. *Got to get myself together, get over to the town hall. Can't miss this chance to look for Joy.* Ed eyed his banjo that lay on a chair across the room. *Was looking forward to playing with that band. Wanted to show these hick farmers some real talent.*

Sarah and Ben had watched the exchange between Joy and Julib. "He'll be asking to come courting and when he does, I hope we'll have wisdom to know what the answer should be," Ben said.

"I agree, Ben," Sarah said as she looped her arm through her husband's and pulled him close. "This is something we need to pray about, seek God's guidance. I thought we had a few years yet to prepare for this grown-up stuff. Having a sixteen-year-old young woman in our home has us in a position to parent in a way we aren't yet prepared for."

"I heard you say, aren't prepared for," Jeb Carter interjected as he walked up to stand next to Ben and Sarah. "If it's Humes a showin' up you're thinkin' about, I got that covered. Me and Red," Jeb turned and pointed to his deputy who was at the food table piling a plate high, "we just come in from makin' multiple rounds about town. I don't think we got nothin' to worry about tonight. We ain't seen hide nor hair of any strangers. We felt comfortable enough to come on in and socialize a bit ourselves."

"Glad to see you, Husband," Judith Carter said as she came up alongside and took Jeb's hand. "I've been waiting for a chance to dance with my best beau."

"Your best beau," Jeb teased. "I'd better be your only beau, Woman"

Zeke had been biding his time. The matches in his pocket were near burning a hole, both figuratively and literally, he'd been fingering them so much. The boy had seen Jeb Carter and Red Buttman come in. He'd noticed Julib Carter talking to Joy and figured he'd stay occupied. Zeke's pa and ma looked like they'd settled into a conversation that would hold their attention. Abe was busy fetching punch, Luke and Josh were chowing down over in a corner.

Now's my chance. Zeke walked fast, he knew better than to draw attention by running from the building. Once outside he made a beeline to the jail and Marshal Carter's wood pile.

***

Ed forced himself to a standing position then walked to a pitcher and poured water into a bowl. He washed his face and underarms before putting on his *go to meetin'* set of clothing. After combing his hair, he threaded his belt with the large silver buckle through the loops on his pants. He patted the shiny surface as he contemplated using it to exact revenge on Joy.

***

Zeke was gathering a load of wood when he saw a man coming down the street carrying a banjo. *Who's that? Might be comin' to play in the band.* Zeke could hear the music start up again. *Band's break must be over. Good, folks will be busy dancin' again.*

Ed Humes headed for the back door of the town hall, one he knew would provide a behind the stage entrance to the building.

The band finished playing *She'll Be Coming Round the Mountain.* Slim Kilty walked center stage. "This next song, ladies and gentlemen," he called out. "will be a slow one. Link yourselves up with someone special. Them that don't, pull out your hankies 'cause this next tune has been known to draw a tear or two. Me and the boys will be playin' *I'll Take You Home Again, Kathleen*."

Ben asked Sarah to dance and Jeb took Judith by the arm. Abe asked Breanna to the floor to try out his practiced two step and Julib swallowed hard and held a hand out to Joy. "Miss Joy," he said as he stuck his finger under his collar to loosen it a bit, "I'd be honored if you'd join me on the dance floor."

"I'm not very good at dancing," Joy timidly said. "But, if we move slowly, I think I can manage to keep off of your feet."

Julib's eyes were full of tenderness when he responded, "I plan to take it real slow, Miss Joy."

***

Ed Humes came from behind the stage and mounted the steps. Slim Kilty saw him, smiled, and nodded for Ed to come join in. Before doing so, Humes surveyed the room. He spied Joy dancing with a young man.

A glint in Joy's peripheral vision caused her to look toward the stage. She saw the belt buckle. There was no need to take time to look up at the face on the body wearing it, she knew.

Joy gasped, jerked away from Julib and ran toward the door. Humes dropped his banjo and took after her.

Sarah had been discretely keeping an eye on Joy and Julib. She saw Joy look to the stage then jerk away from Julib. Sarah turned toward the stage, saw a man drop a banjo and run down the stairs. Sarah yelled, "It's him," pushed away from Ben and started running.

Josh had seen the man come up on the stage but had been so focused on his harmonica playing that it didn't, at first, register that he was Joy's father. When he saw his mother start to run, he caught on and took off after Humes.

Zeke had his arms full, with a third load of wood, when he saw Joy come running out of the town hall. In hot pursuit he saw a man. His mind made a connection that the man was the one who'd been carrying a banjo. When it clicked in his mind that it must be the feared Edward J. Humes, Joy's father, he dropped his load. Two large pieces landed on his foot and he fell to the ground groaning.

Joy ran past Zeke, close enough that he could see the terror in her eyes. He looked up to see that the predator was gaining ground. In his peripheral vison he saw a woman with her skirt hiked up, bloomers showing, running from the town hall. He wiped his hand over his eyes then strained to look more intently. "Ma," he yelled. "Stay back, I'll stop him."

Humes flew past Zeke. Zeke picked up a stick of wood and limped into the space between Humes and his mother.

Sarah saw Zeke and screamed, "No! Stay back, he's dangerous."

By this time the rest of the family and friends had realized what was transpiring.

Julib was the first of them to respond. Cutting off Josh's approach, he ran from the building immediately behind Sarah. "Sarah, stay back, I'm coming," he yelled.

While Humes' long legs closed the distance between him and Joy, he was ripping off his belt. He caught the girl by her hair and jerked her to a stop and down on the ground where he straddled her. "Thought you could run from me, you worthless piece of shit. How dare you scratch your name in my banjo," he yelled as he drew back the belt.

Before he could bring the buckle down on the girl's tender flesh, Zeke jumped up on Ed Humes' back and tried hitting him with his stick of wood. Humes easily flicked the boy off, Zeke hit the ground hard.

Ed again secured the belt around his hand, positioning the buckle over his knuckles. Humes held Joy down with a hand on her throat. The girl thrashed and kicked. Humes drew his weapon back. Before he could swing downward, Sarah landed on his back and wrapped her arms around his neck. Humes let go of Joy's throat and grabbed Sarah's hands. He raised up while prying her hands off. Then he flung Sarah from his back. Joy started scooting backward.

"Where do you think you're going?" Humes said grabbing the hem of Joy's dress. He was pulling her toward him when Julib Carter arrived on the scene. Julib stomped on Ed Humes' hand. Ed let go of Joy's dress, she scrambled a distance and got to her feet.

Humes tried to stand and Julib kicked him in the ribs. Ed fell, Julib jumped on him and began pummeling the man's face. Jeb ran up and jerked Julib off Humes. "Enough, Son," he yelled.

Zeke was on his knees crawling toward his mother. Sarah was lying on her side with one hand outstretched to her son, the other holding her stomach.

Ben skidded to her side, "Sarah, Sarah. Dear, God, Sarah!"

Zeke sobbed, "Is Ma hurt?"

Ben softened his voice. "Sarah, you're safe now. Can you tell us where it hurts?"

"Not, uh, not hurt," she gasped. "…got wind knocked out."

Marshal Cater handcuffed Ed Humes and jerked him to his feet. "Doc is Sarah gonna be okay?" he called out.

Sarah, who now had been able to draw in a full breath, answered. "Jeb, I'm okay." Sarah clutched Ben's arm, "I'll tend to Zeke. You go check on Joy."

Ben looked over to see that Joy was sobbing in Julib Carter's arms.

"Zeke are you all right, Son?" Sarah asked.

Zeke got to his feet, pulled his shoulders back, and used his shirtsleeve to swipe away his tears. "You can leave me be," he said. "Go see to Joy, she's the one that's a bawlin' like a baby."

Abe, Josh and Luke came to Zeke. "You gonna be okay, little brother?" Abe asked as he put his arm around the boy's shoulders.

"No, I ain't," Zeke said, now crying again.

"Where are you hurt?" Luke asked.

"My foot's a throbbin', dropped firewood on it. But it hurts worser here," Zeke said clutching his heart.

"Your hearts a hurtin'," Josh said eyes wide, eyebrows raised. "I'd better fetch Ben."

Abe grabbed Josh's arm. "Hold up a minute," he said. "Zeke, do you think you need a doctor?"

"No, it ain't that kind of hurtin'," the boy said. "It just, well… I had me a perfect Halloween trickdition planned," he said as he pulled a fist full of matches from his pocket, "and that man," he pointed to Ed Humes who was being hauled off to jail, "that man done went and spoilt it for me."

Abe looked at the matches, then the pile of wood stacked a few feet away. "You beat all, brother," Abe said. "You just beat all.

"Luke, Josh, grab up that wood, get it out of the street and back over yonder on Marshal Carter's wood pile." Abe pointed to where he wanted the wood moved. "If we get the mess cleared before anyone notices we might be able to save our brother's hide."

Luke and Josh caught on and rushed to do their older brother's bidding. Their arms were loaded with wood when Red Buttman tapped one, then the other on the shoulder. "What's up boys?" he said.

Chapter 36

While Abe, Josh, and Luke were dealing with Zeke, Sarah went to join Doc who was examining Joy. "Is she hurt anywhere?" Sarah asked.

"My shoulder hurts," Joy responded. "Skin on my back is burning,"

Ben looked at the girl's back. "Your dress is torn, and you've got some scrapes that are oozing blood."

"My dress-torn!" Joy cried out, slumped and started shivering uncontrollably.

Julib whipped off his jacket and wrapped it around Joy's shoulders. Ben started barking orders. "She's in shock. Someone go get her water to drink? Got to get her warm, need more than Julib's jacket. Anyone got a blanket?"

"I'll fetch one," Julib said as he took off running. Sarah got to the ground and pulled the child close to share her body's warmth. An onlooker brought a glass of water, Sarah gave Joy sips.

Julib was quickly back with a blanket. Ben grabbed it and swaddled the girl. "This should stop her shivering in short order," Ben said.

After a few minutes, the girl's body relaxed in Sarah's arms. "Julib, where'd you get the blanket?" Sarah asked.

"The jail," Julib responded. "Ripped it off Humes. Pa already had him in a cell. He was laying on the cot, covered up. Hope the temperature drops below thirty-two degrees tonight, I'd like to see the bastard freeze." As soon as he said it, Julib's hand flew to cover his mouth. "Oh, sorry ladies, I forgot myself."

"You're forgiven," Sarah replied. "I wouldn't have said it, but, Lord, forgive me, my thinking of Ed Humes isn't very pure either right now."

"She's going to need to rest the remainder of the night," Ben said to Sarah.

"Abe," Sarah called to her son who was hovering near. "Please get our things gathered up. We need to take Joy home."

"Sarah," Ben said. "The scrapes on Joy's back aren't deep. They'll scab over quickly. She can move her shoulder, so I think it's bruised, not displaced or broken. It'll be tender for a couple of weeks but there isn't much we can do for it."

"What about pain medication?" Sarah asked.

I'd rather not give her anything if she can tolerate the discomfort and I think she should be able to. I'd give her some sugar tea before she goes to bed," Ben said. "That will help counteract the residual effects of her shock experience."

"Does that sound okay to you, Joy?" Sarah asked as she caressed the girl's cheek.

"Yes. I don't need anything, I've made it through pain much worse than this, many times," Joy reassured her.

"I hate to not be there to help you get everyone settled in tonight, but duty calls for me to go check on Hume's injuries," Ben said. "Would it be all right if I asked your father to take you and the children home?"

"I understand," Sarah responded while she gently picked debris from Joy's hair. "I'm sure Ma and Pa will be willing to do that."

"No need to ask your parents to go out of their way when I can take you," Julib said.

"That sounds like a good idea, Julib," Ben replied. "Sarah, that okay with you?"

"Yes, that would be fine," Sarah responded, "Thank you, Julib."

"Uh, Ben," Abe said, "Could I have a word with you…over yonder," the boy pointed off in the distance.

Ben followed. When the pair were several feet away Abe spoke. "We got us a bit of a problem."

"You mean something more than this business with Ed Humes?" Ben asked.

"Afraid so," Abe replied. He proceeded to tell Doc about Zeke's planned Halloween prank and that Josh and Luke got caught by Red Buttman when they were, on Abe's orders, trying to clean up their little brother's mess.

"Well, Son, you said it best. Zeke sure does beat all," Ben said scratching his head.

"I told Red we saw the pile of wood in the street and that my brothers were just cleaning it up," Abe explained. "That wasn't a lie, just not the whole truth. Thought maybe we could keep the fact that Zeke was behind it all in the family."

"Quick thinking. This issue with Joy has already brought more attention to our family than comfortable. So, did that bode well with Red?"

"No such luck. Zeke blurted out his plan to set the wood on fire. He wanted credit for the idea…didn't seem to catch on that he might be in trouble with Red and Marshal Carter, or Ma."

"I'll talk to Red. Zeke didn't get to perpetrate the act, so, no real harm done. I'll have to let your mother know, but not now. I'm sure the little dickens won't escape some type of punishment, but it'll come from his mother, not the law."

Sarah and the children, plus Breanna, were loaded into the Carter's wagon. Sarah had asked Breanna to spend the night with Joy. Her plan was to move Hathaway downstairs with the twins for the night and give the three-year-old's room to Joy and Breanna to use. Sarah knew that having her friend close by would bring comfort to Joy.

When Ben got to the jail, Jeb and Red were discussing plans for guarding their *houseguest* for the night. "Red, are you sure you don't mind takin' the night shift?" Jeb asked the deputy.

"It'll suit me better than you. Meanin' no offense, but you got a few years on me and sleepin' in that chair yonder," Red pointed to Jeb's swivel desk chair, "ain't gonna do that bad back of yours any favors. 'Sides, you need to get on home and be with your missus. Ain't nobody gonna miss me if I stay here tonight."

"Thanks, Red," Jeb replied. "My back and my wife will be in your debt."

Before Jeb left for home, Ben discussed Zeke's situation with the two law officers. It was readily agreed that given Zeke's age, punishment for his foiled intent was a family matter.

Jeb left and Red unlocked the cell for Ben to examine Ed Humes. "Mr. Humes," Ben said, "I'm the doctor here in town and I've come to see about the injuries you sustained in the fight tonight."

Ed was lying on his cot shivering. "Red," Ben called out, "please grab that blanket from the other cell's cot and bring it in here."

Red complied with the request. Ed sat up on the side of the bed and Ben wrapped the blanket around his shoulders. A chair was brought in and Ben sat down in front of Humes. "I'm going to check this cut on your cheek first," Doc said as he palpated the wound site.

"It's superficial, no stitches needed. Your hand looks swollen," Ben stated as he took Humes' right hand in his.

"That big brute that attacked me, stomped on it," Humes said. "The way it hurts, I think my fingers might be broken. If they are, I won't be able to play the banjo. Think I'll sue the guy."

Ben stayed silent while he examined Ed's hand. "Your fingers are badly bruised, but not broken. I recommend wearing the affected arm in a sling for a week, keep the hand mobilized and protected. Are you in pain anywhere else?" Ben inquired.

"My ribs hurt when I breathe," Ed said, clutching at his right side. "Lummox kicked me."

"Your ribs are probably just bruised," Doc counseled. "They might be cracked. Either way, treatment is the same. I'll go over to my office and get some supplies, wrap your ribs for you. Having them bound will help with the pain. It will take a few weeks for them to heal."

"Hey, it just clicked with me," Ed Humes said. "The doctor over in Banquo that treated me for dysentery, said he learned about the cure he gave me from a doc here in LaFontaine. Guess that must have been you."

"If you had dysentery from drinking some tainted moonshine, then, yes, that would have been me. We had a couple of severe cases here. We tracked the source to a still in Banquo. I was able to find an herbal tea that soothed the gut enough to get the diarrhea and vomiting curtailed. I shared the remedy with Banquo's doctor. He told me he had a fellow that was near death when he was brought to his office. Was that you?"

"Likely it was. They said I was as near death as anyone they'd ever seen, yet still breathing," Humes replied.

"You know Humes, the irony is, it was your daughter, Joy, who told me about the herbal tea treatment for dysentery. She showed me the pictured herb guide she'd made with her mother. Her knowledge of herbs and holistic healing was so impressive I decided that it couldn't hurt to give the brew a try. It did the trick for my two sick patients and it worked for you too. You might not be alive if it weren't for your daughter."

"Her one good deed doesn't make up for the way the girl wronged me," Humes said. "I shouldn't be locked up behind bars. A father aught to be able to discipline his child when it's called for.

Joy damaged my banjo. Scratched her name into its veneer. It was a willful, hateful act and she needs to be punished for it."

"Humes," Ben said, "my family and I found your daughter in our barn, battered and bruised, and suffering from starvation. Her condition spoke of prolonged neglect and abuse. We know that abuse came from you. What you, her father, the one who should have cherished and protected her, did to her, is beyond reprehension. It's criminal."

Hume's rebuttal was quick, "You have no right..."

"Mr. Humes, I suggest you shut that filthy mouth of yours before I shut it for you," Ben said, now trembling with anger. "Physician or no, I've got my limits." He tapped his chest, "That was my son and my wife that you flung off your back tonight when they tried to protect Joy."

Humes couldn't leave it alone, "They had no business inter...."

Ben jumped to his feet. "Red," he called out, "I need to put some distance between this man and me." Doc started to leave the cell then turned. "They had every right to stop you from hurting Joy. You discarded the girl and she's a part of our family now and we take care of our own. Red, I'll be back with some binding for Humes' ribs and a sling for his arm," Ben informed the deputy.

"I'm going to need some laudanum to get me through the night," Ed called to Ben's back.

Ben stopped but didn't turn to face Humes. "Your injuries aren't life threatening. I'll give it some thought, but the way I'm seeing it right now, I don't think I can spare any laudanum for the likes of you."

It was nearly midnight by the time Ben got home. He'd spent some time on his knees, in his office praying before he went back to the jail. The result had been a refocus on his role as a physician and his right to mete out punishment. In the end, he'd taken laudanum for Red to give to Humes throughout the night as needed for pain.

When Doc entered the kitchen, he found Sarah sitting in a chair by the fireplace. Her feet were propped up on a footstool and she had an afghan spread over her lap. She was sipping from a cup of chamomile tea. Ben went to her, leaned down and gave her a tender kiss. "How's it going?" he asked.

"Everyone is asleep," Sarah said. "The twins and Hathaway were dead to the world by the time we got home. We put them to bed without them waking. I sent Breanna and Joy up to Hathaway's room and put her in with the babies. The older girls were subdued, but I could hear murmuring coming from their room. Hopefully Joy shared her feelings with Breanna."

"Did she talk to you about what happened?" Ben asked Sarah.

"No, and I didn't press, didn't think tonight was the time. Hopefully tomorrow she and I can talk things through," Sarah replied.

"What about the boys? Did they discuss the evening's events, the fight, or other things?" Ben asked.

"I could hear them chattering, sometimes it sounded as if they were arguing. They seemed excited, but not worried or afraid. I decided to leave them be, let them talk it out amongst themselves. I had personal issues to deal with."

"Personal issues?" Ben asked.

"Ben," Sarah said, "you commented this morning that you'd seen me holding my stomach, you wondered if it was hurting me."

"Yes, I recall," Ben asked. "You said it wasn't. Is it now? Did the fall cause you some harm beyond getting your wind knocked out?"

"I wasn't even aware that I'd been holding my stomach when you asked me about it. I guess it was my thoughts of possible pregnancy that had me doing it. It had been ten weeks since my last monthly. I wanted to wait until I was at least three months gone before I said anything to you."

Ben grabbed Sarah's hand, "That's wonderful news."

"I'm sorry, Ben," Sarah said kissing the back of Ben's hand. "As of a couple of hours ago, there isn't any news."

"What do you mean?"

"I had a backache when we left LaFontine tonight. Some mild cramping before we got home. A flow of blood started after we arrived, and the cramping got quite severe. The flow increased and I passed some tissue that was near half-dollar size," Sarah said as a tear ran down her cheek.

"Oh, no, that sounds like a miscarriage," Ben lamented.

"That was my conclusion too," Sarah said.

"It likely was caused when Ed Humes threw you off of his back," Ben said, his hands now fisted.

"Ben," Sarah softly said, "If I had it to do over, I don't think I could have reacted any differently. My only thought was to keep Ed Humes from hurting Joy. I didn't take time to count the cost. I had to protect her."

"I know," Ben said, again taking Sarah's hand. "I knew from the first time I saw you with your children that you'd fight like a banty rooster to protect them. You've come to think of Joy as your daughter, so, no, I'm not surprised you reacted as you did."

"My heart near stopped when I saw Zeke take after Humes," Sarah said. "I yelled for him to stop, but he kept right on going. Truth be told, if Zeke hadn't jumped on Ed's back, slowed him down so I could get there, the man would have struck a vicious blow to Joy."

"Yes, and if Julib hadn't intervened when you got tossed aside, well, I think Humes might have killed her," Ben said. "He seemed to be in a blind rage. He must have gone crazy to attack her with so many people around. If he'd thought it out, he'd have known others would come to her rescue."

"Would you have believed that Zeke would be the first to take action?" Sarah said shaking her head. "It reminded me of when he jumped on Ernie Brown when he attacked Abe on the school grounds."

"The boy's a wildcat when it comes to protecting his family, that's for sure. Sarah," Ben said. "That other title you've given the boy still applies too."

"What title is that, Ben?" Sarah asked, tilting her head and furrowing her brow.

"Loose Cannon," was Ben's reply.

Sarah let out a sigh and sat straight up in her chair. "I'm guessing something happened tonight that I haven't yet been told. I caught a couple of comments that came from the boys overhead, before they went to sleep. I wondered if they were talking about an issue other than Ed Humes' attack on Joy but decided I'd find out later if it was important enough for me to know."

"I've no doubt they were talking about it," Ben said.

"Don't keep me in suspense," was Sarah's plea, "let's hear it."

Ben gave Sarah an accounting of the foiled Halloween prank. "… that's the story as told to me, by Abe," Ben said. "I haven't spoken to Zeke about it. I did breech the subject with Jeb and Red and they assured me that, with no harm done, they were fine with letting us handle Zeke," Ben said. "But we don't have to figure that out tonight. Let's get you to bed."

"I don't even know where to begin with bringing Zeke in line. And, we've got a lot more to talk about before Joy and the conflict with her father are resolved," Sarah said as she got up from her chair. "I need to spend some time in prayer on both subjects.

"But, enough for tonight. Bed does sound inviting," Sarah said holding her stomach.

"Is your bleeding under control? Has your cramping stopped?" Ben asked.

"Yes, I've only a slight flow now, no pain," Sarah said.

Ben took Sarah into his arms. "Sarah, I'm so sorry about the miscarriage. I'd have welcomed another child, and, yes, it would have been nice to raise one I fathered. But, Sarah, the family you've already given me is more than any man could wish for. Please know that if we never have a child together, I'm perfectly content to help you parent the ones we already have."

"And," Sarah said, hugging Ben tightly, "the sixteen-year-old that I hope you'll agree is now our eighth child."

Chapter 37

Ben yawned and stretched as Sarah poured him his second cup of coffee. After she returned the pot to the stove and came back to the table, he pulled her to his lap. "Forgive me, I wasn't thinking. I should be the one doing the fetching and toting. How are you this morning? Any pain?"

"No pain, I am a little tired and I'll have to admit melancholy. I guess I hadn't realized how much I was looking forward to another baby until there was no longer the prospect."

Ben hugged Sarah close. "I'm feeling a sense of loss too. And, we can't discount the drama of last night. I still have an unsettled feeling and I'm sure I'm not alone."

Sarah kissed Ben on the cheek, "No, you're not alone," she said getting up from his lap. She took a seat next to him and folded her hands, resting them on the table. "God will see us through this. We've no time to indulge our feelings right now. There's a lot to discuss before the children wake up."

"Are we all going to church this morning?" Ben asked.

"No, I was thinking that I'd stay home with Joy. Keep the twins here too. You could take the boys and Hathaway and go on to service, let the children stay for Sunday School. Would that be okay with you?" Sarah asked.

"That sounds like a good plan. There'll be talk about last night, no doubt. Joy doesn't need to hear any of that today," Ben said. "What about Breanna? You said she spent the night."

"Josephine will expect to see her at church. Besides, I'd like the alone time to draw Joy out, get her to talk about what happened," Sarah said.

Ben took a sip of coffee. "That's how we'll do it then. I'm not worried about Joy's physical condition, but I will check on her injuries before we leave. It's her emotional status that concerns me. It may well need some attention."

"I agree. I've been giving it some thought, and I believe we should encourage Joy to face her father, while he's in Jeb's custody."

"I can see the value in that. If she faces him, she might come to see him as the pathetic person he is, not some looming threat."

"Can't we take some type of legal action to assure he never again is a threat to her?" Sarah asked.

Ben scratched his head. "I don't know. He is her father and I've no doubt the law would think that carries weight. She's only sixteen and with her being a girl, Humes might be able to maintain say over the child."

"I want us to consult with a lawyer. Wonder if the one I used a few years back still comes to LaFontaine?"

"If you're talking about Pettigrew and Pettigrew Law Offices, yes, they still come from Wabash weekly and hold consultations at Parker's store. They could advise us on how to protect Joy and on the practicality of filing charges against Ed Humes. He did after all, attack her and assault you and Zeke," Ben said.

Sarah eyes flew open wide and she grabbed Ben's arm. "What if we offered Humes a deal?" she said.

Ben furrowed his brow. "A deal, what do you mean?"

"We tell Humes that if he'll sign over parental control of Joy to us, make her legally our ward, we won't press any charges against him for the attacks," Sarah said.

Ben scratched his chin, "It might work. Pettigrew will be at Parkers on Tuesday morning. Do you think you could come into town then?"

"Yes, I'll ask Josephine to watch Hathaway and the twins. Before we see the lawyer, we need to present our plan to Joy and ask her if she'd like to become our legal ward. Let her know that means living with us for as long as she wants, joining the family…"

"Being our eighth child," Ben interrupted.

Sarah smiled. "Exactly. If Joy were the one to get Humes to sign, relinquishing his parental rights, that might instill some confidence in her, help her feel as if she has taken control of her destiny so to speak," Sarah said.

Ben shook his head. "Sarah, can you imagine a father giving up his parental control?"

"I can imagine Ed Humes doing that," Sarah said. "He's out for himself and no other. If he can see even a measure of personal gain out of the transaction, he'll go for it."

"Transaction," Ben said. "That's a harsh word."

"Yes, but it fits. Joy's father sees her as chattel. Something he owns, something he can do with as he pleases. The prospect of getting out of legal trouble might make the offer attractive to him."

"What do you think is wrong with Humes? Why do you think he hates the child so much?"

"I think Ed Humes is a dark and depraved soul, and he knows it," Sarah said. "John 3:19 says, and I'm paraphrasing, Christ was the light that came into our world, but people shunned the light because of their evil deeds and evil wants to stay hidden…stay in the dark."

"But, what does that have to do with Joy?" Ben asked.

"Joy represents light," Sarah explained. "In 2 Corinthians 6:14, it says that righteousness and wickedness have nothing in common. That there can be no fellowship between those that walk in the light and those that hide in the darkness. Joy came into this world pure, she brought light into Humes life. He shuns light."

"Humes is a self-centered man. He may, at one time, have seen Joy as competition for his wife's attention, jealous of her," Ben interjected.

"But deeper than that," Sarah continued. "Deeper than Humes may have been able to realize, and still won't admit, Joy's purity, her light, is a threat to him. He's afraid it will invade his darkness and bring about what he fears most of all."

"What's that?" Ben asked.

"What he fears most," Sarah said, "is that he'll see through his own pretend persona and come face to face with his true self."

"So, he shunned her, still shuns her," Ben said. "He pushed her away, but worse, he was and still is frightened by her light, so he wants to snuff it out."

Tears were running down Sarah's cheeks. "Yes, he fears her light so much he literally feels the need to snuff it out."

Chapter 38

Sarah and Joy had a meaningful conversation on Sunday morning while Ben and the older children went to church. Joy cried tears of joy over the suggestion she become a ward of Sarah and Ben and thus a permanent member of the family.

The girl was fearful over the suggestion that she confront her father. After reassurance from Sarah that she, Ben, and the marshal would be there to protect her, she agreed. It was decided that she would go to see Clint Pettigrew, the lawyer, with Ben and Sarah so that he could be assured that Joy's wishes were being followed.

If all went according to plan with the legal aspects of their scheme, they would challenge Humes on Thursday morning. The Wabash County Circuit Judge was scheduled to hold court in LaFontaine that same afternoon. Marshal Carter had placed Ed Humes' arraignment on the docket. It was hoped that the threat of facing the judge would influence Humes' decision regarding the custody proposal.

***

The mood at the breakfast table Thursday morning was somber. Zeke had been forced to pass the plater of bacon on to Luke without taking even a single slice. His punishment for planning his foiled Halloween prank was no bacon for three weeks. Sarah had thought long and prayerfully about how to deal with Zeke and his rebellious nature. She'd conclude that her past attempts at bringing the boy in line by assigning him extra chores hadn't been successful. This time she thought she'd act where it would make the most lasting impression, his voracious appetite for bacon.

When she'd sat Zeke down and lectured him on the perils of deception, getting him to realize that a finger cross didn't give lying a pass, the boy had acquiesced and showed contrition. When Sarah explained the punishment he was to receive, Zeke laid his head down on the kitchen table and sobbed. "You might as well just take me down to the barn and shoot me," the boy had lamented. "Life ain't gonna be worth livin' ifin I don't get me bacon to eat of a mornin'."

Thursday was Zeke's forth day of punishment and although the tears had ceased, his glum mood persisted. "Zeke," Sarah said, "I'm requesting that you wipe that sour look off your face. You chose your path of disobedience for which you're being punished. The rest of us at this table weren't intended to be involved in your sentence."

"I ain't gettin' my bacon and now your expectin' me to take it with a smile on my face. If you ask me, that's too much…."

Up came Sarah's finger along with the stern stare and arched eyebrows. "Pass the biscuits please," Zeke said with a forced smile on his face that extended ear to ear.

"Ma, can me, Luke and Josh be at the jail when Joy gives her Pa 'what for'?" Abe asked.

"I think not," Sarah responded. "Joy knows you will be with her in spirit. It will be best if you go on to school." Sarah gave Joy a reassuring smile. If she feels up to it, after we're finished meeting with her father, Joy can attend afternoon classes."

Joy's eyes were brimming with tears when she spoke. "Just knowing that all of you want to be there for support is enough. Your mother has prayed with me about going, but truthfully, I have no idea what I'm going to say to him. I hope it will be what it takes to get him to sign that paper releasing his control over me. Whatever happens, I intend for this to be the last time I lay eyes on him. From this day forward, he will be dead to me."

Joy's words clutched at Sarah's heart. *Peace won't come for the girl until she can forgive. I pray that through God's grace that will happen.*

Sarah saw Ben flinch when Joy said that Ed Humes would be dead to her. When Ben immediately bowed his head, she felt sure he too was praying that the child could come to experience the healing power of forgiveness.

***

Jeb Carter arranged three chairs facing a single chair. To the right Clint Pettigrew sat waiting behind the marshal's desk. At ten o'clock Sarah, Ben and Joy arrived at the jail. The trio took the three chairs, Joy in the middle, flanked on her right side by Sarah, Ben on her left. Red Buttman was off to the side holding his shotgun, broken open, across his arms. Sarah held Joy's hand as Jeb unlocked the cell, then escorted Edward J. Humes to his stand-alone seat. Jeb took up position immediately behind Humes.

The Marshal had allowed Humes to bathe and shave. The cut at Ed's brow was scabbed over and his affected eye was framed in hues of green and yellow. His hair was combed but his pants were wrinkled and his shirt unwashed. It was day five for the prisoner and he hadn't had any alcohol to drink since Saturday past. His jerks and tics indicated that the creepy crawlies had invaded his body.

As Humes proceeded to take his seat, he glanced over at the line up directly in front of him. He immediately flung an arm across his eyes. "Too bright in here, hurts my eyes," he cried out.

"Red, go ahead and pull the shades," Jeb instructed.

"Mr. Humes, we're here this morning to discuss a legal transaction," Lawyer Clint Pettigrew said. "Marshal Carter has informed me that you've been afforded the opportunity to have counsel present to represent you, but you declined. Is that true?"

"Yes. As I told the Marshal, I don't need anyone to speak for me," Humes said with a sneer.

Pettigrew looked at his watch. "Then let's get started. As you know you are being held on charges of fighting with the intent to cause bodily harm to a child. In the perpetration of that crime you also assaulted Mrs. Adams," Clint pointed to Sarah, "and her six-year-old son who both intervened to protect your daughter." Pettigrew pointed to Joy.

In addition, you are charged with resisting an officer of the law."

Humes whipped around to look at Jeb. "I did no such thing. When the Marshal went to handcuff me, I did not resist."

"It isn't Marshal Jeb Carter I'm referring to," Pettigrew said. "It was Julib Carter, his deputized son that you tangled with."

The look Humes returned was one of disgust. "Railroad job through and through." He mumbled.

The attorney continued, "If found guilty, these offenses carry a penalty of up to one-year in jail and a fine of fifty-dollars."

Humes started to interject but was cut off by Pettigrew. "Let me finish Mr. Humes, then you may speak your piece. Judge Mittegan will be here at one o'clock his afternoon to hold circuit court. Your case is on the docket with these charges I've just outlined so stipulated."

"So, why are we here now? I'm prepared to defend myself to the judge, but I've nothing to say to these people," Humes said with a fast, backhanded gesture toward Joy, Sarah and Ben.

Always on guard when around her father, Joy flinched and started to tremble when Humes made the familiar air assault. Sarah took the child's hand in hers and Ben wrapped his arm around her shoulders.

Humes taunted Joy, "Go ahead, shake and cower like the frightened scared-cat you've always been. Spineless piece of shi…"

Humes was stopped midsentence when Jeb Carter slapped him on the side of his head. "Shut your trap, Humes. Mr. Pettigrew will let you know when it's your turn to speak."

The lawyer cleared his throat. "Let's all calm down." He cut a look at Jeb. "We're here to discuss a legal transaction. We need to stay focused.

"Doctor Adams, why don't you go ahead and tell Mr. Humes what you're proposing," the lawyer said.

Doc tightened his arm around Joy and Sarah bowed her head in prayer. "We've come with a document, which, if you sign, would relinquish your parental rights over Joy. She would become a ward of myself and my wife." Ben said nodding to Sarah.

Humes shook his head with a look of incredulousness on his face, "It's not going to happen. She's my daughter and she'll be leaving town with me. I'll be the one to decide what happens to her."

Jeb butted in, "The only thing you're gonna be doin' is coolin' your heels in jail."

Again, Clint Pettigrew cleared his throat and cut a look at Jeb. "In exchange for you signing the agreement, relinquishing your parental rights, Doctor Adams, his wife and your daughter would agree to drop their charges against you."

Humes looked at the lawyer and made a double take before nodding toward Joy. You mean if I let her go, I won't have to face the judge this afternoon for charges related to the incident Saturday night."

"That's what we're saying, Mr. Humes," Pettigrew reiterated.

"What about the claim that I resisted an officer of the law?" Humes asked.

Jeb chimed in, "I'll make that go away too if you sign the agreement."

"I've heard the doctor speak, but not the woman…need to know if she's in agreement. She's been sitting there with her head bowed and eyes closed. Is she dumb and mute, or maybe she's too cowered to look at me?" Humes spewed.

Sarah's head came up and she looked Ed Humes square in the eyes. "Be assured, Mr. Humes, I'm not afraid of you. In my view you are a weak, pathetic, disgusting excuse for a man. Only a coward would raise his hand to a child knowing full well she couldn't defend herself. My eyes were closed, and my head bowed because I was praying. I was asking God to allow me to see you as He does.

"By faith I accept that you matter to God. I'm awestruck by the capacity of our Heavenly Father's grace to see, even you, as one of His lost sheep. I believe that you count to Him, but, as I sit here, I'm struggling to glimpse even a particle of anything redeemable in you."

Clint Pettigrew turned to Humes and raised his eyebrows. "Mr. Humes, do you have any further questions to ask Mrs. Adams?"

With squinted eyes trained on Sarah and nostrils flared, Ed gave a shake of his head.

"Hearing no further questions, I'll continue," the lawyer said. "If you sign the agreement, I'll send a telegraph to Wabash to let the judge know he can remove your case, for the aforesaid charges, from his docket for this afternoon."

Humes folded his arms across his chest, leaned back in his chair, stretched his legs and crossed his ankles. "What's to be done about my scratched banjo?"

"You have the right to make a claim for damages through the court," the lawyer advised.

Ben kept one arm securely around Joy while he used the other to take a draw-string pouch, containing thirty sliver twenty-five cent pieces, out of his pocket. "I figured you'd be asking for compensation." He held the money out to Humes. "I believe the going rate for a mahogany veneered banjo is seven dollars and fifty cents."

Humes continued to keep his arms folded and his countenance held a sneer as he looked from Joy to Ben, to Sarah and back at Joy. He moved to the edge of his chair, his lip curled as he reached out and took the thirty pieces of silver. "You can have her, where do I sign?"

Joy pulled her body rigid, let go of Sarah's hand and scooted forward, taking herself from under Ben's protective arm. She locked eyes on her father. "There's one other thing I want from you. I want an agreement that you won't try to prevent me changing my name from Humes to my mother's maiden name. And, I want you to know that from this day forward, I will no longer consider you my father. You will be nothing and nobody to me."

Humes appeared stunned over Joy's boldness. He pulled his shoulders back and jutted out his chin, "I tried to be a good fath…"

Joy leaped to her feet and shouted, "You never loved me. All my life you've done nothing but show cruelty to me, lie to me, neglect me. You don't know the meaning of the word father, so don't you dare use it in front of me. If you do, I'll tear up that piece of paper and walk out of here," she pointed to the document Clint Pettigrew was holding. "I'll leave and take my chances that you'll get locked up where you will rot while you shake and shiver. Because behind bars you won't get a drop of alcohol to drink."

The girl pulled herself tall and took a step toward Humes, hand held out. "Give the money back or I'll go to the judge and tell him how you've beaten and neglected me the past five years. I'll ask him to make you pay *me* compensation for the way you've damaged me."

With the bag of coins fisted, Humes used the back of his hand to swipe across his mouth. He locked eyes with Joy and tried to swallow the terror that surfaced at the prospect of being locked up for a year without access to alcohol. Beads of sweat popped out on his forehead. He used his shirtsleeve to catch the droplets that trickled down to his nose and threatened to drop like tears of fear. "I'll agree to the name change and to relinquishing my parental rights," Ed said as he handed the money to Joy. The girl turned and gave it to Ben.

Clint Pettigrew slid the papers to the edge of the desk and Humes walked over and signed where indicated. "There, done! I'm out of here and out of this hick town," Humes said grabbing his jacket and banjo and moving toward the door.

This time it was Jeb Carter who cleared his throat. Upon the cue, Red Buttman moved to block the exit. He closed and cocked his shotgun. "Edward J. Humes," Jeb said, "I'm arresting you on an outstanding warrant for running out on gambling debt and hotel fees in the city of Wabash."

Jeb turned and pointed to the wanted poster of Humes. While Ed had been in the cell, Jeb kept it turned face-side in. As per their choreographed arrangement, Clint Pettigrew walked over and flipped it face outward.

Humes looked wild eyed, "You can't, we had an agreement."

"This ain't got nothin' to do with the agreement you made with your daughter, Doc and Sarah," Jeb said. "This is county sheriff business." He took Humes by the seat of his pants and high-stepped the man into a cell then slammed the door shut. The click of the lock rang out with a note of finality.

Chapter 39

Saturday morning, two days after the confrontation with Ed Humes at the jail, Ben and Sarah sat at the kitchen table enjoying their early morning quiet time. "How about a refill on that coffee?" Sarah asked.

"Sure, might as well. This will be my fourth cup this morning. I suppose since I'm a doctor I should be more careful about my consumption."

"Why?"

"As you know, coffee contains caffeine and caffeine is a stimulant...," Ben was cut off before he could finish.

"Say no more," was Sarah's quick interjection. "You, my dear husband, do not need a stimulant."

Ben had a coy smile on his face when he countered, "Wish we had the house to ourselves this morning."

Sarah's laugh was full scale. "House to ourselves! How could it ever happen?"

"One day, they'll all be grown and hopefully in homes of their own," Ben replied.

"Let me calculate the years," Sarah teasingly said. "The twins are the youngest at seventeen months. Add seventeen years to that and they'll be approaching nineteen. They hopefully will be on their own by then."

Ben spread his arms wide and splayed his hands, palm sides up, "See, there's hope," he said.

"Yes, but, add seventeen years to your current age of thirty-eight. You'll be fifty-seven years old by then. Do you really think you'll still be wishing for the house to ourselves at that age?" Sarah asked with a giggle.

"Well...," Ben drawled, "maybe not without a sixth or seventh cup of coffee under my belt."

A whimper could be heard coming from the parlor/nursery. "Sounds as if Henry is awake," Sarah said.

"I'll go tend to him," Ben said hopping up from the table.

Directly Ben returned, baby boy in arms. Sarah had the child's high chair positioned at the table. A double handled cup full of warm milk was waiting for him. The baby guzzled it down. Sarah handed him a day-old biscuit to chew.

Ben took a seat and extracted a folded piece of paper from his inside vest pocket. "What's that you've got there?" Sarah asked.

Ben unfolded the paper to reveal a sketch. "It's an idea for adding an addition to the house. With Joy staying on permanently, she needs a room of her own."

"We could move her upstairs to share a room with Hathaway," Sarah said.

"I'm not too fond of that idea," Ben said. "First off, the difference in the girl's ages makes that difficult."

"You're right, Hathaway would be getting in to Joy's things. She's still a toddler with a lot of curiosity and little ability to maintain boundaries. Another problem with having Joy upstairs is the boy's bedroom is right next door." Sarah said.

"Now you're thinking like me. Adolescent boys have a budding curiosity about the female form. The temptation to invade Joy's privacy might be too great. What I'm saying is, let's not put the forbidden fruit where it's easy pickin'."

"Ben Adams," Sarah exclaimed, "those are my sweet boys you're talking about. They wouldn't..."

"Oh, yes, they would, Sarah," was Ben's retort. "Take my word for it, the male specie thinks differently than the female. Trust me, I was an adolescent boy once myself," Ben schooled.

"Well, I refuse to think about my boys that way," Sarah responded with a fake haughtiness. "But I do support your idea of an addition to the house. Maybe add a couple of rooms. One for Joy and one that would initially be used for the twins. In a year or so, we could send Henry upstairs to bunk with Zeke, let Abe have his own room. Hathaway could share Naomi's downstairs bedroom."

"Aside from the bedroom needs," Ben interjected, "we have two teenagers on our hands. We need a parlor for them to entertain their friends. And, what if Julib Carter wants to come courting Joy? We've many reasons to get a proper parlor set up again."

"How soon can we get started?" Sarah asked.

"I'll stop by Benner's lumberyard tomorrow, see if Mr. Benner can recommend someone to do the work. With my inheritance, money isn't a problem, so, we can start soon. If the foundation can get laid before a hard freeze, the construction can move ahead on days the temperature is tolerable." Ben said. Sarah clapped her hands and baby Henry joined in.

"On a serious issue," Sarah said, her smile now gone, "how's Ed Humes doing? Are you ready to let him be transferred to Wabash's jail?"

"He's had a pretty bad case of alcohol withdrawal. I've been tending to him daily since you saw him on Thursday. The most I've been able to do for the man is push fluids, give him light doses of laudanum to help him sleep through the experience. Humes knows the dance, he's been through this, countless times before. To answer your question, I plan to release him for travel this coming Monday. He should be able to finish his drying out in Wabash."

"Ben, you're a kind man," Sarah said patting her husband's arm. "Not many could minister to someone as despicable as Ed Humes." Baby Henry banged his spoon on his tray as if in agreement.

"I'll have to admit my ethics have been challenged lately. But my position is clear, I can't think of the man as other than a human being that needs doctoring," Ben replied. "As long as I carry the bag, I'm bound to the oath I took.

"On another subject," Ben continued, "do you have a date in mind to hold a celebration to honor Joy officially becoming a member of this family?"

"I was thinking we should wait until we have the sealed documents back from the court," Sarah said. "Clint Pettigrew thought that'd take a couple of weeks. Two weeks from last Thursday will be November 16th. That's a week day, but, if the papers come in the mail close to then we could plan it for Saturday November the 18th, or Sunday, November the 19th."

"Let's get it planned for the Sunday date. Make it an afternoon celebration. If we wait much longer, we'll be into Thanksgiving then Christmas. This will be our first opportunity to celebrate the holiday season with Joy."

"Good idea, we want to keep her special day separate," Sarah said. "But what if the papers aren't returned from the court by then?"

"If we don't have them by November 14th, I'll take the train to Wabash and fetch them myself," Ben said.

"Wonderful," Sarah responded. "I'll send out invitations to our friends and family. I want to give early notice to Ma and Pa Whitcome. I'd like for them to come and meet Joy, if they're up to the travel." Sarah's excitement was growing, "Let's frame the documents. They'll be two, one making her our ward and one that changes her name to Anderson, her mother's maiden name. She can hang them in her new room once it's built."

Ben reached over and squeezed Sarah's hand. "It's wonderful to see you so happy and excited Sarah. I've been watching Joy. I've seen no indication that she's found peace."

"No, and she won't as long as she harbors anger and hatred for Ed Humes. This afternoon she and I are going to work on taking her torn dress apart. I've enough material to cut a new back piece.

Should be able to fix it. I plan on using our time together to talk to her about forgiveness," Sarah said.

***

Saturday afternoon Ben had a couple of house calls to make, the boys were outside playing ball and Hathaway and the twins were down for a nap. Sarah and Joy were at the task of repairing the girl's torn dress.

"If you cut a new back for my dress, it doesn't look as if they'll be enough yardage left to make a dress for Naomi," Joy said.

Sarah laid the dress pattern's back piece on the fabric. "You're right. But this is the best use of the material for now. If we don't fix this, the dress isn't wearable. Once we get this back section replaced, the dress will be as good as new."

"Hathaway was counting on all three of us girls having dresses alike," Joy said. "Now that isn't possible."

"Yes, it's still possible. Next time I'm in town I'll go by Parker's store and pick up another length of the cloth. I'll eventually get a dress made for Naomi," Sarah said.

"The three of us with dresses alike, I can't wait," Joy responded.

"So, tell me, is there anyone specific you'd like me to invite to your celebration?" Sarah asked Joy.

The girl took a moment to contemplate. "Brenna and her family, of course. I'm sure you'll include your parents and your brother Jack and family. The mailman, Elmo Jones and his lady friend Miss Peterson would be nice, I like them both. What about the Carters? Will you be inviting them?" Joy asked, her face blushing.

"I'd thought we would, the Carters are good friends of ours. Is it alright with you if they come?" Sarah asked.

"I'd like to have them here," Joy said releasing a big sigh. "I feel as if Julib saved my life. The girl's eyes welled, "Sarah, I haven't been able to put into words how much I appreciate you coming to my rescue that night. And, Zeke! I've, never known anyone as fierce as he is and he's just a little boy. I know he's a handful for you to mother, but don't give up on him, he's worth every minute of your time."

Now it was Sarah who had tears running down her cheeks. "You're right about Zeke. When he was just a little tyke, I remember telling my father that I'd rather have a child that needed their reins pulled in, than one that needed gumption instilled in them. Zeke isn't lacking in the gumption area, that's for sure. And, I know his heart is pure, it's just that his will is strong. Hopefully when he's an adult that tenacity will carry him far."

"Your whole family has been kind to me, especially Ben. He's a kind man and a wonderful father to the children."

"Speaking of fathers," Sarah said. "I want to talk to you about yours."

"I don't have a father," Joy said. "My father is dead to me."

"Okay, then let's talk about Ed Humes," Sarah said. "Joy, if you continue to harbor hatred for the man, you allow him to have power over you."

"I don't understand what you're saying," the girl responded.

"Let me ask you, how many times since last Thursday, when you saw him at the jail, have you thought of him and replayed his hateful words over in your mind?" Sarah asked.

"Countless times, truly, those words are constantly on my mind. He called me a worthless piece of, uh, I don't have to say it, you were there."

"That's my point. Because you haven't forgiven him, you are harboring those hurtful thoughts. In doing that, you hear the words in your head and each time you do, you allow him to hurt you again." Sarah explained.

"I don't know how to stop the thoughts," Joy said. "I've never understood why he hates me so much."

"Joy, one can only speculate. I'm not sure even Ed Humes knows. He might not be able to love anyone because he doesn't love himself, nor does he have enough of a relationship with God to feel His love. Whatever the reason, it isn't your fault.

"You aren't the first, nor will you be the last, to have an earthly father who doesn't live up to the title and the responsibilities it carries. But you do have a father who will be with you always. A father whose love is all encompassing, and everlasting."

"Sarah, that description is the way I see Ben. Are you talking about him?" Joy asked.

"No, although Ben does love you and will live up to the honor of being called your father, if you choose to address him as such, he's not the one I'm referring to. I'm speaking about your Heavenly Father, God. Joy, above all else, you are a child of God."

Joy sat quietly for a time, before speaking. "That's a lot to take in Sarah. Right now, hating Ed Humes is on my mind and I can't stop those thoughts. Do you know how I can get rid of them?"

"Through prayer and forgiveness," was Sarah's response. "Each Sunday we recite the Lord's Prayer together in church. We've said it so often, most of us have committed it to memory. What many haven't done is really listen to the words and their meaning and application to our lives today. God gave us that prayer because in those sixty-five words, he outlines for us a model to live by."

Joy's brow furrowed, "I don't understand."

"I'll try to explain," Sarah said. "The prayer starts with *Our Father who art in heaven, Hallowed be thy name. They kingdom come, thy will be done, on earth as it is in heaven.* When we recite it, we're recognizing God's dominion over us in heaven and here on earth. We're pledging to honor His will. The next part, *Give us this day our daily bread,* is our opportunity to ask God for whatever we need to make it through the day. It isn't merely just the food we eat, but rather those attributes such as patience, love, forgiveness, that we need to live amongst one another. The specific attributes, and their levels, vary from day to day. When we wake in the morning, we don't know what the day will bring. But, when we pray *give us this day our daily bread,* we're asking God to give us any and all the, uh, the tools, in the amount needed, to make it through the day in accordance with His will. I was struggling for the word, but it may well help if you think of attributes as tools, instruments to help us complete the work of living and loving one another.

"Some days, such as recently with Zeke, I've needed a lot of patience and understanding. I don't have to spell that out to God, he just knows what I need. My responsibility is to *ask for the daily bread,* God honors His promise and provides what I need."

"I've never thought about that prayer like you've just explained."

"There's more," Sarah said. "This next part is what I'm hoping to help you understand right now…*and forgive us our debts as we forgive our debtors.* This isn't speaking of a monetary debt, but rather our transgressions, our sins. We ask God to forgive us because we all, knowingly, sometimes unknowingly, sin or wrong others and that second part is us saying that we know that if we expect God to forgive us, we must be willing to forgive others."

"So, are you saying that if I want God to forgive me when I sin, make a mistake, mess up, I have to be willing to forgive Ed Humes?" Joy asked.

"That's it exactly. The Lord's Prayer covers other areas, but the forgiveness part is what I wanted you to understand today. There's another scripture that helps explain it," Sarah said as she reached for her Bible. She thumbed through finding the familiar passage. "Here it is, Matthew 6:14-15, *For if you forgive other people when they sin against you, your heavenly Father will also forgive you. But if you do not forgive others their sins, your Father will not forgive your sins.*

"Joy, you may never want to see Ed Humes again. Whether you do or not, is between you and the Lord. But you do need to forgive Ed in your heart. I want you to do it not for him, but for you. If you forgive him, that space in your heart that is harboring those bad memories and bad feelings will be freed. Don't allow that man to continue to have power over you. It takes a lot of energy to hate. Don't spend your good energy on him."

The discussion was interrupted when Hathaway came walking into the room. "Ma, I'm hungry, can I have some milk and cookies?" the toddler asked.

"I'll get them for her," Joy said jumping to her feet. As she was getting cookies from the jar she called over to Sarah, "What you've told me makes sense. The last thing I want is to allow Ed Humes to have any power or place in my life moving forward. I promise, I'll give our discussion a lot of thought."

Chapter 40

Sunday, November 19, 1905 dawned to a clear, bright sky. The temperatures promised to be in the high forty degrees. The climate outside matched the sunny disposition of the ten inhabitants of Sarah's farm house. Energy levels were high and excitement for the celebration that lay ahead was intense.

"Hathaway, please stand still," Joy pleaded. "I can't get your dress buttoned with you hopping up and down."

"Joy, ain't you excited about bein' my big sister?" Hathaway asked.

"Yes, and I'm very happy that we're having a party today. But the celebration is this afternoon. Right now, we need to get ready for church. Your Pa just called the ten-minute warning. If we aren't climbing in the wagon in ten minutes time, we'll get left behind," Joy said.

"Joy, can you help me?" Zeke said tugging on the girl's arm. The boy stood waiting, tie in hand, his hair slicked down, his face scrubbed so clean it shined.

"Let me get Hathaway's dress buttoned, then I'll help you," Joy said.

"Here brother, I'll do it," Abe said, taking the tie and looping it around his younger brother's neck.

"Allllll, aboard," Ben called from the kitchen. Multiple pairs of shoes and one four-legged companion answered the call, scrambled out the door and climbed up in the wagon.

Lancy dived between bodies and burrowed under Josh's legs attempting to stay hidden from those that might thwart his plan to ride into town with the family.

"Josh," Sarah called out, "I know your dog jumped up in the wagon. No point helping him hide, he can't go with us to church."

"Nice try, boy," Josh said as he shooed the dog off the wagon. "You stay here and hold down the fort, we'll be home in a couple of hours."

Ben called, "Walk" to the team and they took off down the lane. As he ordered "Gee", signaling the team to make a right turn onto America road, the family was singing, *Buffalo Gal Won't You Come Out Tonight.* Since the night they'd practiced dancing, a few days before the infamous fall festival, it had become the family's signature song.

"I'm fine with singing this song on the way in to church," Ben said to Sarah, leaning in for only her ears to hear. "But we need to cut it off when we hit main street or switch to a chorus of *Bringing In the Sheaves.* If the church deacons hear, they'll think we're a family of heathens."

"That don't make me no never mind," Sarah said in jest. "This is a special day and ain't nothin' or nobody gonna dampen this family's spirits."

At three o'clock in the afternoon the guests started arriving. No one came empty handed. Arms were laden with contributions of food and tokens of acknowledgement in honor of Joy's special day. The girl was handed so many gifts it took Breanna's help to accept them all.

Hathaway and Joy were wearing their matching dresses. The toddler was at the height of her glory and Johnny on the Spot when the knocks came. She was eager to introduce folks to her *new, official big sister.* After each introduction the small child helped carry hats and coats, dragging many of them, to be laid on Sarah and Ben's bed.

When Mister and Missus Jeb Carter arrived, Judith gave Joy a hug and Jeb patted her on the back. "Where's that big boy of yours, *Marshtal* Carter?" Hathaway asked.

"He'll be here directly, he's finishin' up evenin' chores," Jeb replied.

Jonas and Emma Whitcome, Sarah's first husband's, Henry's, parents and grandparents to her children arrived. They were enthusiastically greeted by the family. Due to their age, they'd had their hired hand bring them. The trio would spend the night and make the hour-long trek home the next morning.

Extra chairs had been gathered from various rooms in the house and brought to the kitchen. A couple of makeshift benches had been created with stacked bricks for legs and board planks for seats.

The kitchen table held a virtual feast of eclectic dishes of vegetables, canned fruits and relishes. Sarah had baked a huge ham that took center stage. The sideboard was burdened with the cakes, pies and puddings that were eyed in eager anticipation. Loaves of bread, dishes of butter and compotes of jam sat on a table riding shotgun to the sideboard. Pitchers of sweet tea and milk rested on the dry sink's counter top. Coffee, perked and ready, waited on the cookstove's back burner.

The children playing outside were called in and Zeke was given the honor of getting everyone's attention. He hammed it up by banging a spoon on a tin pie plate and calling out, "Hear ye, Hear ye."

"Welcome to our home," Sarah said. "We're so pleased to have you here today to celebrate this special occasion. Joy," Sarah called out, "come on over here, Dear."

The girl complied and took a stand between Sarah and Ben. Each took one of Joy's hands.

"Would you all please bow your heads," Ben said. "Father in heaven," he prayed, "we come to you today praising you for the blessing of permanently welcoming Joy into our home. We're honored to have friends and family here with us to help us celebrate this occasion. Father, we ask for your blessings on Joy and this family. Sarah and I pray for your guidance as we strive to be good parents to all our children…which now, count to eight.

"Oh, Lord, bless this food we are about to partake of to the nourishment of our bodies and bless the hands that have prepared it. In Jesus' name, Amen." The Amen echoed about the room.

"Children, line up in age order, youngest first," Sarah instructed.

"Ma, 'Omi and Henry is the youngest," Hathaway yelled, "I think them plates is too heavy for 'em to carry."

"Don't worry, Dear," Mary Riley, Sarah's mother, interjected. "Grandpa Tom has the twins loaded into their high chairs and I'll fix their food for them."

There was a knock at the door and Joy rushed to greet the late arriving guest. As she had anticipated, Julib Carter was standing on the stoop, hat in hand. "Come in," Joy said, "we've been expecting you." He handed her his hat, then took off his coat.

"Grace has been said, so go on and line up, you'll find plates and eating utensils in yonder," the girl said pointing toward the food spread. "I'll put your things in on the bed then come join you."

"Wait." With a blush on his face Julib placed a small package in Joy's hand. "It's a blue ribbon for your hair, the color suits you real nice." Joy's cheeks took on a hew that matched that of the gift giver when she said, "Thank you, Julib."

Abe and Breanna, Joy and Julib sat on the makeshift benches facing one another. The younger Whitcome boys ate with their cousins, taking seats on the floor. Hathaway pulled a small footstool up close to Naomi's high chair and chatted with her baby sister while they ate.

It was near six o'clock in the evening when, with conversations spent, congratulations made and stomachs full to bursting, guests began gathering belongs to make their departures. The three Carters were the last to leave. Joy gave Julib a warm smile when she bid him goodbye. The girl handed Jeb Carter his hat and coat. When he turned to leave, she placed a hand on his arm.

"Marshal Carter," Joy said pulling an envelope from her pocket, "I'd appreciate it if you could get this to Ed Humes." She didn't divulge the contents, she'd decided she'd keep that to herself, as least for a while longer. The words she'd penned were few. The letter simply read. *Dear Ed Humes, I forgive you.* Her closing was, *Goodbye forever,* bringing closure to her painful childhood.

She signed it *Joy Anderson, A Child of God.*

I'm honored that you read *The Shelter of the Dove's Wings.* I'm an unaccompanied author and trust in you to tell others about the book, the second in the Sarah series. If you enjoyed reading it, please let your friends and family know. I also would like to hear from you. Whatever your means of obtaining the book, please take a minute to give it a brief review on Amazon. Thanks for your time. May you too experience The Dove's sheltering wings. Melody

"On the Wings of a Dove", book one in the Sarah trilogy. At the turn of the 20th century, Sarah Whitcome, a wife and young mother of five is happy and content in her rural Indiana farming community. A catastrophic event thrusts her into the role of head of the household. Butting heads with social convention for a woman in 1903, Sarah faces the daunting task of maintaining their farm while finding a way to eke out a living for her family.

The family's distinctive personalities jump to life, make you laugh and steal your affection. Reading their story will warm your heart and uplift your soul.

Book available through Amazon.com, Barns & Nobel, and Balboa Press in paperback and Kindle. However, you procured the book, your rating on Amazon would be much appreciated.

Printed in the United States
By Bookmasters